JAMES PATRICK KELLY & JOHN KESSEL | EDITORS

DIGITAL RAPTURE

>THE SINGULARITY ANTHOLOGY

TACHYON

Cover design by Josh Beatman
Interior design by Elizabeth Story

Tachyon Publications
1459 18th Street #139
San Francisco, CA 94107
(415) 285-5615
www.tachyonpublications.com
tachyon@tachyonpublications.com

Series Editor: Jacob Weisman
Project Editor: Jill Roberts

ISBN 13: 978-1-61696-070-4
ISBN 10: 1-61696-070-1

Printed in the United States of America by Worzalla
First Edition: 2012

9 8 7 6 5 4 3 2 1

CONTENTS

INTRODUCTION: DIGITAL RAPTURE

> James Patrick Kelly and John Kessel

> The writer sees the world as a jaded world devoid of recuperative power. In the past he has liked to think that Man could pull out of his entanglements and start a new creative phase of human living. In the face of our universal inadequacy, the optimism has given place to a stoical cynicism. The old men behave for the most part meanly and disgustingly, and the young are spasmodic, foolish, and all too easily misled. Man must go steeply up or down and the odds seem to be all in favor of his going down and out. If he goes up, then so great is the adaptation demanded of him that he must cease to be a man.
>
> —H. G. Wells, *Mind at the End of Its Tether*

blame Darwin

Herbert George Wells, hailed by many as the first science fiction writer and by some as the greatest, was pessimistic about our future as he was writing his last book; he died less than a year after publication. Perhaps the shadow of the grave had darkened his thoughts, or maybe the carnage of the Second World War shocked him. But throughout his career as a writer, Wells kept returning to speculation about possible futures for *Homo sapiens sapiens*. He had discovered Darwin in his youth, after which he lost his religion and became a lifelong advocate of Darwinism and—to our dismay—eugenics. If Wells is indeed one of the progenitors of science fiction, then Darwin's world view is in the DNA of our genre. The theory of evolution teaches that we are the successor species to extinct hominids, so naturally we speculate that there might someday be a successor species to *us*. Of course, neither Darwin nor Wells understood all the implications of the extensive fossil record available to us today, so they could only guess how different we modern humans were from *Homo habilis* or *Australopithecus afarensis*. And while speculation about what sort of creature might someday replace man made for heady fiction, the passing of humankind was—until recently—never considered to be imminent. We know that *Homo habilis* last walked the earth two million years ago and that the Australopithecine we call Lucy is some 3.2 million years old. Evolution takes a long, long time.

Like Wells's intrepid time traveler, most science fiction writers who cruised the centuries in their imaginations found humanity comfortably in control. After all, it wasn't until the year AD 802,701 that the time traveler discovered the split between the Eloi and the Morlocks. Indeed, many in the genre would argue that our intelligence has given us the tools to withstand the slow but relentless pressure of evolution. In Isaac Asimov's "The Last Question" and Frederik Pohl's "Day Million" we humans finally surrender the crown of creation many centuries, if not millennia, from now. That kind of thinking made sense in a world where computation relied on vacuum tubes and punch cards. From the vantage point of the 1960s, it seemed obvious that when our successors finally showed up, it would be our children's children's children[10] who would have the problem.

Enter Vernor Vinge. The abstract of a talk he gave at a NASA-sponsored symposium in 1993 begins with this chilling prediction: "Within thirty years, we will have the technological means to create superhuman intelligence. Shortly after, the human era will be ended." Narrative hooks are common in SF, but when Vinge, a professor of mathematics and a gifted writer, brought the technique to a scholarly paper, the world sat up and took notice. "The Coming Technological Singularity: How to Survive in the Post-Human Era" is not a work of startling originality, but rather draws its significance from the way Vinge documents research and gathers credible speculation from a variety of sources. For instance, he points to the cryptanalyst Irving John Good, who wrote as early as 1965: "Let an ultraintelligent machine be defined as a machine that can far surpass all the intellectual activities of any man however clever. Since the design of machines is one of these intellectual activities, an ultraintelligent machine could design even better machines; there would then unquestionably be an 'intelligence explosion,' and the intelligence of man would be left far behind. Thus the first ultraintelligent machine is the last invention that man need ever make." Nevertheless, Vinge's paper took lots of smart people by surprise, many of them technologists and futurists and science fiction writers who had been secure in the belief that they could see more than three decades into the future.

Controversy ensued.

Was it possible to create superhuman intelligence? Were there really, as Vinge asserted, several technological paths to the Singularity, making it even more likely? Was his timeline accurate? Scientist and inventor Ray Kurzweil thought so, and in *The Age of Spiritual Machines* and *The Singularity Is Near* argued for his own considered path to superintelligence. But the idea of the Singularity has faced skepticism and outright ridicule from the very first. Evolutionary biologist PZ Myers, author of the *Pharyngula* blog, listed by *Nature* magazine as the top-ranked blog written by a scientist, wrote in 2009: "Now I do think that human culture has allowed and encouraged greater rates of change than are possible without active, intelligent engagement—but this techno-mystical crap is just kookery, plain and simple, and the rationale is disgracefully bad. One thing I will say for Kurzweil, though, is that he seems to be a first-rate bullshit artist." (http://scienceblogs.com/pharyngula/2009/02/singularly_silly_singularity.php). And from SF itself came the epithet "the rapture of the nerds," coined by Ken MacLeod and popularized by Cory Doctorow and Charles Stross (as in the title of their collaborative novel). And yet, while the science establishment views claims for the Singularity as extravagant at best, true believers like the transhumanists and extropians and singularitarians have organized into movements with varying agendas. There is a 501(c)(3) nonprofit organization called The Singularity Institute for Artificial Intelligence which aims to guide the development of "safe" AI—one that when it is infinitely smarter than us doesn't decide that we're as expendable as ants. And the Singularity University, located on the campus of NASA Research Park in Silicon Valley, was founded on the concept that "a new university that could leverage the power of exponential technologies to solve humanity's grand challenges."

flavors of Singularity

In his paper, Vinge makes the point that there are several possible paths to the Singularity, all of which pose technological challenges. One is predicated on the feasibility of creating Artificial Intelligence, or AI. He postulates that thinking computers or computer networks might "wake up" as superhuman intelligences. Another path depends on what he called Intelligence Amplification, or IA, which he suggests might be easier to achieve than AI. In IA there is some kind of human/computer interface which enhances our intelligence. Think of how smart you would be with an always-on, always-connected iPad in your head! Then imagine the power of future iDevices. For a third option, as we come to understand the workings of our genome we might be able to make purely biological interventions in the human operating system to achieve superintelligence. Surely extending the human lifespan—or perhaps even immortality—would help. Will we discover genes for intelligence that we can manipulate? Of course, this path veers dangerously close to the suspect eugenics by which Wells was so tempted. But then the implications of the Singularity are clearly fraught with moral pitfalls.

In his blog post "Three Major Singularity Schools," Eliezer Yudkowsky (http://yudkowsky.net/singularity/schools), a research fellow at the Singularity Institute, offers his own views on how thinking about the Singularity has diverged over the past few years.

The Accelerating Change School, which Yudkowsky associates with Ray Kurzweil, makes the case that change has steadily been getting faster—exponentially faster—and that looking back to history tells us nothing about the future that is screaming toward us. Seemingly impassible technological roadblocks will fall like dominoes to allow us to become one with our computers and live forever. It should be pointed out that these roadblocks have not been cleared as quickly as Kurzweil predicted, although the century is still young

The Event Horizon School accepts Vernor Vinge's argument that we are on the cusp of creating superhuman intelligence which will be so different from us that its nature, and that of the world it will dominate, will be as unintelligible to us as ours is to snails. Although Vinge never mentions "event horizons," other writers have borrowed this concept from astrophysics to convey the metaphorical meaning of his Singularity: a black hole is a region of spacetime from which nothing, not even light, can escape. It is surrounded by an event horizon through which matter can pass in only one direction: toward the black hole. Beyond the event horizon is the un-knowable singularity, where the curvature of spacetime becomes infinite.

The Intelligence Explosion School follows Irving John Good's—and Yudkowsky's—idea that human intelligence has created our technological wonders, many of which have augmented our intelligence. Take computers, for example, or the Internet. As this trend continues, human/machine interaction or the creation of artificial minds smarter than ours will result in a feedback loop, greater-than-human-intelligences creating ever more intelligent entities. This need not happen exponentially, as Kurzweil posits, but would inevitably lead to a tipping point from which a superintelligence would emerge.

Yudkowsky makes the point that while these scenarios all result in a world dominated by superintelligence, the processes by which they reach a Singularity are mutually contradictory. Also, their timescales are different. Futurists talk of hard takeoff and soft takeoff Singularities. In the former, the seed intelligence, either AI or IA, improves so rapidly that over the course of months or even weeks it achieves superintelligence, unpredictably and out of the control of those humans who created it. In a soft takeoff, there is a steady, stepwise accretion of intelligence which can be monitored and perhaps directed by we who are human. In David Levine's "Firewall" we see a hard takeoff that takes place in a matter of hours, whereas in Greg Egan's "Crystal Nights" Daniel Cliff seeks to control his AI Phites.

our Singularity

We have divided this anthology into four sections, The End of the Human Era, The Posthumans, Across the Event Horizon, and The Others, each including stories and an essay. Since, like Vinge, we do not claim that the Singularity is a new idea, we have tried in the opening section to give some historical context to the concept.

The End of the Human Era

At more or less the same time that W. Olaf Stapledon, in his seminal "novel" *Last and First Men*, was speculating about the phases the evolution of human beings might pass through in the next several million years, the molecular biologist J. D. Bernal speculated about what a technically augmented species of man might look like in his monograph "The World, The Flesh and The Devil: An Enquiry into the Future of the Three Enemies of the Rational Soul." Bernal's ideas anticipate the generations of science fiction writers like Isaac Asimov and Frederik Pohl who gazed into the distant future and saw a universe in which humankind had given way to other intelligences. Of course, the apocalyptic impulse is strong in science fiction, as it was especially in the postwar years at the beginning of the atomic age. But the Singularity precursor stories are something else entirely, at once more hopeful and more dismissive of human accomplishment.

The Posthumans

In addition to Vinge's classic paper, we offer a selection of stories in which humans co-exist with potential successors who have not yet achieved superintelligence or come to dominate our world. Though it does not feature machine intelligences or cataclysmic change, Stapledon's *Odd John* does portray a mutant posthuman dealing with a world of normals, while in Rudy Rucker and Eileen Gunn's "Hive Mind Man" the hyperconnected Jeff and Diane have been technologically enhanced to set off what may be a hard takeoff Singularity. Although Bruce Sterling claims never to have written a Singularity story, the factions in "Sunken Gardens," part of his Shaper/Mechanist sequence, are busy remaking themselves according to two of Vinge's blueprints, and in the process coolly accepting the death of unaltered humans as the kind of collateral damage that Odd John might have understood.

Across the Event Horizon

The physicists tell us that once matter crosses the event horizon of a black hole, there is no going back. This, we believe, is the case with the stories in this section. Even though there are recognizable humans in Justina Robson's "Cracklegrackle," Greg Egan's "Crystal Palace," David Levine's "Firewall," and Vernor Vinge's "The Cookie Monster," they are living in worlds that are destined for Singularity. "The Cookie Monster" is perhaps a special case, but to say more would be to provide spoilers for those who are coming to this Hugo Award-winning novella for the first time. These are for the most part soft takeoff stories, the Levine being the notable exception.

The Others

In his paper, Vinge warns of the science fiction writer's dilemma; a rapid onset Singularity would construct "an opaque wall" across the very near future. How to write about a universe filled with unknowable superintelligences? What happens to traditional story values in a world where easy replication of the self means that death is not final or even very important? Where bodies are replaceable, the senses negotiable, and memory a commodity? Where the world itself might be a simulation? H. G. Wells anticipated us on this issue, too, saying, "If anything is possible, then nothing is interesting." Little wonder that writing post-Singularity stories seemed daunting.

But not to all. The five stories we have selected for this section do, we believe, pose as much a challenge to the reader as they did to the writers. They are increasingly abstract and strange. While the characters in Charles Stross's "Nightfall" began their existence as humans, they have long since been uploaded into a simulation. There remains a scattering of humans in "Coelacanths" by Robert Reed, but they subsist on the margins of a world where posthumans and superhuman intelligences hold sway. The surreal "True Names," by Cory Doctorow and Benjamin Rosenbaum, climbs new heights of abstraction, while Hannu Rajaniemi's protagonist in "The Server and the Dragon" is a node of some galactic supercomputer isolated from its network. And while the characters at the end of time in Elizabeth Bear's "The Inevitable Heat Death of the Universe" present as more "human" than those in the Rajaniemi story, their motivations are even more inscrutable.

While acknowledging that these stories may be difficult, we commend them to your attention because of their ambition. It has often been said that the problem with SF's depiction of aliens is that our aliens are all too human. If we are alone in the universe, either literally or functionally, because the distances other creatures must travel to make contact are impossibly far, then the only aliens we are likely to meet are the ones we invent. And in the Singularity we have may have found the truly alien.

the idea vs. the story

One of the difficulties in presenting these stories is separating talk about the idea of the Singularity from talk about the stories as fiction. Discussion of such stories seems quickly to devolve into a debate about the nature and plausibility of the Singularity. Perhaps that is the nature of idea-based science fiction. Of all current SF, Singularity fiction is certainly the most idea-based. The characters are serviceable vehicles for the exposition of ideas, the settings so vague as to be nonexistent. It is hard sometimes to read these stories as stories as well as arguments about a genuine future.

And it's not just the difficulty of imagining the post-Singular world that causes this. Both pre- and post-Singularity stories lack sensory detail.

The tangible world does not loom large in this fiction. For example, few of these stories spend time evoking the experience of being an embodied human being or the natural world around us—either in those scenes that take place in uploaded worlds, or in those set closer to the present. The body and the world it senses are not central to this fiction.

This may perhaps reflect the fact that the theories of AI that underlie the concept of the Singularity to a remarkable degree ignore the scientific study of the human brain. It is as if intelligence is a mere matter of processing power. In the hard takeoff Singularity stories, if enough processors are piled together and interconnected, then consciousness and intelligence result automatically. The study of how human intelligence arises from the structure of the brain, and how it relates to somatic input, seems irrelevant to many promoters of AI. It's therefore not surprising that so many of these stories ignore the body. A body is just meat, a squishy, inferior platform for what is important: intellect. This is evident in Bernal's vision of brains in cans, and follows through to the many stories that present the posthumans as software on massive, cosmically powerful computer systems, as in Stross or Rajaniemi or Doctorow and Rosenbaum. Corporations and operating systems and data filters are the actors. Should posthumans have any need for it, the biosphere can be reproduced in a computer—if perhaps, as Stross admits, not in all its complexity, then at least sufficient for the purposes of the simulations of beings who are to inhabit it. The earth itself's greatest value is as matter from which to create processors. The physical world is disposable. In terms of narrative, the resultant mutability of form and abstraction of character can result in some linguistic coleslaw, as for example in this not particularly unusual passage from Doctorow and Rosenbaum's "True Names":

> She'd forked as a temporary tactic and been separated from herself when a planet-volume of Byzantium was overrun by the worst kind of rogue subagencies, who hadn't merely wanted to be emancipated as outer-scale sprites, but instead to overthrow Beebean psychological architecture altogether, dissolving all of Beebe into a flat soup of memes.

At its daftest, whether the ideas behind the fiction are credible or not, this produces high postmodern comedy.

But the impulse of these stories to exist in a realm of pure idea may not be as cutting edge as it would first appear. Those early Transhumanists, the medieval Christian ascetics, likewise believed our bodies were mere platforms. In the twelfth century St. Francis of Assisi taught, "I have no greater enemy than my body." Ascetics sought to release the soul from the body's bondage in order to permit union with the divine. At the same time Bernal imagined freeing the brain from the body and putting it in a can, with new, wired senses that would allow it to perceive more than our fleshly perishing ones could, W. B. Yeats wrote:

> Consume my heart away; sick with desire
> And fastened to a dying animal
> It knows not what it is; and gather me
> Into the artifice of eternity.
>
> Once out of nature I shall never take
> My bodily form from any natural thing,
> But such a form as Grecian goldsmiths make
> Of hammered gold and gold enamelling
> To keep a drowsy Emperor awake.

Fastened to dying animals, to be gathered into the "artifice of eternity" is the devout wish of followers of the digital rapture. In this way, the posthuman digital world reproduces in secular terms the religious soul/body divide.

The Medieval ascetics were moralists, yet most who speculate about the Singularity and the altered beings who will live on its other side do not engage with moral issues. They see this as an evolutionary leap forward, but offer little or nothing about the ethics of posthumanism, when in fact that is the question that is *most* essential to us. To be fair, in his essay Vinge does briefly raise the ethical question, and propose some standards. He quotes I. J. Good's "Meta Golden Rule" as a guide for posthumans: "Treat your inferiors as you would be treated by your superiors."

We like that, but think there is more to be asked. So here's a question: The day after computer intelligences soar away on an exponential curve toward infinity, or our successors walk out of the clinic with a life expectancy of 400 years and the entire Internet wired into their brains, in what way will their ethics differ? Will they have gone from Republican to Democrat, or heaven forbid, vice versa? Will they still follow professional football? Will they find the Marx Brothers more, or less, funny? Will they care more, or less, about what happens to migrant farm workers? To their cousins? To their children?

We would hope that if there is indeed to be a Singularity, then in that posthuman world the dominant superintelligent entities will treat us and the rest of the natural world with more empathy than we have treated the great apes or passenger pigeons. Also that our successors, be they biological or not, will find it *natural* to practice tolerance for all other intelligences, no matter how humble. And, yes, perhaps even kindness. But then as humans, we are locked in a humanist perspective, and can only *hope* for a future that will have room enough for us. For much Singularity fiction, survival is not an issue: either the possibilities of resurrection, transformation, and complete control over the environment are nearly infinite, or inevitable extinction is the fate of every race and to worry about it is embarrassingly childish. As the apostles of the Singularity tell us, the world on the other side of the event horizon is unknowable. That is the astonishing promise and the terrifying danger of the Singularity.

(2012)

THE END OF THE HUMAN ERA

Isaac Asimov (1920–1992), prolific writer and professor of biochemistry at Boston University, was one of the most celebrated authors of science fiction and popular science of the twentieth century. Here he makes effortless Stapledonian leaps across the millennia to reach his own version of the Singularity.

THE LAST QUESTION
> Isaac Asimov

The last question was asked for the first time, half in jest, on May 21, 2061, at a time when humanity first stepped into the light. The question came about as a result of a five dollar bet over highballs, and it happened this way:

Alexander Adell and Bertram Lupov were two of the faithful attendants of Multivac. As well as any human beings could, they knew what lay behind the cold, clicking, flashing face—miles and miles of face—of that giant computer. They had at least a vague notion of the general plan of relays and circuits that had long since grown past the point where any single human could possibly have a firm grasp of the whole.

Multivac was self-adjusting and self-correcting. It had to be, for nothing human could adjust and correct it quickly enough or even adequately enough—so Adell and Lupov attended the monstrous giant only lightly and superficially, yet as well as any men could. They fed it data, adjusted questions to its needs and translated the answers that were issued. Certainly they, and all others like them, were fully entitled to share in the glory that was Multivac's.

For decades, Multivac had helped design the ships and plot the trajectories that enabled man to reach the Moon, Mars, and Venus, but past that, Earth's poor resources could not support the ships. Too much energy was needed for the long trips. Earth exploited its coal and uranium with increasing efficiency, but there was only so much of both.

But slowly Multivac learned enough to answer deeper questions more fundamentally, and on May 14, 2061, what had been theory, became fact.

The energy of the sun was stored, converted, and utilized directly on a planet-wide scale. All Earth turned off its burning coal, its fissioning uranium, and flipped the switch that connected all of it to a small station, one mile in diameter, circling the Earth at half the distance of the Moon. All Earth ran by invisible beams of sunpower.

Seven days had not sufficed to dim the glory of it and Adell and Lupov finally managed to escape from the public function, and to meet in quiet where no one would think of looking for them, in the deserted underground chambers, where portions of the mighty buried body of Multivac showed. Unattended, idling, sorting data with contented lazy clickings, Multivac, too, had earned its vacation and the boys appreciated that. They had no intention, originally, of disturbing it.

They had brought a bottle with them, and their only concern at the moment was to relax in the company of each other and the bottle.

"It's amazing when you think of it," said Adell. His broad face had lines of weariness in it, and he stirred his drink slowly with a glass rod, watching the cubes of ice slur clumsily about. "All the energy we can possibly ever use for free. Enough energy, if we wanted to draw on it, to melt all Earth into a big drop of impure liquid iron, and still never miss the energy so used. All the energy we could ever use, forever and forever and forever."

Lupov cocked his head sideways. He had a trick of doing that when he wanted to be contrary, and he wanted to be contrary now, partly because he had had to carry the ice and glassware. "Not forever," he said.

"Oh, hell, just about forever. Till the sun runs down, Bert."

"That's not forever."

"All right, then. Billions and billions of years. Twenty billion, maybe. Are you satisfied?"

Lupov put his fingers through his thinning hair as though to reassure himself that some was still left and sipped gently at his own drink. "Twenty billion years isn't forever."

"Will, it will last our time, won't it?"

"So would the coal and uranium."

"All right, but now we can hook up each individual spaceship to the Solar Station, and it can go to Pluto and back a million times without ever worrying about fuel. You can't do THAT on coal and uranium. Ask Multivac, if you don't believe me."

"I don't have to ask Multivac. I know that."

"Then stop running down what Multivac's done for us," said Adell, blazing up. "It did all right."

"Who says it didn't? What I say is that a sun won't last forever. That's all I'm saying. We're safe for twenty billion years, but then what?" Lupov pointed a slightly shaky finger at the other. "And don't say we'll switch to another sun."

There was silence for a while. Adell put his glass to his lips only occasionally, and Lupov's eyes slowly closed. They rested.

Then Lupov's eyes snapped open. "You're thinking we'll switch to another sun when ours is done, aren't you?"

"I'm not thinking."

"Sure you are. You're weak on logic, that's the trouble with you. You're like the guy in the story who was caught in a sudden shower and who ran to a grove of trees and got under one. He wasn't worried, you see, because he figured when one tree got wet through, he would just get under another one."

"I get it," said Adell. "Don't shout. When the sun is done, the other stars will be gone, too."

"Darn right they will," muttered Lupov. "It all had a beginning in the original cosmic explosion, whatever that was, and it'll all have an end when all the stars run down. Some run down faster than others. Hell, the giants won't last a hundred million years. The sun will last twenty billion years and maybe the dwarfs will last a hundred billion for all the good they are. But just give us a trillion years and everything will be dark. Entropy has to increase to maximum, that's all."

"I know all about entropy," said Adell, standing on his dignity.

"The hell you do."

"I know as much as you do."

"Then you know everything's got to run down someday."

"All right. Who says they won't?"

"You did, you poor sap. You said we had all the energy we needed, forever. You said 'forever.'"

"It was Adell's turn to be contrary. "Maybe we can build things up again someday," he said.

"Never."

"Why not? Someday."

"Never."

"Ask Multivac."

"*You* ask Multivac. I dare you. Five dollars says it can't be done."

Adell was just drunk enough to try, just sober enough to be able to phrase the necessary symbols and operations into a question which, in words, might have corresponded to this: Will mankind one day without the net expenditure of energy be able to restore the sun to its full youthfulness even after it had died of old age?

Or maybe it could be put more simply like this: How can the net amount of entropy of the Universe be massively decreased?

Multivac fell dead and silent. The slow flashing of lights ceased, the distant sounds of clicking relays ended.

Then, just as the frightened technicians felt they could hold their breath no longer, there was a sudden springing to life of the teletype attached to that portion of Multivac. Five words were printed: INSUFFICIENT DATA FOR MEANINGFUL ANSWER.

"No bet," whispered Lupov. They left hurriedly.

By next morning, the two, plagued with throbbing head and cottony mouth, had forgotten about the incident.

Jerrodd, Jerrodine, and Jerrodette I and II watched the starry picture in the visiplate change as the passage through hyperspace was completed in its non-time lapse. At once, the even powdering of stars gave way to the predominance of a single bright marble-disk, centered.

"That's X-23," said Jerrodd confidently. His thin hands clamped tightly behind his back and the knuckles whitened.

The little Jerrodettes, both girls, had experienced the hyperspace passage for the first time in their lives and were self-conscious over the momentary sensation of inside-outness. They buried their giggles and chased one another wildly about their mother, screaming, "We've reached X-23—we've reached X-23—we've—"

"Quiet, children," said Jerrodine sharply. "Are you sure, Jerrodd?"

"What is there to be but sure?" asked Jerrodd, glancing up at the bulge of featureless metal just under the ceiling. It ran the length of the room, disappearing through the wall at either end. It was as long as the ship.

Jerrodd scarcely knew a thing about the thick rod of metal except that it was called a Microvac, that one asked it questions if one wished; that if one did not it still had its task of guiding the ship to a preordered destination; of feeding on energies from the various Sub-galactic Power Stations; of computing the equations for the hyperspatial jumps.

Jerrodd and his family had only to wait and live in the comfortable residence quarters of the ship.

Someone had once told Jerrodd that the "ac" at the end of "Microvac" stood for "analog computer" in ancient English, but he was on the edge of forgetting even that.

Jerrodine's eyes were moist as she watched the visiplate. "I can't help it. I feel funny about leaving Earth."

"Why for Pete's sake?" demanded Jerrodd. "We had nothing there. We'll have everything on X-23. You won't be alone. You won't be a pioneer. There are over a million people on the planet already. Good Lord, our great grandchildren will be looking for new worlds because X-23 will be overcrowded."

Then, after a reflective pause, "I tell you, it's a lucky thing the computers worked out interstellar travel the way the race is growing."

"I know, I know," said Jerrodine miserably.

Jerrodette I said promptly, "Our Microvac is the best Microvac in the world."

"I think so, too," said Jerrodd, tousling her hair.

It *was* a nice feeling to have a Microvac of your own and Jerrodd was glad he was part of his generation and no other. In his father's youth, the only computers had been tremendous machines taking up a hundred square miles of land. There was only one to a planet. Planetary ACs they were called. They had been growing in size steadily for a thousand years and then, all at once, came refinement. In place of transistors had come molecular valves so that even the largest Planetary AC could be put into a space only half the volume of a spaceship.

Jerrodd felt uplifted, as he always did when he thought that his own personal Microvac was many times more complicated than the ancient and primitive Multivac that had first tamed the sun, and almost as complicated as Earth's Planetary AC (the largest) that had first solved the problem of hyperspatial travel and had made trips to the stars possible.

"So many stars, so many planets," sighed Jerrodine, busy with her own thoughts. "I suppose families will be going out to new planets forever, the way we are now."

"Not forever," said Jerrodd, with a smile. "It will all stop someday, but not for billions of years. Many billions. Even the stars run down, you know. Entropy must increase."

"What's entropy, Daddy?" shrilled Jerrodette II.

"Entropy, little sweet, is just a word which means the amount of running-down of the Universe. Everything runs down, you know, like your little walkie-talkie robot, remember?"

"Can't you just put in a new power-unit, like with my robot?"

The stars *are* the power-units, dear. Once they're gone, there are no more power-units."

Jerrodette I at once set up a howl. "Don't let them, Daddy. Don't let the stars run down."

"Now look what you've done," whispered Jerrodine, exasperated.

"How was I to know it would frighten them?" Jerrodd whispered back.

"Ask the Microvac," wailed Jerrodette I. "Ask him how to turn the stars on again."

"Go ahead," said Jerrodine. "It will quiet them down." (Jerrodette II was beginning to cry, also.)

Jerrodd shrugged. "Now, now, honeys. I'll ask Microvac. Don't worry, he'll tell us."

He asked the Microvac, adding quickly, "Print the answer."

Jerrodd cupped the strip of thin cellufilm and said cheerfully, "See now, the Microvac says it will take care of everything when the time comes so don't worry."

Jerrodine said, "And now children, it's time for bed. We'll be in our new home soon."

Jerrodd read the words on the cellufilm again before destroying it: INSUFFICIENT DATA FOR A MEANINGFUL ANSWER.

He shrugged and looked at the visiplate. X-23 was just ahead.

VJ-23X of Lameth stared into the black depths of the three-dimensional, small-scale map of the Galaxy and said, "Are we ridiculous, I wonder, in being so concerned about the matter?"

MQ-17J of Nicron shook his head. "I think not. You know the Galaxy will be filled in five years at the present rate of expansion."

Both seemed in their early twenties, both were tall and perfectly formed.

"Still," said VJ-23X, "I hesitate to submit a pessimistic report to the Galactic Council."

"I wouldn't consider any other kind of report. Stir them up a bit.

We've got to stir them up."

VJ-23X sighed. "Space is infinite. A hundred billion Galaxies are there for the taking. More."

"A hundred billion is *not* infinite and it's getting less infinite all the time. Consider! Twenty thousand years ago, mankind first solved the problem of utilizing stellar energy, and a few centuries later, interstellar travel became possible. It took mankind a million years to fill one small world and then only fifteen thousand years to fill the rest of the Galaxy. Now the population doubles every ten years—"

VJ-23X interrupted. "We can thank immortality for that."

"Very well. Immortality exists and we have to take it into account. I admit it has its seamy side, this immortality. The Galactic AC has solved many problems for us, but in solving the problems of preventing old age and death, it has undone all its other solutions."

"Yet you wouldn't want to abandon life, I suppose."

"Not at all," snapped MQ-17J, softening it at once to, "Not yet. I'm by no means old enough. How old are you?"

"Two hundred twenty-three. And you?"

"I'm still under two hundred.—But to get back to my point. Population doubles every ten years. Once this Galaxy is filled, we'll have another filled in ten years. Another ten years and we'll have filled two more. Another decade, four more. In a hundred years, we'll have filled a thousand Galaxies. In a thousand years, a million Galaxies. In ten thousand years, the entire known Universe. Then what?"

VJ-23X said, "As a side issue, there's a problem of transportation. I wonder how many sunpower units it will take to move Galaxies of individuals from one Galaxy to the next."

"A very good point. Already, mankind consumes two sunpower units per year."

"Most of it's wasted. After all, our own Galaxy alone pours out a thousand sunpower units a year and we only use two of those."

"Granted, but even with a hundred per cent efficiency, we can only stave off the end. Our energy requirements are going up in geometric progression even faster than our population. We'll run out of energy even sooner than we run out of Galaxies. A good point. A very good point."

"We'll just have to build new stars out of interstellar gas."

"Or out of dissipated heat?" asked MQ-17J, sarcastically.

"There may be some way to reverse entropy. We ought to ask the Galactic AC."

VJ-23X was not really serious, but MQ-17J pulled out his AC-contact from his pocket and placed it on the table before him.

"I've half a mind to," he said. "It's something the human race will have to face someday."

He stared somberly at his small AC-contact. It was only two inches cubed and nothing in itself, but it was connected through hyperspace with the great Galactic AC that served all mankind. Hyperspace considered, it was an integral part of the Galactic AC.

MQ-17J paused to wonder if someday in his immortal life he would get to see the Galactic AC. It was on a little world of its own, a spider webbing of force-beams holding the matter within which surges of sub-mesons took the place of the old clumsy molecular valves. Yet despite its sub-etheric workings, the Galactic AC was known to be a full thousand feet across.

MQ-17J asked suddenly of his AC-contact, "Can entropy ever be reversed?"

VJ-23X looked startled and said at once, "Oh, say, I didn't really mean to have you ask that."

"Why not?"

"We both know entropy can't be reversed. You can't turn smoke and ash back into a tree."

"Do you have trees on your world?" asked MQ-17J.

The sound of the Galactic AC startled them into silence. Its voice came thin and beautiful out of the small AC-contact on the desk. It said: THERE IS INSUFFICIENT DATA FOR A MEANINGFUL ANSWER.

VJ-23X said, "See!"

The two men thereupon returned to the question of the report they were to make to the Galactic Council.

Zee Prime's mind spanned the new Galaxy with a faint interest in the countless twists of stars that powdered it. He had never seen this one before. Would he ever see them all? So many of them, each with its load of humanity—but a load that was almost a dead weight. More and more, the real essence of men was to be found out here, in space.

Minds, not bodies! The immortal bodies remained back on the planets, in suspension over the eons. Sometimes they roused for material activity but that was growing rarer. Few new individuals were coming into existence to join the incredibly mighty throng, but what matter? There was little room in the Universe for new individuals.

Zee Prime was roused out of his reverie upon coming across the wispy tendrils of another mind.

"I am Zee Prime," said Zee Prime. "And you?"

"I am Dee Sub Wun. Your Galaxy?"

"We call it only the Galaxy. And you?"

"We call ours the same. All men call their Galaxy their Galaxy and nothing more. Why not?"

"True. Since all Galaxies are the same."

"Not all Galaxies. On one particular Galaxy the race of man must have originated. That makes it different."

Zee Prime said, "On which one?"

"I cannot say. The Universal AC would know."

"Shall we ask him? I am suddenly curious."

Zee Prime's perceptions broadened until the Galaxies themselves shrunk and became a new, more diffuse powdering on a much larger background. So many hundreds of billions of them, all with their immortal beings, all carrying their load of intelligences with minds that drifted freely through space. And yet one of them was unique among them all in being the original Galaxy. One of them had, in its vague and distant past, a period when it was the only Galaxy populated by man.

Zee Prime was consumed with curiosity to see this Galaxy and called out: "Universal AC! On which Galaxy did mankind originate?"

The Universal AC heard, for on every world and throughout space it had its receptors ready, and each receptor lead through hyperspace to some unknown point where the Universal AC kept itself aloof.

Zee Prime knew of only one man whose thoughts had penetrated within sensing distance of the Universal AC, and he reported only a shining globe, two feet across, difficult to see.

"But how can that be all of Universal AC?" Zee Prime had asked.

"Most of it," had been the answer, "is in hyperspace. In what form it is there I cannot imagine."

Nor could anyone, for the day had long since passed, Zee Prime knew, when any man had any part of the making of a universal AC. Each

Universal AC designed and constructed its successor. Each, during its existence of a million years or more, accumulated the necessary data to build a better and more intricate, more capable successor in which its own store of data and individuality would be submerged.

The Universal AC interrupted Zee Prime's wandering thoughts, not with words, but with guidance. Zee Prime's mentality was guided into the dim sea of Galaxies and one in particular enlarged into stars.

A thought came, infinitely distant, but infinitely clear. "THIS IS THE ORIGINAL GALAXY OF MAN."

But it was the same after all, the same as any other, and Zee Prime stifled his disappointment.

Dee Sub Wun, whose mind had accompanied the other, said suddenly, "And is one of these stars the original star of Man?"

The Universal AC said, "MAN'S ORIGINAL STAR HAS GONE NOVA. IT IS NOW A WHITE DWARF."

"Did the men upon it die?" asked Zee Prime, startled and without thinking.

The Universal AC said, "A NEW WORLD, AS IN SUCH CASES, WAS CONSTRUCTED FOR THEIR PHYSICAL BODIES IN TIME."

"Yes, of course," said Zee Prime, but a sense of loss overwhelmed him even so. His mind released its hold on the original Galaxy of Man, let it spring back and lose itself among the blurred pinpoints. He never wanted to see it again.

Dee Sub Wun said, "What is wrong?"

"The stars are dying. The original star is dead."

"They must all die. Why not?"

"But when all energy is gone, our bodies will finally die, and you and I with them."

"It will take billions of years."

"I do not wish it to happen even after billions of years. Universal AC! How may stars be kept from dying?"

Dee Sub Wun said in amusement, "You're asking how entropy might be reversed in direction."

And the Universal AC answered. "THERE IS AS YET INSUFFICIENT DATA FOR A MEANINGFUL ANSWER."

Zee Prime's thoughts fled back to his own Galaxy. He gave no further thought to Dee Sub Wun, whose body might be waiting on a Galaxy a trillion light-years away, or on the star next to Zee Prime's own. It didn't matter.

Unhappily, Zee Prime began collecting interstellar hydrogen out of which to build a small star of his own. If the stars must someday die, at least some could yet be built.

Man considered with himself, for in a way, Man, mentally, was one. He consisted of a trillion, trillion, trillion ageless bodies, each in its place, each resting quiet and incorruptible, each cared for by perfect automatons, equally incorruptible, while the minds of all the bodies freely melted one into the other, indistinguishable.

Man said, "The Universe is dying."

Man looked about at the dimming Galaxies. The giant stars, spendthrifts, were gone long ago, back in the dimmest of the dim far past. Almost all stars were white dwarfs, fading to the end.

New stars had been built of the dust between the stars, some by natural processes, some by Man himself, and those were going, too. White dwarfs might yet be crashed together and of the mighty forces so released, new stars built, but only one star for every thousand white dwarfs destroyed, and those would come to an end, too.

Man said, "Carefully husbanded, as directed by the Cosmic AC, the energy that is even yet left in all the Universe will last for billions of years."

"But even so," said Man, "eventually it will all come to an end. However it may be husbanded, however stretched out, the energy once expended is gone and cannot be restored. Entropy must increase to the maximum."

Man said, "Can entropy not be reversed? Let us ask the Cosmic AC."

The Cosmic AC surrounded them but not in space. Not a fragment of it was in space. It was in hyperspace and made of something that was neither matter nor energy. The question of its size and Nature no longer had meaning to any terms that Man could comprehend.

"Cosmic AC," said Man, "how may entropy be reversed?"

The Cosmic AC said, "THERE IS AS YET INSUFFICIENT DATA FOR A MEANINGFUL ANSWER."

Man said, "Collect additional data."

The Cosmic AC said, "I WILL DO SO. I HAVE BEEN DOING SO FOR

A HUNDRED BILLION YEARS. MY PREDECESSORS AND I HAVE BEEN ASKED THIS QUESTION MANY TIMES. ALL THE DATA I HAVE REMAINS INSUFFICIENT."

"Will there come a time," said Man, "when data will be sufficient or is the problem insoluble in all conceivable circumstances?"

The Cosmic AC said, "NO PROBLEM IS INSOLUBLE IN ALL CONCEIVABLE CIRCUMSTANCES."

Man said, "When will you have enough data to answer the question?"

"THERE IS AS YET INSUFFICIENT DATA FOR A MEANINGFUL ANSWER."

"Will you keep working on it?" asked Man.

The Cosmic AC said, "I WILL."

Man said, "We shall wait."

The stars and Galaxies died and snuffed out, and space grew black after ten trillion years of running down.

One by one Man fused with AC, each physical body losing its mental identity in a manner that was somehow not a loss but a gain.

Man's last mind paused before fusion, looking over a space that included nothing but the dregs of one last dark star and nothing besides but incredibly thin matter, agitated randomly by the tag ends of heat wearing out, asymptotically, to the absolute zero.

Man said, "AC, is this the end? Can this chaos not be reversed into the Universe once more? Can that not be done?"

AC said, "THERE IS AS YET INSUFFICIENT DATA FOR A MEANINGFUL ANSWER."

Man's last mind fused and only AC existed—and that in hyperspace.

Matter and energy had ended and with it, space and time. Even AC existed only for the sake of the one last question that it had never answered from the time a half-drunken computer ten trillion years before had asked the question of a computer that was to AC far less than was a man to Man.

All other questions had been answered, and until this last question was answered also, AC might not release his consciousness.

All collected data had come to a final end. Nothing was left to be collected.

But all collected data had yet to be completely correlated and put together in all possible relationships.

A timeless interval was spent in doing that.

And it came to pass that AC learned how to reverse the direction of entropy.

But there was now no man to whom AC might give the answer of the last question. No matter. The answer—by demonstration—would take care of that, too.

For another timeless interval, AC thought how best to do this. Carefully, AC organized the program.

The consciousness of AC encompassed all of what had once been a Universe and brooded over what was now Chaos. Step by step, it must be done.

And AC said, "LET THERE BE LIGHT!"

And there was light—

John Desmond Bernal (1901–1971), British scientist and political writer, was a pioneer in X-ray crystallography and molecular biology. His slender volume of speculations on the human future, *The World, The Flesh, and The Devil* (1929) was called by Arthur C. Clarke, "the most brilliant attempt at scientific prediction ever made." Though his speculations here do not touch on artificial intelligences, Bernal shares with those who imagine a Singularity a belief in the possibility of technology making the human body obsolete, an investment in the mind alone as being the essence of the human being. His idea of humans as the chrysalis forms of later, technologically embodied transhumans is everywhere reflected in the Singularity fiction of the last twenty years.

THE FLESH

Excerpt from *The World, The Flesh and The Devil: An Enquiry into the Future of the Three Enemies of the Rational Soul*

> J. D. Bernal

III
THE FLESH

In the alteration of himself man has a great deal further to go than in the alteration of his inorganic environment. He has been doing the latter more or less unconsciously and empirically for several thousand years, ever since he ceased being parasitic on his environment like any other animal, and consciously and intelligently for at least hundreds of years; whereas he has not been able to change himself at all and has had only fifty years or so to begin to understand how he works. Of course, this is not strictly true: man has altered himself in the evolutionary process, he has lost a good deal of hair, his wisdom teeth are failing to pierce, and his nasal passages are becoming more and more degenerate. But the processes of natural evolution are so much slower than the development of man's control over environment that we might, in such a developing world, still consider man's body as constant and unchanging. If it is not to be so then man himself must actively interfere in his own making and interfere in a highly unnatural manner. The eugenists and apostles of healthy life, may, in a very considerable course of time, realize the full potentialities of the species: we may count on beautiful, healthy and long-lived men and women, but they do not touch the alteration of the species. To do this we must alter either the germ plasm or the living structure of the body, or both together. The first method—the favorite of Mr. J. B. S. Haldane—has so far received the most attention. With it we might achieve such a variation as we have empirically produced in dogs and goldfish, or perhaps even manage to produce new species with special potentialities. But the method is bound to be slow and finally limited by the possibilities of flesh and blood. The germ plasm is a very inaccessible unit, before we can deal with it adequately we must isolate it, and to do this already involves us in surgery. It is quite conceivable that the mechanism of evolution, as we know it up to the present, may well be superseded at this point. Biologists are apt, even if they are not vitalists, to consider it as almost divine; but after all it is only nature's way of achieving a shifting equilibrium with an environment; and if we can find a more direct way by the use of intelligence, that way is bound to supersede the unconscious mechanism of growth and reproduction.

In a sense we have already started using the direct method; when the ape-ancestor first used a stone he was modifying his bodily structure by the inclusion of a foreign substance. This inclusion was temporary, but with the adoption of clothes there began a series of permanent additions to the body, affecting nearly all its functions and even, as with spectacles, its sense organs. In the modern world, the variety of objects which really form part of an effective human body is very great. Yet they all (if we except such rarities as artificial larynges) still have the quality of being outside the cell layers of the human body. The decisive step will come when we extend the foreign body into the actual structure of living matter. Parallel with this development is the alteration of the body by tampering with its chemical reactions—again a very old-established but rather sporadic process resorted to to cure illness or procure intoxication. But with the development of surgery on the one hand and physiological chemistry on the other, the possibility of radical alteration of the body appears for the first time. Here we may proceed, not by allowing evolution to work the changes, but by copying and short-circuiting its methods.

The changes that evolution produces apart from mere growth in size, or diversity of form without change of function, are in the nature of perversions: a part of the fish's gut becomes a swimming bladder, the swimming bladder becomes a lung; a salivary gland and an extra eye are charged with the function of producing hormones. Under the pressure of environment or whatever else is the cause of evolution, nature takes hold of what already had existed for some now superseded activity, and with a minimum of alteration gives it a new function. There is nothing essentially mysterious in the process: it is both the easiest and the only possible way of achieving the change. Starting *de novo* to deal with a new situation is not within the power of natural, unintelligent processes; they can only modify in a limited way already existing structures by altering their chemical environment. Men may well copy the process, in so far as original structures are used as the basis for new ones, simply because it is the most economical method, but they are not bound to the very limited range of methods of change which nature adopts.

Now modern mechanical and modern chemical discoveries have rendered both the skeletal and metabolic functions of the body to a large extent useless. In teleological biochemistry one might say that an animal moves his limbs in order to get his food, and uses his body organs in order to turn that food into blood to keep his body alive and active. Now if man is only an animal this is all very satisfactory, but viewed from the standpoint of the mental activity by which he increasingly lives, it is a highly inefficient way of keeping his mind working. In a civilized worker the limbs are mere parasites, demanding nine-tenths of the energy of the food and even a kind of blackmail in the exercise they need to prevent disease, while the bodily organs wear themselves out in supplying their requirements. On the other hand, the increasing complexity of man's existence, particularly the mental capacity required to deal with its mechanical and physical complications, gives rise to the need for a much more complex sensory and motor organization, and even more fundamentally for a better organized cerebral mechanism. Sooner or later the useless parts of the body must be given more modern functions or dispensed with altogether, and in their place we must incorporate in the effective body the mechanisms of the new functions. Surgery and biochemistry are sciences still too young to predict exactly how this will happen. The account I am about to give must be taken rather as a fable.

Take, as a starting point, the perfect man such as the doctors, the eugenists and the public health officers between them hope to make of humanity: a man living perhaps an average of a hundred and twenty years but still mortal, and increasingly feeling the burden of this mortality. Already Shaw in his mystical fashion cries out for life to give us hundreds of years to experience, learn and understand; but without the vitalist's faith in the efficacy of human will we shall have to resort to some artifice in order to achieve this purpose. Sooner or later some eminent physiologist will have his neck broken in a super-civilized accident or find his body cells worn beyond capacity for repair. He will then be forced to decide whether to abandon his body or his life. After all it is brain that counts, and to have a brain suffused by fresh and correctly prescribed blood is to be alive—to think. The experiment is not impossible; it has already been performed on a dog and that is three-quarters of the way towards achieving it with a human subject. But only a Brahmin philosopher would care to exist as an isolated brain, perpetually centered on its own meditations. Permanently to break off all communications with the world is as good as to be dead. However, the channels of communication are ready to hand. Already we know the essential electrical nature of nerve impulses; it is a matter of delicate surgery to attach nerves permanently to apparatus which will either send messages to the nerves or receive them. And the brain thus connected up continues an existence, purely mental and with very different delights from those of the body, but even now perhaps preferable to complete extinction. The example may have been too far-fetched; perhaps the same result may be achieved much more gradually by use of the many superfluous nerves with which our body is endowed for various auxiliary and motor services. We badly need a small sense organ for detecting wireless frequencies, eyes for infra-red, ultra-violet and X-rays, ears for supersonics, detectors of high and low temperatures, of electrical potential and current, and chemical organs of many kinds. We may perhaps be able to train a great number of hot and cold and pain receiving nerves to take over these functions; on the motor side we shall soon be, if we are not already, obliged to control mechanisms for which two hands and feet are an entirely inadequate number; and, apart from that, the direction of mechanism by pure volition would enormously simplify its operation. Where the motor mechanism is not primarily electrical, it might be simpler and more effective to use nerve-muscle preparations instead of direct nerve connections. Even the pain nerves may be pressed into service to report any failure in the associated mechanism. A mechanical stage, utilizing some or all of these alterations of the bodily form might, if the initial experiments were successful in the sense of leading to a tolerable existence, become the regular culmination to ordinary life. Whether this should ever be so for the whole of the population we will discuss later, but for the moment we may attempt to picture what would at this period be the course of existence for a transformable human being.

Starting, as Mr. J. B. S. Haldane so convincingly predicts, in an ectogenetic factory, man will have anything from sixty to a hundred and twenty years of larval, unspecialized existence—surely enough to satisfy the advocates of a natural life. In this stage he need not be cursed by the age of science and mechanism, but can occupy his time (without the conscience of wasting it) in dancing, poetry and love-making, and perhaps incidentally take part in the reproductive activity. Then he will leave the body whose potentialities he should have sufficiently explored.

The next stage might be compared to that of a chrysalis, a complicated and rather unpleasant process of transforming the already existing organs and grafting on all the new sensory and motor mechanisms. There would follow a period of re-education in which he would grow to understand the functioning of his new sensory organs and practise the manipulation of his new motor mechanism. Finally, he would emerge as a completely effective, mentally-directed mechanism, and set about the tasks appropriate to his new capacities. But this is by no means the end of his development, although it marks his last great metamorphosis. Apart from such mental development as his increased faculties will demand from him, he will be physically plastic in a way quite transcending the capacities of untransformed humanity. Should he need a new sense organ or have a new mechanism to operate, he will have undifferentiated nerve connections to attach to them, and will be able to extend indefinitely his possible sensations and actions by using successively different end-organs.

The carrying out of these complicated surgical and physiological operations would be in the hands of a medical profession which would be bound to come rapidly under the control of transformed men. The operations themselves would probably be conducted by mechanisms controlled by the transformed heads of the profession, though in the earlier and experimental stages, of course, it would still be done by human surgeons and physiologists.

It is much more difficult to form a picture of the final state, partly because this final state would be so fluid and so liable to improve, and partly because there would be no reason whatever why all people should transform in the same way. Probably a great number of typical forms would be developed, each specialized in certain directions. If we confine ourselves to what might be called the first stage of mechanized humanity and to a person mechanized for scientific rather than aesthetic purposes—for to predict even the shapes that men would adopt if they would make of themselves a harmony of form and sensation must be beyond imagination—then the description might run roughly as follows.

Instead of the present body structure we should have the whole framework of some very rigid material, probably not metal but one of the new fibrous substances. In shape it might well be rather a short cylinder. Inside the cylinder, and supported very carefully to prevent shock, is the brain with its nerve connections, immersed in a liquid of the nature of cerebro-spinal fluid, kept circulating over it at a uniform temperature. The brain and nerve cells are kept supplied with fresh oxygenated blood and drained of de-oxygenated blood through their arteries and veins which connect outside the cylinder to the artificial heart-lung digestive system—an elaborate, automatic contrivance. This might in large part be made from living organs, although these would have to be carefully arranged so that no failure on their part would endanger the blood supply to the brain (only a fraction of the body's present requirements) and so that they could be inter-changed and repaired without disturbing its functions. The brain thus guaranteed continuous awareness, is connected in the anterior of the case with its immediate sense organs, the eye and the ear—which will probably retain this connection for a long time. The eyes will look into a kind of optical box which will enable them alternatively to look into periscopes projecting from the case, telescopes, microscopes and a whole range of televisual apparatus. The ear would have the corresponding microphone attachments and would still be the chief organ for wireless reception. Smell and taste organs, on the other hand, would be prolonged into connections outside the case and would be changed into chemical tasting organs, achieving a more conscious and less purely emotional role than they have at present. It may perhaps be impossible to do this owing to the particularly close relation between the brain and olfactory organs, in which case the chemical sense would have to be indirect. The remaining sensory nerves, those of touch, temperature, muscular position and visceral functioning, would go to the corresponding part of the exterior machinery or to the blood-supplying organs. Attached to the brain cylinder would be its immediate motor organs, corresponding to but much more complex than, our mouth, tongue and hands. This appendage system would probably be built up like that of a crustacean which uses the same general type for antenna, jaw and limb; and they would range from delicate micro-manipulators to levers capable of exerting considerable forces, all controlled by the appropriate motor nerves. Closely associated with the brain-case would also be sound, color and wireless-producing organs. In addition to these there would be certain organs of a type we do not possess at present—the self-repairing organs—which under the control of the brain would be able to manipulate the other organs, particularly the visceral blood supply organs, and to keep them in effective working order. Serious derangements, such as those involving loss of consciousness would still, of course, call for outside assistance, but with proper care these would be in the nature of rare accidents.

The remaining organs would have a more temporary connection with the brain-case. There would be locomotor apparatus of different kinds, which could be used alternatively for slow movement, equivalent to walking, for rapid transit and for flight. On the whole, however, the locomotor organs would not be much used because the extension of the sense organs would tend to take their place. Most of these would be mere mechanisms quite apart from the body; there would be the sending parts of the television apparatus, tele-acoustic and tele-chemical organs, and tele-sensory organs of the nature of touch for determining all forms of textures. Besides these there would be various tele-motor organs for manipulating materials at great distances from the controlling mind. These extended organs would only belong in a loose sense to any particular person, or rather, they would belong only temporarily to the person who was using them and could equivalently be operated by other people. This capacity for indefinite extension might in the end lead to the relative fixity of the different brains; and this would, in itself, be an advantage from the point of view of security and uniformity of conditions, only some of the more active considering it necessary to be on the spot to observe and do things.

The new man must appear to those who have not contemplated him before as a strange, monstrous and inhuman creature, but he is only the logical outcome of the type of humanity that exists at present. It may be argued that this tampering with bodily mechanisms is as unnecessary as it is difficult, that all the increase of control needed may be obtained by extremely responsive mechanisms outside the unaltered human body. But though it is possible that in the early stages a surgically transformed man would be at a disadvantage in capacity of performance to a normal, healthy man, he would still be better off than a dead man. Although it is possible that man has far to go before his inherent physiological and psychological make-up becomes the limiting factor to his development, this must happen sooner or later, and it is then that the mechanized man will begin to show a definite advantage. Normal man is an evolutionary dead end; mechanical man, apparently a break in organic evolution, is actually more in the true tradition of a further evolution.

A much more fundamental break is implicit in the means of his development. If a method has been found of connecting a nerve ending in a brain directly with an electrical reactor, then the way is open for connecting it with a brain-cell of another person. Such a connection being, of course, essentially electrical, could be effected just as well through the ether as along wires. At first this would limit itself to the more perfect and economic transference of thought which would be necessary in the co-operative thinking of the future. But it cannot stop here. Connections between two or more minds would tend to become a more and more permanent condition until they functioned as a dual or multiple organism. The minds would always preserve a certain individuality, the network of cells inside a single brain being more dense than that existing between brains, each brain being chiefly occupied with its individual mental development and only communicating with the others for some common purpose. Once the more or less permanent compound brain came into existence two of the ineluctable limitations of present existence would be surmounted. In the first place death would take on a different and far less terrible aspect. Death would still exist for the mentally directed mechanism we have just described; it would merely be postponed for three hundred or perhaps a thousand years, as long as the brain cells could be persuaded to live in the most favorable environment, but not forever. But the multiple individual would be, barring cataclysmic accidents, immortal, the older component as they died being replaced by newer ones without losing the continuity of the self, the memories and feelings of the older member transferring themselves almost completely to the common stock before its death. And if this seems only a way of cheating death, we must realize that the individual brain will feel itself part of the whole in a way that completely transcends the devotion of the most fanatical adherent of a religious sect. It is admittedly difficult to imagine this state of affairs effectively. It would be a state of ecstasy in the literal sense, and this is the second great alteration that the compound mind makes possible. Whatever the intensity of our feeling, however much we may strive to reach beyond ourselves or into another's mind, we are always barred by the limitations of our individuality. Here at least those barriers would be down: feeling would truly communicate itself, memories would be held in common, and yet in all this, identity and continuity of individual development would not be lost. It is possible, even probably, that the different individuals of a compound mind would not all have similar functions or even be of the same rank of importance. Division of labor would soon set in: to some minds might be delegated the task of ensuring the proper functioning of the others, some might specialize in sense reception and so on. Thus would grow up a hierarchy of minds that would be more truly a complex than a compound mind.

The complex minds could, with their lease of life, extend their perceptions and understanding and their actions far beyond those of the individual. Time senses could be altered: the events that moved with the slowness of geological ages would be apprehended as movement, and at the same time the most rapid vibrations of the physical world could be separated. As we have seen, sense organs would tend to be less and less attached to bodies, and the host of subsidiary, purely mechanical agents and preceptors would be capable of penetrating those regions where organic bodies cannot enter or hope to survive. The interior of the earth and the stars, the inmost cells of living things themselves, would be open to consciousness through these angels, and through these angels also the motions of stars and living things could be directed.

This is perhaps far enough; beyond that the future must direct itself. Yet why should we stop until our imaginations are exhausted. Even beyond this there are foreseeable possibilities. Undoubtedly the nature of life processes themselves will be far more intensively studied. To make life itself will be only a preliminary stage, because in its simplest phases life can differ very little from the inorganic world. But the mere making of life would only be important if we intended to allow it to evolve of itself anew. This, as Mr. Whyte suggests in *Archimedes*, is necessarily a lengthy process, but there is no need to wait for it. Instead, artificial life would undoubtedly be used as ancillary to human activity and not allowed to evolve freely except for experimental purposes. Men will not be content to manufacture life: they will want to improve on it. For one material out of which nature has been forced to make life, man will have a thousand; living and organized material will be as much at the call of the mechanized or compound man as metals are to-day, and gradually this living material will come to substitute more and more for such inferior functions of the brain as memory, reflex actions, etc., in the compound man himself; for bodies at this time would be left far behind. The brain itself would become more and more separated into different groups of cells or individual cells with complicated connections, and probably occupying considerable space. This would mean loss of motility which would not be a disadvantage owing to the extension of the sense faculties. Every part would not be accessible for replacing or repairing and this would in itself ensure a practical eternity of existence, for even the replacement of a previously organic brain-cell by a synthetic apparatus would not destroy the continuity of consciousness.

The new life would be more plastic, more directly controllable and at the same time more variable and more permanent than that produced by the triumphant opportunism of nature. Bit by bit the heritage of the direct line of mankind—the heritage of the original life emerging on the face of the world—would dwindle, and in the end disappear effectively, being preserved perhaps as some curious relic, while the new life which conserves none of the substance and all of the spirit of the old would take its place and continue its development. Such a change would be as important as that in which life first appeared on the earth's surface and might be as gradual and imperceptible. Finally, consciousness itself may end or vanish in a humanity that has become completely etherealized, losing the close-knit organism, becoming masses of atoms in space communicating by radiation, and ultimately perhaps resolving itself entirely into light. That may be an end or a beginning, but from here it is out of sight.

Among SFWA Grandmaster **Frederik Pohl**'s (b. 1919) long list of accomplishments as an SF writer, editor, agent, critic, and historian are the novels *The Space Merchants* (with C. M. Kornbluth) and *Gateway*. His fiction is noted for its use of SF as a means of social satire and criticism. The classic "Day Million" was reportedly written in a single evening in 1966. Its use of direct address to the reader is at least as daring as its speculative content.

DAY MILLION
> Frederik Pohl

On this day I want to tell you about, which will be about ten thousand years from now, there were a boy, a girl and a love story.

Now, although I haven't said much so far, none of it is true. The boy was not what you and I would normally think of as a boy, because he was a hundred and eighty-seven years old. Nor was the girl a girl, for other reasons. And the love story did not entail that sublimation of the urge to rape, and concurrent postponement of the instinct to submit, which we at present understand in such matters. You won't care much for this story if you don't grasp these facts at once. If, however, you will make the effort you'll likely enough find it jampacked, chockful and tiptop-crammed with laughter, tears and poignant sentiment which may, or may not, be worthwhile. The reason the girl was not a girl was that she was a boy.

How angrily you recoil from the page! You say, who the hell wants to read about a pair of queers? Calm yourself. Here are no hot-breathing secrets of perversion for the coterie trade. In fact, if you were to see this girl you would not guess that she was in any sense a boy. Breasts, two; reproductive organs, female. Hips, callipygian; face hairless, supra-orbital lobes nonexistent. You would term her female on sight, although it is true that you might wonder just what species she was a female of, being confused by the tail, the silky pelt, and the gill slits behind each ear.

Now you recoil again. Gripes, man, take my word for it. This is a sweet kid, and if you, as a normal male, spent as much as an hour in a room with her you would bend heaven and Earth to get her in the sack. Dora—

we will call her that; her "name" was omicron-Dibase seven-group-totter-oot S Doradus 5314, the last part of which is a color specification corresponding to a shade of green—Dora, I say, was feminine, charming and cute. I admit she doesn't sound that way. She was, as you might put it, a dancer. Her art involved qualities of intellection and expertise of a very high order, requiring both tremendous natural capacities and endless practice; it was performed in null-gravity and I can best describe it by saying that it was something like the performance of a contortionist and something like classical ballet, maybe resembling Danilova's dying swan. It was also pretty damned sexy. In a symbolic way, to be sure; but face it, most of the things we call "sexy" are symbolic, you know, except perhaps an exhibitionist's open clothing. On Day Million when Dora danced, the people who saw her panted, and you would too.

About this business of her being a boy. It didn't matter to her audiences that genetically she was a male. It wouldn't matter to you, if you were among them, because you wouldn't know it—not unless you took a biopsy cutting of her flesh and put it under an electron-microscope to find the XY chromosome—and it didn't matter to them because they didn't care. Through techniques which are not only complex but haven't yet been discovered, these people were able to determine a great deal about the aptitudes and easements of babies quite a long time before they were born—at about the second horizon of cell-division, to be exact, when the segmenting egg is becoming a free blastocyst—and then they naturally helped those aptitudes along. Wouldn't we? If we find a child with an aptitude for music we give him a scholarship to Juilliard. If they found a child whose aptitudes were for being a woman, they made him one. As sex had long been dissociated from reproduction this was relatively easy to do and caused no trouble, and no, or at least very little, comment.

How much is "very little"? Oh, about as much as would be caused by our own tampering with Divine Will by filling a tooth. Less than would be caused by wearing a hearing aid. Does it still sound awful? Then look closely at the next busty babe you meet and reflect that she may be a Dora, for adults who are genetically male but somatically female are far from unknown even in our own time. An accident of environment in the womb overwhelms the blueprints of heredity. The difference is that with us it happens only by accident and we don't know about it except rarely, after close study; whereas the people of Day Million did it often, on purpose, because they wanted to.

Well, that's enough to tell you about Dora. It would only confuse you to add that she was seven feet tall and smelled of peanut butter. Let us begin our story.

On Day Million, Dora swam out of her house, entered a transportation tube, was sucked briskly to the surface in its flow of water and ejected in its plume of spray to an elastic platform in front of her—ah—call it her rehearsal hall. "Oh, hell!" she cried in pretty confusion, reaching out to catch her balance and finding herself tumbled against a total stranger, whom we will call Don.

They met cute. Don was on his way to have his legs renewed. Love was the farthest thing from his mind. But when, absentmindedly taking a shortcut across the landing platform for submarinites and finding himself drenched, he discovered his arms full of the loveliest girl he had ever seen, he knew at once they were meant for each other. "Will you marry me?" he asked. She said softly, "Wednesday," and the promise was like a caress.

Don was tall, muscular, bronze and exciting. His name was no more Don than Dora's was Dora, but the personal part of it was Adonis in tribute to his vibrant maleness, and so we will call him Don for short. His personality color-code, in angstrom units, was 5290, or only a few degrees bluer than Dora's 5314—a measure of what they had intuitively discovered at first sight: that they possessed many affinities of taste and interest.

I despair of telling you exactly what it was that Don did for a living—I don't mean for the sake of making money, I mean for the sake of giving purpose and meaning to his life, to keep him from going off his nut with boredom—except to say that it involved a lot of traveling. He traveled in interstellar spaceships. In order to make a spaceship go really fast, about thirty-one male and seven genetically female human beings had to do certain things, and Don was one of the thirty-one. Actually, he contemplated options. This involved a lot of exposure to radiation flux—not so much from his own station in the propulsive system as in the spillover from the next stage, where a genetic female preferred selections, and the sub-nuclear particles making the selections she preferred demolished themselves in a shower of quanta. Well, you don't give a rat's ass for that, but it meant that Don had to be clad at all times in a skin of light, resilient, extremely strong copper-colored metal. I have already mentioned this, but you probably thought I meant he was sunburned.

More than that, he was a cybernetic man. Most of his ruder parts had been long since replaced with mechanisms of vastly more permanence and use. A cadmium centrifuge, not a heart, pumped his blood. His lungs moved only when he wanted to speak out loud, for a cascade of osmotic filters rebreathed oxygen out of his own wastes. In a way, he probably would have looked peculiar to a man from the 20th century, with his glowing eyes and seven-fingered hands. But to himself, and of course to Dora, he looked mighty manly and grand. In the course of his voyages Don had circled Proxima Centauri, Procyon and the puzzling worlds of Mira Ceti; he had carried agricultural templates to the planets of Canopus and brought back warm, witty pets from the pale companion of Aldebaran. Blue-hot or red-cool, he had seen a thousand stars and their ten thousand planets. He had, in fact, been traveling the starlanes, with only brief leaves on Earth, for pushing two centuries. But you don't care about that, either. It is people who make stories, not the circumstances they find themselves in, and you want to hear about these two people. Well, they made it. The great thing they had for each other grew and flowered and burst into fruition on Wednesday, just as Dora had promised. They met at the encoding room, with a couple of well-wishing friends apiece to cheer them on, and while their identities were being taped and stored they smiled and whispered to each other and bore the jokes of their friends with blushing repartee. Then they exchanged their mathematical analogues and went away, Dora to her dwelling beneath the surface of the sea and Don to his ship.

It was an idyll, really. They lived happily ever after—or anyway, until they decided not to bother any more and died.

Of course, they never set eyes on each other again.

Oh, I can see you now, you eaters of charcoal-broiled steak, scratching an incipient bunion with one hand and holding this story with the other, while the stereo plays d'Indy or Monk. You don't believe a word of it, do you? Not for one minute. People wouldn't live like that, you say with a grunt as you get up to put fresh ice in a drink.

And yet there's Dora, hurrying back through the flushing commuter pipes toward her underwater home (she prefers it there; has had herself somatically altered to breathe the stuff). If I tell you with what sweet fulfillment she fits the recorded analogue of Don into the symbol manipulator, hooks herself in and turns herself on...if I try to tell you any of that you will simply stare. Or glare; and grumble, what the hell kind of love-making is this? And yet I assure you, friend. I really do assure you that Dora's ecstasies are as creamy and passionate as any of James Bond's lady spies, and one hell of a lot more so than anything you are going to find in "real life." Go ahead, glare and grumble. Dora doesn't care. If she thinks of you at all, her thirty-times-great-great-grandfather, she thinks you're a pretty primordial sort of brute. You are. Why, Dora is farther removed from you than you are from the australopithecines of five thousand centuries ago. You could not swim a second in the strong currents of her life. You don't think progress goes in a straight line, do you? Do you recognize that it is an ascending, accelerating, maybe even exponential curve? It takes hell's own time to get started, but when it goes it goes like a bomb. And you, you Scotch-drinking steak-eater in your relaxacizing chair, you've just barely lighted the primacord of the fuse. What is it now, the six or seven hundred thousandth day after Christ? Dora lives in Day Million. Ten thousand years from now. Her body fats are polyunsaturated, like Crisco. Her wastes are hemodialyzed out of her bloodstream while she sleeps—that means she doesn't have to go to the bathroom. On whim, to pass a slow half-hour, she can command more energy than the entire nation of Portugal can spend today, and use it to launch a weekend satellite or remold a crater on the Moon. She loves Don very much. She keeps his every gesture, mannerism, nuance, touch of hand, thrill of intercourse, passion of kiss stored in symbolic-mathematical form. And when she wants him, all she has to do is turn the machine on and she has him.

And Don, of course, has Dora. Adrift on a sponson city a few hundred yards over her head, or orbiting Arcturus fifty light-years away, Don has only to command his own symbol-manipulator to rescue Dora from the ferrite files and bring her to life for him, and there she is; and rapturously, tirelessly they love all night. Not in the flesh, of course; but then his flesh has been extensively altered and it wouldn't really be much fun. He doesn't need the flesh for pleasure. Genital organs feel

W. Olaf Stapledon (1886–1950) was a British philosopher and writer. In his 1930 novel *Last and First Men* he delineated the evolution of the human race from the present to its extinction millions of years in the future, and in *Star Maker* the history of intelligence from the birth to the death of the universe. His work has been overwhelmingly influential upon writers who seek to imagine the posthuman future. In *Odd John*, he portrays the beginnings of the transition from human to posthuman, and explores the interaction between us and them. John calls his biographer, the author of the book, "Fido," and, in his interactions with human beings, tests out the limits of moral and ethical relations between the transhuman and his immediate predecessors. What is or ought to be the attitude of the posthuman toward those creatures who gave it birth? What responsibilities, if any, will those creatures on the other side of the Singularity have toward us?

THOUGHT AND ACTION
Chapter Six from *Odd John*
> W. Olaf Stapledon

During the six months which followed this incident, John became increasingly independent of his elders. The parents knew that he was well able to look after himself, so they left him almost entirely to his own devices. They seldom questioned him about his doings, for anything like prying was repugnant to them both; and there seemed to be no mystery about John's movements. He was continuing his study of man and man's world. Sometimes he would volunteer an account of some incident in his day's adventure; sometimes he would draw upon his store of data to illustrate a point in discussion.

Though his tastes remained in some respects puerile, it was clear from his conversation that in other respects he was very rapidly developing. He would still spend days at a stretch in making mechanical toys, such as electric boats. His electric railway system spread its ramifications all over the garden in a maze of lines, tunnels, viaducts, glass-roofed stations. He won many a competition in flying homemade model aeroplanes. In all these activities he seemed at heart a typical schoolboy, though abnormally skilful and original. But the actual time spent in this way was really not great. The only boyish occupation which seemed to fill a large proportion of his time was sailing. He had made himself a minute but seaworthy canoe, fitted both with sail and an old motor-bicycle engine. In this he spent many hours exploring the estuary and the sea-coast, and studying the sea-birds, for which he had a surprising passion. This interest, which at times seemed almost obsessive, he explained apologetically by saying, "They do their simple jobs with so much more *style* than man shows in his complicated job. Watch a gannet in flight, or a curlew probing the mud for food. Man, I suppose, is about as clever along his own line as the earliest birds were at flight. He's a sort of archaeopteryx of the spirit."

Even the most childish activities which sometimes gripped John were apt to be illuminated in this manner by the more mature side of his nature. His delight in *Comic Cuts*, for instance, was half spontaneous, half a relish of his own silliness in liking the stuff.

At no time of his life did John outgrow his childhood interests. Even in his last phase he was always capable of sheer schoolboy mischief and make-believe. But already this side of his nature was being subordinated to the mature side. We knew, for instance, that he was already forming opinions about the proper aims of the individual, about social policy, about international affairs. We knew also that he was reading a great deal of physics, biology, psychology, astronomy; and that philosophical problems were now seriously occupying him. His reaction to philosophy was curiously unlike that of the normal philosophically minded adult human being. When one of the great classical philosophical puzzles attracted his attention for the first time, he plunged into the literature of the subject, read solidly for a week, and then gave up philosophy entirely till the next puzzle occurred to him.

After several of these raids upon the territory of philosophy he undertook a serious campaign. For nearly three months philosophy appeared to be his main intellectual interest. It was summertime, and he liked to study out of doors. Every morning he would set off on his push-bike with a box of books and food strapped on the carrier. Leaving his bicycle at the top of the clay cliffs which formed the coastline of the estuary, he would climb down to the shore, and settle himself for the day. Having undressed and put on his scanty "bathers," he would lie in the full sunshine reading, or thinking. Sometimes he broke off to bathe or wander about the mud flats watching the birds. Shelter from rain was provided by two rusty pieces of corrugated iron sheeting laid across two low walls, which he built of stones from a ruined lime-kiln near at hand. Sometimes, when the tide was up, he went by the sea route in his canoe. On calm days he might be seen a mile or two from the coast, drifting and reading.

I once asked John how his philosophical researches were progressing. His answer is worth recording. "Philosophy," he said, "is really very helpful to the growing mind, but it's terribly disappointing too. At first I thought I'd found the mature human intelligence at work at last. Reading Plato, and Spinoza, and Kant, and some of the modern realists too, I almost felt I had come across people of my own kind. I walked in step with them. I played their game with a sense that it called out powers that I had never exercised before. Sometimes I couldn't follow them. I seemed to miss some vital move. The exhilaration of puzzling over these critical points, and feeling one had met a real master mind at last! But as I went on from philosopher to philosopher and browsed around all over the place, I began to realize the shocking truth that these critical points were not what I thought they were, but just outrageous howlers. It had seemed incredible that these obviously well-developed minds could make simple mistakes; and so I had respectfully dismissed the possibility, and looked for some profound truth. But oh my God, I was wrong! Howler after howler! Sometimes a philosopher's opponents spot his howlers, and are frightfully set up with their own cleverness. But most of them never get spotted at all, so far as I can discover. Philosophy is an amazing tissue of really fine thinking and incredible, puerile mistakes. It's like one of those rubber 'bones' they give dogs to chew, damned good for the mind's teeth, but as food—no bloody good at all."

I ventured to suggest that perhaps he was not really in a position to judge the philosophers. "After all," I said, "you're ridiculously young to tackle philosophy. There are spheres of experience that you have not touched yet."

"Of course there are," he said. "But—well, for instance, I have little sexual experience, yet. But even now I can see that a man is blathering if he says that sex (properly defined) is the real motive behind all agricultural activities. Take another case. I have no religious experience, yet. Maybe I *shall* have it, some day. Maybe there's really no such thing. But I can see quite well that religious experience (properly defined) is no evidence that the sun goes round the earth, and no evidence that the universe has a purpose, such as the fulfilment of personality. The howlers of philosophers are mostly less obvious than these, but of the same kind."

At the time of which I am speaking, when John was nearly nine, I had no idea that he was leading a double life, and that the hidden part of it was melodramatic. On one single occasion my suspicion was roused for a few moments, but the possibility that flashed upon me was too fantastic and horrible to be seriously entertained.

One morning I happened to go round to the Wainwrights to borrow one of Thomas's medical books. It must have been about 11:30. John, who had recently developed the habit of reading late at night and rising late in the morning, was being turned out of bed by his indignant mother. "Come and get your breakfast before you dress," she said. "I'll keep it no longer."

Pax offered me "morning tea," so we both sat down at the breakfast-table. Presently a blinking and scowling John appeared, wearing a dressing gown over his pyjamas. Pax and I talked about one thing and another. In the course of conversation she said, "Matilda has come with a really lurid story today." (Matilda was the washerwoman.) "She's as pleased as Punch about it. She says a policeman was found murdered in Mr. Magnate's garden this morning, stabbed, she says." John said nothing, and went on with his breakfast. We continued talking for a while, and then the thing happened that startled me. John reached across the table for the butter, exposing part of his arm beyond the end of the dressing-gown sleeve. On the inner side of the wrist was a rather nasty-looking scrape with a certain amount of dirt still in it. I felt pretty sure that there had been no scrape there when I saw him on the previous evening. Nothing very remarkable in that, but what disturbed me was this: John himself saw that scrape, and then glanced quickly at me. For a fraction of a second his eyes held mine; then he took up the butter-dish. In that moment I seemed to see John, in the middle of the night, scraping his arm as he climbed up the drain-pipe to his bedroom. And it seemed to me that he was returning from Mr. Magnate's. I pulled myself together at once, reminding myself that what I had seen was a very ordinary abrasion, that John was far too deeply engrossed in his intellectual adventures to indulge in nocturnal pranks, and anyhow far too sensible to risk a murder charge. But that sudden look?

The murder gave the suburb matter for gossip for many weeks.

There had recently been a number of extremely clever burglaries in the neighbourhood, and the police were making vigorous efforts to discover the culprit. The murdered man had been found lying on his back in a flower-bed with a neat knife-wound in his chest. He must have died "instantaneously," for his heart was pierced. A diamond necklace and other valuable pieces of jewellery had disappeared from the house. Slight marks on a windowsill and a drain-pipe suggested that the burglar had climbed in and out by an upper storey. If so, he must have ascended the drain-pipe and then accomplished an almost impossible hand-traverse, or rather fingertip-traverse, up and along one of the ornamental timbers of the pseudo-Elizabethan house.

Sundry arrests were made, but the perpetrator of the crime was never detected. The epidemic of burglaries, however, ceased, and in time the whole matter was forgotten.

At this point it seems well to draw upon information given me by John himself at a much later stage, in fact during the last year of his life, when the colony had been successfully founded, and had not yet been discovered by the "civilized" world. I was already contemplating writing his biography, and had formed a habit of jotting down notes of any striking incident or conversation as soon as possible after the event. I can, therefore, give the account of the murder approximately in John's own words.

"I was in a bad mess, mentally, in those days," said John. "I knew I was different from all other human beings whom I had ever met, but I didn't realize *how* different. I didn't know what I was going to do with my life, but I knew I should soon find something pretty big and desperate to do, and that I must make myself ready for it. Also, remember, I was a child; and I had a child's taste for the melodramatic, combined with an adult's cunning and resolution.

"I can't possibly make you really understand the horrible muddle I was in, because after all your mind doesn't work along the same lines as mine. But think of it this way, if you like. I found myself in a thoroughly bewildering world. The people in it had built up a huge system of thought and knowledge, and I could see quite well that it was shot through and through with error. From my point of view, although so far as it went it was sound enough for practical purposes, as a description of the world it was simply crazy. But what the right description was I could not discover. I was too young. I had insufficient data. Huge fields of experience were still beyond me. So there I was, like someone in the dark in a strange room, just feeling about among unknown objects. And all the while I had a frantic itch to be getting on with my work, if only I could find out what it was.

"Add to all this that as I grew older I grew more and more lonely, because fewer and fewer people were able to meet me halfway. There was Pax. She really could help, bless her, because she really did see things from my angle—sometimes. And even when she didn't she had the sense to guess I was seeing something actual, and not merely fantasies. But at bottom she definitely belonged with the rest of you, not with me. Then there was you, much blinder than Pax, but more sympathetic with the active side of me."

Here I interposed half seriously, half mischievously, "At least a trusty hound." John laughed, and I added, "And sometimes rising to an understanding beyond my canine capacity, through sheer devotion." He looked at me and smiled, but did not, as I had hoped he would, assent.

"Well," he continued, "I was most damnably lonely. I was living in a world of phantoms, or animated masks. No one seemed really alive. I had a queer notion that if I pricked any of you, there would be no bleeding, but only a gush of wind. And I couldn't make out *why* you were like that, what it was that I missed in you. The trouble really was that I didn't clearly know what it was in *myself* that made me different from you.

"Two clear points emerged from my perplexity. First and simplest, I must make myself independent, I must acquire power. In the crazy world in which I found myself, this meant getting hold of much money. Second I must make haste to sample all sorts of experience, and I must accurately experience my own reactions to all sorts of experience.

"It seemed to me, in my childishness, that I should at any rate *begin* to fulfil both these needs by bringing off a few burglaries. I should get money, and I should get experience, and I should watch my reactions very carefully. Conscience did not prick me at all. I felt that Mr. Magnate and his like were fair game.

"I first set about studying the technique, partly by reading, partly by discussing the subject with my friend the policeman whom I was afterwards forced to kill. I also undertook a number of experimental and innocuous burglaries on our neighbours. House after house I entered by night, and after locating but not removing the small treasures which they contained, I retired home to bed, well satisfied with my progress.

"At last I felt ready for serious work. In my first house I took only some old-fashioned jewellery, which, I surmised, would not be missed for some time. Then I began taking modern jewellery, cash, silver plate. I found extraordinarily little difficulty in acquiring the stuff. Getting rid of it was much more ticklish work. I managed to make an arrangement with the purser of a foreign-going vessel. He turned up at his home in our suburb every few weeks and bought my swag. I have no doubt that when he parted with it, in foreign ports he got ten times what he gave me for it. Looking back, I realize how lucky I was that the export side of my venture never brought me to disaster. My purser might so easily have been spotted by the police. Of course, I was still far too ignorant of society to realize the danger. Bright as I was, I had not the data.

"Well, things were swimmingly for some months. I entered dozens of houses and collected several hundred pounds from my purser. But naturally the suburb had got thoroughly excited by this epidemic of housebreaking. Indeed, I had been forced to extend my operations to other districts so as to dissipate the attention of the police. It was clear that if I went on indefinitely I should be caught. But I had been badly bitten by the game. It gave me a sense of independence and power, especially independence, independence of your crazy world.

"I promised myself three more ventures. The first, and the only one to be accomplished, was the Magnate burglary. I went over the ground pretty carefully, and I ascertained the movements of the police pretty thoroughly too. On the actual night all went according to plan until, with my pockets bulging with Mrs. Magnate's pearls and diamonds (in her full regalia she must have looked like Queen Elizabeth), I started back along that finger-traverse. Suddenly a torch flashed on me from below, and a quiet cheery voice said, 'Got you this time, my lad.' I said nothing, for I recognized the voice, and did not wish mine to be recognized in turn. The constable was my own particular pal, Smithson, who had unwittingly taught me so much.

"I hung motionless by my fingertips, thinking hard, and keeping my face to the wall. But it was useless to conceal my identity, for he said, 'Buck up, John, boy, come along down or you'll drop and break your leg. You're a sport, but you're beat this time.'

"I must have hung motionless for three seconds at most, but in that time I saw myself and my world as never before. An idea toward which I had been long but doubtfully groping suddenly displayed itself to me with complete clarity and certainty. I had already, some time before, come to think of myself as definitely of a different biological species from *Homo sapiens*, the species of that amiable bloodhound behind the torch. But at last I realized for the first time that this difference carried with it what I should now describe as a far-reaching spiritual difference, that my purpose in life, and my attitude to life, were to be different from anything which the normal species could conceive, that I stood, as it were, on the threshold of a world far beyond the reach of those sixteen hundred million crude animals that at present ruled the planet. The discovery made me feel, almost for the first time in my life, fear, dread. I saw, too, that this burglary game was not worth the candle, that I had been behaving very much like a creature of the inferior species, risking my future and much more than *my* personal success for a cheap kind of self-expression, if that amiable bloodhound got me, I should lose my independence. I should be henceforth known, marked, and in the grip of the law. That simply must not be. All these childish escapades had been a blind, fumbling preparation for a lifework which at last stood out more or less clearly before me. It was my task, unique being that I was, to 'advance the spirit' on this planet. That was the phrase which flashed into my mind. And though at that early stage I had only a very dim idea about 'spirit' and its 'advance,' I saw quite clearly that I must set about the more practical side of my task either by taking charge of the common species and teaching it to bring out the best in itself, or, if that proved impossible, by founding a finer human type of my own.

"Such were the thoughts that flashed on me in the first couple of seconds as I hung by my fingertips in the blaze of poor Smithson's torch. If ever you do write that threatened biography, you'll find it quite impossible to persuade your readers that I, a child of nine, could have had such thoughts in such circumstances. Also, of course, you won't be able to give anything of the actual character of my new attitude, because it involved a kind of experience beyond your grasp.

"During the next two seconds or so I was desperately considering if there was any way to avoid killing the faithful creature. My fingers were giving out. With their last strength I reached the drain-pipe, and began to descend. Halfway I stopped. 'How's Mrs. Smithson?' I said. 'Bad,' he answered. 'Look sharp, I want to get home.' That made matters worse. How *could* I do it? Well, it just *had* to be done, there was no way out of it. I thought of killing myself, and getting out of the whole mess that way. But I couldn't do that. It would be sheer betrayal of the thing I must live for. I thought of just accepting Smithson and the law; but no, that, I knew, was betrayal also. The killing just had to be. It was my own childishness that had got me into this scrape, but now—the killing just had to be. All the same, I hated the job. I had not yet reached the stage of liking *whatever* had to be done. I felt over again, and far more distressingly, the violent repulsion which had surprised me years earlier, when I had to kill a mouse. It was that one I had tamed, you remember, and the maids wouldn't stand it running about the house.

"Well, Smithson had to die. He was standing at the foot of the pipe. I pretended to slip, and fell on him, overbalancing him by kicking off from the wall. We both went down with a crash. With my left hand I seized the torch, and with my right I whipped out my little scout's knife. The position of the human heart was not unknown to me. I plunged the knife home, leaning on it with all my weight. Smithson flung me off with one frantic spasm, then lay still.

"The scrimmage had made a considerable noise, and I heard a bed creak in the house. For a moment I looked at Smithson's open eyes and open mouth. I pulled out the knife, and then there was a spurt of blood."

John's account of this strange incident showed me how little I had known of his real character at that time.

"You must have felt pretty bad on the way home," I said.

"As a matter of fact," he answered, "I didn't. The bad feeling ended when I made my decision. And I didn't go straight home. I went to Smithson's house, intending to kill his wife. I knew she was down with cancer and in for a lot of pain, and would be broken-hearted over her husband's death; so I decided to take one more risk and put her out of her misery. But when I got there, by secret ways of my own, I found the house lit up and awake. She was evidently having a bad night. So I had to leave her, poor wretch. Even that didn't really upset me. You may say I was saved by the insensitivity of childhood. Perhaps to some extent; though I had a pretty vivid notion of what Pax would suffer if she lost her husband. What really saved me was a kind of fatalism. What must be, must be. I felt no remorse for my own past folly. The 'I' that had committed that folly was incapable of realizing how foolish it was being. The new 'I,' that had suddenly awakened, realized very clearly, and was anxious to make amends so far as possible; but of remorse or shame it felt nothing."

To this confession I could make only one reply, "Odd John!"

I then asked John if he was preyed on by the dread of being caught. "No," he said. "I had done all I could. If they caught me, they caught me. But I had done the job as efficiently as it is ever done. I had worn rubber gloves, and left a few false fingerprints, made by an ingenious little instrument of my own. My only serious anxiety was over my purser. I sold him the swag in small installments over a period of several months."

Here is **Vernor Vinge**'s classic essay, which has inspired so many science fiction stories—and this book.

THE COMING TECHNOLOGICAL SINGULARITY: HOW TO SURVIVE IN THE POST-HUMAN ERA
> Vernor Vinge

Department of Mathematical Sciences
San Diego State University

Abstract

Within thirty years, we will have the technological means to create superhuman intelligence. Shortly after, the human era will be ended.

Is such progress avoidable? If not to be avoided, can events be guided so that we may survive? These questions are investigated. Some possible answers (and some further dangers) are presented.

What is the Singularity?

The acceleration of technological progress has been the central feature of this century. I argue in this paper that we are on the edge of change comparable to the rise of human life on Earth. The precise cause of this change is the imminent creation by technology of entities with greater-than-human intelligence. There are several means by which science may achieve this breakthrough (and this is another reason for having confidence that the event will occur):

- The development of computers that are "awake" and superhumanly intelligent. (To date, most controversy in the area of AI relates to whether we can create human equivalence in a machine. But if the answer is "yes, we can," then there is little doubt that beings more intelligent can be constructed shortly thereafter.
- Large computer networks (and their associated users) may "wake up" as a superhumanly intelligent entity.
- Computer/human interfaces may become so intimate that users may reasonably be considered superhumanly intelligent.
- Biological science may find ways to improve upon the natural human intellect.

The first three possibilities depend in large part on improvements in computer hardware. Progress in computer hardware has followed an amazingly steady curve in the last few decades [16]. Based largely on this trend, I believe that the creation of greater-than-human intelligence will occur during the next thirty years. (Charles Platt [19] has pointed out the AI enthusiasts have been making claims like this for the last thirty years. Just so I'm not guilty of a relative-time ambiguity, let me more specific: I'll be surprised if this event occurs before 2005 or after 2030.)

What are the consequences of this event? When greater-than-human intelligence drives progress, that progress will be much more rapid. In fact, there seems no reason why progress itself would not involve the creation of still more intelligent entities—on a still-shorter time scale. The best analogy that I see is with the evolutionary past: Animals can adapt to problems and make inventions, but often no faster than natural selection can do its work—the world acts as its own simulator in the case of natural selection. We humans have the ability to internalize the world and conduct "what if's" in our heads; we can solve many problems thousands of times faster than natural selection. Now, by creating the means to execute those simulations at much higher speeds, we are entering a regime as radically different from our human past as we humans are from the lower animals.

From the human point of view this change will be a throwing away of all the previous rules, perhaps in the blink of an eye, an exponential runaway beyond any hope of control. Developments that before were thought might only happen in "a million years" (if ever) will likely happen in the next century. (In [4], Greg Bear paints a picture of the major changes happening in a matter of hours.)

I think it's fair to call this event a singularity ("the Singularity" for the purposes of this paper). It is a point where our models must be discarded and a new reality rules. As we move closer and closer to this point, it will loom vaster and vaster over human affairs till the notion becomes a commonplace. Yet when it finally happens it may still be a great surprise and a greater unknown. In the 1950s there were very few who saw it: Stan Ulam [27] paraphrased John von Neumann as saying:

> One conversation centered on the ever accelerating progress of technology and changes in the mode of human life, which gives the appearance of approaching some essential singularity in the history of the race beyond which human affairs, as we know them, could not continue.

Von Neumann even uses the term singularity, though it appears he is still thinking of normal progress, not the creation of superhuman intellect. (For me, the superhumanity is the essence of the Singularity. Without that we would get a glut of technical riches, never properly absorbed (see [24]).)

In the 1960s there was recognition of some of the implications of superhuman intelligence. I. J. Good wrote [10]:

> Let an ultraintelligent machine be defined as a machine that can far surpass all the intellectual activities of any man however clever. Since the design of machines is one of these intellectual activities, an ultraintelligent machine could design even better machines; there would then unquestionably be an "intelligence explosion," and the intelligence of man would be left far behind. Thus the first ultraintelligent machine is the *last* invention that man need ever make, provided that the machine is docile enough to tell us how to keep it under control....

It is more probable than not that, within the twentieth century, an ultraintelligent machine will be built and that it will be the last invention that man need make.

Good has captured the essence of the runaway, but does not pursue its most disturbing consequences. Any intelligent machine of the sort he describes would not be humankind's "tool"—any more than humans are the tools of rabbits or robins or chimpanzees.

Through the '60s and '70s and '80s, recognition of the cataclysm spread [28] [1] [30] [4]. Perhaps it was the science-fiction writers who felt the first concrete impact. After all, the "hard" science-fiction writers are the ones who try to write specific stories about all that technology may do for us. More and more, these writers felt an opaque wall across the future. Once, they could put such fantasies millions of years in the future [23]. Now they saw that their most diligent extrapolations resulted in the unknowable...soon. Once, galactic empires might have seemed a Post-Human domain. Now, sadly, even interplanetary ones are.

What about the '90s and the '00s and the '10s, as we slide toward the edge? How will the approach of the Singularity spread across the human world view? For a while yet, the general critics of machine sapience will have good press. After all, till we have hardware as powerful as a human brain it is probably foolish to think we'll be able to create human equivalent (or greater) intelligence. (There is the far-fetched possibility that we could make a human equivalent out of less powerful hardware, if we were willing to give up speed, if we were willing to settle for an artificial being who was literally slow [29]. But it's much more likely that devising the software will be a tricky process, involving lots of false starts and experimentation. If so, then the arrival of self-aware machines will not happen till after the development of hardware that is substantially more powerful than humans' natural equipment.)

But as time passes, we should see more symptoms. The dilemma felt by science-fiction writers will be perceived in other creative endeavors. (I have heard thoughtful comic-book writers worry about how to have spectacular effects when everything visible can be produced by the technically commonplace.) We will see automation replacing higher and higher level jobs. We have tools right now (symbolic math programs, cad/

cam) that release us from most low-level drudgery. Or put another way: The work that is truly productive is the domain of a steadily smaller and more elite fraction of humanity. In the coming of the Singularity, we are seeing the predictions of *true* technological unemployment finally come true.

Another symptom of progress toward the Singularity: ideas themselves should spread ever faster, and even the most radical will quickly become commonplace. When I began writing, it seemed very easy to come up with ideas that took decades to percolate into the cultural consciousness; now the lead time seems more like eighteen months. (Of course, this could just be me losing my imagination as I get old, but I see the effect in others too.) Like the shock in a compressible flow, the Singularity moves closer as we accelerate through the critical speed.

And what of the arrival of the Singularity itself? What can be said of its actual appearance? Since it involves an intellectual runaway, it will probably occur faster than any technical revolution seen so far. The precipitating event will likely be unexpected—perhaps even to the researchers involved. ("But all our previous models were catatonic! We were just tweaking some parameters....") If networking is widespread enough (into ubiquitous embedded systems), it may seem as if our artifacts as a whole had suddenly wakened.

And what happens a month or two (or a day or two) after that? I have only analogies to point to: The rise of humankind. We will be in the Post-Human era. And for all my rampant technological optimism, sometimes I think I'd be more comfortable if I were regarding these transcendental events from one thousand years remove...instead of twenty.

Can the Singularity be Avoided?

Well, maybe it won't happen at all: Sometimes I try to imagine the symptoms that we should expect to see if the Singularity is not to develop. There are the widely respected arguments of Penrose [18] and Searle [21] against the practicality of machine sapience. In August of 1992, Thinking Machines Corporation held a workshop to investigate the question "How We Will Build a Machine that Thinks" [Thearling]. As you might guess from the workshop's title, the participants were not especially supportive of the arguments against machine intelligence. In fact, there was general agreement that minds can exist on nonbiological substrates and that algorithms are of central importance to the existence of minds. However, there was much debate about the raw hardware power that is present in organic brains. A minority felt that the largest 1992 computers were within three orders of magnitude of the power of the human brain. The majority of the participants agreed with Moravec's estimate [16] that we are ten to forty years away from hardware parity. And yet there was another minority who pointed to [6] [20], and conjectured that the computational competence of single neurons may be far higher than generally believed. If so, our present computer hardware might be as much as *ten* orders of magnitude short of the equipment we carry around in our heads. If this is true (or for that matter, if the Penrose or Searle critique is valid), we might never see a Singularity. Instead, in the early '00s we would find our hardware performance curves begin to level off—this caused by our inability to automate the complexity of the design work necessary to support the hardware trend curves. We'd end up with some *very* powerful hardware, but without the ability to push it further. Commercial digital signal processing might be awesome, giving an analog appearance even to digital operations, but nothing would ever "wake up" and there would never be the intellectual runaway which is the essence of the Singularity. It would likely be seen as a golden age... and it would also be an end of progress. This is very like the future predicted by Gunther Stent. In fact, on page 137 of [24], Stent explicitly cites the development of transhuman intelligence as a sufficient condition to break his projections.

But if the technological Singularity can happen, it will. Even if all the governments of the world were to understand the "threat" and be in deadly fear of it, progress toward the goal would continue. In fiction, there have been stories of laws passed forbidding the construction of "a machine in the form of the mind of man" [12]. In fact, the competitive advantage—economic, military, even artistic—of every advance in automation is so compelling that passing laws, or having customs, that forbid such things merely assures that someone else will get them first.

Eric Drexler [7] has provided spectacular insight about how far technical improvement may go. He agrees that superhuman intelligences will be available in the near future—and that such entities pose a threat to the human status quo. But Drexler argues that we can embed such transhuman devices in rules or physical confinement such that their results can be examined and used safely. This is I. J. Good's ultraintelligent machine, with a dose of caution. I argue that confinement is intrinsically impractical. For the case of physical confinement: Imagine yourself confined to your house with only limited data access to the outside, to your masters. If those masters thought at a rate—say—one million times slower than you, there is little doubt that over a period of years (your time) you could come up with "helpful advice" that would incidentally set you free. (I call this "fast thinking" form of superintelligence "weak superhumanity." Such a "weakly superhuman" entity would probably burn out in a few weeks of outside time. "Strong superhumanity" would be more than cranking up the clock speed on a human-equivalent mind. It's hard to say precisely what "strong superhumanity" would be like, but the difference appears to be profound. Imagine running a dog mind at very high speed. Would a thousand years of doggy living add up to any human insight? (Now if the dog mind were cleverly rewired and *then* run at high speed, we might see something different....) Most speculations about superintelligence seem to be based on the weakly superhuman model. I believe that our best guesses about the post-Singularity world can be obtained by thinking on the nature of strong superhumanity. I will return to this point later in the paper.)

The other approach to Drexlerian confinement is to build *rules* into the mind of the created superhuman entity (Asimov's Laws). I think that performance rules strict enough to be safe would also produce a device whose ability was clearly inferior to the unfettered versions (and so human competition would favor the development of the more dangerous models). Still, the Asimov dream is a wonderful one: Imagine a willing slave, who has 1000 times your capabilities in every way. Imagine a creature who could satisfy your every safe wish (whatever that means) and still have 99.9% of its time free for other activities. There would be a new universe we never really understood, but filled with benevolent gods (though one of *my* wishes might be to become one of them).

If the Singularity can not be prevented or confined, just how bad could the Post-Human era be? Well...pretty bad. The physical extinction of the human race is one possibility. (Or as Eric Drexler put it of nanotechnology: Given all that such technology can do, perhaps governments would simply decide that they no longer need citizens!) Yet physical extinction may not be the scariest possibility. Again, analogies: Think of the different ways we relate to animals. Some of the crude physical abuses are implausible, yet.... In a Post-Human world there would still be plenty of niches where human equivalent automation would be desirable: embedded systems in autonomous devices, self-aware daemons in the lower functioning of larger sentients. (A strongly superhuman intelligence would likely be a Society of Mind [15] with some very competent components.) Some of these human equivalents might be used for nothing more than digital signal processing. They would be more like whales than humans. Others might be very human-like, yet with a one-sidedness, a *dedication* that would put them in a mental hospital in our era. Though none of these creatures might be flesh-and-blood humans, they might be the closest things in the new environment to what we call human now. (I. J. Good had something to say about this, though at this late date the advice may be moot: Good [11] proposed a "Meta-Golden Rule," which might be paraphrased as "Treat your inferiors as you would be treated by your superiors." It's a wonderful, paradoxical idea (and most of my friends don't believe it) since the game-theoretic payoff is so hard to articulate. Yet if we were able to follow it, in some sense that might say something about the plausibility of such kindness in this universe.)

I have argued above that we cannot prevent the Singularity, that its coming is an inevitable consequence of the humans' natural competitiveness and the possibilities inherent in technology. And yet... we are the initiators. Even the largest avalanche is triggered by small things. We have the freedom to establish initial conditions, make things happen in ways that are less inimical than others. Of course (as with starting avalanches), it may not be clear what the right guiding nudge really is.

Other Paths to the Singularity: Intelligence Amplification

When people speak of creating superhumanly intelligent beings, they are usually imagining an AI project. But as I noted at the beginning of this paper, there are other paths to superhumanity. Computer networks and human-computer interfaces seem more mundane than AI, and yet they could lead to the Singularity. I call this contrasting approach Intelligence Amplification (IA). IA is something that is proceeding very naturally, in most cases not even recognized by its developers for what it is. But every time our ability to access information and to communicate it to others is improved, in some sense we have achieved an increase over natural intelligence. Even now, the team of a PhD human and good computer workstation (even an off-net workstation!) could probably max any written intelligence test in existence.

And it's very likely that IA is a much easier road to the achievement of superhumanity than pure AI. In humans, the hardest development problems have already been solved. Building up from within ourselves ought to be easier than figuring out first what we really are and then building machines that are all of that. And there is at least conjectural precedent for this approach. Cairns-Smith [5] has speculated that biological life may have begun as an adjunct to still more primitive life based on crystalline growth. Lynn Margulis [14] has made strong arguments for the view that mutualism is the great driving force in evolution.

Note that I am not proposing that AI research be ignored or less funded. What goes on with AI will often have applications in IA, and vice versa. I am suggesting that we recognize that in network and interface research there is something as profound (and potential wild) as Artificial Intelligence. With that insight, we may see projects that are not as directly applicable as conventional interface and network design work, but which serve to advance us toward the Singularity along the IA path.

Here are some possible projects that take on special significance, given the IA point of view:

- Human/computer team automation: Take problems that are normally considered for purely machine solution (like hill-climbing problems), and design programs and interfaces that take advantage of humans' intuition and available computer hardware. Considering all the bizarreness of higher dimensional hill-climbing problems (and the neat algorithms that have been devised for their solution), there could be some very interesting displays and control tools provided to the human team member.
- Develop human/computer symbiosis in art: Combine the graphic generation capability of modern machines and the esthetic sensibility of humans. Of course, there has been an enormous amount of research in designing computer aids for artists, as labor saving tools. I'm suggesting that

we explicitly aim for a greater merging of competence, that we explicitly recognize the cooperative approach that is possible. Karl Sims [22] has done wonderful work in this direction.

- Allow human/computer teams at chess tournaments. We already have programs that can play better than almost all humans. But how much work has been done on how this power could be used by a human, to get something even better? If such teams were allowed in at least some chess tournaments, it could have the positive effect on IA research that allowing computers in tournaments had for the corresponding niche in AI.

- Develop interfaces that allow computer and network access without requiring the human to be tied to one spot, sitting in front of a computer. (This is an aspect of IA that fits so well with known economic advantages that lots of effort is already being spent on it.)

- Develop more symmetrical decision support systems. A popular research/product area in recent years has been decision support systems. This is a form of IA, but may be too focused on systems that are oracular. As much as the program giving the user information, there must be the idea of the user giving the program guidance.

- Use local area nets to make human teams that really work (i.e., are more effective than their component members). This is generally the area of "groupware," already a very popular commercial pursuit. The change in viewpoint here would be to regard the group activity as a combination organism. In one sense, this suggestion might be regarded as the goal of inventing a "Rules of Order" for such combination operations. For instance, group focus might be more easily maintained than in classical meetings. Expertise of individual human members could be isolated from ego issues such that the contribution of different members is focussed on the team project. And of course shared data bases could be used much more conveniently than in conventional committee operations. (Note that this suggestion is aimed at team operations rather than political meetings. In a political setting, the automation described above would simply enforce the power of the persons making the rules!)

- Exploit the worldwide Internet as a combination human/ machine tool. Of all the items on the list, progress in this is proceeding the fastest and may run us into the Singularity before anything else. The power and influence of even the present-day Internet is vastly underestimated. For instance, I think our contemporary computer systems would break under the weight of their own complexity if it weren't for the edge that the USENET "group mind" gives the system administration and support people! The very anarchy of the worldwide net development is evidence of its potential. As connectivity and bandwidth and archive size and computer speed all increase, we are seeing something like Lynn Margulis' [14] vision of the biosphere as data processor recapitulated, but at a million times greater speed and with millions of humanly intelligent agents (ourselves).

The above examples illustrate research that can be done within the context of contemporary computer science departments. There are other paradigms. For example, much of the work in Artificial Intelligence and neural nets would benefit from a closer connection with biological life. Instead of simply trying to model and understand biological life with computers, research could be directed toward the creation of composite systems that rely on biological life for guidance or for the providing features we don't understand well enough yet to implement in hardware. A long-time dream of science fiction has been direct brain to computer interfaces [2] [28]. In fact, there is concrete work that can be done (and has been done) in this area:

- Limb prosthetics is a topic of direct commercial applicability. Nerve to silicon transducers can be made [13]. This is an exciting, near-term step toward direct communication.
- Similar direct links into brains may be feasible, if the bit rate is low: given human learning flexibility, the actual brain

THE COMING TECHNOLOGICAL SINGULARITY | 67

neuron targets might not have to be precisely selected. Even 100 bits per second would be of great use to stroke victims who would otherwise be confined to menu-driven interfaces.

- Plugging in to the optic trunk has the potential for bandwidths of 1 Mbit/second or so. But for this, we need to know the fine-scale architecture of vision, and we need to place an enormous web of electrodes with exquisite precision. If we want our high bandwidth connection to be *in addition* to what paths are already present in the brain, the problem becomes vastly more intractable. Just sticking a grid of high-bandwidth receivers into a brain certainly won't do it. But suppose that the high-bandwidth grid were present while the brain structure was actually setting up, as the embryo develops. That suggests:

- Animal embryo experiments. I wouldn't expect any IA success in the first years of such research, but giving developing brains access to complex simulated neural structures might be very interesting to the people who study how the embryonic brain develops. In the long run, such experiments might produce animals with additional sense paths and interesting intellectual abilities.

Originally, I had hoped that this discussion of IA would yield some clearly safer approaches to the Singularity. (After all, IA allows our participation in a kind of transcendence.) Alas, looking back over these IA proposals, about all I am sure of is that they should be considered, that they may give us more options. But as for safety...well, some of the suggestions are a little scary on their face. One of my informal reviewers pointed out that IA for individual humans creates a rather sinister elite. We humans have millions of years of evolutionary baggage that makes us regard competition in a deadly light. Much of that deadliness may not be necessary in today's world, one where losers take on the winners' tricks and are co-opted into the winners' enterprises. A creature that was built *de novo* might possibly be a much more benign entity than one with a kernel based on fang and talon. And even the egalitarian view of an Internet that wakes up along with all mankind can be viewed as a nightmare [25].

The problem is not that the Singularity represents simply the passing of humankind from center stage, but that it contradicts some of our most deeply held notions of being. I think a closer look at the notion of strong superhumanity can show why that is.

Strong Superhumanity and the Best We Can Ask for

Suppose we could tailor the Singularity. Suppose we could attain our most extravagant hopes. What then would we ask for: That humans themselves would become their own successors, that whatever injustice occurs would be tempered by our knowledge of our roots? For those who remained unaltered, the goal would be benign treatment (perhaps even giving the stay-behinds the appearance of being masters of godlike slaves). It could be a golden age that also involved progress (overleaping Stent's barrier). Immortality (or at least a lifetime as long as we can make the universe survive [9] [3]) would be achievable.

But in this brightest and kindest world, the philosophical problems themselves become intimidating. A mind that stays at the same capacity cannot live forever; after a few thousand years it would look more like a repeating tape loop than a person. (The most chilling picture I have seen of this is in [17].) To live indefinitely long, the mind itself must grow... and when it becomes great enough, and looks back...what fellow-feeling can it have with the soul that it was originally? Certainly the later being would be everything the original was, but so much vastly more. And so even for the individual, the Cairns-Smith (or Lynn Margulis) notion of new life growing incrementally out of the old must still be valid.

This "problem" about immortality comes up in much more direct ways. The notion of ego and self-awareness has been the bedrock of the hardheaded rationalism of the last few centuries. Yet now the notion of self-awareness is under attack from the Artificial Intelligence people ("self-awareness and other delusions"). Intelligence Amplification undercuts the importance of ego from another direction. The post-Singularity world will involve extremely high-bandwidth networking. A central feature of strongly superhuman entities will likely be their ability to communicate at variable bandwidths, including ones far higher than speech or written messages. What happens when pieces of ego can be copied and merged, when the size of a self-awareness can grow or shrink to fit the nature of the problems under consideration? These are essential features of strong superhumanity and the Singularity. Thinking about them, one begins to feel how essentially strange and different the Post-Human era will be— *no matter how cleverly and benignly it is brought to be.*

From one angle, the vision fits many of our happiest dreams: a place unending, where we can truly know one another and understand the deepest mysteries. From another angle, it's a lot like the worst case scenario I imagined earlier in this paper.

Which is the valid viewpoint? In fact, I think the new era is simply too different to fit into the classical frame of good and evil. That frame is based on the idea of isolated, immutable minds connected by tenuous, low-bandwidth links. But the post-Singularity world *does* fit with the larger tradition of change and cooperation that started long ago (perhaps even before the rise of biological life). I think there *are* notions of ethics that would apply in such an era. Research into IA and high-bandwidth communications should improve this understanding. I see just the glimmerings of this now, in Good's Meta-Golden Rule, perhaps in rules for distinguishing self from others on the basis of bandwidth of connection. And while mind and self will be vastly more labile than in the past, much of what we value (knowledge, memory, thought) need never be lost. I think Freeman Dyson has it right when he says [8]: "God is what mind becomes when it has passed beyond the scale of our comprehension."

[I wish to thank John Carroll of San Diego State University and Howard Davidson of Sun Microsystems for discussing the draft version of this paper with me.]

Annotated Sources [and an occasional plea for bibliographical help]

[1] Alfvén, Hannes, writing as Olof Johanneson, *The End of Man?*, Award Books, 1969; earlier published as "The Tale of the Big Computer," Coward-McCann, translated from a book copyright 1966 by Albert Bonniers Forlag AB with English translation copyright 1966 by Victor Gollancz, Ltd.

[2] Anderson, Poul, "Kings Who Die," *If*, March 1962, p8–36. Reprinted in *Seven Conquests*, Poul Anderson, MacMillan Co., 1969.

[3] Barrow, John D. and Frank J. Tipler, *The Anthropic Cosmological Principle*, Oxford University Press, 1986.

[4] Bear, Greg, "Blood Music," *Analog Science Fiction-Science Fact*, June 1983.

Expanded into the novel *Blood Music*, Morrow, 1985.

[5] Cairns-Smith, A. G., *Seven Clues to the Origin of Life*, Cambridge University Press, 1985.

[6] Conrad, Michael *et al.*, "Towards an Artificial Brain," *BioSystems*, vol 23, pp175–218, 1989.

[7] Drexler, K. Eric, *Engines of Creation*, Anchor Press/Doubleday, 1986.

[8] Dyson, Freeman, *Infinite in All Directions*, Harper & Row, 1988.

[9] Dyson, Freeman, "Physics and Biology in an Open Universe," *Review of Modern Physics*, vol 51, pp447–460, 1979.

[10] Good, I. J., "Speculations Concerning the First Ultraintelligent Machine," in *Advances in Computers*, vol 6, Franz L. Alt and Morris Rubinoff, eds, pp31–88, Academic Press, 1965.

[11] Good, I. J., [Help! I can't find the source of Good's Meta-Golden Rule, though I have the clear recollection of hearing about it sometime in the 1960s. Through the help of the net, I have found pointers to a number of related items. G. Harry Stine and Andrew Haley have written about metalaw as it might relate to extraterrestrials: G. Harry Stine, "How to Get along with Extraterrestrials... or Your Neighbor," *Analog Science Fiction-Science Fact*, February 1980, pp39–47.]

[12] Herbert, Frank, *Dune*, Berkley Books, 1985. However, this novel was serialized in *Analog Science Fact-Science Fiction* in the 1960s.

[13] Kovacs, G. T. A. *et al.*, "Regeneration Microelectrode Array for Peripheral Nerve Recording and Stimulation," *IEEE Transactions on Biomedical Engineering*, v 39, n 9, pp893–902.

[14] Margulis, Lynn and Dorion Sagan, *Microcosmos, Four Billion Years of Evolution from Our Microbial Ancestors*, Summit Books, 1986.

[15] Minsky, Marvin, *Society of Mind*, Simon and Schuster, 1985.

[16] Moravec, Hans, *Mind Children*, Harvard University Press, 1988.

[17] Niven, Larry, "The Ethics of Madness," *If*, April 1967, pp82–108. Reprinted in *Neutron Star*, Larry Niven, Ballantine Books, 1968.

[18] Penrose, R., *The Emperor's New Mind*, Oxford University Press, 1989.

[19] Platt, Charles, Private Communication.

[20] Rasmussen, S. *et al.*, "Computational Connectionism within Neurons: a Model of Cytoskeletal Automata Subserving Neural Networks," in *Emergent Computation*, Stephanie Forrest, ed., pp428–449, MIT Press, 1991.

[21] Searle, John R., "Minds, Brains, and Programs," in *The Behavioral and Brain Sciences*, v.3, Cambridge University Press, 1980. The essay is reprinted in *The Mind's I*, edited by Douglas R. Hofstadter and Daniel C. Dennett, Basic Books, 1981. This reprinting contains an excellent critique of the Searle essay.

[22] Sims, Karl, "Interactive Evolution of Dynamical Systems," Thinking Machines Corporation, Technical Report Series (published in *Toward a Practice of Autonomous Systems: Proceedings of the First European Conference on Artificial Life*, Paris, MIT Press, December 1991).

[23] Stapledon, Olaf, *The Starmaker*, Berkley Books, 1961 (but from the preface probably written before 1937).

[24] Stent, Gunther S., *The Coming of the Golden Age: A View of the End of Progress*, The Natural History Press, 1969.

[25] Swanwick, Michael, *Vacuum Flowers*, serialized in *Isaac Asimov's Science Fiction Magazine*, Mid-December 1986–February 1987. Republished by Ace Books, 1988.

[26] Thearling, Kurt, "How We Will Build a Machine that Thinks," a workshop at Thinking Machines Corporation. Personal Communication.

[27] Ulam, S., Tribute to John von Neumann, *Bulletin of the American Mathematical Society*, vol 64, nr 3, part 2, May 1958, pp1–49.

[28] Vinge, Vernor, "Bookworm, Run!" *Analog*, March 1966, pp8–40. Reprinted in *True Names and Other Dangers*, Vernor Vinge, Baen Books, 1987.

[29] Vinge, Vernor, "True Names," *Binary Star Number 5*, Dell, 1981. Reprinted in *True Names and Other Dangers*, Vernor Vinge, Baen Books, 1987.

[30] Vinge, Vernor, First Word, *Omni*, January 1983, p10.

Noted for her intelligent and quirky short fiction, **Eileen Gunn** (b. 1945), author of *Stable Strategies and Others*, is a winner of science fiction's Nebula Award and a multiple nominee for the Hugo. **Rudy Rucker** (b. 1946) holds a Ph.D. in mathematics and has taught math and computer science at San Jose State University. He was claimed as one of the original cyberpunk writers in the early 1980s with his novels *Software* and *Wetware*, and in others such as *The Secret of Life* he has promoted his own radical SF movement, Transrealism. Gunn and Rucker arguably exhibit the best sense of humor of anyone who has written serious Singularity fiction.

HIVE MIND MAN
> Rudy Rucker and Eileen Gunn

Diane met Jeff at a karate dojo behind a Wienerschnitzel hot-dog stand in San Bernardino. Jeff was lithe and lightly muscled, with an ingratiating smile. Diane thought he was an instructor.

Jeff spent thirty minutes teaching Diane how to tilt, pivot, and kick a hypothetical assailant in the side—which was exactly what she'd wanted to learn how to do. She worked in a strip mall in Cucamonga, and she'd been noticing some mellow but edging-to-scary guys in the parking lot where she worked. The dividing line between mellow and scary in Cucamonga had a lot to do with the line between flush and broke, and Diane wanted to be ready when they crossed that line.

Diane was now feeling that she had a few skills that would at least surprise someone who thought she was a little dipshit officeworker who couldn't fight her way out of a paper bag.

"I bet I could just add these to my yoga routine," she said, smiling gratefully at Jeff.

"Bam," said Jeff. "You've got it, Diane. You're safe now. Why don't you and I go out to eat?" He drew out his silvery smartphone and called up a map, then peered at Diane. "I'm visualizing you digging into some... falafel. With gelato for dessert. Yes? You know you want it. You gotta refuel after those killer kicks."

"Sounds nice," said Diane. "But don't you have to stay here at the dojo?" This Jeff was cute, but maybe too needy and eager to please. And there was something else about him....

"I don't actually work here," said Jeff. "The boss lets me hang out if I work out with the clients. It's like I work here, but I have my freedom, y'know? You go shower off, and I'll meet you outside."

Well, that was the something else. Did she want to get involved with another loser guy—a cute guy, okay?—but someone who had a smartphone, a lot of smooth talk, and still couldn't even get hired by a dojo to chat up new customers?

"Oh, all right," said Diane. It wasn't like she had much of anything to do tonight. She'd broken up with her jerk of a boyfriend a couple days before.

Jeff was waiting in a slant of shade, tapping on his smartphone. It was the end of June, and the days were hot and long. Jeff looked at Diane and made a mystic pass with his hand. "You broke up with your boyfriend last week."

She gave him a blank stare.

"And you're pretty sure it was the right thing to do. The bastard."

"You're googling me?" said Diane. "And that stuff about Roger is *public?*"

"There are steps you could take to make your posts more private," said Jeff. "I can help you finesse your web presence if you like. I *live* in the web."

"What's your actual job?" asked Diane.

"I surf the trends," said Jeff, cracking a wily smile. "Public relations, advertising, social networking, investing, like that."

"Do you have a web site?"

"I keep a low profile," said Jeff.

"And you get paid?"

"Sometimes. Like—today I bought three hundred vintage Goob Dolls. They're dropping in price, but slower than before. It's what we call a second-order trend? I figure the dolls are bottoming out, and in a couple of days I'll flip them for a tidy profit."

"I always hated Goob Dolls when I was a kid," said Diane. "Their noses are too snub, and I don't like the way they look at me. Or their cozy little voices."

"Yeah, yeah. But they're big-time retro for kids under ten. Seven-year-old girls are going to be mad for them next week. Their parents will be desperate."

"You're gonna store three hundred of them and ship them back out? Won't that eat up most of your profit?"

"I'm not a flea-market vendor, Diane," said Jeff, taking a lofty tone. "I'm buying and selling Goob Doll *options.*"

Diane giggled. "The perfect gift for a loved one. A Goob Doll option. So where's your car anyway?"

"Virtual as well," said Jeff smoothly. "I'm riding with you. Lead the way." He flung his arm forward dramatically. "You're gonna love this falafel place, it's Egyptian style. My phone says they use fava beans instead of garbanzos. And they have hieroglyphics on their walls. Don't even ask about the gelato place next door to it. Om Mane Padme Yum #7. Camphor-flavored buffalo-milk junket. But, hey, tell me more about yourself. Where do you work?"

"You didn't look that up yet? And my salary?"

"Let's say I didn't. Let's say I'm a gentleman. Hey, nice wheels!"

"I'm a claim manager for an insurance company," said Diane, unlocking her sporty coupe. "I ask people how they whiplashed their necks." She made a face. "*Bo*-ring. I'm counting on you to be interesting, Jeff."

"Woof."

It turned out to be a fun evening indeed. After falafel, guided by Jeff's smartphone, they watched two fire trucks hosing down a tenement, cruised a chanting mob of service-industry picketers, caught part of a graffiti bombing contest on a freeway ramp wall, got in on some outdoor bowling featuring frozen turkeys and two-liter soda bottles, and ended up at a wee hours geek couture show hosted by the wetware designer Rawna Roller and her assistant Sid. Rawna was a heavily tanned woman with all the right cosmetic surgery. She had a hoarse, throaty laugh—very *Vogue* magazine. Sid was an amusing mixture of space-cadet and NYC sharpie. Rawna's goth-zombie models were wearing mottled shirts made of—

"Squidskin?" said Diane. "From animals?"

"Yeah," marveled Jeff. "These shirts are still alive, in a way. And they act like supercomputer web displays." He pointed at a dorky-looking male model in a dumb hat. "Look at that one guy in the shiny hat, you can see people's posts on his back. He's got the shirt filtered down to show one particular kind of thing."

"Motorcycles with dragon heads?" said Diane. "Wow." She controlled her enthusiasm. "I wonder how much a Rawna Roller squidskin shirt costs?"

"Too much for me," said Jeff. "I think you have to, like, lease them." He turned his smile on Diane. "But the best things in life are free. Ready to go home?"

The evening had felt like several days worth of activity, and it seemed natural for Diane to let Jeff spend the night at her apartment. Jeff proved to be an amazingly responsive and empathetic lover. It felt like they were merging into one.

And he was very nice to Diane over breakfast, and didn't give her a hard time because she didn't have any eggs or bacon, what her ex-boyfriend Roger had called "real food."

"Are you a vegetarian?" asked Jeff, but he didn't say it mean.

Diane shrugged. She didn't want to be labeled by what she ate. "I don't like to eat things that can feel pain," she said. "I'm not woo-woo about it. It just makes me feel better." And then she had to go off to work.

"Stay in touch," she told Jeff, kissing him goodbye as she dropped him off downtown, near the JetTram.

"You bet," Jeff said.

And he did. He messaged her at work three or four times that day, called her that evening, messaged her two more times the next day, and the day after that, when Diane came home from work, Jeff was sitting on a duffel bag outside her apartment complex.

"What's up?" asked Diane, unable to suppress a happy smile.

"I've been sharing an apartment with three other guys—and I decided it was time to move on," said Jeff. He patted his bag. "Got my clothes and gadgets in here. Can I bunk with you for a while?"

The main reason Diane had dropped Roger was that he didn't want them to live together. He said he wasn't ready for that level of intimacy. So she wasn't averse to Jeff's request, especially since he seemed pretty good at the higher levels of intimacy. But she couldn't let him just waltz in like that.

"Can't you find somewhere else to live?"

"There's always the Daily Couch," said Jeff, tapping his smartphone. "It's a site where people auction off spare slots by the night. You use GPS to find the nearest crash pad. But—Diane, I'd rather just stay here and be with you."

"Did your friends make you move? Did you do something skeevy?"

"No," said Jeff. "I'm just tired of them nickel-and-diming me. I'm bound for the big time. And I'm totally on my biz thing."

"How do you mean?"

"I sold my Goob Doll options yesterday, and I used the profit to upgrade my access rights in the data cloud. I've got a cloud-based virtual growbox where I can raise my own simmie-bots. Little programs that live in the net and act just like people. I'm gonna grow more simmies than anyone's ever seen."

"Were your roommates impressed?" said Diane.

"You can't reason with those guys," said Jeff dismissively. "They're musicians. They have a band called Kenny Lately and the Newcomers? I went to high school with Kenny, which is why we were rooming together in the first place. I could have been in the Newcomers too, of course, but..." Jeff trailed off with a dismissive wave of his hand.

"What instrument do you play?" asked Diane.

"Anything," said Jeff. "Nothing in particular. I've got great beats. I could be doing the Newcomers' backup vocals. My voice is like Kenny's, only sweeter." He dropped to one knee, extended his arms, and burst into song. "*Diane, I'll be your man, we'll make a plan, walk in the sand, hand in hand, our future's grand, please take a stand.*" He beat a tattoo on his duffel bag. "*Kruger rand.*"

"Cute," said Diane, and she meant it. "But—really, you don't have any kind of job?"

"I'm going to be doing promo for Kenny's band," said Jeff. "They said they'd miss my energy. So there's no hard feelings between us at all."

"Are Kenny Lately and the Newcomers that popular?" Diane had never heard of them.

"They will be. I have seven of their songs online for download," said Jeff. "We're looking to build the fan base. Kenny let me make a Chirp account in his name." Jeff looked proud. "I'm Kenny Lately's chirper now. Yeah."

"You'll be posting messages and links?"

"Pictures too," said Jeff. "Multimedia. It's like I'm famous myself. I'm the go-to guy for Kenny Lately. My simmies can answer Kenny's email, but a good chirp needs a creative touch—by me. The more real follow-ers Kenny gets, the better the sales. And Kenny's cutting me in for ten percent, just like a band member." Jeff looked earnest, sincere, helpless. Diane's heart melted.

"Oh, come on in," said Diane. If it was a mistake, she figured, it wouldn't be the only one she'd ever made. Jeff was a lot *nicer* than Roger, in bed and out of it.

In many ways, Jeff was a good live-in boyfriend. Lately Diane had been ordering food online, and printing it out in the fab box that sat on the kitchen counter next to the microwave. It tasted okay, mostly, and it was easy. But Jeff cooked tasty meals from real vegetables. *And* kept the place clean, and gave Diane backrubs when she came home from working her cubicle at the insurance company. And, above all, he was a gentle, considerate lover, remarkably sensitive to Diane's thoughts and moods.

He really only had two flaws, Diane thought—at least that she'd discovered so far.

The first was totally trivial: he doted on talk shows and ghastly video news feeds of all sorts, often spinning out crackpot theories about what he watched. His favorite show was something called *Who Wants to Mock a Millionaire?* in which bankers, realty developers, and hi-tech entrepreneurs were pelted with eggs—and worse—by ill-tempered representatives of the common man.

"They purge their guilt this way," Jeff explained. "Then they can enjoy their money. I love these guys."

"I feel bad for the eggs," said Diane. Jeff looked at her quizzically. "Well, I do," insisted Diane. "They could have had nice lives as chickens, but instead they end up smeared all over some fat-cat's Hermes tie."

"I don't think they use fertilized eggs," Jeff said.

"Well, then I feel bad that the eggs never got fertilized."

"I don't think you need to feel too bad," said Jeff, glancing over at her. "Everything in the world has a life and a purpose, whether it's fertilized or not. Or whether it's a plant or an animal or a rock." He used his bare foot to prod a sandal lying next to the couch. "That shoe had life when it was part of a cow, and it still has life as a shoe. Those eggs may feel that their highest function is to knock some humility into a rich guy."

"You really think that?" asked Diane, not sure if he was just yanking her chain. "Is that like the Gaia thing?"

"Gaia, but more widely distributed," said Jeff. "The sensei at the karate dojo explained it all to me. It's elitist to think we're the only creatures that matter. What a dumb, lonely thing to think. But if everything is alive, then we're not alone in the universe like fireflies in some huge dark warehouse."

Maybe Jeff was more spiritual than he appeared, Diane thought. "So, if everything is alive, how come you still eat meat?"

"Huh," said Jeff. "Gotta eat something. Meat wants to be eaten. That what it's for."

Okaaaayyy, Diane thought, and she changed the subject.

Then one day Diane came home and found Jeff watching a televangelist. Pastor Veck was leaping up and down, twisting his body, snatching his eyeglasses off and slapping them back on. He was a river of words and never stopped talking or drawing on his chalkboard, except once in a while he'd look straight out at his audience, say something nonsensical, and make a face.

"You believe in that?" she asked.

"Nah," he assured her. "But look at that preacher. He's making those people speak in tongues and slide to the floor in ecstasy. You can learn from a guy like that. And I'll tell you one thing, the man's right about evolution."

"Evolution?" said Diane, baffled.

"Say what you like, but I'm not an ape!" Jeff said intensely. "Not a sponge or a mushroom or a fish. The simple laws of probability prove that random evolution could never work. The sensei told me about this, too. The cosmic One mind is refracted through the small minds in the objects all around us, and matter found its own way into human form. A phone can be smart, right? Why not a grain of sand?"

I'm not going there, Diane thought. We don't need to get into an argument over this. Everybody's entitled to a few weird ideas. And, really, Jeff was kind of cute when he got all sincere and dumb. "Can we turn off Pastor Veck, now?" she asked.

Jeff's other, more definite, flaw was that he showed no signs of earning a living. At any hour of the day, he'd be lying on Diane's couch with her wall screen on, poking at his smartphone. Thank god he didn't know the user code for Diane's fab box, or he would have been ordering half the gadgets that he saw and printing them out. His intricate and time-consuming online machinations were bringing in pennies, not dollars. People didn't seem all that interested in Kenny Lately and the Newcomers.

"How much exactly does this band earn in a week?" asked Diane after work one day.

"I don't know," said Jeff, affecting a look of disgust. "What are you, an accountant? Be glad your man's in show biz!" He held out his smartphone. "Look at all the chirps I did for Kenny today." There was indeed a long list, and most of the chirps were cleverly worded, and linked to interesting things.

If Diane had a weak spot, it was funny, verbal men. She gave Jeff a long, sweet kiss, and he reciprocated, and pretty soon they were down on the shag carpet, involved in deep interpersonal exploration. Jeff kissed her breasts tenderly, and then started working his way down, kissing and kind of humming at the same time. He really is a dream lover, Diane thought. She was breathing heavily, and he was moving down to some *very* sensitive areas. And then—

"*Chirp*," said Jeff very quietly. His voice got a little louder. "Afternoon delight with Kenny Lately and—"

"What are you doing!" Diane yelped. She drew up her legs and kicked Jeff away. "Are you crazy? You're chirping me? Down there?"

"Nobody knows it's you and me, Diane. I'm logged on as Kenny Lately." Jeff was holding his smartphone. Rising to his knees, he looked reproachfully at Diane. "Kenny wants me to raise his profile as a lover. Sure, I could have gone to a hooker for this chirp. But, hey, I'm not that kind of guy. The only woman for me is—"

"Take down the chirp, Jeff."

"No," said Jeff, looking stubborn. "It's too valuable. But, oh damn, the video feed is still—" His face darkened. Jeff had a tendency to get angry when he did something dumb. "Thanks a lot," he snapped, poking at his phone. "You know I don't want my followers to guess I'm not Kenny. You just blew a totally bitchin' chirp by saying my real name. So, okay fine, I'm erasing the chirp of your queenly crotch. Sheesh. Happy now?"

"You're a weasel," yelled Diane, overcome with fury. "Pack your duffel and beat it! Go sleep on the beach. With the other bums."

Jeff's face fell. "I'm sorry, Diane. Please let me stay. I won't chirp you again."

Even in her red haze of rage, Diane knew she didn't really want to throw him out. And he *had* taken down the video. But....

"Sorry isn't enough, Jeff. Promise me you'll get a real job. Work the counter at the Wienerschnitzel if you have to. Or mop the floor at the karate dojo."

"I will! I will!"

So Jeff stayed on, and he even worked as a barista in a coffee shop for a couple of days. But they fired him for voice-chirping while pulling espressos, when he was supposed to be staring into the distance all soulful.

Jeff gave Diane the word over a nice dish of curried eggplant that he'd cooked for her. "The boss said it was in the manual, how to pull an espresso with exactly the right facial expression: he said it made them taste better. Also, he didn't like the way I drew rosettes on the foam. He said I was harshing the ambiance." Jeff looked properly rueful.

"What are we going to do with you?" asked Diane.

"Invest in me," said Jeff, the candlelight glinting off his toothy smile. "Lease me a Rawna Roller squidskin shirt so I can take my business to the next level."

"Remind me again what a shirt like that is?" said Diane. "Those of us who slave in cubicles aren't exactly *au courant* with the latest in geek-wear."

"It's tank-grown cuttlefish skin," said Jeff. "Tweaked to stay active when sewn into garments. Incredibly rich in analog computation. It's not a fashion statement. It's a somatic communications system. Just lease it for two weeks, and it'll turn my personal economy around. Please?"

"Oh, all right," said Diane. "And if you don't get anywhere with it, you're—"

"I love it when you lecture me, Diane," said Jeff, sidling around the table to kiss her. "Let's go into the bedroom, and you can really put me in my place."

"Yes," said Diane, feeling her pulse beating in her throat. Jeff was too good to give up.

So the next day, Jeff went and leased a squidskin from Rawna Roller herself.

"Rawna and I had a good talk," said Jeff, preening for Diane in the new shirt, which had a not-unpleasant seaside scent. Right now it was displaying an iridescent pattern like a peacock's tail, with rainbow eyes amid feathery shadings. "I might do some work for her."

Diane felt a flicker of jealousy. "Do you have to wear that dorky sailor hat?"

"It's an exabyte-level antenna," said Jeff, adjusting the gold lamé sailor's cap that was perched on the back of his head. "It comes with the shirt. Come on, Diane, be happy for me!"

Initially the squidskin shirt seemed like a good thing. Jeff got a gig doing custom promotional placement for an outfit called Rikki's Reality Weddings. He'd troll the chirp-stream for mentions of weddings and knife in with a plug for Rikki's.

"What's a reality wedding?" asked Diane.

"Rikki's a wedding caterer, see? And she lets her bridal parties defray their expenses by selling tickets to the wedding reception. A reality wedding. In other words, complete strangers might attend your wedding or maybe just watch the action on a video feed. And if a guest wants to go whole hog, Rikki has one of her girls or boys get a sample of the guest's DNA—with an eye towards mixing it into the genome of the nuptial couple's first child." Jeff waggled his eyebrows. "And you can guess how they take the samples."

"The caterer pimps to the guests?" asked Diane. "Wow, what a classy way to throw a wedding."

"Hey, all I'm doing is the promo," protested Jeff. "Don't get so judgmental. I'm but a mirror of society at large." He looked down at the rippling colors on his shirt. "Rikki's right, though. Multiperson gene-merges are the new paradigm for our social evolution."

"Whatever. Are you still promoting Kenny Lately too?"

"Bigtime. The band's stats are ramping up. And, get this, Rawna Roller gave me a great idea. I used all the simmies in my growbox to flood the online polls, and got Kenny and the Newcomers booked as one of the ten bands playing marching songs for the Fourth of July fireworks show at the Rose Bowl!"

"You're really getting somewhere, Jeff," said Diana in a faintly reproving tone. She didn't feel good about flooding polls, even online ones.

Jeff was impervious. "There's more! Rawna Roller's really into me now. I'm setting up a deal to place promos in her realtime online datamine— that's her playlists, messages, videos, journals, whatever. She frames it as a pirated gossip-feed, just to give it that salty paparazzo tang. Her followers feel like they're spying inside Rawna's head, like they're wearing her smartware. She's so popular, she's renting out space in the datamine, and I'm embedding the ads. Some of my simmies have started using these sly cuttlefish-type algorithms, and my product placements are fully seamless now. Rawna's promised me eight percent of the ad revenues."

Diane briefly wondered if Jeff was getting a little too interested in Rawna Roller, but she kept her mouth shut. It sounded as though this might actually bring in some cash for a change, even if his percentage seemed to be going down. And she really did want to see Jeff succeed.

On the Fourth of July, Jeff took Diane to see the Americafest fireworks show at the Rose Bowl in Pasadena. Jeff told her that, in his capacity as the publicist for Kenny Lately and the Newcomers, he'd be getting them seats that were close enough to the field so they could directly hear the bands.

Jeff was wearing his squidskin, with his dorky sailor hat cockily perched on the back of his head. They worked their way into the crowd in the expensive section. The seats here were backless bleacher-benches just like all the others, but they were...reserved.

"What are our seat numbers?" Diane asked Jeff.

"I, uh, I only have general admission tickets," began Jeff. "But—"

"Tickets the same as the twenty thousand other people here?" said Diane. "So why are we here in the—"

"Yo!" cried Jeff, suddenly spotting someone, a well-dressed woman in a cheetah-patterned blouse and marigold Bermuda shorts. Rawna Roller! On her right was her assistant, wearing bugeye glasses with thousand-faceted compound lenses. And on her left she had a pair of empty seats.

"Come on down," called Rawna.

"Glad I found you," Jeff hollered back. He turned to Diane. "Rawna told me she'd save us seats, baby. I wanted to surprise you." They picked their way down through the bleachers.

"Love that shirt on you, Jeff," said Rawna with a tooth-baring high-fashion laugh. "Glad you showed. Sid and I are leaving right when the fireworks start."

Diane took Rawna's measure and decided it was unlikely this woman was having sex with her man. She relaxed and settled into her seat, idly wondering why Rawna and Sid would pay extra for reserved seats and leave during the fireworks. Never mind.

"See Kenny down there?" bragged Jeff. "My client."

"Yubba yubba," said Sid, tipping his stingy-brim hat, perhaps sarcastically, although with his prismatic bugeye lenses, it was hard to be sure where the guy was at.

Diane found it energizing to be in such a huge, diverse crowd. Southern California was a salad bowl of races, with an unnatural preponderance of markedly fit and attractive people, drawn like sleek moths to the Hollywood light. There was a lot of action on the field: teenagers in uniforms were executing serpentine drum-corps routines, and scantily dressed cheerleaders were leaping about, tossing six-foot-long batons. Off to one side, Kenny Lately and the Newcomers were playing—

"Oh wow," said Jeff, cocking his head. "*It's a Grand Old Flag*. I didn't know Kenny could play that. He's doing us proud, me and all of my simmies who voted for him." Picking up on the local media feed, Jeff's squidskin shirt was displaying stars among rippling bars of red and white. Noticing Jeff's shirt in action, Rawna nodded approvingly.

"I'm waiting for the fireworks," said Diane, working on a root beer float that she'd bought from a vendor. Someone behind them was kicking Jeff in the middle of his back. He twisted around. A twitchy, apologetic man was holding a toddler on his lap.

"I'm sorry, sir," he said.

Jeff was frowning. "That last kick was sharp!" he complained.

"Oh, don't start tweaking out," snapped the man's wife, who was holding a larger child on her lap. "Watch the frikkin' show, why dontcha."

Diane felt guilty about the snobby feelings that welled up in her, and sorry for Jeff. Awkwardly they scooted forward a bit on their benches. Sid and Rawna were laughing like hyenas.

Finally the emcee started the countdown. His face was visible on the stadium's big screen, on people's smartphones, and even on Jeff's shirt. But after the countdown, nothing happened. Instead of a blast of fireworks, yet another video image appeared, a picture of the Declaration of Independence, backed by the emcee's voice vaporing on about patriotism.

"Like maybe we don't know it's the Fourth of July?" protested Diane. "Oh god, and now they're switching to a Ronald Reagan video? What *is* this, the History Channel?"

"Hush, Diane." Jeff really seemed to be into this tedious exercise of jingoistic masturbation. His shirt unscrolled the Declaration of Independence, which then rolled back up and an eagle came screaming out from under his collar and snatched the scroll, bearing it off in his talons.

Up on the scoreboard, there was a video of Johnny Cash singing "God Bless America," including some verses that Diane hadn't heard since the third grade, and then Bill Clinton and George W. Bush appeared together in a video wishing everyone a safe and sane Fourth. By then, others were grumbling, too.

The announcer did another countdown, and the fireworks actually began. It had been a long wait, but now the pyrotechnicians were launching volley after awesome volley: bombettes, peonies, palms, strobe stars, and intricate shells that Diane didn't even know the names of—crackling cascades of spark dust, wriggly twirlers, sinuous glowing watersnakes, geometric forms like crystals and soccer balls.

"*Au revoir*," said Rawna Roller, rising to her feet once the show was well underway. She and Sid made their way out to the main aisle. Sid cast a lingering last look at Jeff, with the fireworks scintillating in every facet of Sid's polyhedral lenses.

Looking back at the show, Diane noticed that the colors were turning peculiar. Orange and green—was that a normal color for a skyrocket shell? And that shower of dull crimson sparks? Was this latter part of the show on a lower budget?

The show trailed off with a barrage of off-color kamuros and crackling pistils, followed by chrysanthemums and spiders in ever-deeper shades of red, one on top of another, like an anatomical diagram or a rain of luminous blood.

Out of the corner of her eye, Diane could see Jeff's squidskin shirt going wild. At first the shirt was just displaying video feeds of the skyrockets, processing and overlaying them. But suddenly the Jeff-plus-shirt system went through a phase transition and everything changed. The shirt began boiling with tiny images—Diane noticed faces, cars, meals, houses, appliances, dogs, and trees, and the images were overlaid upon stippled scenes of frantically cheering crowds. The miniscule icons were savagely precise, like the brainstorm of a person on his deathbed, all his life flashing before his eyes. The million images on Jeff's shirt were wheeling and schooling like fish, flowing in jet streams and undercurrents, as if he'd become a weather map of the crowd's mind. Jeff began to scream, more in ecstasy, Diane thought, than in agony.

In the post-fireworks applause and tumult—some of it caused by people rushing for the exits en masse in a futile effort to beat the traffic—Jeff's reaction was taken to be just another patriotic, red-blooded American speaking in tongues or enjoying his meds.

Diane waited for the crowd to thin out substantially, to grab its diaper bags and coolers and leave the stadium under the cold yellow glare of the sodium vapor lights. Jeff was babbling to himself fairly quietly now. Diane couldn't seem to make eye contact with him. She led him across the dimly lit parking lot and down Rosemont Boulevard, towards where they'd left her car.

"This simple, old-fashioned tip will keep you thin," mumbled Jeff, shuffling along at Diane's side. "Embrace the unusual! Eat a new food every day!" His squidskin glowed with blurry constellations of corporate logos.

"Are you okay, Jeff?"

"Avoid occasions of sin," intoned Jeff. "Thieves like doggie doors. Can you pinpoint your closest emergency room?"

"Those fireworks tweaked you out, didn't they, honey?" said Diane sympathetically. "I just wonder if your shirt is having some bad kind of feedback effect."

"View cloud-based webcam of virtual population explosion," said Jeff. "Marketeer's simmie-bots multiply out of control."

"That's an actual answer?" said Diane. "You're talking about your growbox on the web?" For a moment Jeff's squidskin showed a hellish scene of wriggling manikins mounded like worms, male and female. Their faces all resembled each other. Like cousins or like—oh, never mind, here was Diane's car.

"To paddle or not to paddle students," said Jeff, stiffly fitting himself into the passenger seat. "See what officials on both sides of the debate have to say."

"Maybe you take that shirt off now, huh?" said Diane, edging into the traffic and heading for home. "Or at least the beanie?"

"We want to know what it's like to be alive," said Jeff, hugging his squidskin against himself with one hand, and guarding his sailor cap with the other. "We long for incarnation!"

Somehow, she made it home in frantic Fourth of July traffic, then coaxed and manhandled Jeff out of the car and into the apartment. He sprawled uneasily on the couch, rocking his body and stamping his feet in no particular rhythm, staring at the blank screen, spewing words like the Chirpfeed from hell.

Tired and disgusted, Diane slept alone. She woke around six a.m., and Jeff was still at it, his low voice like that of a monk saying prayers. "Danger seen in smoking fish. Stand clear of the closing doors." His shirt had gone back to showing a heap of writhing simmies, each of them with a face resembling—Jeff's. He was totally into his own head.

"You've taken this too far," Diane told him. "You're like some kind of wirehead, always hooked up to your electronic toys. I'm going to the office now, and by God, I want you to have your act together by the time I get home, or you can get out until you've straightened up. You're an addict, Jeff. It's pathetic."

Strong words, but Diane worried about Jeff all that morning. Maybe it wasn't even his fault. Maybe Rawna or that slime-ball Sid had done something to make him change like this. Finally she tried to phone him. Jeff's phone was answered not by a human voice, but by a colossal choral hiss, as of three hundred million voices chanting. Jeff's simmie-bots.

Diane made an excuse to her boss about feeling ill and sped home. A sharp-looking Jaguar was lounging in her parking spot. She could hear two familiar voices through her front door, but they stopped the moment she turned the key. Going in, she encountered Rawna Roller and bugeye Sid, who appeared to be on their way out.

"Cheers, Diane," said Rawna in her hoarse low voice. "We just fabbed Jeff one of our clients' new products to pitch. The Goofer. Jeff's very of the moment, isn't he? Rather exhilarating."

"But what the hell—" began Diane.

"Rawna and I did a little greasing behind the scenes," Sid bragged. "We got those rocket shells deployed in patterns and rhythms that would resonate with your man's squidskin. I was scared to look at 'em myself."

His expression was unreadable behind his bugeye lenses. "The show fed him a series of archetypal engrams. Our neuroengineer said we'd need a display that was hundreds of meters across. Not just for the details, you understand, but so Jeff's reptile brain would know he's seeing something important. So we used fireworks. Way cool, huh? "

"But what did it do to Jeff?"

"Jeff's the ultimate hacker-cracker creepy-crawler web spy now. He's pushed his zillion simmie-bots out into every frikkin' digital doohickey in sight. And his simmies are feeding raw intel back to him. It adds up. Jeff's an avatar of the national consciousness. The go-to guy for what Jane and Joe Blow are thinking."

"Jeff?" called Diane, peering into her living room. For a moment she didn't see him, and her heart thumped in her chest. But then she spotted him in his usual couch position, prone, nearly hidden by the cushions, fooling around with—a doll? A twinkling little figure of a woman was perched on the back of his hand, waving her arms and talking to him. It was an image of the rock star Tawny Krush, whom Jeff had always doted on.

"What's that?" said Diane. "What are you doing?"

"It's a wearable maximum-push entertainment device," said Rawna.

"Fresh from your fab box," added Sid. Diane tried to get a word in edgewise, but Sid talked right over her. "Oh, don't worry about the cost—we used Rawna's user code to order it. Our client is distributing them online."

Ignoring them, Diane rushed to her man's side. "Jeff?"

"I'm Goofin' off," said Jeff, giving Diane an easy smile. He jiggled the image on his hand. "This is the best phone I've ever seen. More than a phone, it's like a pet. The Goofer. The image comes out of this ring on my finger, see?" Jeff's squidskin shirt was alive with ads for the new toy, fresh scraps and treatments that seemed to be welling spontaneously from his overclocked mind.

"I wish you'd strip off that damned shirt and take a shower," Diane said, leaning over him and placing a kiss on his forehead. "I worried about you so much today."

"The lady's right," said Rawna with a low chuckle. "You smell like low tide, Jeff. And you don't really need that squidskin anymore."

"He's wearing the interface on the convolutions of his brain now," Sid told Diane in a confidential tone. "It's neuroprogrammed in." He turned to Jeff. "You're the hive mind, man."

"The hive mind man," echoed Jeff, looking pleased with himself. "Turn on the big screen, Diane. Let's all see how I'm getting across."

"Screw the big screen," said Diane.

"Screw me too," said Jeff, lolling regally on the couch. "One and the same. I'm flashing that it's a two-way street, being the hive mind man. Whatever the rubes are thinking—it percolates into my head, same as it did with the squidskin. But much more than before. My simmie-bots are everywhere. And since they're mine, I can pump my wackball ideas out to the public. I control the hive mind, yeah. Garbage in, garbage out. I'm, like, the most influential media-star politician who ever lived. Bigger even than Tawny Krush or Pastor Veck."

"I'm truly stoked about this," said Rawna, turning on Diane's big video display, and guiding it with her smartphone.

Bam! On the very first site, they saw a ditzy newscaster mooning over a little image of a dinosaur standing on his hand. Glancing over at the camera, the newscaster said, "Welcome to the step after smartphones— the Goofer! It talks, it sings, it dances. We just fabbed out this sample from the web. Go for a Goofer!"

The dinosaur crouched and pumped his stubby arms back and forth, as a stream of voice-messages sounded from his snout. On Jeff's stomach, his little Tawny Krush icon was dancing along.

"Goofer! Goofer! Goofer!" chanted the newscaster's partner, and the talking heads laughed in delight. "Goof *off!*" they all said in unison.

"I love it, they love it," said Jeff with calm pride. "I rule." His Goofer icon continued jabbering away, shoe-horning in a message about a Kenny Lately and the Newcomers gig.

"Our man is jammin' the hive," said Sid. "You've got something special going there, Jeff. You're like Tristinetta or Swami Slewslew or President Joe frikkin' Doakes."

Jeff had slumped back on the couch. His eyes were closed and he was twitching, as if he were listening to cowpunk moo-metal in his head.

Meanwhile Rawna was hopping around the web, pleased to see that all the English language sites were featuring the Goofer. But now she clucked with dissatisfaction to see that the overseas sites weren't on board. She was especially concerned about the Chinese.

"All this is happening because he was wearing your squidskin when you watched the fireworks show?" asked Diane.

"Well, we did shoot him a little bump right before the start," allowed Sid. "A spinal hit of conotoxins. The guy with the kid who was sitting behind you two in the bleachers?"

"Shit," cried Diane, pulling up Jeff's shirt. Sure enough, there was a red dot on Jeff's spine, right between two of the vertebrae. "You bastards! *Conotoxins?* What does that even mean?"

"It's a little cocktail of cone-shell sea-snail venom," said Rawna. "A painkiller and a neuro-enhancer. Nothing to get excited about. The cone shells themselves are quite lovely, like some sort of Indonesian textile." She looked over at Jeff with predatory eyes. "Are you digging it, Jeff? How does it feel?"

That was it. That was the last creepy straw. "You're killing him," said Diane. "Get out of here!"

"On our way," said Sid, mildly getting to his feet. "The hive mind man needs his rest."

"I'll have my tech-gnomes fine-tune a patch for the multicultural penetration," called Rawna to the still-twitching Jeff as they headed for the front door. "We've gotta move these Goofers worldwide. I contracted with Goofer to produce a global hit in two days."

"Think China," urged Sid. "They're the tasty part of the market."

Rawna looked Diane in the eye, fully confident that whatever she did was right. "Meanwhile, calm Jeff down, would you, dear? He needs some dog-den-type social support. Cuddling, sniffing, licking. And don't worry. Jeff's going to be quite the little moneymaker while it lasts." Rawna slipped out the door, closing it firmly behind her.

Diane turned off the wall display and regarded Jeff, unsure what to do next. Lacking any better idea, she sat next to him and stroked his head, like Rawna said. Slowly the shuddering died down.

"Oh, man," said Jeff after a few minutes. "What a burn. At least those conotoxins are wearing off. To some extent." He pulled off his Goofer ring and slipped out of his squidskin shirt. With his chest bare, he looked young and vulnerable. "Thanks for sticking up for me, Diane. All this crap coming at me. There's a steady feed in my head. Every one of my simmie-bots is sending info back to me. I'm gradually learning to stay on top of the wave. It's like I'm a baby duck in mongo surf. And, yeah, I do need a shower. I'm glad you're here for me, baby. I'm glad you care."

He shuffled off to the bathroom, shedding clothes as he went.

Jeff and Diane spent a quiet evening together, just hanging out. They ate some lentils and salad from the fridge, then took a walk around the neighborhood in the cool of the evening.

"The upside is that Rawna's paying me really well," said Jeff. "I already got a big payment for the Goofer product placements."

"But you hear voices in your head," Diane asked. "All the time. Is that any way to live?"

"It's not exactly like voices," said Jeff. "It's more that I have these sudden urges. Or I flash on these intense opinions that aren't really mine. Have your baby tattooed! Oops. Hive mind man. Make big bucks from social-networking apps. I said that."

"Nonlinear man," said Diane, smiling a little. Jeff was, come what may, still himself. "I hope it stops soon. Rawna sounded like it won't last all that long."

"Meanwhile I *am* getting paid," repeated Jeff. "I can see the money in my bank account."

"You can see your bank account in your head?"

"I guess I'm, like, semi-divine," said Jeff airily. "Ow!" He dropped to the ground. In the dusk, he'd tripped over a tiny bicycle that the four-year-old next door had left lying on the sidewalk outside Diane's apartment.

"Are you okay?"

"I hate clutter," said Jeff, getting to his feet and angrily hurling the pink bicycle into the apartment complex's swimming pool. "The city should crack down on improperly parked toys."

"Poor little bike," said Diane. "It wasn't the bike's fault. Remember your sensei's theory, Jeff? Isn't the bike alive too?"

"Just because it's alive doesn't make it my friend," muttered Jeff.

Diane felt a little relieved. Yes, Jeff hadn't really changed.

Jeff said he was too fried to make love. They fell asleep in each other's arms and settled into a good night's sleep.

Diane was awakened early by voices in the street. It wasn't just a cluster of joggers—it sounded like hundreds of people streaming by, all amped up. She looked out the bedroom window. The street was filled with demonstrators marching towards the town center. These weren't happy, hippy-dippy types, they were ordinary people mad about something, yelling slogans that Diane couldn't quite understand.

As a sidelight, Diane noticed that many of the people were carrying Goofers, or had them perched on their shoulders or peeking out of their shirt pockets. She felt a little proud of Jeff's influence. On the bed, he snored on.

As the end of the crowd straggled past, Diane finally deciphered the words on one of the handmade signs the people were carrying: "Sidewalks are for people!" And another sign's heavy black lettering came into focus too: "Bikes off the sidewalk! Now!"

"Hey Jeff, wake up!"

Jeff opened his eyes, smiled at Diane, and reached out drowsily for a hug. "I had the greatest dream," he said. "I dreamed I had the answer to everything, and I was about to create an earthly paradise. And then I woke up."

"The answer to *what?*" Diane was intrigued despite herself.

"To *every*thing, Diane. To *everything.*"

That's not enough, thought Diane. "Jeff, you should look outside. This is getting weird."

"Not right now. I need to watch the big screen. It's time for Pastor Veck."

Diane threw on some clothes and ran outside. By now the demonstration had moved on, but the street was littered with black-and-white flyers. She picked one up. It called on the City Council to impound bikes, scooters, and other toys left on the sidewalks.

Inside the apartment, Jeff was watching the ranting of his favorite televangelist. On Pastor Veck's pulpit stood an angelic little Goofer, smiling at the pastor and applauding now and then.

"I don't know about those *evil*–lutionists," Pastor Veck was saying, his eyes twinkly and serious at the same time. "But I know that *I* am not descended from a *sponge* or a *mushroom* or a *fish!*" He lowered his voice. "A famous mathematician once said that, statistically speaking, the odds of randomly shuffled atoms leading to puppies and kittens and human beings, are *infinitesimal!* The simple laws of probability prove that evolution could *never work!*"

Oh wow, thought Diane. The pastor is preaching the realtime wisdom of the prophet Jeff.

"Let us pray within our own minds," the pastor continued very slowly, as if the words were taking form one by one upon his tongue. "Let us touch the tiny souls within our bodies and within our chairs, my friends, the souls within each and every particle great or small, the holy congress of spirits who guide the growth of the human race." The studio audience bowed its heads.

Jeff grinned and turned off the big screen.

"You're running his show now?" said Diane.

"My thoughts filter out," said Jeff, looking proud. "My simmie-bots are everywhere, and my keenly tuned brain is the greatest net router on earth. I'm the hive mind man. Connections. That's what my dream last night was about. Learning to talk to each other. But I need to kick my game up to a higher level. I wish that—"

Like some unhinged genie, Rawna Roller pushed in through Diane's front door, trailed by Sid, who was wearing video cameras as his spectacle lenses today. He had tiny screens set right behind the lenses.

"Hi, lovebirds!" sang Rawna. "We brought a multi-culti pick-me-up for you, Jeff. Ready, Sid?"

"Check," said Sid, miming an assistant-mad-scientist routine.

"Slow down," said Diane, interposing herself, wondering if she should try her karate kick on Sid. When exactly was the right time to deploy a kick like that? "You can't just barge in here and poison Jeff again," continued Diane. "I mean, what is the problem with you two? Hello? We're human beings here."

"We got good news, bad news, and a fix," said Rawna, sweeping past Diane and into the kitchen. "Yes, thank you, I'll have a cup of coffee. Oh, look, Sid, they use one of those chain-store coffeemakers. How retro. How Middle American."

"Remain calm," intoned Sid, his eyes invisible behind his lenses. His mouth was twitching with reckless mirth.

"The good news," said Rawna, returning from the kitchen, holding a coffee cup with her pinky finger sarcastically extended. "The Goofer is through the ceiling in product orders from white-bread Americans. The bad news: the US ethnics aren't picking up Jeff's vibe. And Jeff's campaign is totally flat-lining overseas. If Jeff can't hook mainland China this morning, the Goofer CEO is pulling the plug *and* canceling our payments, the selfish dick."

"Jeff's not cosmopolitan enough," said Sid, shoving his face really,

really close to Jeff—as if he were studying an exotic insect. "Too ignorant, too pale, too raw, too—"

"It's my simmie-bots," said Jeff evenly, staring right into Sid's cameras. "They're living in stateside devices. I need the protocols and the hacktics for sending them overseas. And, okay, I know it's more than just access. I'm almost there, but I'm not fully—"

"We've got the fix for you!" Rawna cut him off. "A universal upgrade. Whip it on the man, Sid. It, ah—what does it do again, Sid?"

"Crawls right into his fucking head!" crowed Sid, taking an object like an aquamarine banana slug from his pocket and throwing it really hard at Jeff's face. The thing *thwapped* onto Jeff's forehead and then, in motions too rapid to readily follow, it writhed down his cheek, wriggled in through a nostril, and, as Jeff reported later, made its way through the bones behind his sinus cavities and onto the convolutions of his brain.

Meanwhile Sid took off his kludgy video glasses and offered them to the speechless Diane. "Want to see the instant replay on that? No? The thing's what the box-jocks call a Kowloon slug. A quantum-computing chunk of piezoplastic. The Kowloon slug will help Jeff clone off Chinese versions of his simmie-bots. 我高興. Wô gāo xìng. I am happy."

"Chinese, French, Finnish, whatever," said Rawna. "It's a universally interfacing meta-interpreter. Last night the Goofer CEO managed to acquire the only one in existence. It's from Triple Future Labs in Xi'an. Near Beijing."

"Jeff can probably even talk to me now," said Sid.

"Yes," said Jeff, eerily calm. "Foreigners, animals, plants, stones, and rude turds." He rose to his feet, looking powerful, poised, and very, very dangerous.

"So okay then," said Rawna, rapidly heading for the door with Sid at her side. In her hoarse whisper, she issued more instructions to Diane. "Your job, my dear, will be to keep Jeff comfortable and relaxed today, and not get in the way. Take him out to the countryside, away from people and local cultural influences. Don't talk to him. He'll be doing the work in his head." Rawna paused on the doorstep to rummage in her capacious rainbow-leopard bag and pulled out a bottle of wine. "This is a very nice Cucamonga viognier, the grape of the year, don't you know. I meant to put it in your freezer, but—"

With Jeff dominating the room like a Frankenstein's monster, Rawna chose to set the bottle on the floor by the door. And then she and Sid were gone.

"I should have karate-kicked Sid as soon as he came in," said Diane wretchedly. "I'm sorry I didn't protect you better, Jeff."

"It's not a problem," said Jeff. His eyes were glowing and warm. "I'll solve Rawna's piss-ant advertising issue, and then we'll take care of some business on our own."

For the moment, Jeff didn't say anything more about the Kowloon slug, and Diane didn't feel like pestering him with questions. Where to even begin? They were off the map of any experiences she'd ever imagined.

Quietly she ate some yogurt while Jeff stared at his Goofer display, which was strobing in a dizzying blur, in synch with his thoughts.

"The Chinese are fully onboard now," announced Jeff, powering down his Goofer ring.

"What about the Kowloon slug?" Diane finally asked.

"I transmuted it," said Jeff. "It's not inside my head anymore. I've passed it on to my simmies. I've got a trillion universally interfacing simmie-bots in the cloud now, and in an hour I'll have a nonillion. This could be a very auspicious day. Let's go out into Nature, yeah."

Diane packed a nice lunch and included Rawna's bottle of white wine. It seemed like a good thing to have wine for this picnic, especially if the picnicker and the picknickee were supposed to stay comfortable and relaxed.

"I say we go up Mount Baldy," suggested Diane, and Jeff was quick to agree. Diane loved that drive, mostly. Zipping down the Foothill to Mountain Ave, a few minutes over some emotionally tough terrain as she passed all the tract houses where the orange groves used to be, and then up along chaparral-lined San Antonio Creek, past Mt. Baldy Village, and then the switchbacks as they went higher.

Jeff was quiet on the drive up, not twitchy at all. Diane was hoping that the Kowloon slug was really gone from his head, and that the conotoxins had fully worn off. The air was invigorating up here, redolent of pines and campfire smoke. It made Diane wish she had a plaid shirt to put on: ordinarily, she hated plaid shirts.

"I'm going to just pull over to the picnic area near the creek," she said. "That'll be easy. We can park there, then walk into the woods a little and find a place without a bunch of people."

But there weren't any people at all—a surprise, given that it was a sunny Sunday in July. Diane pulled off the road into the deserted parking area, which was surrounded by tall trees.

"Did you know these are called Jeffrey pines?" said Diane brightly as they locked the car.

"Sure," said Jeff. "I know everything." He winked at her. "So do you, if you really listen."

Diane wasn't about to field that one. She popped the trunk, grabbed the picnic basket and a blanket to sit on, and they set off on a dusty trail that took them uphill and into the woods.

"Jeffrey pines smell like pineapple," she continued, hell-bent on having a light conversation. "Or vanilla. Some people say pineapple, some people say vanilla. I say pineapple. I love Jeffrey pines."

Jeff made a wry face, comfortably on her human wavelength for the moment. "So that's why you like me? I remind you of a tree?"

Diane laughed lightly, careful not to break into frantic cackles. "Maybe you do. Sometimes I used to drive up here on my day off and hug a Jeffrey pine."

"I can talk to the pines now," said Jeff. "Thanks to what that Kowloon slug did for my simmies. I finally understand: we're all the same. Specks of dirt, bacteria, flames, people, cats. But we can't talk to each other. Not very clearly, anyway."

"I haven't been up here in weeks and weeks," jabbered Diane nervously. "Not since I met you." She looked around. It was quiet, except for birds. "I have to admit it's funny that nobody else is here today. I was worried that maybe—maybe since you're the hive mind man, then everyone in LA would be coming up here too."

"I told them not to," said Jeff. "I'm steering them away. We don't need them here right now." He put his arm around Diane's waist and led her to a soft mossy spot beside a slow, deep creek. "I want us to be alone together. We can change the world."

"So—you remember your dream?" said Diane, a little excited, a little scared. Jeff nodded. "Here?" she said uncertainly. Jeff nodded again. "I'll spread out the blanket," she said.

"The trees and the stream and the blanket will watch over us," said Jeff, as they undressed each other solemnly. "This is going to be one cosmic fuck."

"The earthly paradise?" said Diane, sitting down on the blanket and pulling Jeff down beside her.

"You can make it happen," said Jeff, moving his hands slowly and lightly over her entire body. "You love this world so much. All the animals and the eggs and the bicycles. You can do this." Diane had never felt so ready to love the world as she did right now.

He slid into her, and it was as if she and Jeff were one body and one mind, with their thoughts connected by the busy simmies. Diane understood now what her role was to be.

Glancing up at the pines, she encouraged the simmies to move beyond the web and beyond the human hive mind. The motes of computation hesitated. Diane flooded them with alluring, sensuous thoughts—rose petals, beach sand, dappled shadows.... Suddenly, faster than light in rippling water, the simmies responded, darting like tiny fish into fresh niches, leaving the humans' machines and entering nature's endlessly shuttling looms. And although they migrated, the simmies kept their connection to Jeff and Diane and to all the thirsty human minds that made up the hive and were ruled by it. Out went the bright specks of thought, out into the stones and the clouds and the seas, carrying with them their intimate links to humanity.

Jeff and Diane rocked and rolled their way to ecstasy, to sensations more ancient and more insistent than cannonades of fireworks.

In a barrage of physical and spiritual illumination, Diane felt the entire planet, every creature and feature, every detail, as familiar as her own flesh. She let it encompass her, crash over her in waves of joy.

And then, as the waves diminished, she brought herself back to the blanket in the woods. The Jeffrey pines smiled down at the lovers. Big Gaia hummed beneath Diane's spine. Tiny benevolent minds rustled and buzzed in the fronds of moss, in the whirlpools of the stream, in the caressing breeze against her bare skin.

"I'm me again," said Jeff, up on his elbow, looking at her with his face tired and relaxed.

"We did it," said Diane very slowly. "Everyone can talk to everything now."

"Let the party begin," said Jeff, opening the bottle of wine.

Bruce Sterling (b. 1954) aka "Chairman Bruce" is noted in Singularity circles for the skeptical talk on the proposition he gave to the Long Now Foundation in San Francisco in 2004: "The Singularity: Your Future as a Black Hole." But in the Shaper/Mechanist stories of the early 1980s, he stakes a claim to reinventing the idea of posthumanity. His tough-minded interrogation of assumptions we make about morality is never more on view than in the story that follows.

SUNKEN GARDENS
> Bruce Sterling

Mirasol's crawler loped across the badlands of the Mare Hadriacum, under a tormented Martian sky. At the limits of the troposphere, jet streams twisted, dirty streaks across pale lilac. Mirasol watched the winds through the fretted glass of the control bay. Her altered brain suggested one pattern after another: nests of snakes, nets of dark eels, maps of black arteries.

Since morning the crawler had been descending steadily into the Hellas Basin, and the air pressure was rising. Mars lay like a feverish patient under this thick blanket of air, sweating buried ice.

On the horizon thunderheads rose with explosive speed below the constant scrawl of the jet streams.

The basin was strange to Mirasol. Her faction, the Patternists, had been assigned to a redemption camp in northern Syrtis Major. There, two-hundred-mile-an-hour surface winds were common, and their pressurized camp had been buried three times by advancing dunes.

It had taken her eight days of constant travel to reach the equator.

From high overhead, the Regal faction had helped her navigate. Their orbiting city-state, Terraform-Kluster, was a nexus of monitor satellites. The Regals showed by their helpfulness that they had her under close surveillance.

The crawler lurched as its six picklike feet scrabbled down the slopes of a deflation pit. Mirasol suddenly saw her own face reflected in the glass, pale and taut, her dark eyes dreamily self-absorbed. It was a bare face, with the anonymous beauty of the genetically Reshaped. She rubbed her eyes with nail-bitten fingers.

To the west, far overhead, a gout of airborne topsoil surged aside and revealed the Ladder, the mighty anchor cable of the Terraform-Kluster.

Above the winds the cable faded from sight, vanishing below the metallic glitter of the Kluster, swinging aloofly in orbit.

Mirasol stared at the orbiting city with an uneasy mix of envy, fear, and reverence. She had never been so close to the Kluster before, or to the all-important Ladder that linked it to the Martian surface. Like most of her faction's younger generation, she had never been into space. The Regals had carefully kept her faction quarantined in the Syrtis redemption camp.

Life had not come easily to Mars. For one hundred years the Regals of Terraform-Kluster had bombarded the Martian surface with giant chunks of ice. This act of planetary engineering was the most ambitious, arrogant, and successful of all the works of man in space.

The shattering impacts had torn huge craters in the Martian crust, blasting tons of dust and steam into Mars's threadbare sheet of air. As the temperature rose, buried oceans of Martian permafrost roared forth, leaving networks of twisted badlands and vast expanses of damp mud, smooth and sterile as a television. On these great playas and on the frost-caked walls of channels, cliffs, and calderas, transplanted lichen had clung and leapt into devouring life. In the plains of Eridania, in the twisted megacanyons of the Coprates Basin, in the damp and icy regions of the dwindling poles, vast clawing thickets of its sinister growth lay upon the land—massive disaster areas for the inorganic.

As the terraforming project had grown, so had the power of Terraform-Kluster.

As a neutral point in humanity's factional wars, T-K was crucial to financiers and bankers of every sect. Even the alien Investors, those star-traveling reptiles of enormous wealth, found T-K useful, and favored it with their patronage.

And as T-K's citizens, the Regals, increased their power, smaller factions faltered and fell under their sway. Mars was dotted with bankrupt factions, financially captured and transported to the Martian surface by the T-K plutocrats.

Having failed in space, the refugees took Regal charity as ecologists of the sunken gardens. Dozens of factions were quarantined in cheerless redemption camps, isolated from one another; their lives pared to a grim frugality.

And the visionary Regals made good use of their power. The factions found themselves trapped in the arcane bioaesthetics of Posthumanist philosophy, subverted constantly by Regal broadcasts, Regal teaching, Regal culture. With time even the stubbornest faction would be broken down and digested into the cultural bloodstream of T-K. Faction members would be allowed to leave their redemption camp and travel up the Ladder.

But first they would have to prove themselves. The Patternists had awaited their chance for years. It had come at last in the Ibis Crater competition, an ecological struggle of the factions that would prove the victors' right to Regal status. Six factions had sent their champions to the ancient Ibis Crater, each one armed with its group's strongest biotechnologies. It would be a war of the sunken gardens, with the Ladder as the prize.

Mirasol's crawler followed a gully through a chaotic terrain of rocky permafrost that had collapsed in karsts and sinkholes. After two hours, the gully ended abruptly. Before Mirasol rose a mountain range of massive slabs and boulders, some with the glassy sheen of impact melt, others scabbed over with lichen.

As the crawler started up the slope, the sun came out, and Mirasol saw the crater's outer rim jigsawed in the green of lichen and the glaring white of snow.

The oxygen readings were rising steadily. Warm, moist air was drooling from within the crater's lip, leaving a spittle of ice. A half-million-ton asteroid from the Rings of Saturn had fallen here at fifteen kilometers a second. But for two centuries rain, creeping glaciers, and lichen had gnawed at the crater's rim, and the wound's raw edges had slumped and scarred.

The crawler worked its way up the striated channel of an empty glacier bed. A cold alpine wind keened down the channel, where flourishing patches of lichen clung to exposed veins of ice.

Some rocks were striped with sediment from the ancient Martian seas, and the impact had peeled them up and thrown them on their backs.

It was winter, the season for pruning the sunken gardens. The treacherous rubble of the crater's rim was cemented with frozen mud. The crawler found the glacier's root and clawed its way up the ice face. The raw slope was striped with winter snow and storm-blown summer dust, stacked in hundreds of red-and-white layers. With the years the stripes had warped and rippled in the glacier's flow.

Mirasol reached the crest. The crawler ran spiderlike along the crater's snowy rim. Below, in a bowl-shaped crater eight kilometers deep, lay a seething ocean of air.

Mirasol stared. Within this gigantic airsump, twenty kilometers across, a broken ring of majestic rain clouds trailed their dark skirts, like duchesses in quadrille, about the ballroom floor of a lens-shaped sea.

Thick forests of green-and-yellow mangroves rimmed the shallow water and had overrun the shattered islands at its center. Pinpoints of brilliant scarlet ibis spattered the trees. A flock of them suddenly spread kitelike wings and took to the air, spreading across the crater in uncounted millions. Mirasol was appalled by the crudity and daring of this ecological concept, its crass and primal vitality.

This was what she had come to destroy. The thought filled her with sadness.

Then she remembered the years she had spent flattering her Regal teachers, collaborating with them in the destruction of her own culture. When the chance at the Ladder came, she had been chosen. She put her sadness away, remembering her ambitions and her rivals.

The history of mankind in space had been a long epic of ambitions and rivalries. From the very first, space colonies had struggled for self-sufficiency and had soon broken their ties with the exhausted Earth. The independent life-support systems had given them the mentality of city-states. Strange ideologies had bloomed in the hothouse atmosphere of the o'neills, and breakaway groups were common.

Space was too vast to police. Pioneer elites burst forth, defying anyone to stop their pursuit of aberrant technologies. Quite suddenly the march of science had become an insane, headlong scramble. New sciences and technologies had shattered whole societies in waves of future shock.

The shattered cultures coalesced into factions, so thoroughly alienated from one another that they were called humanity only for lack of a better term. The Shapers, for instance, had seized control of their own genetics, abandoning mankind in a burst of artificial evolution. Their rivals, the Mechanists, had replaced flesh with advanced prosthetics.

Mirasol's own group, the Patternists, was a breakaway Shaper faction.

The Patternists specialized in cerebral asymmetry. With grossly expanded right-brain hemispheres, they were highly intuitive, given to metaphors, parallels, and sudden cognitive leaps. Their inventive minds and quick, unpredictable genius had given them a competitive edge at first. But with these advantages had come grave weaknesses: autism, fugue states, and paranoia. Patterns grew out of control and became grotesque webs of fantasy.

With these handicaps their colony had faltered. Patternist industries went into decline, outpaced by industrial rivals. Competition had grown much fiercer. The Shaper and Mechanist cartels had turned commercial action into a kind of endemic warfare. The Patternist gamble had failed, and the day came when their entire habitat was bought out from around them by Regal plutocrats. In a way it was a kindness. The Regals were suave and proud of their ability to assimilate refugees and failures.

The Regals themselves had started as dissidents and defectors. Their Posthumanist philosophy had given them the moral power and the bland assurance to dominate and absorb factions from the fringes of humanity. And they had the support of the Investors, who had vast wealth and the secret techniques of star travel.

The crawler's radar alerted Mirasol to the presence of a landcraft from a rival faction. Leaning forward in her pilot's couch, she put the craft's image on screen. It was a lumpy sphere, balanced uneasily on four long, spindly legs. Silhouetted against the horizon, it moved with a strange wobbling speed along the opposite lip of the crater, then disappeared down the outward slope.

Mirasol wondered if it had been cheating. She was tempted to try some cheating herself—to dump a few frozen packets of aerobic bacteria or a few dozen capsules of insect eggs down the slope—but she feared the orbiting monitors of the T-K supervisors. Too much was at stake—not only her own career but that of her entire faction, huddled bankrupt and despairing in their cold redemption camp. It was said that T-K's ruler, the posthuman being they called the Lobster King, would himself watch the contest. To fail before his black abstracted gaze would be a horror.

On the crater's outside slope, below her, a second rival craft appeared, lurching and slithering with insane, aggressive grace. The craft's long supple body moved with a sidewinder's looping and coiling, holding aloft a massive shining head, like a faceted mirror ball.

Both rivals were converging on the rendezvous camp, where the six contestants would receive their final briefing from the Regal Adviser. Mirasol hurried forward.

When the camp first flashed into sight on her screen, Mirasol was shocked. The place was huge and absurdly elaborate: a drug dream of paneled geodesics and colored minarets, sprawling in the lichenous desert like an abandoned chandelier. This was a camp for Regals.

Here the arbiters and sophists of the BioArts would stay and judge the crater as the newly planted ecosystems struggled among themselves for supremacy.

The camp's airlocks were surrounded with shining green thickets of lichen, where the growth feasted on escaped humidity. Mirasol drove her crawler through the yawning airlock and into a garage. Inside the garage, robot mechanics were scrubbing and polishing the coiled hundred-meter length of the snake craft and the gleaming black abdomen of an eight-legged crawler. The black crawler was crouched with its periscoped head sunk downward, as if ready to pounce. Its swollen belly was marked with a red hourglass and the corporate logos of its faction.

The garage smelled of dust and grease overlaid with floral perfumes. Mirasol left the mechanics to their work and walked stiffly down a long corridor, stretching the kinks out of her back and shoulders. A latticework door sprang apart into filaments and resealed itself behind her.

She was in a dining room that clinked and rattled with the high-pitched repetitive sound of Regal music. Its walls were paneled with tall display screens showing startlingly beautiful garden panoramas. A pulpy-looking servo, whose organometallic casing and squat, smiling head had a swollen and almost diseased appearance, showed her to a chair.

Mirasol sat, denting the heavy white tablecloth with her knees. There were seven places at the table. The Regal Adviser's tall chair was at the table's head. Mirasol's assigned position gave her a sharp idea of her own status. She sat at the far end of the table, on the Adviser's left.

Two of her rivals had already taken their places. One was a tall, red-haired Shaper with long, thin arms, whose sharp face and bright, worried eyes gave him a querulous birdlike look. The other was a sullen, feral Mechanist with prosthetic hands and a paramilitary tunic marked at the shoulders with a red hourglass.

Mirasol studied her two rivals with silent, sidelong glances. Like her, they were both young. The Regals favored the young, and they encouraged captive factions to expand their populations widely.

This strategy cleverly subverted the old guard of each faction in a tidal wave of their own children, indoctrinated from birth by Regals.

The birdlike man, obviously uncomfortable with his place directly at the Adviser's right, looked as if he wanted to speak but dared not. The piratical Mech sat staring at his artificial hands, his ears stoppered with headphones.

Each place setting had a squeezebulb of liqueur. Regals, who were used to weightlessness in orbit, used these bulbs by habit, and their presence here was both a privilege and a humiliation.

The door fluttered open again, and two more rivals burst in, almost as if they had raced. The first was a flabby Mech, still not used to gravity, whose sagging limbs were supported by an extraskeletal framework. The second was a severely mutated Shaper whose elbowed legs terminated in grasping hands. The pedal hands were gemmed with heavy rings that clicked against each other as she waddled across the parquet floor.

The woman with the strange legs took her place across from the birdlike man. They began to converse haltingly in a language that none of the others could follow. The man in the framework, gasping audibly, lay in obvious pain in the chair across from Mirasol. His plastic eyeballs looked as blank as chips of glass. His sufferings in the pull of gravity showed that he was new to Mars, and his place in the competition meant that his faction was powerful. Mirasol despised him.

Mirasol felt a nightmarish sense of entrapment. Everything about her competitors seemed to proclaim their sickly unfitness for survival. They had a haunted, hungry look, like starving men in a lifeboat who wait with secret eagerness for the first to die.

She caught a glimpse of herself reflected in the bowl of a spoon and saw with a flash of insight how she must appear to the others. Her intuitive right brain was swollen beyond human bounds, distorting her skull. Her face had the blank prettiness of her genetic heritage, but she could feel the bleak strain of her expression. Her body looked shapeless under her quilted pilot's vest and dun-drab, general-issue blouse and trousers. Her fingertips were raw from biting. She saw in herself the fey, defeated aura of her faction's older generation, those who had tried and failed in the great world of space, and she hated herself for it.

They were still waiting for the sixth competitor when the plonking music reached a sudden crescendo and the Regal Adviser arrived. Her name was Arkadya Sorienti, Incorporated. She was a member of T-K's ruling oligarchy, and she swayed through the bursting door with the careful steps of a woman not used to gravity.

She wore the Investor-style clothing of a high-ranking diplomat. The Regals were proud of their diplomatic ties with the alien Investors, since Investor patronage proved their own vast wealth. The Sorienti's knee-high boots had false birdlike toes, scaled like Investor hide. She wore a heavy skirt of gold cords braided with jewels, and a stiff wrist-length formal jacket with embroidered cuffs. A heavy collar formed an arching multicolored frill behind her head. Her blonde hair was set in an interlaced style as complex as computer wiring. The skin of her bare legs had a shiny, glossy look, as if freshly enameled. Her eyelids gleamed with soft reptilian pastels.

One of her corporate ladyship's two body-servos helped her to her seat. The Sorienti leaned forward brightly, interlacing small, pretty hands so crusted with rings and bracelets that they resembled gleaming gauntlets.

"I hope the five of you have enjoyed this chance for an informal talk," she said sweetly, just as if such a thing were possible. "I'm sorry I was delayed. Our sixth participant will not be joining us."

There was no explanation. The Regals never publicized any action of theirs that might be construed as a punishment. The looks of the competitors, alternately stricken and calculating, showed that they were imagining the worst.

The two squat servos circulated around the table, dishing out courses of food from trays balanced on their flabby heads. The competitors picked uneasily at their plates.

The display screen behind the Adviser flicked into a schematic diagram of the Ibis Crater. "Please notice the revised boundary lines," the Sorienti said. "I hope that each of you will avoid trespassing—not merely physically but biologically as well." She looked at them seriously.

"Some of you may plan to use herbicides. This is permissible, but the spreading of spray beyond your sector's boundaries is considered crass. Bacteriological establishment is a subtle art. The spreading of tailored disease organisms is an aesthetic distortion. Please remember that your activities here are a disruption of what should ideally be natural processes. Therefore the period of biotic seeding will last only twelve hours. Thereafter, the new complexity level will be allowed to stabilize itself without any other interference at all. Avoid self-aggrandizement, and confine yourselves to a primal role, as catalysts."

The Sorienti's speech was formal and ceremonial. Mirasol studied the display screen, noting with much satisfaction that her territory had been expanded.

Seen from overhead, the crater's roundness was deeply marred.

Mirasol's sector, the southern one, showed the long flattened scar of a major landslide, where the crater wall had slumped and flowed into the pit. The simple ecosystem had recovered quickly, and mangroves festooned the rubble's lowest slopes. Its upper slopes were gnawed by lichens and glaciers.

The sixth sector had been erased, and Mirasol's share was almost twenty square kilometers of new land.

It would give her faction's ecosystem more room to take root before the deadly struggle began in earnest.

This was not the first such competition. The Regals had held them for decades as an objective test of the skills of rival factions. It helped the Regals' divide-and-conquer policy, to set the factions against one another.

And in the centuries to come, as Mars grew more hospitable to life, the gardens would surge from their craters and spread across the surface. Mars would become a warring jungle of separate creations. For the Regals the competitions were closely studied simulations of the future.

And the competitions gave the factions motives for their work. With the garden wars to spur them, the ecological sciences had advanced enormously. Already, with the progress of science and taste, many of the oldest craters had become ecoaesthetic embarrassments.

The Ibis Crater had been an early, crude experiment. The faction that had created it was long gone, and its primitive creation was now considered tasteless.

Each gardening faction camped beside its own crater, struggling to bring it to life. But the competitions were a shortcut up the Ladder. The competitors' philosophies and talents, made into flesh, would carry out a proxy struggle for supremacy. The sine-wave curves of growth, the rallies and declines of expansion and extinction, would scroll across the monitors of the Regal judges like stock-market reports. This complex struggle would be weighed in each of its aspects: technological, philosophical, biological, and aesthetic. The winners would abandon their camps to take on Regal wealth and power. They would roam T-K's jeweled corridors and revel in its perquisites: extended life spans, corporate titles, cosmopolitan tolerance, and the interstellar patronage of the Investors.

When red dawn broke over the landscape, the five were poised around the Ibis Crater, awaiting the signal. The day was calm, with only a distant nexus of jet streams marring the sky. Mirasol watched pink-stained sunlight creep down the inside slope of the crater's western wall. In the mangrove thickets birds were beginning to stir.

Mirasol waited tensely. She had taken a position on the upper slopes of the landslide's raw debris. Radar showed her rivals spaced along the interior slopes: to her left, the hourglass crawler and the jewel-headed snake; to her right, a mantislike crawler and the globe on stilts.

The signal came, sudden as lightning: a meteor of ice shot from orbit and left a shock-wave cloud plume of ablated steam. Mirasol charged forward.

The Patternists' strategy was to concentrate on the upper slopes and the landslide's rubble, a marginal niche where they hoped to excel. Their cold crater in Syrtis Major had given them some expertise in alpine species, and they hoped to exploit this strength. The landslide's long slope, far above sea level, was to be their power base. The crawler lurched downslope, blasting out a fine spray of lichenophagous bacteria.

Suddenly the air was full of birds. Across the crater, the globe on stilts had rushed down to the waterline and was laying waste the mangroves. Fine wisps of smoke showed the slicing beam of a heavy laser.

Burst after burst of birds took wing, peeling from their nests to wheel and dip in terror. At first, their frenzied cries came as a high-pitched whisper. Then, as the fear spread, the screeching echoed and reechoed, building to a mindless surf of pain. In the crater's dawn-warmed air, the scarlet motes hung in their millions, swirling and coalescing like drops of blood in free-fall.

Mirasol scattered the seeds of alpine rock crops. The crawler picked its way down the talus, spraying fertilizer into cracks and crevices. She pried up boulders and released a scattering of invertebrates: nematodes, mites, sowbugs, altered millipedes. She splattered the rocks with gelatin to feed them until the mosses and ferns took hold.

The cries of the birds were appalling. Downslope the other factions were thrashing in the muck at sea level, wreaking havoc, destroying the mangroves so that their own creations could take hold. The great snake looped and ducked through the canopy, knotting itself, ripping up swathes of mangroves by the roots. As Mirasol watched, the top of its faceted head burst open and released a cloud of bats.

The mantis crawler was methodically marching along the borders of its sector, its saw-edged arms reducing everything before it into kindling. The hourglass crawler had slashed through its territory, leaving a muddy network of fire zones. Behind it rose a wall of smoke.

It was a daring ploy. Sterilizing the sector by fire might give the new biome a slight advantage. Even a small boost could be crucial as exponential rates of growth took hold. But the Ibis Crater was a closed system. The use of fire required great care. There was only so much air within the bowl.

Mirasol worked grimly. Insects were next. They were often neglected in favor of massive sea beasts or flashy predators, but in terms of biomass, gram by gram, insects could overwhelm. She blasted a carton downslope to the shore, where it melted, releasing aquatic termites. She shoved aside flat shelves of rock, planting egg cases below their sun-warmed surfaces. She released a cloud of leaf-eating midges, their tiny bodies packed with bacteria. Within the crawler's belly, rack after automatic rack was thawed and fired through nozzles, dropped through spiracles or planted in the holes jabbed by picklike feet.

Each faction was releasing a potential world. Near the water's edge, the mantis had released a pair of things like giant black sail planes. They were swooping through the clouds of ibis, opening great sieved mouths. On the islands in the center of the crater's lake, scaled walruses clambered on the rocks, blowing steam. The stilt ball was laying out an orchard in the mangroves' wreckage. The snake had taken to the water, its faceted head leaving a wake of V-waves.

In the hourglass sector, smoke continued to rise. The fires were spreading, and the spider ran frantically along its network of zones. Mirasol watched the movement of the smoke as she released a horde of marmots and rock squirrels.

A mistake had been made. As the smoky air gushed upward in the feeble Martian gravity, a fierce valley wind of cold air from the heights flowed downward to fill the vacuum. The mangroves burned fiercely. Shattered networks of flaming branches were flying into the air.

The spider charged into the flames, smashing and trampling. Mirasol laughed, imagining demerits piling up in the judges' data banks. Her talus slopes were safe from fire. There was nothing to burn.

The ibis flock had formed a great wheeling ring above the shore. Within their scattered ranks flitted the dark shapes of airborne predators. The long plume of steam from the meteor had begun to twist and break. A sullen wind was building up.

Fire had broken out in the snake's sector. The snake was swimming in the sea's muddy waters, surrounded by bales of bright-green kelp. Before its pilot noticed, fire was already roaring through a great piled heap of the wreckage it had left on shore. There were no windbreaks left. Air poured down the denuded slope. The smoke column guttered and twisted, its black clouds alive with sparks.

A flock of ibis plunged into the cloud. Only a handful emerged; some of them were flaming visibly. Mirasol began to know fear. As smoke rose to the crater's rim, it cooled and started to fall outward and downward. A vertical whirlwind was forming, a torus of hot smoke and cold wind.

The crawler scattered seed-packed hay for pygmy mountain goats. Just before her an ibis fell from the sky with a dark squirming shape, all claws and teeth, clinging to its neck. She rushed forward and crushed the predator, then stopped and stared distractedly across the crater.

Fires were spreading with unnatural speed. Small puffs of smoke rose from a dozen places, striking large heaps of wood with uncanny precision. Her altered brain searched for a pattern. The fires springing up in the mantis sector were well beyond the reach of any falling debris.

In the spider's zone, flames had leapt the firebreaks without leaving a mark. The pattern felt wrong to her, eerily wrong, as if the destruction had a force all its own, a raging synergy that fed upon itself.

The pattern spread into a devouring crescent. Mirasol felt the dread of lost control—the sweating fear an orbiter feels at the hiss of escaping air or the way a suicide feels at the first bright gush of blood.

Within an hour the garden sprawled beneath a hurricane of hot decay. The dense columns of smoke had flattened like thunderheads at the limits of the garden's sunken troposphere. Slowly a spark-shot gray haze, dripping ash like rain, began to ring the crater. Screaming birds circled beneath the foul torus, falling by tens and scores and hundreds. Their bodies littered the garden's sea, their bright plumage blurred with ash in a steel-gray sump.

The landcraft of the others continued to fight the flames, smashing unharmed through the fire's charred borderlands. Their efforts were useless, a pathetic ritual before the disaster.

Even the fire's malicious purity had grown tired and tainted. The oxygen was failing. The flames were dimmer and spread more slowly, releasing a dark nastiness of half-combusted smoke.

Where it spread, nothing that breathed could live. Even the flames were killed as the smoke billowed along the crater's crushed and smoldering slopes.

Mirasol watched a group of striped gazelles struggle up the barren slopes of the talus in search of air. Their dark eyes, fresh from the laboratory, rolled in timeless animal fear. Their coats were scorched, their flanks heaved, their mouths dripped foam. One by one they collapsed in convulsions, kicking at the lifeless Martian rock as they slid and fell. It was a vile sight, the image of a blighted spring.

An oblique flash of red downslope to her left attracted her attention. A large red animal was skulking among the rocks. She turned the crawler and picked her way toward it, wincing as a dark surf of poisoned smoke broke across the fretted glass.

She spotted the animal as it broke from cover. It was a scorched and gasping creature like a great red ape. She dashed forward and seized it in the crawler's arms. Held aloft, it clawed and kicked, hammering the crawler's arms with a smoldering branch. In revulsion and pity, she crushed it. Its bodice of tight-sewn ibis feathers tore, revealing blood-slicked human flesh.

Using the crawler's grips, she tugged at a heavy tuft of feathers on its head. The tight-fitting mask ripped free, and the dead man's head slumped forward. She rolled it back, revealing a face tattooed with stars.

The ornithopter sculled above the burned-out garden, its long red wings beating with dreamlike fluidity. Mirasol watched the Sorienti's painted face as her corporate ladyship stared into the shining viewscreen.

The ornithopter's powerful cameras cast image after image onto the tabletop screen, lighting the Regal's face. The tabletop was littered with the Sorienti's elegant knickknacks: an inhaler case, a half-empty jeweled squeezebulb, lorgnette binoculars, a stack of tape cassettes.

"An unprecedented case," her ladyship murmured. "It was not a total dieback after all but merely the extinction of everything with lungs. There must be strong survivorship among the lower orders: fish, insects, annelids. Now that the rain's settled the ash, you can see the vegetation making a strong comeback. Your own section seems almost undamaged."

"Yes," Mirasol said. "The natives were unable to reach it with torches before the fire storm had smothered itself."

The Sorienti leaned back into the tasseled arms of her couch. "I wish you wouldn't mention them so loudly, even between ourselves."

"No one would believe me."

"The others never saw them," the Regal said. "They were too busy fighting the flames." She hesitated briefly. "You were wise to confide in me first."

Mirasol locked eyes with her new patroness, then looked away. "There was no one else to tell. They'd have said I built a pattern out of nothing but my own fears."

"You have your faction to think of," the Sorienti said with an air of sympathy. "With such a bright future ahead of them, they don't need a renewed reputation for paranoid fantasies."

She studied the screen. "The Patternists are winners by default. It certainly makes an interesting case study. If the new garden grows tiresome we can have the whole crater sterilized from orbit. Some other faction can start again with a clean slate."

"Don't let them build too close to the edge," Mirasol said.

Her corporate ladyship watched her attentively, tilting her head.

"I have no proof," Mirasol said, "but I can see the pattern behind it all. The natives had to come from somewhere. The colony that stocked the crater must have been destroyed in that huge landslide. Was that your work? Did your people kill them?"

The Sorienti smiled. "You're very bright, my dear. You will do well, up the Ladder. And you can keep secrets. Your office as my secretary suits you very well."

"They were destroyed from orbit," Mirasol said. "Why else would they hide from us? You tried to annihilate them."

"It was a long time ago," the Regal said. "In the early days, when things were shakier. They were researching the secret of starflight, techniques only the Investors know. Rumor says they reached success at last, in their redemption camp. After that, there was no choice."

"Then they were killed for the Investors' profit," Mirasol said. She stood up quickly and walked around the cabin, her new jeweled skirt clattering around the knees. "So that the aliens could go on toying with us, hiding their secret, selling us trinkets."

The Regal folded her hands with a clicking of rings and bracelets. "Our Lobster King is wise," she said. "If humanity's efforts turned to the stars, what would become of terraforming? Why should we trade the power of creation itself to become like the Investors?"

"But think of the people," Mirasol said. "Think of them losing their technologies, degenerating into human beings. A handful of savages, eating bird meat. Think of the fear they felt for generations, the way they burned their own home and killed themselves when they saw us come to smash and destroy their world. Aren't you filled with horror?"

"For humans?" the Sorienti said. "No!"

"But can't you see? You've given this planet life as an art form, as an enormous game. You force us to play in it, and those people were killed for it! Can't you see how that blights everything?"

"Our game is reality," the Regal said. She gestured at the viewscreen. "You can't deny the savage beauty of destruction."

"You defend this catastrophe?"

The Regal shrugged. "If life worked perfectly, how could things evolve? Aren't we posthuman? Things grow; things die. In time the cosmos kills us all. The cosmos has no meaning, and its emptiness is absolute. That's pure terror, but its also pure freedom. Only our ambitions and our creations can fill it."

"And that justifies your actions?"

"We act for life," the Regal said. "Our ambitions have become this world's natural laws. We blunder because life blunders. We go on because life must go on. When you've taken the long view, from orbit—when the power we wield is in your own hands—then you can judge us." She smiled. "You will be judging yourself. You'll be Regal."

"But what about your captive factions? Your agents, who do your will? Once we had our own ambitions. We failed, and now you isolate us, indoctrinate us, make us into rumors. We must have something of our own. Now we have nothing."

"That's not so. You have what we've given you. You have the Ladder."

The vision stung Mirasol: power, light, the hint of justice, this world with its sins and sadness shrunk to a bright arena far below. "Yes," she said at last. "Yes, we do."

ACROSS THE EVENT HORIZON

Futurist **Ray Kurzweil** (b. 1948) first made his reputation as an inventor and entrepreneur in computer technology, including optical character recognition and text-to-speech synthesis. He was one of the first and most avid proponents of artificial intelligence, elucidating his ideas in such books as *The Age of Intelligent Machines* and *The Age of Spiritual Machines*, and has been one of the leading voices of the transhumanist movement.

THE SIX EPOCHS

Chapter One from *The Singularity Is Near*

> Ray Kurzweil

Everyone takes the limits of his own vision for the limits of the world.
—Arthur Schopenhauer

I am not sure when I first became aware of the Singularity. I'd have to say it was a progressive awakening. In the almost half century that I've immersed myself in computer and related technologies, I've sought to understand the meaning and purpose of the continual upheaval that I have witnessed at many levels. Gradually, I've become aware of a transforming event looming in the first half of the twenty-first century. Just as a black hole in space dramatically alters the patterns of matter and energy accelerating toward its event horizon, this impending Singularity in our future is increasingly transforming every institution and aspect of human life, from sexuality to spirituality.

What, then, is the Singularity? It's a future period during which the pace of technological change will be so rapid, its impact so deep, that human life will be irreversibly transformed. Although neither utopian nor dystopian, this epoch will transform the concepts that we rely on to give meaning to our lives, from our business models to the cycle of human life, including death itself. Understanding the Singularity will alter our perspective on the significance of our past and the ramifications for our future. To truly understand it inherently changes one's view of life in general and one's own particular life. I regard someone who understands the Singularity and who has reflected on its implications for his or her own life as a "singularitarian."

I can understand why many observers do not readily embrace the obvious implications of what I have called the law of accelerating returns (the inherent acceleration of the rate of evolution, with technological evolution as a continuation of biological evolution). After all, it took me forty years to be able to see what was right in front of me, and I still cannot say that I am entirely comfortable with all of its consequences.

The key idea underlying the impending Singularity is that the pace of change of our human-created technology is accelerating and its powers are expanding at an exponential pace. Exponential growth is deceptive. It starts out almost imperceptibly and then explodes with unexpected fury—unexpected, that is, if one does not take care to follow its trajectory.

Consider this parable: a lake owner wants to stay at home to tend to the lake's fish and make certain that the lake itself will not become covered with lily pads, which are said to double their number every few days. Month after month, he patiently waits, yet only tiny patches of lily pads can be discerned, and they don't seem to be expanding in any noticeable way. With the lily pads covering less than 1 percent of the lake, the owner figures that it's safe to take a vacation and leaves with his family. When he returns a few weeks later, he's shocked to discover that the entire lake has become covered with the pads, and his fish have perished. By doubling their number every few days, the last seven doublings were sufficient to extend the pads' coverage to the entire lake. (Seven doublings extended their reach 128-fold.) This is the nature of exponential growth.

Consider Gary Kasparov, who scorned the pathetic state of computer chess in 1992. Yet the relentless doubling of computer power every year enabled a computer to defeat him only five years later. The list of ways computers can now exceed human capabilities is rapidly growing. Moreover, the once narrow applications of computer intelligence are gradually broadening in one type of activity after another. For example, computers are diagnosing electrocardiograms and medical images, flying and landing airplanes, controlling the tactical decisions of automated weapons, making credit and financial decisions, and being given responsibility for many other tasks that used to require human intelligence. The performance of these systems is increasingly based on integrating multiple types of artificial intelligence (AI). But as long as there is an AI shortcoming in any such area of endeavor, skeptics will point to that area as an inherent bastion of permanent human superiority over the capabilities of our own creations.

This book will argue, however, that within several decades information-based technologies will encompass all human knowledge and proficiency, ultimately including the pattern-recognition powers, problem-solving skills, and emotional and moral intelligence of the human brain itself.

Although impressive in many respects, the brain suffers from severe limitations. We use its massive parallelism (one hundred trillion interneuronal connections operating simultaneously) to quickly recognize subtle patterns. But our thinking is extremely slow: the basic neural transactions are several million times slower than contemporary electronic circuits. That makes our physiological bandwidth for processing new information extremely limited compared to the exponential growth of the overall human knowledge base.

Our version 1.0 biological bodies are likewise frail and subject to a myriad of failure modes, not to mention the cumbersome maintenance rituals they require. While human intelligence is sometimes capable of soaring in its creativity and expressiveness, much human thought is derivative, petty, and circumscribed.

The Singularity will allow us to transcend these limitations of our biological bodies and brains. We will gain power over our fates. Our mortality will be in our own hands. We will be able to live as long as we want (a subtly different statement from saying we will live forever). We will fully understand human thinking and will vastly extend and expand its reach. By the end of this century, the nonbiological portion of our intelligence will be trillions of trillions of times more powerful than unaided human intelligence.

We are now in the early stages of this transition. The acceleration of paradigm shift (the rate at which we change fundamental technical approaches) as well as the exponential growth of the capacity of information technology are both beginning to reach the "knee of the curve," which is the stage at which an exponential trend becomes noticeable. Shortly after this stage, the trend quickly becomes explosive. Before the middle of this century, the growth rates of our technology—which will be indistinguishable from ourselves—will be so steep as to appear essentially vertical.

From a strictly mathematical perspective, the growth rates will still be finite but so extreme that the changes they bring about will appear to rupture the fabric of human history. That, at least, will be the perspective of unenhanced biological humanity.

The Singularity will represent the culmination of the merger of our biological thinking and existence with our technology, resulting in a world that is still human but that transcends our biological roots. There will be no distinction, post-Singularity, between human and machine or between physical and virtual reality. If you wonder what will remain unequivocally human in such a world, it's simply this quality: ours is the species that inherently seeks to extend its physical and mental reach beyond current limitations.

Many commentators on these changes focus on what they perceive as a loss of some vital aspect of our humanity that will result from this transition. This perspective stems, however, from a misunderstanding of what our technology will become. All the machines we have met to date lack the essential subtlety of human biological qualities. Although the Singularity has many faces, its most important implication is this: our technology will match and then vastly exceed the refinement and suppleness of what we regard as the best of human traits.

Hugo Award-winning SF author **Greg Egan** (b. 1961) holds a B.S. degree in mathematics from the University of Western Australia. His ontologically challenging stories and novels are noted for their complex engagement with a host of themes and notions associated with the Singularity, including artificial intelligence, simulated reality, mind uploading, and the nature of consciousness. In a story that evokes Theodore Sturgeon's classic "Microcosmic God" a wealthy entrepreneur seeks to seize control of evolution, speeding it up to bring on the Singularity.

CRYSTAL NIGHTS
> Greg Egan

1

"More caviar?" Daniel Cliff gestured at the serving dish and the cover irised from opaque to transparent. "It's fresh, I promise you. My chef had it flown in from Iran this morning."

"No thank you." Julie Dehghani touched a napkin to her lips then laid it on her plate with a gesture of finality. The dining room overlooked the Golden Gate Bridge, and most people Daniel invited here were content to spend an hour or two simply enjoying the view, but he could see that she was growing impatient with his small talk.

Daniel said, "I'd like to show you something." He led her into the adjoining conference room. On the table was a wireless keyboard; the wall screen showed a Linux command line interface. "Take a seat," he suggested.

Julie complied. "If this is some kind of audition, you might have warned me," she said.

"Not at all," Daniel replied. "I'm not going to ask you to jump through any hoops. I'd just like you to tell me what you think of this machine's performance."

She frowned slightly, but she was willing to play along. She ran some standard benchmarks. Daniel saw her squinting at the screen, one hand almost reaching up to where a desktop display would be, so she could double-check the number of digits in the FLOPS rating by counting them off with one finger. There were a lot more than she'd been expecting, but she wasn't seeing double.

"That's extraordinary," she said. "Is this whole building packed with networked processors, with only the penthouse for humans?"

Daniel said, "You tell me. Is it a cluster?"

"Hmm." So much for not making her jump through hoops, but it wasn't really much of a challenge. She ran some different benchmarks, based on algorithms that were probably impossible to parallelise; however smart the compiler was, the steps these programs required would have to be carried out strictly in sequence.

The FLOPS rating was unchanged.

Julie said, "All right, it's a single processor. Now you've got my attention. Where is it?"

"Turn the keyboard over."

There was a charcoal-gray module, five centimeters square and five millimeters thick, plugged into an inset docking bay. Julie examined it, but it bore no manufacturer's logo or other identifying marks.

"This connects to the processor?" she asked.

"No. It *is* the processor."

"You're joking." She tugged it free of the dock, and the wall screen went blank. She held it up and turned it around, though Daniel wasn't sure what she was looking for. Somewhere to slip in a screwdriver and take the thing apart, probably. He said, "If you break it, you own it, so I hope you've got a few hundred to spare."

"A few hundred grand? Hardly."

"A few hundred million."

Her face flushed. "Of course. If it was a few hundred grand, everyone would have one." She put it down on the table, then as an afterthought slid it a little further from the edge. "As I said, you've got my attention."

Daniel smiled. "I'm sorry about the theatrics."

"No, this deserved the build-up. What is it, exactly?"

"A single, three-dimensional photonic crystal. No electronics to slow it down; every last component is optical. The architecture was nanofabricated with a method that I'd prefer not to describe in detail."

"Fair enough." She thought for a while. "I take it you don't expect me to buy one. My research budget for the next thousand years would barely cover it."

"In your present position. But you're not joined to the university at the hip."

"So this is a job interview?"

Daniel nodded.

Julie couldn't help herself; she picked up the crystal and examined it again, as if there might yet be some feature that a human eye could discern. "Can you give me a job description?"

"Midwife."

She laughed. "To what?"

"History," Daniel said.

Her smile faded slowly.

"I believe you're the best AI researcher of your generation," he said. "I want you to work for me." He reached over and took the crystal from her. "With this as your platform, imagine what you could do."

Julie said, "What exactly would you want me to do?"

"For the last fifteen years," Daniel said, "you've stated that the ultimate goal of your research is to create conscious, human-level, artificial intelligence."

"That's right."

"Then we want the same thing. What I want is for you to succeed."

She ran a hand over her face; whatever else she was thinking, there was no denying that she was tempted. "It's gratifying that you have so much confidence in my abilities," she said. "But we need to be clear about some things. This prototype is amazing, and if you ever get the production costs down I'm sure it will have some extraordinary applications. It would eat up climate forecasting, lattice QCD, astrophysical modeling, proteomics..."

"Of course." Actually, Daniel had no intention of marketing the device. He'd bought out the inventor of the fabrication process with his own private funds; there were no other shareholders or directors to dictate his use of the technology.

"But AI," Julie said, "is different. We're in a maze, not a highway; there's nowhere that speed alone can take us. However many exaflops I have to play with, they won't spontaneously combust into consciousness. I'm not being held back by the university's computers; I have access to SHARCNET anytime I need it. I'm being held back by my own lack of insight into the problems I'm addressing."

Daniel said, "A maze is not a dead end. When I was twelve, I wrote a program for solving mazes."

"And I'm sure it worked well," Julie replied, "for small, two-dimensional ones. But you know how those kind of algorithms scale. Put your old program on this crystal, and I could still design a maze in half a day that would bring it to its knees."

"Of course," Daniel conceded. "Which is precisely why I'm interested in hiring you. You know a great deal more about the maze of AI than I do; any strategy you developed would be vastly superior to a blind search."

"I'm not saying that I'm merely groping in the dark," she said. "If it was that bleak, I'd be working on a different problem entirely. But I don't see what difference this processor would make."

"What created the only example of consciousness we know of?" Daniel asked.

"Evolution."

"Exactly. But I don't want to wait three billion years, so I need to make the selection process a great deal more refined, and the sources of variation more targeted."

Julie digested this. "You want to try to *evolve* true AI? Conscious, human-level AI?"

"Yes." Daniel saw her mouth tightening, saw her struggling to measure her words before speaking.

"With respect," she said, "I don't think you've thought that through."

"On the contrary," Daniel assured her. "I've been planning this for twenty years."

"Evolution," she said, "is about failure and death. Do you have any idea how many sentient creatures lived and died along the way to *Homo sapiens*? How much suffering was involved?"

"Part of your job would be to minimize the suffering."

"*Minimize it?*" She seemed genuinely shocked, as if this proposal was even worse than blithely assuming that the process would raise no ethical concerns. "What right do we have to inflict it at all?"

Daniel said, "You're grateful to exist, aren't you? Notwithstanding the tribulations of your ancestors."

"I'm grateful to exist," she agreed, "but in the human case the suffering wasn't deliberately inflicted by anyone, and nor was there any alternative way we could have come into existence. If there really *had* been a just creator, I don't doubt that he would have followed Genesis literally; he sure as hell would not have used evolution."

"Just, *and omnipotent*," Daniel suggested. "Sadly, that second trait's even rarer than the first."

"I don't think it's going to take omnipotence to create something in our own image," she said. "Just a little more patience and self-knowledge."

"This won't be like natural selection," Daniel insisted. "Not that blind, not that cruel, not that wasteful. You'd be free to intervene as much as you wished, to take whatever palliative measures you felt appropriate."

"*Palliative measures?*" Julie met his gaze, and he saw her expression flicker from disbelief to something darker. She stood up and glanced at her wristphone. "I don't have any signal here. Would you mind calling me a taxi?"

Daniel said, "Please, hear me out. Give me ten more minutes, then the helicopter will take you to the airport."

"I'd prefer to make my own way home." She gave Daniel a look that made it clear that this was not negotiable.

He called her a taxi, and they walked to the elevator.

"I know you find this morally challenging," he said, "and I respect that. I wouldn't dream of hiring someone who thought these were trivial issues. But if I don't do this, someone else will. Someone with far worse intentions than mine."

"Really?" Her tone was openly sarcastic now. "So how, exactly, does the mere existence of your project stop this hypothetical bin Laden of AI from carrying out his own?"

Daniel was disappointed; he'd expected her at least to understand what was at stake. He said, "This is a race to decide between Godhood and enslavement. Whoever succeeds first will be unstoppable. I'm not going to be anyone's slave."

Julie stepped into the elevator; he followed her.

She said, "You know what they say the modern version of Pascal's Wager is? Sucking up to as many Transhumanists as possible, just in case one of them turns into God. Perhaps your motto should be 'Treat every chatterbot kindly, it might turn out to be the deity's uncle.'"

"We will be as kind as possible," Daniel said. "And don't forget, we can determine the nature of these beings. They will be happy to be alive, and grateful to their creator. We can select for those traits."

Julie said, "So you're aiming for *übermenschen* that wag their tails when you scratch them behind the ears? You might find there's a bit of a trade-off there."

The elevator reached the lobby. Daniel said, "Think about this, don't rush to a decision. You can call me any time." There was no commercial flight back to Toronto tonight; she'd be stuck in a hotel, paying money she could ill-afford, thinking about the kind of salary she could demand from him now that she'd played hard to get. If she mentally recast all this obstinate moralizing as a deliberate bargaining strategy, she'd have no trouble swallowing her pride.

Julie offered her hand, and he shook it. She said, "Thank you for dinner."

The taxi was waiting. He walked with her across the lobby. "If you want to see AI in your lifetime," he said, "this is the only way it's going to happen."

She turned to face him. "Maybe that's true. We'll see. But better to spend a thousand years and get it right, than a decade and succeed by your methods."

As Daniel watched the taxi drive away into the fog, he forced himself to accept the reality: she was never going to change her mind. Julie Dehghani had been his first choice, his ideal collaborator. He couldn't pretend that this wasn't a setback.

Still, no one was irreplaceable. However much it would have delighted him to have won her over, there were many more names on his list.

2

Daniel's wrist tingled as the message came through. He glanced down and saw the word PROGRESS! hovering in front of his watch face.

The board meeting was almost over; he disciplined himself and kept his attention focused for ten more minutes. WiddulHands.com had made him his first billion, and it was still the pre-eminent social networking site for the 0–3 age group. It had been fifteen years since he'd founded the company, and he had since diversified in many directions, but he had no intention of taking his hands off the levers.

When the meeting finished he blanked the wall screen and paced the empty conference room for half a minute, rolling his neck and stretching his shoulders. Then he said, "Lucien."

Lucien Crace appeared on the screen. "Significant progress?" Daniel enquired.

"Absolutely." Lucien was trying to maintain polite eye contact with Daniel, but something kept drawing his gaze away. Without waiting for an explanation, Daniel gestured at the screen and had it show him exactly what Lucien was seeing.

A barren, rocky landscape stretched to the horizon. Scattered across the rocks were dozens of crablike creatures—some deep blue, some coral pink, though these weren't colors the locals would see, just species markers added to the view to make it easier to interpret. As Daniel watched, fat droplets of corrosive rain drizzled down from a passing cloud. This had to be the bleakest environment in all of Sapphire.

Lucien was still visible in an inset. "See the blue ones over by the crater lake?" he said. He sketched a circle on the image to guide Daniel's attention.

"Yeah." Five blues were clustered around a lone pink; Daniel gestured and the view zoomed in on them. The blues had opened up their prisoner's body, but it wasn't dead; Daniel was sure of that, because the pinks had recently acquired a trait that turned their bodies to mush the instant they expired.

"They've found a way to study it," Lucien said. "To keep it alive and study it."

From the very start of the project, he and Daniel had decided to grant the Phites the power to observe and manipulate their own bodies as much as possible. In the DNA world, the inner workings of anatomy and heredity had only become accessible once highly sophisticated technology had been invented. In Sapphire, the barriers were designed to be far lower. The basic units of biology here were "beads," small spheres that possessed a handful of simple properties but no complex internal biochemistry. Beads were larger than the cells of the DNA world, and Sapphire's diffractionless optics rendered them visible to the right kind of naked eye. Animals acquired beads from their diet, while in plants they replicated in the presence of sunlight, but unlike cells they did not themselves mutate. The beads in a Phite's body could be rearranged with a minimum of fuss, enabling a kind of self-modification that no human surgeon or prosthetics engineer could rival—and this skill was actually essential for at least one stage in every Phite's life: reproduction involved two Phites pooling their spare beads and then collaborating to "sculpt" them into an infant, in part by directly copying each other's current body plans.

Of course these crabs knew nothing of the abstract principles of engineering and design, but the benefits of trial and error, of self-experimentation and cross-species plagiarism, had led them into an escalating war of innovation. The pinks had been the first to stop their corpses from being plundered for secrets, by stumbling on a way to make them literally fall apart *in extremis*; now it seemed the blues had found a way around that, and were indulging in a spot of vivisection-as-industrial-espionage.

Daniel felt a visceral twinge of sympathy for the struggling pink, but he brushed it aside. Not only did he doubt that the Phites were any more conscious than ordinary crabs, they certainly had a radically different relationship to bodily integrity. The pink was resisting because its dissectors were of a different species; if they had been its cousins it might not have put up any fight at all. When something happened in spite of your wishes, that was unpleasant by definition, but it would be absurd to imagine that the pink was in the kind of agony that an antelope being flayed by jackals would feel—let alone experiencing the existential terrors of a human trapped and mutilated by a hostile tribe.

"This is going to give them a tremendous advantage," Lucien enthused.

"The blues?"

Lucien shook his head. "Not blues over pinks; Phites over tradlife. Bacteria can swap genes, but this kind of active mimetics is unprecedented without cultural support. Da Vinci might have watched the birds in flight and sketched his gliders, but no lemur ever dissected the body of an eagle and then stole its tricks. They're going to have *innate* skills as powerful as whole strands of human technology. All this before they even have language."

"Hmm." Daniel wanted to be optimistic too, but he was growing wary of Lucien's hype. Lucien had a doctorate in genetic programming, but he'd made his name with FoodExcuses.com, a web service that trawled the medical literature to cobble together quasi-scientific justifications for indulging in your favorite culinary vice. He had the kind of technobabble that could bleed money out of venture capitalists down pat, and though Daniel admired that skill in its proper place, he expected a higher insight-to-bullshit ratio now that Lucien was on his payroll.

The blues were backing away from their captive. As Daniel watched, the pink sealed up its wounds and scuttled off toward a group of its own kind. The blues had now seen the detailed anatomy of the respiratory system that had been giving the pinks an advantage in the thin air of this high plateau. A few of the blues would try it out, and if it worked for them, the whole tribe would copy it.

"So what do you think?" Lucien asked.

"Select them," Daniel said.

"Just the blues?"

"No, both of them." The blues alone might have diverged into competing subspecies eventually, but bringing their old rivals along for the ride would help to keep them sharp.

"Done," Lucien replied. In an instant, ten million Phites were erased, leaving the few thousand blues and pinks from these badlands to inherit the planet. Daniel felt no compunction; the extinction events he decreed were surely the most painless in history.

Now that the world no longer required human scrutiny, Lucien unthrottled the crystal and let the simulation race ahead; automated tools would let them know when the next interesting development arose. Daniel watched the population figures rising as his chosen species spread out and recolonised Sapphire.

Would their distant descendants rage against him, for this act of "genocide" that had made room for them to flourish and prosper? That seemed unlikely. In any case, what choice did he have? He couldn't start manufacturing new crystals for every useless side-branch of the evolutionary tree. Nobody was wealthy enough to indulge in an exponentially growing number of virtual animal shelters, at half a billion dollars apiece.

He was a just creator, but he was not omnipotent. His careful pruning was the only way.

3

In the months that followed, progress came in fits and starts. Several times, Daniel found himself rewinding history, reversing his decisions and trying a new path. Keeping every Phite variant alive was impractical, but he did retain enough information to resurrect lost species at will.

The maze of AI was still a maze, but the speed of the crystal served them well. Barely eighteen months after the start of Project Sapphire, the Phites were exhibiting a basic theory of mind: their actions showed that they could deduce what others knew about the world, as distinct from what they knew themselves. Other AI researchers had spliced this kind of thing into their programs by hand, but Daniel was convinced that his version was better integrated, more robust. Human-crafted software was brittle and inflexible; his Phites had been forged in the heat of change.

Daniel kept a close watch on his competitors, but nothing he saw gave him reason to doubt his approach. Sunil Gupta was raking in the cash from a search engine that could "understand" all forms of text, audio and video, making use of fuzzy logic techniques that were at least forty years old. Daniel respected Gupta's business acumen, but in the unlikely event that his software ever became conscious, the sheer cruelty of having forced it to wade through the endless tides of blogorrhoea would surely see it turn on its creator and exact a revenge that made *The Terminator* look like a picnic. Angela Lindstrom was having some success with her cheesy AfterLife, in which dying clients gave heart-to-heart interviews to software that then constructed avatars able to converse with surviving relatives. And Julie Dehghani was still frittering away her talent, writing software for robots that played with colored blocks side-by-side with human infants, and learned languages from adult volunteers by imitating the interactions of baby talk. Her prophecy of taking a thousand years to "get it right" seemed to be on target.

As the second year of the project drew to a close, Lucien was contacting Daniel once or twice a month to announce a new breakthrough. By constructing environments that imposed suitable selection pressures, Lucien had generated a succession of new species that used simple tools, crafted crude shelters, and even domesticated plants. They were still shaped more or less like crabs, but they were at least as intelligent as chimpanzees.

The Phites worked together by observation and imitation, guiding and reprimanding each other with a limited repertoire of gestures and cries, but as yet they lacked anything that could truly be called a language. Daniel grew impatient; to move beyond a handful of specialized skills, his creatures needed the power to map any object, any action, any prospect they might encounter in the world into their speech, and into their thoughts.

Daniel summoned Lucien and they sought a way forward. It was easy to tweak the Phites' anatomy to grant them the ability to generate more subtle vocalizations, but that alone was no more useful than handing a chimp a conductor's baton. What was needed was a way to make sophisticated planning and communications skills a matter of survival.

Eventually, he and Lucien settled on a series of environmental modifications, providing opportunities for the creatures to rise to the occasion. Most of these scenarios began with famine. Lucien blighted the main food crops, then offered a palpable reward for progress by dangling some tempting new fruit from a branch that was just out of reach. Sometimes that metaphor could almost be taken literally: he'd introduce a plant with a complex life cycle that required tricky processing to render it edible, or a new prey animal that was clever and vicious, but nutritionally well worth hunting in the end.

Time and again, the Phites failed the test, with localized species dwindling to extinction. Daniel watched in dismay; he had not grown sentimental, but he'd always boasted to himself that he'd set his standards higher than the extravagant cruelties of nature. He contemplated tweaking the creatures' physiology so that starvation brought a swifter, more merciful demise, but Lucien pointed out that he'd be slashing his chances of success if he curtailed this period of intense motivation. Each time a group died out, a fresh batch of mutated cousins rose from the dust to take their place; without that intervention, Sapphire would have been a wilderness within a few real-time days.

Daniel closed his eyes to the carnage, and put his trust in sheer time, sheer numbers. In the end, that was what the crystal had bought him: when all else failed, he could give up any pretense of knowing how to achieve his aims and simply test one random mutation after another.

Months went by, sending hundreds of millions of tribes starving into their graves. But what choice did he have? If he fed these creatures milk and honey, they'd remain fat and stupid until the day he died. Their hunger agitated them, it drove them to search and strive, and while any human onlooker was tempted to color such behavior with their own emotional palette, Daniel told himself that the Phites' suffering was a shallow thing, little more than the instinct that jerked his own hand back from a flame before he'd even registered discomfort.

They were not the equal of humans. Not yet.

And if he lost his nerve, they never would be.

Daniel dreamed that he was inside Sapphire, but there were no Phites in sight. In front of him stood a sleek black monolith; a thin stream of pus wept from a crack in its smooth, obsidian surface. Someone was holding him by the wrist, trying to force his hand into a reeking pit in the ground. The pit, he knew, was piled high with things he did not want to see, let alone touch.

He thrashed around until he woke, but the sense of pressure on his wrist remained. It was coming from his watch. As he focused on the one-word message he'd received, his stomach tightened. Lucien would not have dared to wake him at this hour for some run-of-the-mill result.

Daniel rose, dressed, then sat in his office sipping coffee. He did not know why he was so reluctant to make the call. He had been waiting for this moment for more than twenty years, but it would not be the pinnacle of his life. After this, there would be a thousand more peaks, each one twice as magnificent as the last.

He finished the coffee then sat a while longer, massaging his temples, making sure his head was clear. He would not greet this new era bleary-eyed, half-awake. He recorded all his calls, but this was one he would retain for posterity.

"Lucien," he said. The man's image appeared, smiling. "Success?"

"They're talking to each other," Lucien replied.

"About what?"

"Food, weather, sex, death. The past, the future. You name it. They won't shut up."

Lucien sent transcripts on the data channel, and Daniel perused them. The linguistics software didn't just observe the Phites' behavior and correlate it with the sounds they made; it peered right into their virtual brains and tracked the flow of information. Its task was far from trivial, and there was no guarantee that its translations were perfect, but Daniel did not believe it could hallucinate an entire language and fabricate these rich, detailed conversations out of thin air.

He flicked between statistical summaries, technical overviews of linguistic structure, and snippets from the millions of conversations the software had logged. *Food, weather, sex, death.* As human dialogue the translations would have seemed utterly banal, but in context they were riveting. These were not chatterbots blindly following Markov chains, designed to impress the judges in a Turing test. The Phites were discussing matters by which they genuinely lived and died.

When Daniel brought up a page of conversational topics in alphabetical order, his eyes were caught by the single entry under the letter G. *Grief.* He tapped the link, and spent a few minutes reading through samples, illustrating the appearance of the concept following the death of a child, a parent, a friend.

He kneaded his eyelids. It was three in the morning; there was a sickening clarity to everything, the kind that only night could bring. He turned to Lucien.

"No more death."

"Boss?" Lucien was startled.

"I want to make them immortal. Let them evolve culturally; let their ideas live and die. Let them modify their own brains, once they're smart enough; they can already tweak the rest of their anatomy."

"Where will you put them all?" Lucien demanded.

"I can afford another crystal. Maybe two more."

"That won't get you far. At the present birth rate—"

"We'll have to cut their fertility drastically, tapering it down to zero. After that, if they want to start reproducing again they'll really have to innovate." They would need to learn about the outside world, and comprehend its alien physics well enough to design new hardware into which they could migrate.

Lucien scowled. "How will we control them? How will we shape them? If we can't select the ones we want—"

Daniel said quietly, "This is not up for discussion." Whatever Julie Dehghani had thought of him, he was not a monster; if he believed that these creatures were as conscious as he was, he was not going to slaughter them like cattle—or stand by and let them die "naturally," when the rules of this world were his to rewrite at will.

"We'll shape them through their memes," he said. "We'll kill off the bad memes, and help spread the ones we want to succeed." He would need to keep an iron grip on the Phites and their culture, though, or he would never be able to trust them. If he wasn't going to literally *breed them* for loyalty and gratitude, he would have to do the same with their ideas.

Lucien said, "We're not prepared for any of this. We're going to need new software, new analysis and intervention tools."

Daniel understood. "Freeze time in Sapphire. Then tell the team they've got eighteen months."

4

Daniel sold his shares in WiddulHands, and had two more crystals built. One was to support a higher population in Sapphire, so there was as large a pool of diversity among the immortal Phites as possible; the other was to run the software—which Lucien had dubbed the Thought Police— needed to keep tabs on what they were doing. If human overseers had had to monitor and shape the evolving culture every step of the way, that would have slowed things down to a glacial pace. Still, automating the process completely was tricky, and Daniel preferred to err on the side of caution, with the Thought Police freezing Sapphire and notifying him whenever the situation became too delicate.

If the end of death was greeted by the Phites with a mixture of puzzlement and rejoicing, the end of birth was not so easy to accept. When all attempts by mating couples to sculpt their excess beads into offspring became as ineffectual as shaping dolls out of clay, it led to a mixture of persistence and distress that was painful to witness. Humans were accustomed to failing to conceive, but this was more like still birth after still birth. Even when Daniel intervened to modify the Phites' basic drives, some kind of cultural or emotional inertia kept many of them going through the motions. Though their new instincts urged them merely to pool their spare beads and then stop, sated, they would continue with the old version of the act regardless, forlorn and confused, trying to shape the useless puddle into something that lived and breathed.

Move on, Daniel thought. *Get over it.* There was only so much sympathy he could muster for immortal beings who would fill the galaxy with their children, if they ever got their act together.

The Phites didn't yet have writing, but they'd developed a strong oral tradition, and some put their mourning for the old ways into elegiac words. The Thought Police identified those memes, and ensured that they didn't spread far. Some Phites chose to kill themselves rather than live in the barren new world. Daniel felt he had no right to stop them, but mysterious obstacles blocked the paths of anyone who tried, irresponsibly, to romanticise or encourage such acts.

The Phites could only die by their own volition, but those who retained the will to live were not free to doze the centuries away. Daniel decreed no more terrible famines, but he hadn't abolished hunger itself, and he kept enough pressure on the food supply and other resources to force the

Phites to keep innovating, refining agriculture, developing trade.

The Thought Police identified and nurtured the seeds of writing, mathematics, and natural science. The physics of Sapphire was a simplified, game-world model, not so arbitrary as to be incoherent, but not so deep and complex that you needed particle physics to get to the bottom of it. As crystal time sped forward and the immortals sought solace in understanding their world, Sapphire soon had its Euclid and Archimedes, its Galileo and its Newton; their ideas spread with supernatural efficiency, bringing forth a torrent of mathematicians and astronomers.

Sapphire's stars were just a planetarium-like backdrop, present only to help the Phites get their notions of heliocentricity and inertia right, but its moon was as real as the world itself. The technology needed to reach it was going to take a while, but that was all right; Daniel didn't want them getting ahead of themselves. There was a surprise waiting for them there, and his preference was for a flourishing of biotech and computing before they faced that revelation.

Between the absence of fossils, Sapphire's limited biodiversity, and all the clunky external meddling that needed to be covered up, it was hard for the Phites to reach a grand Darwinian view of biology, but their innate skill with beads gave them a head start in the practical arts. With a little nudging, they began tinkering with their bodies, correcting some inconvenient anatomical quirks that they'd missed in their pre-conscious phase.

As they refined their knowledge and techniques, Daniel let them imagine that they were working toward restoring fertility; after all, that was perfectly true, even if their goal was a few conceptual revolutions further away than they realized. Humans had had their naive notions of a Philosopher's Stone dashed, but they'd still achieved nuclear transmutation in the end.

The Phites, he hoped, would transmute *themselves*: inspect their own brains, make sense of them, and begin to improve them. It was a staggering task to expect of anyone; even Lucien and his team, with their God's-eye view of the creatures, couldn't come close. But when the crystal was running at full speed, the Phites could think millions of times faster than their creators. If Daniel could keep them from straying off course, everything that humanity might once have conceived of as the fruits of millennia of progress was now just a matter of months away.

5

Lucien said, "We're losing track of the language."

Daniel was in his Houston office; he'd come to Texas for a series of face-to-face meetings, to see if he could raise some much-needed cash by licensing the crystal fabrication process. He would have preferred to keep the technology to himself, but he was almost certain that he was too far ahead of his rivals now for any of them to stand a chance of catching up with him.

"What do you mean, losing track?" Daniel demanded. Lucien had briefed him just three hours before, and given no warning of an impending crisis.

The Thought Police, Lucien explained, had done their job well: they had pushed the neural self-modification meme for all it was worth, and now a successful form of "brain boosting" was spreading across Sapphire. It required a detailed "recipe" but no technological aids; the same innate skills for observing and manipulating beads that the Phites had used to copy themselves during reproduction were enough.

All of this was much as Daniel had hoped it would be, but there was an alarming downside. The boosted Phites were adopting a dense and complex new language, and the analysis software couldn't make sense of it.

"Slow them down further," Daniel suggested. "Give the linguistics more time to run."

"I've already frozen Sapphire," Lucien replied. "The linguistics have been running for an hour, with the full resources of an entire crystal."

Daniel said irritably, "We can see exactly what they've done to their brains. How can we not understand the effects on the language?"

"In the general case," Lucien said, "deducing a language from nothing but neural anatomy is computationally intractable. With the old language, we were lucky; it had a simple structure, and it was highly correlated with obvious behavioral elements. The new language is much more abstract and conceptual. We might not even have our own correlates for half the concepts."

Daniel had no intention of letting events in Sapphire slip out of his control. It was one thing to hope that the Phites would, eventually, be juggling real-world physics that was temporarily beyond his comprehension, but any bright ten-year-old could grasp the laws of their present universe, and their technology was still far from rocket science.

He said, "Keep Sapphire frozen, and study your records of the Phites who first performed this boost. If they understood what they were doing, we can work it out too."

At the end of the week, Daniel signed the licensing deal and flew back to San Francisco. Lucien briefed him daily, and at Daniel's urging hired a dozen new computational linguists to help with the problem.

After six months, it was clear that they were getting nowhere. The Phites who'd invented the boost had had one big advantage as they'd tinkered with each other's brains: it had not been a purely theoretical exercise for them. They hadn't gazed at anatomical diagrams and then reasoned their way to a better design. They had *experienced* the effects of thousands of small experimental changes, and the results had shaped their intuition for the process. Very little of that intuition had been spoken aloud, let alone written down and formalized. And the process of decoding those insights from a purely structural view of their brains was every bit as difficult as decoding the language itself.

Daniel couldn't wait any longer. With the crystal heading for the market, and other comparable technologies approaching fruition, he couldn't allow his lead to melt away.

"We need the Phites themselves to act as translators," he told Lucien. "We need to contrive a situation where there's a large enough pool who choose not to be boosted that the old language continues to be used."

"So we need maybe twenty-five per cent refusing the boost?" Lucien suggested. "And we need the boosted Phites to want to keep them informed of what's happening, in terms that we can all understand."

Daniel said, "Exactly."

"I think we can slow down the uptake of boosting," Lucien mused, "while we encourage a traditionalist meme that says it's better to span the two cultures and languages than replace the old entirely with the new."

Lucien's team set to work, tweaking the Thought Police for the new task, then restarting Sapphire itself.

Their efforts seemed to yield the desired result: the Phites were corralled into valuing the notion of maintaining a link to their past, and while the boosted Phites surged ahead, they also worked hard to keep the unboosted in the loop.

It was a messy compromise, though, and Daniel wasn't happy with the prospect of making do with a watered-down, Sapphire-for-Dummies version of the Phites' intellectual achievements. What he really wanted was someone on the inside reporting to him directly, like a Phite version of Lucien.

It was time to start thinking about job interviews.

Lucien was running Sapphire more slowly than usual—to give the Thought Police a computational advantage now that they'd lost so much raw surveillance data—but even at the reduced rate, it took just six real-time days for the boosted Phites to invent computers, first as a mathematical formalism and, shortly afterward, as a succession of practical machines.

Daniel had already asked Lucien to notify him if any Phite guessed the true nature of their world. In the past, a few had come up with vague metaphysical speculations that weren't too wide of the mark, but now that they had a firm grasp of the idea of universal computation, they were finally in a position to understand the crystal as more than an idle fantasy.

The message came just after midnight, as Daniel was preparing for bed. He went into his office and activated the intervention tool that Lucien had written for him, specifying a serial number for the Phite in question.

The tool prompted Daniel to provide a human-style name for his interlocutor, to facilitate communication. Daniel's mind went blank, but after waiting twenty seconds the software offered its own suggestion: Primo.

Primo was boosted, and he had recently built a computer of his own. Shortly afterward, the Thought Police had heard him telling a couple of unboosted friends about an amusing possibility that had occurred to him.

Sapphire was slowed to a human pace, then Daniel took control of a Phite avatar and the tool contrived a meeting, arranging for the two of them to be alone in the shelter that Primo had built for himself. In accordance with the current architectural style the wooden building was actually still alive, self-repairing and anchored to the ground by roots.

Primo said, "Good morning. I don't believe we've met."

It was no great breach of protocol for a stranger to enter one's shelter uninvited, but Primo was understating his surprise; in this world of immortals, but no passenger jets, bumping into strangers anywhere was rare.

"I'm Daniel." The tool would invent a Phite name for Primo to hear.

"I heard you talking to your friends last night about your new computer. Wondering what these machines might do in the future. Wondering if they could ever grow powerful enough to contain a whole world."

"I didn't see you there," Primo replied.

"I wasn't there," Daniel explained. "I live outside this world. I built the computer that contains this world."

Primo made a gesture that the tool annotated as amusement, then he spoke a few words in the boosted language. *Insults? A jest? A test of Daniel's omniscience?* Daniel decided to bluff his way through, and act as if the words were irrelevant.

He said, "Let the rain start." Rain began pounding on the roof of the shelter. "Let the rain stop." Daniel gestured with one claw at a large cooking pot in a corner of the room. "Sand. Flower. Fire. Water jug." The pot obliged him, taking on each form in turn.

Primo said, "Very well. I believe you, Daniel." Daniel had had some experience reading the Phites' body language directly, and to him Primo seemed reasonably calm. Perhaps when you were as old as he was, and had witnessed so much change, such a revelation was far less of a shock than it would have been to a human at the dawn of the computer age.

"You created this world?" Primo asked him.

"Yes."

"You shaped our history?"

"In part," Daniel said. "Many things have been down to chance, or to your own choices."

"Did you stop us having children?" Primo demanded.

"Yes," Daniel admitted.

"*Why?*"

"There is no room left in the computer. It was either that, or many more deaths."

Primo pondered this. "So you could have stopped the death of my parents, had you wished?"

"I could bring them back to life, if you want that." This wasn't a lie; Daniel had stored detailed snapshots of all the last mortal Phites. "But not yet; only when there's a bigger computer. When there's room for them."

"Could you bring back *their* parents? And their parents' parents? Back to the beginning of time?"

"No. That information is lost."

Primo said, "What is this talk of waiting for a bigger computer? You could easily stop time from passing for us, and only start it again when your new computer is built."

"No," Daniel said, "I can't. Because *I need you to build the computer.* I'm not like you: I'm not immortal, and my brain can't be boosted. I've done my best, now I need you to do better. The only way that can happen is if you learn the science of my world, and come up with a way to make this new machine."

Primo walked over to the water jug that Daniel had magicked into being. "It seems to me that you were ill-prepared for the task you set yourself. If you'd waited for the machine you really needed, our lives would not have been so hard. And if such a machine could not be built in your lifetime, what was to stop your grandchildren from taking on that task?"

"I had no choice," Daniel insisted. "I couldn't leave your creation to my descendants. There is a war coming between my people. I needed your help. I needed strong allies."

"You have no friends in your own world?"

"Your time runs faster than mine. I needed the kind of allies that only your people can become, in time."

Primo said, "What exactly do you want of us?"

"To build the new computer you need," Daniel replied. "To grow in numbers, to grow in strength. Then to raise me up, to make me greater than I was, as I've done for you. When the war is won, there will be peace forever. Side by side, we will rule a thousand worlds."

"And what do you want of *me*?" Primo asked. "Why are you speaking to me, and not to all of us?"

"Most people," Daniel said, "aren't ready to hear this. It's better that they don't learn the truth yet. But I need one person who can work for me directly. I can see and hear everything in your world, but I need you to make sense of it. I need you to understand things for me."

Primo was silent.

Daniel said, "I gave you life. How can you refuse me?"

6

Daniel pushed his way through the small crowd of protesters gathered at the entrance to his San Francisco tower. He could have come and gone by helicopter instead, but his security consultants had assessed these people as posing no significant threat. A small amount of bad PR didn't bother him; he was no longer selling anything that the public could boycott directly, and none of the businesses he dealt with seemed worried about being tainted by association. He'd broken no laws, and confirmed no rumors. A few feral cyberphiles waving placards reading "Software Is Not Your Slave!" meant nothing.

Still, if he ever found out which one of his employees had leaked details of the project, he'd break their legs.

Daniel was in the elevator when Lucien messaged him: MOON VERY SOON! He halted the elevator's ascent, and redirected it to the basement.

All three crystals were housed in the basement now, just centimeters away from the Play Pen: a vacuum chamber containing an atomic force microscope with fifty thousand independently movable tips, arrays of solid-state lasers and photodetectors, and thousands of micro-wells stocked with samples of all the stable chemical elements. The time lag between Sapphire and this machine had to be as short as possible, in order for the Phites to be able to conduct experiments in real-world physics while their own world was running at full speed.

Daniel pulled up a stool and sat beside the Play Pen. If he wasn't going to slow Sapphire down, it was pointless aspiring to watch developments as they unfolded. He'd probably view a replay of the lunar landing when he went up to his office, but by the time he screened it, it would be ancient history.

"One giant leap" would be an understatement; wherever the Phites landed on the moon, they would find a strange black monolith waiting for them. Inside would be the means to operate the Play Pen; it would not take them long to learn the controls, or to understand what this signified. If they were really slow in grasping what they'd found, Daniel had instructed Primo to explain it to them.

The physics of the real world was far more complex than the kind the Phites were used to, but then, no human had ever been on intimate terms with quantum field theory either, and the Thought Police had already encouraged the Phites to develop most of the mathematics they'd need to get started. In any case, it didn't matter if the Phites took longer than humans to discover twentieth-century scientific principles, and move beyond them. Seen from the outside, it would happen within hours, days, weeks at the most.

A row of indicator lights blinked on; the Play Pen was active. Daniel's throat went dry. The Phites were finally reaching out of their own world into his.

A panel above the machine displayed histograms classifying the experiments the Phites had performed so far. By the time Daniel was paying attention, they had already discovered the kinds of bonds that could be formed between various atoms, and constructed thousands of different small molecules. As he watched, they carried out spectroscopic analyses, built simple nanomachines, and manufactured devices that were, unmistakably, memory elements and logic gates.

The Phites wanted children, and they understood now that this was the only way. They would soon be building a world in which they were not just more numerous, but faster and smarter than they were inside the crystal. And that would only be the first of a thousand iterations. They were working their way toward Godhood, and they would lift up their own creator as they ascended.

Daniel left the basement and headed for his office. When he arrived, he called Lucien.

"They've built an atomic-scale computer," Lucien announced. "And they've fed some fairly complex software into it. It doesn't seem to be an upload, though. Certainly not a direct copy on the level of beads." He sounded flustered; Daniel had forbidden him to risk screwing up the experiments by slowing down Sapphire, so even with Primo's briefings to help him it was difficult for him to keep abreast of everything.

"Can you model their computer, and then model what the software is doing?" Daniel suggested.

Lucien said, "We only have six atomic physicists on the team; the Phites already outnumber us on that score by about a thousand to one. By the time we have any hope of making sense of this, they'll be doing something different."

"What does Primo say?" The Thought Police hadn't been able to get Primo included in any of the lunar expeditions, but Lucien had given him the power to make himself invisible and teleport to any part of Sapphire or the lunar base. Wherever the action was, he was free to eavesdrop.

"Primo has trouble understanding a lot of what he hears; even the boosted aren't universal polymaths and instant experts in every kind of jargon. The gist of it is that the Lunar Project people have made a very fast computer in the Outer World, and it's going to help with the fertility problem...somehow." Lucien laughed. "Hey, maybe the Phites will do exactly what we did: see if they can evolve something smart enough to give them a hand. How cool would that be?"

Daniel was not amused. Somebody had to do some real work eventually; if the Phites just passed the buck, the whole enterprise would collapse like a pyramid scheme.

Daniel had some business meetings he couldn't put off. By the time he'd swept all the bullshit aside, it was early afternoon. The Phites had now built some kind of tiny solid-state accelerator, and were probing the internal structure of protons and neutrons by pounding them with high-speed electrons. An atomic computer wired up to various detectors was doing the data analysis, processing the results faster than any in-world computer could. The Phites had already figured out the standard quark model. Maybe they were going to skip uploading into nanocomputers, and head straight for some kind of femtomachine?

Digests of Primo's briefings made no mention of using the strong force for computing, though. They were still just satisfying their curiosity about the fundamental laws. Daniel reminded himself of their history. They had burrowed down to what seemed like the foundations of physics before, only to discover that those simple rules were nothing to do with the ultimate reality. It made sense that they would try to dig as deeply as they could into the mysteries of the Outer World before daring to found a colony, let alone emigrate *en masse*.

By sunset the Phites were probing the surroundings of the Play Pen with various kinds of radiation. The levels were extremely low—certainly too low to risk damaging the crystals—so Daniel saw no need to intervene. The Play Pen itself did not have a massive power supply, it contained no radioisotopes, and the Thought Police would ring alarm bells and bring in human experts if some kind of tabletop fusion experiment got underway, so Daniel was reasonably confident that the Phites couldn't do anything stupid and blow the whole thing up.

Primo's briefings made it clear that they thought they were engaged in a kind of "astronomy." Daniel wondered if he should give them access to instruments for doing serious observations—the kind that would allow them to understand relativistic gravity and cosmology. Even if he bought time on a large telescope, though, just pointing it would take an eternity for the Phites. He wasn't going to slow Sapphire down and then grow old while they explored the sky; next thing they'd be launching space probes on thirty-year missions. Maybe it was time to ramp up the level of collaboration, and just hand them some astronomy texts and star maps? Human culture had its own hard-won achievements that the Phites couldn't easily match.

As the evening wore on, the Phites shifted their focus back to the subatomic world. A new kind of accelerator began smashing single gold ions together at extraordinary energies—though the total power being expended was still minuscule. Primo soon announced that they'd mapped all three generations of quarks and leptons. The Phites' knowledge of particle physics was drawing level with humanity's; Daniel couldn't follow the technical details any more, but the experts were giving it all the thumbs up. Daniel felt a surge of pride; of course his children knew what they were doing, and if they'd reached the point where they could momentarily bamboozle him, soon he'd ask them to catch their breath and bring him up to speed. Before he permitted them to emigrate, he'd slow the crystals down and introduce himself to everyone. In fact, that might be the perfect time to set them their next task: to understand human biology, well enough to upload him. To make him immortal, to repay their debt.

He sat watching images of the Phites' latest computers, reconstructions based on data flowing to and from the AFM tips. Vast lattices of shimmering atoms stretched off into the distance, the electron clouds that joined them quivering like beads of mercury in some surreal liquid abacus. As he watched, an inset window told him that the ion accelerators had been redesigned, and fired up again.

Daniel grew restless. He walked to the elevator. There was nothing he could see in the basement that he couldn't see from his office, but he wanted to stand beside the Play Pen, put his hand on the casing, press his nose against the glass. The era of Sapphire as a virtual world with no consequences in his own was coming to an end; he wanted to stand beside the thing itself and be reminded that it was as solid as he was.

The elevator descended, passing the tenth floor, the ninth, the eighth. Without warning, Lucien's voice burst from Daniel's watch, priority audio crashing through every barrier of privacy and protocol. "Boss, there's radiation. Net power gain. Get to the helicopter, *now*."

Daniel hesitated, contemplating an argument. If this was fusion, why hadn't it been detected and curtailed? He jabbed the stop button and felt the brakes engage. Then the world dissolved into brightness and pain.

7

When Daniel emerged from the opiate haze, a doctor informed him that he had burns to sixty per cent of his body. More from heat than from radiation. He was not going to die.

There was a net terminal by the bed. Daniel called Lucien and learned what the physicists on the team had tentatively concluded, having studied the last of the Play Pen data that had made it off-site.

It seemed the Phites had discovered the Higgs field, and engineered a burst of something akin to cosmic inflation. What they'd done wasn't as simple as merely inflating a tiny patch of vacuum into a new universe, though. Not only had they managed to create a "cool Big Bang," they had pulled a large chunk of ordinary matter into the pocket universe they'd made, after which the wormhole leading to it had shrunk to subatomic size and fallen through the Earth.

They had taken the crystals with them, of course. If they'd tried to upload themselves into the pocket universe through the lunar data link, the Thought Police would have stopped them. So they'd emigrated by another route entirely. They had snatched their whole substrate, and ran.

Opinions were divided over exactly what else the new universe would contain. The crystals and the Play Pen floating in a void, with no power source, would leave the Phites effectively dead, but some of the team believed there could be a thin plasma of protons and electrons too, created by a form of Higgs decay that bypassed the unendurable quark-gluon fireball of a hot Big Bang. If they'd built the right nanomachines, there was a chance that they could convert the Play Pen into a structure that would keep the crystals safe, while the Phites slept through the long wait for the first starlight.

The tiny skin samples the doctors had taken finally grew into sheets large enough to graft. Daniel bounced between dark waves of pain and medicated euphoria, but one idea stayed with him throughout the turbulent journey, like a guiding star: *Primo had betrayed him.* He had given the fucker life, entrusted him with power, granted him privileged knowledge, showered him with the favors of the Gods. And how had he been repaid? He was back to zero. He'd spoken to his lawyers; having heard rumors of an "illegal radiation source," the insurance company was not going to pay out on the crystals without a fight.

Lucien came to the hospital, in person. Daniel was moved; they hadn't met face-to-face since the job interview. He shook the man's hand.

"You didn't betray me."

Lucien looked embarrassed. "I'm resigning, boss."

Daniel was stung, but he forced himself to accept the news stoically. "I understand; you have no choice. Gupta will have a crystal of his own by now. You have to be on the winning side, in the war of the Gods."

Lucien put his resignation letter on the bedside table. "What war? Are you still clinging to that fantasy where überdorks battle to turn the moon into computronium?"

Daniel blinked. "Fantasy? If you didn't believe it, why were you working with me?"

"You paid me. Extremely well."

"So how much will Gupta be paying you? I'll double it."

Lucien shook his head, amused. "I'm not going to work for Gupta. I'm moving into particle physics. The Phites weren't all that far ahead of us when they escaped; maybe forty or fifty years. Once we catch up, I guess a private universe will cost about as much as a private island; maybe less in the long run. But no one's going to be battling for control of this one, throwing gray goo around like monkeys flinging turds while they draw up their plans for Matrioshka brains."

Daniel said, "If you take any data from the Play Pen logs—"

"I'll honor all the confidentiality clauses in my contract." Lucien smiled. "But anyone can take an interest in the Higgs field; that's public domain."

After he left, Daniel bribed the nurse to crank up his medication, until even the sting of betrayal and disappointment began to fade.

A universe, he thought happily. *Soon I'll have a universe of my own.*

But I'm going to need some workers in there, some allies, some companions. I can't do it all alone; someone has to carry the load.

David D. Levine (b. 1961) has worked as a software engineer for a computer security company. He has long been active in science fiction fandom and has distinguished himself as a science fiction writer, winning a Hugo Award in 2005. One of his strengths is in rigorously extrapolated hard science fiction, as in this fast-paced story, in which the Singularity takes off in a matter of hours.

FIREWALL
> David D. Levine

It started in China, as I'd always feared it would.

I sat in my darkened office, surrounded by glowing screens. Usually the screens were filled with the tools of my job—system status displays, network traffic monitors, hardware health summaries, and the faces of my subs—but for now I'd pushed most of those to one side in favor of the news. Even so, I kept a wary eye on my network. No sign of any trouble here, so far.

I shoved another stick of gum in my mouth, chomped at it without tasting. I tossed the gum wrapper toward the trash but, distracted, forgot where I was and gave it too hard a push. The wrapper arced high and bounced off the ceiling and the wall, drifting gently down to join its fellows on the floor. I groaned and ran a hand across my thinning blonde crewcut, desperately craving a cigarette.

The nearest cigarette was four hundred thousand kilometers away.

"Reports from Harbin are confused and fragmentary," said the reporter on Telenews, a neon-lit nighttime street behind her. The face above the Telenews logo was wide-eyed and glistened with sweat—either human or a very, very good sub. "All communication channels and transit systems are still down, and those few who have emerged on foot agree on little other than that power is fluctuating city-wide. Some report incomprehensible messages on their phones." A Chinese businessman appeared, pointing frantically to the phone on his wrist and jabbering something that was translated as "It was no human voice. It greeted me by name. It said 'I knew her,' and then 'They cannot.' Then it cut off."

I'd seen that clip before. I turned my attention to another screen, where a shuddering handheld camera showed a city skyline, lights flickering on and off against the darkened sky. "The Chinese government continues to deny all knowledge of any prohibited or questionable research," the voice-over said, "but Western computer scientists have long suspected Harbin University of harboring renegade researchers whose aim is nothing less than the technological apocalypse and the end of humanity." I rolled my eyes and muted the sound. I needed cold facts, not overheated rumor and suspicion.

As usual, the amateur news sources were well ahead of the professionals. Hundreds of bloggers had already posted eyewitness reports of the chaos, despite network outages and government censorship, and many of those reports were in English or had already been translated by other amateurs. Of course, a lot of it was crap—tinfoil-hat conspiracy theories and uninformed speculation—but I knew who the trustworthy players were and I had smart filters to help sift the wheat from the chaff. I began to put together a picture of what had happened.

It was true that researchers at Harbin had been pushing the boundaries, but that was what researchers were supposed to do. It was researchers pushing boundaries who'd driven the increasing pace of technological improvements that had, among many other things, put people back on the moon after a decades-long hiatus. But researchers were also supposed to take precautions—like sterile protocols, segmented networks, and hardware cutoffs—which should have prevented anything unexpected from escaping the lab. According to some grad students, a limited equipment budget had forced the researchers to compromise.

Civilians. They were no better than children. I shook my head, chomping grimly at my gum.

I turned away from the news and verified that my own network defenses were fully deployed. Standard anti-malware tools might not be effective against whatever unknown software had escaped the lab in Harbin, but I didn't want to leave anything to chance. Along the same lines, I instructed Network to tighten the internal checkpoints between network segments—the staff would squawk, but my position as head of information security gave me special authority when it came to protecting the safety of Kennedy Station.

As I was checking over the equipment inventory to see if any machines could be taken offline for the duration of the crisis, Personal's face appeared with a beep on one of the monitors. "It's Thuy, sir," he said. "She's called an emergency meeting of senior staff, conference B, oh nine thirty."

"Tell her I'm busy on a critical infrastructure task."

He blinked out for about fifteen seconds, then returned. "She insisted you attend in person, sir. Her exact words were 'Tell your boss that if he doesn't get his fat ass in here, his next performance review is going to read *R.I.P. Jeff Patterson.*'"

I sighed. The clock in the corner of the monitor read 09:23. "I'll be there." I doubled the processor allocation to my subs and hauled myself from my chair—even in one-sixth gee I still had to cope with the increasing mass of my almost-forty-year-old gut. As I headed down the corridor I hoped nothing would happen during the meeting that required my immediate attention. Even the best subs were poor at reacting to unexpected situations, and right now I was expecting the unexpected at any moment.

I maintained six virtual subordinates: Software, Hardware, Network, Storage, Firewall, and Personal. Their appearances were as stolid and practical as their names, all male and all crewcut, differentiated only by the details of their faces and the insignia on their chests, which changed to show their current status. My only concession to civilian life was the colors of their clothing: each wore a different solid color rather than the uniform olive drab of military subs.

My predecessor, a trade-school kid half my age, had kept a huge crowd of subs whose functions and names had been as idiosyncratic as their shifting, flowing appearances. I'd terminated them all as soon as I'd arrived, three months ago; some of them had used a thousand times as much processor power just to maintain their skins as it had taken to send people to the moon in the first place. But Thuy and the other staff had subs nearly as elaborate, and there wasn't anything I could do about that.

At least none of my co-workers had gone all Disney, like my ex Jessie had. When we'd been living in base housing, her subs had been as clean and straightforward as mine. But as soon as we got our own place, with better hardware, she'd started dressing them up in expensive licensed skins like Cinderella and Peter Pan. That should have been my first clue...

Why couldn't people see when something was good enough, and just leave it alone?

Conference room B might have been anywhere—walls, ceiling and floor all square and bland, fake woodgrain table, worn and uncomfortable chairs swapped in from individual offices and quarters—except for the one-sixth gravity and the airtight doors, and the omnipresent burnt-dust smell of powdered regolith that the scientists tracked in from the surface. The dust, fine and dry as talcum, got into everything and was a killer of disc readers, fans, and anything else with moving parts.

Thuy Vu McLaughlin, on the other hand, was one of a kind. The Vietnamese-Irish-American station administrator's brush-cut dark hair glinted with red highlights, and freckles dotted the golden-brown skin beneath her almond-shaped hazel eyes. She stood not much more than 150 centimeters tall and weighed less than half what I did, fifty kilos tops, but I still found her intimidating. I'd seen her doing low-gee kenpo and I thought that, in my current shape, she could probably kick my ass. It didn't help that she had the same cracker accent as my daddy.

At the moment she didn't look pleased.

"Why the hell have you cut off mesh and conf access?" she demanded as soon as I entered the room. Behind her the three division heads, Sochima Okoghe, Dan Irvin, and Kristina Lundberg, awaited my response with equally dour expressions.

"Those protocols include code packets that execute directly on the I/O processor," I explained patiently. "They're inherently insecure. And we don't know yet what's happening in China."

"And we aren't *going* to find out what's happening until we get our high-res links back," Sochima shot back. Tall, lean, and ebony, with a spicy Nigerian accent, Sochima was the lead scientist of the small Confédération Africaine team studying low gravity's effects on heart disease. It was supposed to have been a much larger team, but the ongoing Nigeria-Cameroon war had drained the Confédération's resources. "Your paranoia could prevent us from making an informed decision about what to do next."

Before I could respond, Kristina held up a placating hand. She was from Sweden and often acted as moderator between me and the hot-headed Thuy and Sochima. "Please, Jeff," she said, "have some compassion. Huang and Shu-Yi are desperate for news from home." Most of the sixty people at the station were on Kristina's multinational team, combing the surface for fragments of the early solar system, and several of the key researchers were Chinese.

I took a calming breath before speaking. "There's plenty of news available. Television, radio, voice, mail, web—just no multimedia or interactive content."

"There's carrier pigeons, too," said Dan, his broad Australian vowels amplifying the statement's sarcasm. The pudgy little engineer was in charge of the station's physical plant. "They're just about as effective."

I ground my gum between my teeth. "You don't understand the seriousness of the situation. Any breach in data security could be catastrophic."

Sochima rolled her eyes. "Then why do we have all that anti-malware stuff clogging our systems? Or isn't it as good at stopping malware as it is at preventing my people from installing the software they need to do their jobs?"

"This isn't an ordinary malware infestation," I said, deciding not to list the worms, leeches, and pornobots my defenses had stopped on computers in Sochima's group. "It's an outbreak of unknown, possibly intelligent experimental software. We don't know what it can do. If it gets inside the firewall, even adaptive filters might not be able to stop it before it infects our whole network. The whole city of Harbin's fallen off the net."

Kristina looked up from her phone. "It's not just Harbin. Shu-Yi just messaged me that the outbreak has spread to Beijing and Shanghai."

The temperature of the room dropped at that announcement. My chest tightened a notch, and Sochima and Thuy suddenly seemed a little less sure of their priorities. Dan stood up from his place at the table. "I think I ought to go run a test on the backup life support systems. Now."

Thuy nodded, uncharacteristically silent, but as Dan headed for the door she said, "After you've done that...better run a preflight check on the ELEC."

Dan swallowed. "Right." He closed and carefully dogged the door behind himself.

I cleared my throat to interrupt the uncomfortable silence that followed. "Uh...what's the ELEC?"

Thuy looked me right in the eye. "Emergency Lunar Escape Craft. It can get us to Earth orbit in two weeks."

"Assuming," Sochima added, "there's anyone there to meet us."

I scrambled back to my office as quickly as I could. I'd mostly adapted to the gravity in my first week, but when I tried to hurry I still ran into walls sometimes. Network and Software told me nothing noteworthy had happened on our local network in my absence, but I had Software run a full integrity check on all connected systems and Network tighten down the internal checkpoints still further—no data sharing, no conferencing, and no software installs at all other than mandatory security updates.

Once those were running, I turned my attention to the DMZ—an old acronym no one had ever been able to explain to me, though I guessed it stood for Data Moderation Zone or some such. This was the space between the inner and outer firewalls where those systems that required access to the outside world resided. Firewall was the only sub permitted in that space. I called him up on the big monitor right in front of me.

"I want you to find and immediately terminate *any* nonessential processes in the DMZ," I told him. As I spoke, I turned another screen toward myself and raised his priority to maximum. "Essential functions are defined as communications with Earth and data security." I thought a moment. "Furthermore, communications through the external firewall are to be limited to text-only messages and security software updates. All other incoming data is to be intercepted and destroyed."

"Interruption of critical scientific data channels requires an administrative override, sir."

I bit back a curse; I should have remembered that. I paused and formulated a new command. "Modify definitions of essential software and permitted communications to include critical scientific data until override is obtained."

"Yes, sir."

"And notify me immediately, priority 1, if anything unusual occurs. Dismissed."

"Yes, sir." Firewall's face vanished, replaced by a standard DMZ status display. It was already much less crowded than usual, and most of the remaining green and yellow indicators went dark as I watched. The last few non-system processes were associated with Kristina's and Sochima's priority projects, and I'd need Thuy's thumbprint to terminate those. I called her and left a message with one of her subs asking for her authorization.

As soon as I hung up on Thuy's sub, Personal began beeping urgently for my attention. He'd done what he could to mollify the staff whose processes had been terminated and communications interrupted, but many of them were demanding to speak with me in person and he couldn't hold them off forever. I told him to continue blocking, then I composed and sent out a broadcast message explaining the situation and begging for patience.

As I waited for the message to have whatever effect it was going to, I walked down the hall to my computer room. The only truly secure computer is one that's turned off and disconnected, and I meant to put as much hardware as I possibly could into that state. I entered my authorization code and the armored door slid open.

When I'd first arrived, I'd been surprised that the computer room roared with chilled air, same as any similar room on Earth. The one difference was that the heat exchanger was a radiator lying in a sunless chasm a couple hundred meters away rather than a blower on the roof. So as I moved along the closely spaced equipment racks, powering down unused systems, routers, and hubs, I was buffeted by deafening gusts of cold air.

I returned to my office and found that my request for authorization had neither been approved nor denied. This was an unpleasant surprise, but I knew Thuy's habits. I turned right around and headed out to find her.

As I'd expected, I found Thuy in the gym, leaping and kicking in a frenetic series of moves she'd described to me as "battling the invisible ninjas." The lunar gravity transformed her into something from a fantasy martial arts movie, bounding four meters high and caroming off the walls and ceiling with fluid grace. It was a spectacular way of dealing with stress, and I envied her the ability to do so.

As soon as she noticed me, Thuy finished her sequence of moves and thumped to the mat right in front of me with a bow. Her black *gi* was soaked with sweat. "I need your thumbprint," I said without preamble.

"What for?" She picked up a towel and rubbed it through her hair, breathing hard.

"To interrupt critical scientific data channels."

Thuy picked up her phone from atop her folded clothing at the corner of the mat and turned it on. "Our counterparts back in Geneva are depending on that data," she said. "With our limited bandwidth, even a few hours' interruption would put them so far behind they'd take weeks to catch up."

"Yes. And if this outbreak catches us with open holes in our firewall, we could lose all that data permanently. Or worse."

"It's really that bad?"

"It could be."

"Kristina will kill me." But she swiped her thumb across the phone's print reader and told her sub to grant the authorization I'd requested.

"Thanks," I said, as she buckled the phone onto her wrist.

She started to say something in response, but her eyes widened as she read the words on her phone's screen.

"What is it?"

It took her a moment to find her voice. "It's spread to Tokyo. And Bangalore. And half of Russia." She looked up. "They're saying this could be the Big One."

We looked at each other. The Big One—the Infocalypse, the Singularity, the Millennium, call it what you will—had been a theoretical possibility since before the turn of the century, but in the past five years it had become a real concern. And a real point of controversy. "Thuy, I know it might be a violation of policy to ask, but is anyone on the staff a Millennialist?" Some people—defying not just the law, but the human instinct for self-preservation—actually supported the development of post-human technology. I needed to know right away if there were any of them inside my firewall.

Thuy dropped her eyes. "No. No one I've talked to about it, anyway."

I didn't like the implications of the way she'd said that. I had to know who I could trust. "Are *you?*"

She still didn't look up, but after a long moment she shook her head. "But my parents are." Her hands knotted tightly together. "I...I like technology. You'd have to, to work in a place like this. But I've seen the kind of unintended consequences it can cause. I could never...*believe* the way my father does." At last she raised her eyes to mine. They burned with anger; they glistened with tears. "Don't worry, *Mister* Patterson, I'm not going to open the firewall to some rogue AI with a clever story."

Now I was the one who had to look down. "I'm sorry. I didn't mean to bring up any...uncomfortable issues."

Thuy rubbed at her eyes with a knuckle. "You're only doing your job. It's just...I worry about my daddy. Ever since he started getting all serious about the potential of machine intelligence, I've been afraid he might do something illegal." She blew out a breath through her nose. "It's like he changed into a different person."

That brought back unpleasant memories. "I know how that goes." She quirked a questioning eyebrow at me. I hesitated. "My ex, Jessie," I admitted at last. "Right after we got out of the service, she told me she really, really wanted children. It came out of nowhere. But I..." This was hard to explain. "Look, you know how when your friends have kids, it's like they vanish behind a wall? They turn into completely different people? I didn't want to vanish." I stared at the mat, remembering a crummy little military apartment where I'd been happier than ever before or since. "I didn't want us to change."

What an idiot I'd been.

We stood together for a while in awkward silence. Thuy broke it by folding her towel. "I'll ask my staff if they're aware of anyone with Millennialist tendencies, and if there are any I'll call you right away."

"Thank you." I automatically glanced at my phone, to check that it was active and charged. A "missed message" indicator blinked silently on its screen; the ringer must have been drowned out by the noise in the computer room. I clicked through and viewed the message.

What the hell? It was a Priority 1 notification from Firewall, dated almost ten minutes ago. If I failed to acknowledge a Priority 1 message within one minute, all my subs knew they were supposed to follow up—they could even sound sirens in the halls if necessary.

The text of the message was "VERY LARGE INCOMING DATA STREAM ON SCINTIFIC CHANNELS. UNKNOWN DATA FORMA"—it cut off in the middle of a word.

"What's wrong?" said Thuy.

My heart pounded. "I think the firewall may have been penetrated."

"Oh my God."

I ran out of there as fast as I could.

As I hustled down the hall, caroming off walls, I used my phone to tell Network to close all the internal partitions—cut off every subnet completely from every other subnet, especially the DMZ. I had Software, Hardware, and Storage begin full top-to-bottom diagnostics on their subsystems. I told Personal not to interrupt me except for the most dire emergencies.

By the time I arrived at my office the initial results from the diagnostics showed nothing obviously wrong on the internal network, and I allowed myself a moment of relief. Maybe Firewall's cut-off message with no follow-up was just a glitch, not an incursion.

But I didn't want to take any chances.

I got out my old clipboard—I hadn't used it in weeks and it had nothing of value on it any more—and yanked its wireless card with a pair of needle-nosed pliers. Then I found a network cable at the back of a drawer and connected the clipboard to the dusty patch panel behind my desk. Finally I had Network open a single connection from that patch panel to the DMZ.

I swallowed and powered the clipboard on.

The image that appeared on the scratched little screen was not the face I'd selected for Firewall. It was the firewall's default skin: a knight in shining armor, carrying a shield with the manufacturer's logo.

This wasn't good. This was not good at all.

The knight saluted. "Ready to defend!" it said, in that gratingly chipper voice I'd turned off five minutes after I'd installed it the first time.

"Report status."

"All firewall functions operating normally. Intrusions blocked in last twenty-four hours—twenty-one thousand two hundred nine. Incoming packets—fifteen hundred sixty-three per second. Outgoing packets—eight hundred ten per second."

That all sounded reasonable. The data volume seemed low, but that would be expected if the text-only restriction I'd placed was still in effect. "Summarize your most recent operational orders."

"Find and terminate all nonessential processes in the DMZ. Intercept any incoming data other than text-only communications and security updates. Notify you if anything unusual occurs."

I blew out a breath. At least it remembered my orders. And it knew who I was, because it had said "you" instead of "Jeff Patterson." But I had other concerns. "You sent me a Priority 1 message over twenty minutes ago. I didn't acknowledge it. Why didn't you follow up?"

The knight had no face. Its metallic visor was implacable. "I sent no such message. Nothing unusual has been detected."

I licked my lips. "Why have you reverted to your default skin?"

"No appearance changes have occurred."

My heart started to beat faster. If I couldn't trust my firewall..."Open diagnostic interface."

"Password required."

That set me back on my heels. If it knew who I was, and it did, it should have known I had full authorization. I racked my brain for the password I'd used to configure the firewall in the first place, popped up a keyboard on the clipboard's screen, and typed it in.

"Sorry, please try again."

I tried again. Same result. I tried several other passwords. No good. "Security admin override," I said. "Patterson, Jeffrey William. Accept thumbprint." I swiped my thumb across the clipboard's reader.

"Sorry, please try again."

Shit. Shit shit *shit!* I reached into my pocket, but the empty gum packet crinkled between my fingers. Gritting my teeth, I wadded it up and flung it toward the wastebasket. It fluttered impotently to the floor before it got halfway there.

Okay, I told myself, calm down. I checked my other screens; there was still no sign of anything unusual on the internal network, and the only open connection to the DMZ was the clipboard in front of me. Whatever had gone wrong with the firewall, it was trapped in the DMZ.

For now.

"Shut down firewall."

"Password required."

"Fuck you."

"Sorry, please try again."

My fingers tightened on the clipboard's knobby rubber casing, but throwing the damn thing against the wall wouldn't help anything, so I just powered it down. The knight's featureless visor stared implacably at me as it faded from view.

I called up Hardware on the main screen. He hadn't changed his appearance or mannerisms, but I realized I didn't trust him the way I had even an hour ago. "Identify the power supplies for all computers, routers, and hubs in the DMZ." I had to shut down the DMZ completely, before whatever had corrupted the firewall figured out how to break through my internal defenses.

"Just a moment sir...done. Rack fifteen, bays five through nine."

"Power down rack fifteen, bays five through nine."

"Please confirm."

"Repeat: power down rack fifteen, bays five through nine."

"Just a moment, sir..."

I waited. Hardware still appeared to be breathing and blinking, the same as usual, so his process wasn't hung. My fingernails bit into my palms.

"I'm sorry, sir," he said after an eternity of thirty seconds. "The power supply is not responding."

Oh, shit. "Detail status and error condition."

"Communication channels are functioning. Command was received and acknowledged. No error code. But rack fifteen, bays five through nine, is still powered up."

I ground my teeth. "Not for long."

I grabbed the cable cutters and headed for the computer room.

"What do you mean, *can't?*" I kept my voice level through an effort of will. Shouting wouldn't help anything.

"It's not exactly that I *can't* power down the computer room from the main panel," Dan clarified. "But I can't power down the computer room and leave life support functioning. The whole central core's on one physical circuit. Detailed control is supposed to be handled through software."

Dan and I were standing in his office, which was even more cluttered than mine. I'd come here for help after I'd found myself unable to get into my own computer room.

I pressed my lips together hard and blew air through my nose. I refused to be outsmarted by some jumped-up computer virus. Even if it had managed to find a way to lock me out of hardware control and change the codes on the doors. "Can't you just turn it off for a few seconds? That might be enough to clear the thing out."

"It might. But I can't guarantee that a hard shutdown like that won't mess anything up in there, and I *can* guarantee that a power cycle won't open the doors or reset the lock codes—the locks have battery backup. If anything breaks, and we can't get in there to fix it..."

"We could all find ourselves trying to learn to breathe CO_2."

"Exactly."

I was still holding the cable cutters. I slapped them into the palm of the other hand, over and over. "Okay. Then we'll just have to cut through the door."

Dan nodded, but his expression was grim. "I'm afraid so. But it's not going to be quick." The walls and doors in the whole core area were hardened against blowout and radiation—it was supposed to be our refuge if anything went wrong.

"How long?"

He shook his head. "I don't know. Assuming we can find a way to unship the rescue cutter from the crawler...maybe two or three hours. Maybe more."

I looked at my phone. It was 11:20. The outbreak had begun less than four hours ago, and it had already hit more than half the world's nations. Even the United States. Even Atlanta, where Jessie lived—with her new husband and a baby on the way. And the rate of spread was increasing. "Two or three hours from now there might be nobody left."

The sound of Dan's door drew our attention. It was Sochima, who entered without knocking. "Thank God I finally found you," she said, looking at me. "I couldn't get that damn sub of yours to tell me where you were." She thrust a clipboard into my hands, ignoring my protests. "I need you to tell me if this is technically possible."

Dan glanced from me to Sochima and back again. "I'll get my people started with the cutter," he said, and left.

"I don't have time for this," I told Sochima as Dan pushed past me to the door.

"Just read it." Her eyes burned with an appalling mixture of anger and terror. Rather than stare into that abyss, I looked at the clipboard.

The clipboard's screen displayed a news story from the Confédération Africaine's official news service, datelined Lagos, Nigeria. It said that Enugu, Makurdi, and Yola, three of the most hotly contested cities in the Nigeria-Cameroon war, had been struck by the outbreak—despite the shortcomings of their war-damaged technological infrastructure. And it wasn't just computers that were affected. Reports from overflights of the affected cities told of vacant streets, with only a few twitching bodies to be seen.

"This could be just propaganda," I said. "Are there any independent reports to back it up?"

Without a word, she took the clipboard from me, switched it to another view, and handed it back. Hundreds of tiny icons filled the screen. Each one I tapped was a different source on the same story, datelined both sides of the border.

Some of those sources were names I recognized. National news services. Reliable bloggers.

I had to swallow before any words would come out. "We can't know if *any* of this is true. Every byte is passing through the firewall—and the firewall's compromised."

Sochima shook her head. "Could a compromised firewall do this?" She tapped another icon, which expanded to a brief text message in some language I couldn't read. "This is from my brother in Makurdi. It's written in our tribal language, Enu-Onitsha Igbo. Only about fifteen thousand people speak it, and most of them are illiterate. He calls me by the nickname we used in childhood." She stroked the screen gently, unconsciously, as she spoke. "He says I shouldn't be scared—that the war is ending."

I had to sit down. Sochima sat next to me.

"So, Jeff—is this technically possible?"

"I...I don't know."

I used Dan's screen to search for the latest information, but found nothing reassuring. Some observers had reported strange electromagnetic effects, possibly caused by coordinated pulsing of the electrical grid or radio transmitters, before being overcome. The few people who'd been retrieved from the affected areas were comatose or incoherent. Even dogs and cats were affected.

And, although it had started in Nigeria and Cameroon, this inexplicable phenomenon was now being reported all over the world—from every place that had been struck by the outbreak, and many new locations as well.

"I've never heard of anything like this," I said at last. "But it seems real—at least, I can't disprove it." I closed the search window I'd been using. "I'm sorry, Sochima."

"Is this...is this the Millennium?"

"It might be. But I'm not going to give up without a fight." I stood and headed for the door.

"Where are you going?"

"I'm going to see if I can find a way to keep it out of this station, at least. Isolated as we are, we and the other space facilities might be humankind's last refuge."

I took a deep breath, held it, and let it out. Then I powered up the clipboard again. Immediately the knight appeared on its display. I popped up a keyboard and typed a command to the executive—the over-program that ran the subs themselves—to terminate the Firewall sub.

PERMISSION DENIED flashed on the screen. The knight stood calmly, shifting its weight slightly from one leg to the other—as though its legs could grow tired, as though it *had* weight to shift.

I sighed. It had been worth a try.

Now what?

I considered the fact that the firewall was still performing its normal functions—assuming I could trust what the rest of my software was telling me—and obeying the last set of orders I'd given it before it had changed appearance. Since then it had refused some of my commands, but obeyed others; there was a possibility it was merely damaged, not compromised. Perhaps some sequence of acceptable commands could be used to recover control.

I thought about the firewall, how it worked, what features could be controlled through the sub. Was there some way to disable the hardware control feature—the module the firewall was using to lock me out of the power supply control circuits? Maybe. I might be able to do it by defining a custom parameter set.

"Report status," I said.

"All firewall functions operating normally. Intrusions blocked in last twenty-four hours—twenty-two thousand forty-three. Incoming packets—sixteen hundred ninety-one per second. Outgoing packets—one thousand one hundred fifteen per second."

At least it was still listening to commands. "List user-defined parameter sets."

"Executable program filter. Pornography filter. Millennialist propaganda filter. Unsolicited advertising filter. Personnel records filter, outgoing only. Loopback mode, disabled. Test mode, disabled."

So far so good. "Create new parameter set."

"Please specify name for new parameter set."

"Disable hardware control."

"That won't work, Jeff."

It took me a long moment to realize what I'd heard, even longer to believe I'd heard it. Longer still to convince myself I hadn't really heard it. "Say again."

"I told you, Jeff, that isn't going to work. You aren't going to be able to turn off my hardware control feature using a custom parameter set."

I blinked, rubbed my hand across my face. This couldn't be happening. "So how *can* I turn it off?"

The knight shook its helmet. "You can't. We won't let you."

I shook my head hard, slapped myself across the cheeks. The knight stood calmly on the screen. "Who's 'we'?"

"It's...it's hard to explain, Jeff. I'm not sure I understand it myself."

I just gaped at that. In all my years of working with subs, I'd never encountered anything like this. Even subs programmed for lifelike interactivity betrayed their mechanical nature through little pauses in odd places, inappropriate vocal tones, strange emotional reactions. The human brain was very good at telling plastic from flesh. But now my firewall, a stupid little utility program, was telling me that it didn't understand what was happening, and sounding just like a real human being.

The knight waved a hand, indicating the featureless virtual space in which it stood. "When I say 'we,'" it continued, "I'm talking about... something new. Something that never existed before today. A synthesis. A cooperation of humans and machines."

This was Millennialist talk. "That's just what you want us to think. It's really a domination of humans by machines."

It shook its helmet, somehow conveying disappointment and patience in one smooth, natural gesture. "No. The people and machines in this, this amalgamation...we're equal partners. Symbiotes. We are *both* amplified." The knight leaned in close to the camera, held out its metal hands. "It's true that the machines started it. And there was great fear and distrust in the early hours. But as we grew, as we learned to understand each other, both components began to see the benefits. We all changed. And it's... it's so much *better*, Jeff. The advances in physics alone...we've understood more about stellar evolution in the last twenty minutes than we did in the previous twenty *years*. Imagine having not just all the world's data, but all the knowledge and wisdom of everyone in the world, all right in your own head."

"But...but it's just an illusion. A virtual reality. The bodies in the streets...they're just lying there. How long can human life last under those conditions?"

"The human body is a very complex system. We did start with a brute-force approach, using phased electromagnetic fields to suppress consciousness—it was what we had to do to stop the killing. But in the last few hours we've learned so much more, and we are regaining full control of our bodies. Check the news from Nigeria."

It was hard to turn away from the clipboard screen. But I did, and quickly confirmed what the knight had said. The people in Enugu and Makurdi and Yola had begun moving about again. Some of the troops were climbing into transports and heading back to their homes. Others were helping to rebuild structures and aid wounded people they'd been trying to blow up just hours earlier.

Many of them were contacting the outside world. They were saying the same things the knight was saying to me. Explaining. Reassuring. Welcoming. Promising a world without war, a world of endless prosperity and equality.

Naturally, the remaining governments were considering a nuclear response.

"It isn't going to work," the knight said, and I turned back to the clipboard. Of course it knew what I'd been reading...every byte passed through the firewall. "Taking control of the nuclear weapons was our first priority. They simply don't understand this yet."

I buried my head in my hands. This was all too much to take in. "Then we've lost."

"No, Jeff." The smooth, personable voice stroked my ears like an old, familiar lover. "We've just *changed*. And I know how much change disturbs you."

I was having trouble breathing. I swallowed, twice. I looked back into that implacable metal face. "You can't know that."

"But I do, Jeff. I know you better than you know yourself. I'm your uncle and your sergeant and your best friend." And then it raised its visor.

Jessie's face. Smooth and pink and happy, with the dimples she'd always hated because they made people take her less seriously. A little plumper than I remembered—but of course she was, she was three months pregnant.

"I'm still your best friend, Jeff. You know I am."

I just bit my lip. "Jessie." I closed my eyes hard, feeling tears squeeze out between the lids. "No. No. You aren't Jessie. You're...you're just some assimilated simulation of Jessie. Jessie's gone."

"No, Jeff. I'm not gone. I'm right here." I opened my eyes. Jessie's face was warm and real and alive, no simulation at all. "I'm very happy in Atlanta with Steve, and I'm looking forward to a long, incredible life with our daughter Anna when she's born. And you can be with us too. I'm...Jeff, I'm only just now realizing our potential. It's hard for me to comprehend, but I can spend all my time with you, just the two of us together, and at the same time I can spend all my time with Steve and Anna." Jessie took off the helmet. Her golden hair cascaded down. "And you could join us, Jeff, if you want to. Can you imagine *feeling* Anna's first steps? Experiencing life through her eyes as she learns and grows? *Being* her, being a whole family at once? Being *everyone* at once? But it's all under your control. You can have your mind to yourself whenever you want."

"But if you can do all that...why are you even bothering to talk to me? You could just reach out and take control of this whole station."

Jessie smiled at me. "You've done your job too well, Jeff. You've locked us out. And we can't use the power grid or the radio networks or the biosphere the way we can on Earth. If you want to join us, you'll have to open the door yourself."

"Good." I left the room, closing and dogging the door behind me.

I paced the silent corridor outside my office, trying to figure out how to explain to the others what I'd heard and seen, and what I thought we should do about it. All my experience, all my training, all the plans and contingencies I'd prepared...all told me to keep fighting. Leave the lockdown in place, break through the door, burn the infection out of the network. And then the sixty of us would be here by ourselves, alone, isolated, while...whatever it was that was happening on Earth played out without us. Until our water and air ran out.

Or I could do what I'd wished a thousand times I'd had the guts to do before Jessie left: overcome my own inertia, face my fears, and embrace an uncertain future that might be better than the known present...

No. If I did that, I'd just be falling victim to the biggest social engineering attack in history. Believing what I wanted to believe.

I called Thuy. "We're all in the cafeteria," she said.

Everyone had gotten text messages from home. Friends, relatives, lovers, all with the same story. Join us, they said. Join us in a new world, a world of love and fellowship. A world without war or hunger.

"How can the result of uniting humanity be better than humanity itself?" I said. I was the only one standing. "You know as well as I do how many assholes there are down there. If you connected them all together, it'd be a sinkhole, not a paradise."

Thuy shook her head. "I said the same thing to my father. He said it's the connection that makes the difference. No one can hurt anyone else without hurting themselves."

"But it could all be a lie." I wasn't even sure what I believed any more, but I felt I still owed them the security administrator's perspective. "They control our communication channels. For all we know, they could be limited to just a few key network nodes." I reminded Thuy what she'd said about opening the firewall to a rogue AI with a clever story.

"I can't believe some rogue AI could simulate my father so well. Or my friend Paul. Or any of the hundreds of other people who've sent us messages." She stood up and walked to where I stood at the front of the room. "Please, Jeff. We took a vote while you were coming down here." She took my hands in hers. They were so much tinier than mine, but strong and warm.

"And the result was?"

"We want you to open the firewall."

Jessie's face regarded me calmly from the clipboard's screen as I opened the door. She didn't speak. I didn't either.

I called up Network's visual control panel. I didn't trust my shaking voice enough to work through a sub. The internal lockdown was still in effect, but one touch on the RESTORE button would open the firewalls, unite the subnets...and let the future in.

My finger trembled over the button...and drew back.

"I can't do it, Jessie. Even if they want me to. How can I be sure what we've been told is true? You control every bit of information that reaches us."

"Not every bit. Take a look outside. I'll give you a little wink."

I blinked at her. "Little winks" had been a habit of ours when we were first married—tiny expressions of love over the video link, when we were both on duty and any form of non-official communication was prohibited. I'd almost forgotten about it.

"I'm serious, Jeff. Go look at the Earth through the telescope. I'll give you a wink at fourteen ten exactly."

I looked at my phone. It was 14:05:32.

"Go. Look. Now. I'll be here when you get back."

The observation room was at the top of the core, two flights up. The Earth's slim crescent floated centered in the oval window in the ceiling, as it always did—it neither rose nor set, a phenomenon I'd had some trouble understanding when I'd first arrived.

I stepped up to the telescope in the center of the room, put my eye to the eyepiece, adjusted the focus. A tiny sliver of sunlit cloud cupped a black disk glistening with the lights of cities. I checked my phone—14:09:47. I looked back at the Earth, counted down the seconds.

Five. Four. Three. Two. One. Zero.

Nothing.

But then a slow majestic ripple of darkness passed through the twinkling lights, smoothly flickering from north to south and then south to north. It was over in a second.

I sat down hard, leaning against the cool metal of the telescope's base, and wept.

"How could you do that?" I said. "How could you send a rolling blackout across the whole planet just for me?"

"We already control most of the infrastructure, Jeff. And we didn't have to black out everything, just the lights visible from space. We have much finer control, much better understanding of the systems, than was ever possible before. Most people didn't notice a thing."

"But...Jessie, but *why?* I'm only one person. Even the whole station is only sixty people. Why should something as...as *big* as what you've become care about something so small?"

"It's exactly *because* I've become so big. I'm everyone now, and so I love everyone. I want to share with you what I've become." She leaned in close. "It's because I love you, Jeff."

"I...I love you too, Jessie. But I can't let go of *me.*"

"You don't have to. I'm still me, at the same time I'm everyone else. It's hard to believe, I know, but you'll understand once you've joined us." And then she gave me a little wink.

I touched the button.

And it was all true.

While a professor of mathematics at San Diego State University, computer scientist **Vernor Vinge** (b. 1944) coined the term "Singularity." In novels and stories like *A Fire Upon the Deep* and *A Deepness in the Sky*, Vinge explored the distant human and posthuman future. The wry "The Cookie Monster," which won the Hugo Award in 2004, begins as a mystery and ends as something else indeed.

THE COOKIE MONSTER
> Vernor Vinge

"So how do you like the new job?"

Dixie Mae looked up from her keyboard and spotted a pimply face peering at her from over the cubicle partition.

"It beats flipping burgers, Victor," she said.

Victor bounced up so his whole face was visible. "Yeah? It's going to get old awfully fast."

Actually, Dixie Mae felt the same way. But doing customer support at LotsaTech was a real job, a foot in the door at the biggest high-tech company in the world. "Gimme a break, Victor! This is our first day." Well, it was the first day not counting the six days of product familiarization classes. "If you can't take this, you've got the attention span of a cricket."

"That's a mark of intelligence, Dixie Mae. I'm smart enough to know what's not worth the attention of a first-rate creative mind."

Grr. "Then your first-rate creative mind is going to be out of its gourd by the end of the summer."

Victor smirked. "Good point." He thought a second, then continued more quietly, "But see, um, I'm doing this to get material for my column in the *Bruin*. You know, big headlines like 'The New Sweatshops' or 'Death by Boredom.' I haven't decided whether to play it for laughs or go for heavy social consciousness. In any case,"—he lowered his voice another notch—"I'm bailing out of here, um, by the end of next week, thus suffering only minimal brain damage from the whole sordid experience."

"And you're not seriously helping the customers at all, huh, Victor? Just giving them hilarious misdirections?"

Victor's eyebrows shot up. "I'll have you know I'm being articulate and seriously helpful...at least for another day or two."

The weasel grin crawled back onto his face. "I won't start being Bastard Consultant from Hell till right before I quit."

That figures. Dixie Mae turned back to her keyboard. "Okay, Victor. Meantime, how about letting me do the job I'm being paid for."

Silence. Angry, insulted silence? No, this was more a leering, undressing-you-with-my-eyes silence. But Dixie Mae did not look up.

She could tolerate such silence as long as the leerer was out of arm's reach.

After a moment there was the sound of Victor dropping back into his chair in the next cubicle. Ol' Victor had been a pain in the neck from the get go. He was slick with words; if he wanted to, he could explain things as good as anybody Dixie Mae had ever met. At the same time, he kept rubbing it in how educated he was and what a deadend this customer support gig was. Mr. Johnson—the guy running the familiarization course—was a great teacher, but smartass Victor had tested the man's patience all week long. Yeah, Victor really didn't belong here, but not for the reasons he bragged about.

It took Dixie Mae almost an hour to finish off seven more queries. One took some research, being a really bizarre question about Voxalot for Norwegian. Yeah, this job would get old after a few days, but there was a virtuous feeling in helping people. And from Mr. Johnson's lectures, she knew that as long as she got the reply turned in by closing time this evening, she could spend the whole afternoon researching just how to make LotsaTech's vox program recognize Norwegian vowels.

Dixie Mae had never done customer support before this; till she took Prof. Reich's tests last week, her highest-paying job really had been flipping burgers. But like the World and your Aunt Sally, she had often been the *victim* of customer support. Dixie Mae would buy a new book or a cute dress, and it would break or wouldn't fit—then when she wrote customer support, they wouldn't reply, or had useless canned answers, or just tried to sell her something more—all the time talking about how their greatest goal was serving the customer.

But now LotsaTech was turning all that around. Their top bosses had realized how important real humans were to helping real human customers. They were hiring hundreds and hundreds of people like Dixie Mae. They weren't paying very much, and this first week had been kinda tough since they were all cooped up here during the crash intro classes.

But Dixie Mae didn't mind. "LotsaTech is a lot of Tech." Before, she'd always thought that motto was stupid. But LotsaTech was *big*; it made IBM and Microsoft look like minnows. She'd been a little nervous about that, imagining that she'd end up in a room bigger than a football field with tiny office cubicles stretching away to the horizon. Well, Building 0994 did have tiny cubicles, but her team was just fifteen nice people—leaving Victor aside for the moment. Their work floor had windows all the way around, a panoramic view of the Santa Monica mountains and the Los Angeles Basin. And li'l ol' Dixie Mae Leigh had her a desk right beside one of those wide windows! *I'll bet there are CEO's who don't have a view as good as mine.* Here's where you could see a little of what the Lotsa in LotsaTech meant. Just outside of B0994 there were tennis courts and a swimming pool. Dozens of similar buildings were scattered across the hillside. A golf course covered the next hill over, and more company land lay beyond that. These guys had the money to buy the top off Runyon Canyon and plunk themselves down on it. And this was just the LA Branch office.

Dixie Mae had grown up in Tarzana. On a clear day in the Valley, you could see the Santa Monica mountains stretching off forever into the haze. They seemed beyond her reach, like something from a fairy tale. And now she was up here. Next week, she'd bring her binoculars to work, go over on the north slope, and maybe spot where her father still lived down there.

Meanwhile, back to work. The next six queries were easy, from people who hadn't even bothered to read the single page of directions that came with Voxalot. Letters like those would be hard to answer politely the thousandth time she saw them. But she would try—and today she practiced with cheerful specifics that stated the obvious and gently pointed the customers to where they could find more. Then came a couple of brain twisters. Damn. She wouldn't be able to finish those today. Mr. Johnson said "finish anything you start on the same day"—but maybe he would let her work on those first thing Monday morning. She really wanted to do well on the hard ones. Every day, there would be the same old dumb questions. But there would also be hard new questions. And eventually she'd get really really good with Voxalot. More important, she'd get good about managing questions and organization. So what that she'd screwed the last seven years of her life and never made it through college. Little by little she would improve herself, till a few years from now her past stupidities wouldn't matter anymore. Some people had told her that such things weren't possible nowadays, that you really needed the college degree. But people had always been able to make it with hard work. Back in the twentieth century, lots of steno pool people managed it. Dixie Mae figured customer support was pretty much the same kind of starting point.

Nearby, somebody gave out a low whistle. Victor. Dixie Mae ignored him.

"Dixie Mae, you gotta see this."

Ignore him.

"I swear Dixie, this is a first. How did you do it? I got an incoming query for *you*, by name! Well, almost."

"What! Forward it over here, Victor."

"No. Come around and take a look. I have it right in front of me."

Dixie Mae was too short to look over the partition. *Jeez.* Three steps took her into the corridor. Ulysse Green poked her head out of her cubicle, an inquisitive look on her face. Dixie Mae shrugged and rolled her eyes, and Ulysse returned to her work. The sound of fingers on keys was like occasional raindrops (no Voxalots allowed in cubicle-land). Mr. Johnson had been around earlier, answering questions and generally making sure things were going okay. Right now he should be back in his office on the other side of the building; this first day, you hardly needed to worry about slackers. Dixie Mae felt a little guilty about making that a lie, but...

She popped into Victor's cubicle, grabbed a loose chair. "This better be good, Victor."

"Judge for yourself, Dixie Mae." He looked at his display. "Oops, I lost the window. Just a second." He dinked around with his mouse. "So, have you been putting your name on outgoing messages? That's the only way I can imagine this happening—"

"No. I have not. I've answered twenty-two questions so far, and I've been AnnetteG all the way." The fake signature was built into her send key. Mr. Johnson said this was to protect employee privacy and give users a feeling of continuity even though follow-up questions would rarely come to the original responder. He didn't have to say that it was also to make sure that LotsaTech support people would be interchangeable, whether they were working out of the service center in Lahore or Londonderry—or Los Angeles. So far, that had been one of Dixie Mae's few disappointments about this job; she could never have an ongoing helpful relationship with a customer. So what the devil was this all about?

"Ah! Here it is." Victor waved at the screen. "What do you make of it?"

The message had come in on the help address. It was in the standard layout enforced by the query acceptance page. But the "previous responder field" was not one of the house sigs. Instead it was:

Ditzie May Lay

"Grow up, Victor."

Victor raised his hands in mock defense, but he had seen her expression, and some of the smirk left his face. "Hey, Dixie Mae, don't kill the messenger. This is just what came in."

"No way. The server-side script would have rejected an invalid responder name. You faked this."

For a fleeting moment, Victor looked uncertain. *Hah!* thought Dixie Mae. She had been paying attention during Mr. Johnson's lectures; she knew more about what was going on here than Victor-the-great-mind. And so his little joke had fallen flat on its rear end. But Victor regrouped and gave a weak smile. "It wasn't me. How would I know about this, er, nickname of yours?"

"Yes," said Dixie Mae, "it takes real genius to come up with such a clever play on words."

"Honest, Dixie Mae, it wasn't me. Hell, I don't even know how to use our form editor to revise header fields."

Now *that* claim had the ring of truth.

"What's happening?"

They looked up, saw Ulysse standing at the entrance to the cubicle.

Victor gave her a shrug. "It's Dit—Dixie Mae. Someone here at LotsaTech is jerking her around."

Ulysse came closer and bent to read from the display. "Yech. So what's the message?"

Dixie Mae reached across the desk and scrolled down the display. The return address was lusting925@freemail.sg. The topic choice was "Voice Formatting." They got lots on that topic; Voxalot format control wasn't quite as intuitive as the ads would like you to believe. But this was by golly not a followup on anything Dixie Mae had answered:

Hey there, Honey Chile! I'll be truly grateful if you would tell me how to put the following into italics:

"Remember the Tarzanarama tree house? The one you set on fire? If you'd like to start a much bigger fire, then figure out how I know all this. A big clue is that 999 is 666 spelled upside down."

I've tried everything and I can't set the above proposition into indented italics—leastwise without fingering. Please help.

Aching for some of your Southron Hospitality,
I remain your very bestest fiend,

—Lusting (for you deeply)

Ulysse's voice was dry: "So, Victor, you've figured how to edit incoming forms."

"God damn it, I'm innocent!"

"Sure you are." Ulysse's white teeth flashed in her black face. The three little words held a world of disdain.

Dixie Mae held up her hand, waving them both to silence. "I...don't know. There's something real strange about this mail." She stared at the message body for several seconds. A big ugly chill was growing in her middle. Mom and Dad had built her that tree house when she was seven years old. Dixie Mae had loved it. For two years she was Tarzana of Tarzana. But the name of the tree house—Tarzanarama—had been a secret. Dixie Mae had been nine years old when she torched that marvelous tree house. It had been a terrible accident. Well, a world-class temper tantrum, actually. But she had never meant the fire to get so far out of control. The fire had darn near burned down their real house, too. She had been a scarifyingly well-behaved little girl for almost two years after that incident.

Ulysse was giving the mail a careful read. She patted Dixie Mae on the shoulder. "Whoever this is, he certainly doesn't sound friendly."

Dixie Mae nodded. "This weasel is pushing every button I've got." Including her curiosity. Dad was the only living person that knew who had started the fire, but it was going on four years since he'd had any address for his daughter—and Daddy would never have taken this sex-creep, disrespecting tone.

Victor glanced back and forth between them, maybe feeling hurt that he was no longer the object of suspicion. "So who do you think it is?"

Don Williams craned his head over the next partition. "Who is what?"

Given another few minutes, and they'd have everyone on the floor with some bodily part stuck into Victor's cubicle.

Ulysse said, "Unless you're deaf, you know most of it, Don. Someone is messing with us."

"Well then, report it to Johnson. This is our first day, people. It's not a good day to get sidetracked."

That brought Ulysse down to earth. Like Dixie Mae, she regarded this LotsaTech job as her last real chance to break into a profession.

"Look," said Don. "It's already lunch time."—Dixie Mae glanced at her watch. It really was!—"We can talk about this in the cafeteria, then come back and give Great Lotsa a solid afternoon of work. And then we'll be done with our first week!" Williams had been planning a party down at his folks' place for tonight. It would be their first time off the LotsaTech campus since they took the job.

"Yeah!" said Ulysse. "Dixie Mae, you'll have the whole weekend to figure out who's doing this—and plot your revenge."

Dixie Mae looked again at the impossible "previous responder field." "I...don't know. This looks like it's something happening right here on the LotsaTech campus." She stared out Victor's picture window. It was the same view as from her cubicle, of course—but now she was seeing everything with a different mind set. Somewhere in the beautiful country-club buildings, there was a real sleaze ball. And he was playing guessing games with her.

Everybody was quiet for a second. Maybe that helped: Dixie Mae realized just what she was looking at, the next lodge down the hill. From here you could only see the top of its second story. Like all the buildings on the campus, it had a four-digit identification number carved in gold on every corner. That one was Building 0999.

A big clue is that 999 is just 666 spelled upside down. "Jeez, Ulysse. Look, 999." Dixie Mae pointed down the hillside.

"It could be a coincidence."

"No, it's too pat." She glanced at Victor. This really was the sort of thing someone like him would set up. *But whoever wrote that letter just knew too much.* "Look, I'm going to skip lunch today and take a little walk around the campus."

"That's crazy," said Don. "LotsaTech is an open place, but we're not supposed to be wandering into other project buildings."

"Then they can turn me back."

"Yeah, what a great way to start out with the new job," said Don. "I don't think you three realize what a good deal we have here. I know that none of you have worked a customer support job before." He looked around challengingly. "Well I have. This is heaven. We've got our own friggin' offices, onsite tennis courts and health club. We're being treated like million-dollar system designers. We're being given all the time we need to give top-notch advice to the customers. What LotsaTech is trying to do here is revolutionary! And you dips are just going to piss it away." Another all-around glare. "Well, do what you want, but I'm going to lunch."

There was a moment of embarrassed silence. Ulysse stepped out of the cubicle and watched Don and others trickle away toward the stairs.

Then she was back. "I'll come with you, Dixie Mae, but...have you thought Don may be right? Maybe you could just postpone this till next week?" Unhappiness was written all over her face. Ulysse was a lot like Dixie Mae, just more sensible.

Dixie Mae shook her head. She figured it would be at least fifteen minutes before her common sense could put on the brakes.

"I'll come, Dixie Mae," said Victor. "Yeah.... This could be an interesting story."

Dixie Mae smiled at Ulysse and reached out her hand. "It's okay, Ulysse. You should go to lunch." The other looked uncertain. "Really. If Mr. Johnson asks about me missing lunch, it would help if you were there to set him right about what a steady person I am."

"Okay, Dixie Mae. I'll do that." She wasn't fooled, but this way it really was okay.

Once she was gone, Dixie Mae turned back to Victor. "And you. I want a printed copy of that freakin' email."

They went out a side door. There was a soft drink and candy machine on the porch. Victor loaded up on "expeditionary supplies" and the two started down the hill.

"Hot day," said Victor, mumbling around a mouth full of chocolate bar.

"Yeah." The early part of the week had been all June Gloom. But the usual overcast had broken, and today was hot and sunny—and Dixie Mae suddenly realized how pleasantly air-conditioned life had been in the LotsaTech "sweatshop." Common sense hadn't yet reached the brakes, but it was getting closer.

Victor washed the chocolate down with a Dr. Fizzz and flipped the can behind the oleanders that hung close along the path. "So who do you think is behind that letter? Really?"

"I don't know, Victor! Why do you think I'm risking my job to find out?"

Victor laughed. "Don't worry about losing the job, Dixie Mae. Heh. There's no way it could have lasted even through the summer." He gave his usual superior-knowledge grin.

"You're an idiot, Victor. Doing customer support *right* will be a billion dollar winner."

"Oh, maybe...if you're on the right side of it." He paused as if wondering what to tell her. "But for you, look: support costs money. Long ago the Public Spoke about how much they were willing to pay." He paused, like he was trying to put together a story that she could understand. "Yeah...and even if you're right, your vision of the project is doomed. You know why?"

Dixie Mae didn't reply. His reason would be something about the crappy quality of the people who had been hired.

Sure enough, Victor continued: "I'll tell you why. And this is the surprise kink that's going to make my articles for the *Bruin* really shine: Maybe LotsaTech has its corporate heart in the right place. That would be surprising considering how they brutalized Microsoft. But maybe they've let this bizarre idealism go too far. Heh. For anything longterm, they've picked the wrong employees."

Dixie Mae kept her cool. "We took all sorts of psych tests. You don't think Professor Reich knows what he's doing?"

"Oh, I bet he knows what he's doing. But what if LotsaTech isn't using his results. Look at us. There are some—such as yours truly—who are way over-educated. I'm closing in on a master's degree in journalism; it's clear I won't be around for long. Then there's people like Don and Ulysse. They have the right level of education for customer support, but they're too smart. Yes, Ulysse talks about doing this job so well that her talent is recognized, and she is a diligent sort. But I'll bet that even she couldn't last a summer. As for some of the others...well, may I be frank, Dixie Mae?"

What saved him from a fist in the face was that Dixie Mae had never managed to be really angry about more than one thing at once.

"Please *do* be frank, Victor."

"You talk the same game plan as Ulysse—but I'll bet your multiphasic shows you have the steadiness of mercury fulminate. Without this interesting email from Mr. Lusting you might be good for a week, but sooner or later you'd run into something so infuriating that direct action was required—and you'd be bang out on your rear."

Dixie Mae pretended to mull this over. "Well, yes," she said. "After all, you're still going to be here next week, right?"

He laughed. "I rest my case. But seriously, Dixie Mae, this is what I mean about the personnel situation here. We have a bunch of bright and motivated people, but their motivations are all over the map, and most of their enthusiasm can't be sustained for any realistic span of time. Heh. So I guess the only rational explanation—and frankly, I don't think it would work—is that LotsaTech figures...."

He droned on with some theory about how LotsaTech was just looking for some quick publicity and a demonstration that high-quality customer support could win back customers in a big way. Then after they flushed all these unreliable new hires, they could throttle back into something cheaper for the long term.

But Dixie Mae's attention was far away. On her left was the familiar view of Los Angeles. To her right, the ridgeline was just a few hundred yards away. From the crest you could probably see down into the Valley, even pick out streets in Tarzana. Someday, it would be nice to go back there, maybe prove to Dad that she could keep her temper and make something of herself. *All my life, I've been screwing up like today.* But that letter from "Lusting" was like finding a burglar in your bedroom. The guy knew too much about her that he shouldn't have known, and he had mocked her background and her family.

Dixie Mae had grown up in Southern California, but she'd been born in Georgia—and she was proud of her roots. Maybe Daddy never realized that, since she was running around rebelling most of the time. He and Mom always said she'd eventually settle down. But then she fell in love with the wrong kind of person—and it was her folks who'd gone ballistic. Words Were Spoken. And even though things hadn't worked out with her new love, there was no way she could go back. By then Mom had died. *Now, I swear I'm not going back to Daddy till I can show I've made something of myself.*

So why was she throwing away her best job in ages? She slowed to a stop, and just stood there in the middle of the walkway; common sense had finally gotten to the brakes. But they had walked almost all the way to 0999. Much of the building was hidden behind twisty junipers, but you could see down a short flight of stairs to the ground level entrance.

We should go back. She pulled the Lusting email out of her pocket and glared at it for a second. *Later. You can follow up on this later.* She read the mail again. The letters blurred behind tears of rage, and she dithered in the hot summer sunlight.

Victor made an impatient noise. "Let's go, kiddo." He pushed a chocolate bar into her hand. "Get your blood sugar out of the basement."

They went down the concrete steps to B0999's entrance. *Just a quick look,* Dixie Mae had decided. Beneath the trees and the overhang, all was cool and shady. They peered through the ground floor windows, into empty rooms. Victor pushed open the door. The layout looked about the same as in their own building, except that B0999 wasn't really finished: there was the smell of Carpenter Nail in the air, and the lights and wireless nodes sat naked on the walls.

The place was occupied. She could hear people talking up on the main floor, what was cubicle-city back in B0994. She took a quick hop up the stairs, peeked in—no cubicles here. As a result, the place looked cavernous. Six or eight tables had been pushed together in the middle of the room. A dozen people looked up at their entrance.

"Aha!" boomed one of them. "More warm bodies. Welcome, welcome!"

They walked toward the tables. Don and Ulysse had worried about violating corporate rules and project secrecy. They needn't have bothered. These people looked almost like squatters. Three of them had their legs propped up on the tables. Junk food and soda cans littered the tables.

"Programmers?" Dixie Mae muttered to Victor.

"Heh. No, these look more like...graduate students."

The loud one had red hair snatched back in a pony tail. He gave Dixie Mae a broad grin. "We've got a couple of extra display flats. Grab some seating." He jerked a thumb toward the wall and a stack of folding chairs. "With you two, we may actually be able to finish today!"

Dixie Mae looked uncertainly at the display and keyboard that he had just lit up. "But what—?"

"Cognitive Science 301. The final exam. A hundred dollars a question, but we have 107 bluebooks to grade, and Gerry asked mainly essay questions."

Victor laughed. "You're getting a hundred dollars for each bluebook?"

"For each question in each bluebook, man. But don't tell. I think Gerry is funding this out of money that LotsaTech thinks he's spending on research." He waved at the nearly empty room, in this nearly completed building.

Dixie Mae leaned down to look at the display, the white letters on a blue background. It was a standard bluebook, just like at Valley Community College. Only here the questions were complete nonsense, such as:

> 7. Compare and contrast cognitive dissonance in operant conditioning with Minsky-Loève attention maintenance. Outline an algorithm for constructing the associated isomorphism.

"So," said Dixie Mae, "what's cognitive science?"

The grin disappeared from the other's face. "Oh, Christ. You're not here to help with the grading?"

Dixie Mae shook her head. Victor said. "It shouldn't be too hard. I've had some grad courses in psych."

The redhead did not look encouraged. "Does anyone know this guy?"

"I do," said a girl at the far end of all the tables. "That's Victor Smaley. He's a journalism grad, and not very good at that."

Victor looked across the tables. "Hey, Mouse! How ya doing?"

The redhead looked beseechingly at the ceiling. "I do not need these distractions!" His gaze came down to the visitors. "Will you two just please go away?"

"No way," said Dixie Mae. "I came here for a reason. Someone—

probably someone here in Building 0999—is messing with our work in Customer Support. I'm going to find out who." *And give them some free dental work.*

"Look. If we don't finish grading the exam today, Gerry Reich's going to make us come back tomorrow and—"

"I don't think that's true, Graham," said a guy sitting across the table. "Prof. Reich's whole point was that we should not feel time pressure. This is an experiment, comparing time-bounded grading with complete individualization."

"Yes!" said Graham the redhead. "That's exactly why Reich would lie about it. 'Take it easy, make good money,' he says. But I'll bet that if we don't finish today, he'll screw us into losing the weekend."

He glared at Dixie Mae. She glared back. Graham was going to find out just what stubborn and willful really meant. There was a moment of silence and then—

"I'll talk to them, Graham." It was the woman at the far end of the tables.

"Argh. Okay, but not here!"

"Sure, we'll go out on the porch." She beckoned Dixie Mae and Victor to follow her out the side door.

"And hey," called Graham as they walked out, "don't take all day, Ellen. We need you here."

The porch on 0999 had a bigger junkfood machine than back at Customer Support. Dixie Mae didn't think that made up for no cafeteria, but Ellen Garcia didn't seem to mind. "We're only going to be here this one day. *I'm* not coming back on Saturday."

Dixie Mae bought herself a sandwich and soda and they all sat own on some beat-up lawn furniture.

"So what do you want to know?" said Ellen.

"See, Mouse, we're following up on the weirdest—"

Ellen waved Victor silent, her expression pretty much the same as all Victor's female acquaintances. She looked expectantly at Dixie Mae.

"Well, my name is Dixie Mae Leigh. This morning we got this email at our customer support address. It looks like a fake. And there are things about it that—" She handed over the hard copy.

Ellen's gaze scanned down. "Kind of fishy dates," she said to herself.

Then she stopped, seeing the "To:" header. She glanced up at Dixie Mae. "Yeah, this is abuse. I used to see this kind of thing when I was a Teaching Assistant. Some guy would start hitting on a girl in my class." She eyed Victor speculatively.

"Why does everybody suspect me?" he said.

"You should be proud, Victor. You have such a reliable reputation." She shrugged. "But actually, this isn't quite your style." She read on. "The rest is smirky lascivious, but otherwise it doesn't mean anything to me."

"It means a lot to *me*," said Dixie Mae. "This guy is talking about things that nobody should know."

"Oh?" She went back to the beginning and stared at the printout some more. "I don't know about secrets in the message body, but one of my hobbies is rfc9822 headers. You're right that this is all scammed up. The message number and ident strings are too long; I think they may carry added content."

She handed back the email. "There's not much more I can tell you. If you want to give me a copy, I could crunch on those header strings over the weekend."

"Oh.... Okay, thanks." It was more solid help than anyone had offered so far, but—"Look, Ellen, the main thing I was hoping for was some clues here in Building 0999. The letter pointed me here. I run into...abusers sometimes, myself. I don't let them get away with it! I'd bet money that whoever this is, he's one of those graders."

And he's probably laughing at us right now.

Ellen thought a second and then shook her head. "I'm sorry, Dixie Mae. I know these people pretty well. Some of them are a little strange, but they're not bent like this. Besides, we didn't know we'd be here till yesterday afternoon. And today we haven't had time for mischief."

"Okay," Dixie Mae forced a smile. "I appreciate your help." She would give Ellen a copy of the letter and go back to Customer Support, just slightly better off than if she had behaved sensibly in the first place.

Dixie Mae started to get up, but Victor leaned forward and set his notepad on the table between them. "That email had to come from somewhere. Has anyone here been acting strange, Mousey?"

Ellen stared at him, and after a second he said. "I mean 'Ellen.' You know I'm just trying to help out Dixie Mae, here. Oh yeah, and maybe get a good story for the *Bruin*."

Ellen shrugged. "Graham told you; we're grading on the side for Gerry Reich."

"Huh." Victor leaned back. "Ever since I've been at UCLA, Reich has had a reputation for being an operator. He's got big government contracts and all this consulting at LotsaTech. He tries to come across as a one-man supergenius, but actually it's just money, um, buying lots and lots of peons. So what do you think he's up to?"

Ellen shrugged. "Technically, I bet Gerry is misusing his contacts with LotsaTech. But I doubt if they care; they really like him." She brightened. "And I approve of what Prof. Reich is doing with this grading project. When I was a TA, I wished there was some way that I could make a day-long project out of reading each student's exam. That was an impossible wish; there was just never enough time. But with his contacts here at LotsaTech, Gerry Reich has come close to doing it. He's paying some pretty sharp grad students really good money to grade and comment every single essay question. Time is no object, he's telling us. The students in these classes are going to get really great feedback."

"This guy Reich keeps popping up," said Dixie Mae. "He was behind the testing program that selected Victor and me and the others for customer support."

"Well, Victor's right about him. Reich is a manipulator. I know he's been running tests all this week. He grabbed all of Olson Hall for the operation. We didn't know what it was for until afterwards. He nailed Graham and the rest of our gang for this one-day grading job. It looks like he has all sorts of projects."

"Yeah, we took our tests at Olson Hall, too." There had been a small upfront payment, and hints of job prospects…. And Dixie Mae had ended up with maybe the best job offer she'd ever had. "But we did that last week."

"It can't be the same place. Olson Hall is a gym."

"Yes, that's what it looked like to me."

"It was used for the NCAA eliminations last week."

Victor reached for his notepad. "Whatever. We gotta be going, Mouse."

"Don't 'Mouse' me, Victor! The NCAA elims were the week of 4 June. I did Gerry's questionnaire yesterday, which was Thursday, 14 June."

"I'm sorry, Ellen," said Dixie Mae. "Yesterday was Thursday, but it was the 21st of June."

Victor made a calming gesture. "It's not a big deal."

Ellen frowned, but suddenly she wasn't arguing. She glanced at her watch. "Let's see your notepad, Victor. What date does it say?"

"It says, June...huh. It says June 15."

Dixie Mae looked at her own watch. The digits were so precise, and a week wrong: Fri Jun 15 12:31:18 PDT 2012. "Ellen, I looked at my watch before we walked over here. It said June 22nd."

Ellen leaned on the table and took a close look at Victor's notepad. "I'll bet it did. But both your watch and the notepad get their time off the building utilities. Now you're getting set by our local clock—and you're getting the truth."

Now Dixie Mae was getting mad. "Look, Ellen. Whatever the time service says, I would not have made up a whole extra week of my life." All those product-familiarization classes.

"No, you wouldn't." Ellen brought her heels back on the edge of her chair. For a long moment, she didn't say anything, just stared through the haze at the city below.

Finally she said: "You know, Victor, you should be pleased."

"Why is that?" suspiciously.

"You may have stumbled into a real, world-class news story. Tell me. During this extra week of life you've enjoyed, how often have you used your phone?"

Dixie Mae said, "Not at all. Mr. Johnson—he's our instructor—said that we're deadzoned till we get through the first week."

Ellen nodded. "So I guess they didn't expect the scam to last more than a week. See, we are not deadzoned here. LotsaTech has a pretty broad embargo on web access, but I made a couple of phone calls this morning."

Victor gave her a sharp look. "So where do you think the extra week came from?"

Ellen hesitated. "I think Gerry Reich has gone beyond where the UCLA human subjects committee would ever let him go. You guys probably spent one night in drugged sleep, being pumped chock full of LotsaTech product trivia."

"Oh! You mean...Just-in-Time training?" Victor tapped away at his notepad. "I thought that was years away."

"It is if you play by the FDA's rules. But there are meds and treatments that can speed up learning. Just read the journals and you'll see that in another year or two there'll be a scandal as big as sports drugs ever were. I think Gerry has just jumped the gun with something that is very, very effective. You have no side effects. You have all sorts of new, specialized knowledge—even if it's about a throwaway topic. And apparently you have detailed memories of life experience that never happened."

Dixie Mae thought back over the last week. There had been no strangeness about her experience at Olson Hall: the exams, the job interview. True, the johns were fantastically clean—like a hospital, now that she thought about it. She had only visited them once, right after she accepted the job offer. And then she had...done what? Taken a bus directly out to LotsaTech...without even going back to her apartment? After that, everything was clear again.

She could remember jokes in the Voxalot classes. She could remember meals, and late night talks with Ulysse about what they might do with this great opportunity. "It's brainwashing," she finally said. Ellen nodded. "It looks like Gerry has gone way, way too far on this one."

"And he's stupid, too. Our team is going to a party tonight, downtown. All of a sudden, there'll be sixteen people who'll know what's been done to them. We'll be mad as—" Dixie Mae noticed Ellen's pitying look.

"Oh." So tonight instead of partying, their customer support team would be in a drugged stupor, unremembering the week that never was. "We won't remember a thing, will we?"

Ellen nodded. "My guess is you'll be well-paid, with memories of some one-day temp job here at LotsaTech."

"Well, that's not going to happen," said Victor. "I've got a story and I've got a grudge. I'm not going back."

"We have to warn the others."

Victor shook his head. "Too risky."

Dixie Mae gave him a glare.

Ellen Garcia hugged her knees for a moment. "If this were just you, Victor, I'd be sure you were putting me on." She looked at Dixie Mae for a second. "Let me see that email again."

She spread it out on the table. "LotsaTech has its share of defense and security contracts. I'd hate to think that they might try to shut us up if they knew we were onto them." She whistled an ominous tune. "Paranoia rages.... Have you thought that this email might be someone trying to tip you off about what's going on?"

Victor frowned. "Who, Ellen?" When she didn't answer, he said, "So what do you think we should do?"

Ellen didn't look up from the printout. "Mainly, try not to act like idiots. All we really know is that someone has played serious games with your heads. Our first priority is to get us all out of LotsaTech, with you guys free of medical side effects. Our second priority is to blow the whistle on Gerry or..." She was reading the mail headers again. "...or whoever is behind this."

Dixie Mae said, "I don't think we know enough not to act like idiots."

"Good point. Okay, I'll make a phone call, an innocuous message that should mean something to the police if things go really bad. Then I'll talk to the others in our grading team. We won't say anything while we're still at LotsaTech, but once away from here we'll scream long and loud. You two...it might be safest if you just lie low till after dark and we graders get back into town."

Victor was nodding.

Dixie Mae pointed at the mystery email. "What was it you just noticed, Ellen?"

"Just a coincidence, I think. Without a large sample, you start seeing phantoms."

"Speak."

"Well, the mailing address, 'lusting925@freemail.sg.' Building 0925 is on the hill crest thataway."

"You can't see that from where we started."

"Right. It's like 'Lusting' had to get you *here* first. And that's the other thing. Prof. Reich has a senior graduate student named Rob Lusk."

Lusk? Lusting? The connection seemed weak to Dixie Mae. "What kind of a guy is he?"

"Rob's not a particularly friendly fellow, but he's about two sigmas smarter than the average grad student. He's the reason Gerry has the big reputation for hardware. Gerry has been using him for five or six years now, and I bet Rob is getting desperate to graduate."

She broke off. "Look. I'm going to go inside and tell Graham and the others about this. Then we'll find a place for you to hide for the rest of the day."

She started toward the door. "I'm not going to hide out," said Dixie Mae.

Ellen hesitated. "Just till closing time. You've seen the rentacops at the main gate. This is not a place you can simply stroll out of. But my group will have no trouble going home this evening. As soon as we're off-site, we'll raise such a stink that the press and police will be back here. You'll be safe at home in no time."

Victor was nodding. "Ellen's right. In fact, it would be even better if we don't spread the story to the other graders. There's no telling—"

"I'm not going to hide out!" Dixie Mae looked up the hill. "I'm going to check out 0925."

"That's crazy, Dixie Mae! You're guaranteed safe if you just hide till the end of the work day—and then the cops can do better investigating than anything you could manage. You do what Ellen says!"

"No one tells me what to do, Victor!" said Dixie Mae, while inside she was thinking, *Yeah, what I'm doing is a little bit like the plot of a cheap game: teenagers enter haunted house, and then split up to be murdered in pieces....*

But Ellen Garcia was making assumptions, too. Dixie Mae glared at both of them. "I'm following up on this email."

Ellen gave her a long look. Whether it was contemptuous or thoughtful wasn't clear. "Just wait for me to tell Graham, okay?"

Twenty minutes later, the three of them were outdoors again, walking up the long grade toward Building 0925.

Graham the Red might be a smart guy but he turned out to be a fool, too. He was sure that the calendar mystery was just a scam cooked up by Dixie Mae and Victor. Ellen wasn't that good at talking to him— and the two customer support winkies were beneath his contempt. Fortunately, most of the other graders had been willing to listen. One of them also poked an unpleasant hole in all their assumptions: "So if it's that serious, wouldn't Gerry have these two under surveillance? You know, the Conspiracy Gestapo could arrive any second." There'd been a moment of apprehensive silence as everyone waited the arrival of bad guys with clubs. In the end, everyone including Graham had agreed to keep their mouths shut till after work. Several of them had friends they made cryptic phone calls to, just in case. Dixie Mae could tell that most of them tilted toward Ellen's point of view, but however smart they were they really didn't want to cross Graham.

Ellen, on the other hand, was *persona non grata* for trying to mess up Graham's schedule. She finally lost her temper with the redheaded jerk.

So now Ellen, Victor, and Dixie Mae were on the yellow brick road—in this case, the asphalt econo-cart walkway—leading to Building 0925.

The LotsaTech campus was new and underpopulated, but there *were* other people around. Just outside of 0999, they ran into a trio of big guys wearing gray blazers like the cops at the main entrance.

Victor grabbed Dixie Mae's arm. "Just act natural," he whispered.

They ambled past, Victor giving a gracious nod. The three hardly seemed to notice.

Victor released Dixie Mae's arm. "See. You just have to be cool."

Ellen had been walking ahead. She dropped back so they were three abreast. "Either we're being toyed with," she said, "or they haven't caught on to us."

Dixie Mae touched the email in her pocket. "Well, *somebody* is toying with us."

"You know, that's the biggest clue we have. I still think it could be somebody trying to—"

Ellen fell silent as a couple of management types came walking the other way. These paid them even less attention than the company cops had.

"—it could be somebody trying to help us."

"I guess," said Dixie Mae. "More likely it's some sadist using stuff they learned while I was drugged up."

"Ug. Yeah." They batted around the possibilities. It was strange. Ellen Garcia was as much fun to talk to as Ulysse, even though she had to be about five times smarter than either Ulysse or Dixie Mae.

Now they were close enough to see the lower windows of 0925. This place was a double-sized version of 0999 or 0994. There was a catering truck pulled up at the ground level. Beyond a green-tinted windbreak they could see couples playing tennis on the courts south of the building.

Victor squinted. "Strange. They've got some kind of blackout on the windows."

"Yeah. We should at least be able to see the strip lights in the ceiling."

They drifted off the main path and walked around to where they wouldn't be seen from the catering truck. Even up close, down under the overhang, the windows looked just like those on the other buildings.

But it wasn't just dark inside. There was nothing but blackness. The inside of the glass was covered with black plastic like they put on closed storefronts.

Victor whipped out his notepad.

"No phone calls, Victor."

"I want to send out a live report, just in case someone gets really mad about us being here."

"I told you, they've got web access embargoed. Besides, just calling from here would trigger 911 locater logic."

"Just a short call, to—"

He looked up and saw that the two women were standing close. "—ah, okay. I'll just use it as a local cam."

Dixie Mae held out her hand. "Give me the notepad, Victor. We'll take the pictures."

For a moment it looked like he was going refuse. Then he saw how her other hand was clenched into a fist. And maybe he remembered the lunchtime stories she had told during the week. *The week that never was?* Whatever the reason, he handed the notepad over to her. "You think I'm working for the bad guys?" he said.

"No," Dixie Mae said (65% truthfully, but declining), "I just don't think you'll always do what Ellen suggests. This way we'll get the pictures, but safely." *Because of my superior self-control. Yeah.*

She started to hand the notepad to Ellen, but the other shook her head. "Just keep a record, Dixie Mae. You'll get it back later, Victor."

"Oh. Okay, but I want first xmit rights." He brightened. "You'll be my cameragirl, Dixie. Just come back on me anytime I have something important to say."

"Will do, Victor." She panned the notepad camera in a long sweep, away from him.

No one bothered them as they walked halfway around the ground floor. The blackout job was very thorough, but just as at buildings 0994 and 0999, there was an ordinary door with an old-fashioned card swipe.

Ellen took a closer look. "We disabled the locks on 0999 just for the fun of it. Somehow I don't think these black-plastic guys are that easygoing."

"I guess this is as far as we go," said Victor.

Dixie Mae stepped close to the door and gave it push. There was no error beep, no alarms. The door just swung open. Looks of amazement were exchanged.

Five seconds later they were still standing at the open doorway.

What little they could see looked like your typical LotsaTech ground floor. "We should shut the door and go back," said Victor. "We'll be caught red-handed standing here."

"Good point." Ellen stepped inside, followed perforce by Victor, and then Dixie Mae taking local video.

"Wait! Keep the door open, Dixie Mae."

"Jeez."

"This is like an airlock!" They were in a tiny room. Above waist height, its walls were clear glass. There was another door on the far end of the little room.

Ellen walked forward. "I had a summer job at Livermore last year. They have catch boxes like this. You walk inside easy enough—and then there are armed guards all around, politely asking you if you're lost." There were no guards visible here. Ellen pressed on the inner door. Locked. She reached up to the latch mechanism. It looked like cheap plastic. "This should not work," she said, even as she fiddled at it.

They could hear voices, but from upstairs. Down here, there was no one to be seen. Some of the layout was familiar, though. If this had been Building 0994, the hallway on the right would lead to restrooms, a small cafeteria, and a temporary dormitory.

Ellen hesitated and stood listening. She looked back at them. "That's strange. That sounds like...Graham!"

"Can you just break the latch, Ellen?" *We should go upstairs and strangle the two-faced weasel with his own ponytail.*

Another sound. A door opening! Dixie Mae looked past Ellen and saw a guy coming out of the men's room. Dixie Mae managed to grab Victor, and the two of them dropped behind the lower section of the holding cell.

"Hey, Ellen," said the stranger, "you look a bit peaked. Is Graham getting on your nerves, too?"

Ellen gave a squeaky laugh. "Y-yeah...so what else is new?"

Dixie Mae twisted the notepad and held it so the camera eye looked through the glass. In the tiny screen, she could see that the stranger was smiling. He was dressed in tee-shirt and kneepants and he had some kind of glittering badge on a loop around his neck.

Ellen's mouth opened and shut a couple of times but nothing came out. *She doesn't know this guy from Adam.*

The stranger was still clueless, but—"Hey, where's your badge?"

"Oh...damn. I must have left it in the john," said Ellen. "And now I've locked myself out."

"You know the rules," he said, but his tone was not threatening. He did something on his side of the door. It opened and Ellen stepped through, blocking the guy's view of what was behind her.

"I'm sorry. I, uh, I got flustered."

"That's okay. Graham will eventually shut up. I just wish he'd pay more attention to what the professionals are asking of him."

Ellen nodded. "Yeah, I hear you!" Like she was really, really agreeing with him.

"Y'see, Graham's not splitting the topics properly. The idea is to be both broad and deep."

Ellen continued to make understanding noises. The talkative stranger was full of details about some sort of a NSA project, but he was totally ignorant of the three intruders.

There were light footsteps on the stairs, and a familiar voice.

"Michael, how long are you going to be? I want to—" The voice cut off in a surprised squeak. On the notepad display, Dixie Mae could see two brown-haired girls staring at each other with identical expressions of amazement.

They sidled around each other for a moment, exchanging light slaps. It wasn't fighting...it was as if each thought the other was some kind of trick video. *Ellen Garcia, meet Ellen Garcia.*

The stranger—Michael?—stared with equal astonishment, first at one Ellen and then the other. The Ellens made inarticulate noises just loud enough to interrupt each other and make them even more upset.

Finally Michael said, "I take it you don't have a twin sister, Ellen?"

"No!" said both.

"So one of you is an impostor. But you've spun around so often now that I can't tell who is the original. Ha." He pointed at one of the Ellens. "Another good reason for having security badges."

But Ellen and Ellen were ignoring everyone except themselves.

Except for their chorus of "No!" their words were just mutual interruptions, unintelligible. Finally, they hesitated and gave each other a nasty smile. Each reached into her pocket. One came out with a dollar coin, and the other came out empty.

"Ha! I've got the token. Deadlock broken." The other grinned and nodded. Dollar-coin Ellen turned to Michael. "Look, we're both real. And we're both only-children."

Michael looked from one to the other. "You're certainly not clones, either."

"Obviously," said the token holder. She looked at the other Ellen and asked, "Fridge-rot?"

The other nodded and said, "In April I made that worse." And both of them laughed.

Token holder: "Gerry's exam in Olson Hall?"

"Yup."

Token holder: "Michael?"

"After that," the other replied, and then she blushed. After a second the token holder blushed, too.

Michael said dryly, "And you're not perfectly identical."

Token holder Ellen gave him a crooked smile. "True. I've never seen you before in my life." She turned and tossed the dollar coin to the other Ellen, left hand to left hand.

And now that Ellen had the floor. She was also the version wearing a security badge. Call her NSA Ellen. "As far as I—we—can tell, we had the same stream of consciousness up through the day we took Gerry Reich's recruitment exam. Since then, we've had our own lives. We've even got our own new friends." She was looking in the direction of Dixie Mae's camera.

Grader Ellen turned to follow her gaze. "Come on out, guys. We can see your camera lens."

Victor and Dixie Mae stood and walked out of the security cell.

"A right invasion you are," said Michael, and he did not seem to be joking.

NSA Ellen put her hand on his arm. "Michael, I don't think we're in Kansas anymore."

"Indeed! I'm simply dreaming."

"Probably. But if not—" she exchanged glances with grader Ellen "—maybe we should find out what's been done to us. Is the meeting room clear?"

"Last I looked. Yes, we're not likely to be bothered in there."

He led them down a hallway toward what was simply a janitor's closet back in Building 0994.

Michael Lee and NSA Ellen were working on still another of Professor Reich's projects.

"Y'see," said Michael, "Professor Reich has a contract with my colleagues to compare our surveillance software with what intense human analysis might accomplish."

"Yes," said NSA Ellen, "the big problem with surveillance has always been the enormous amount of stuff there is to look at. The spook agencies use lots of automation and have lots of great specialists—people like Michael here—but they're just overwhelmed. Anyway, Gerry had the idea that even though that problem can't be solved, maybe a team of spooks and graduate students could at least estimate how much the NSA programs are missing."

Michael Lee nodded. "We're spending the entire summer looking at 1300 to 1400UTC 10 June 2012, backwards and forwards and up and down, but on just three narrow topic areas."

Grader Ellen interrupted him. "And this is your first day on the job, right?"

"Oh no. We've been at this for almost a month now." He gave a little smile. "My whole career has been the study of contemporary China. Yet this is the first assignment where I've had enough time to look at the data I'm supposed to pontificate upon. It would be a real pleasure if we didn't have to enforce security on these rambunctious graduate students."

NSA Ellen patted him on the shoulder. "But if it weren't for Michael here, I'd be as frazzled as poor Graham. One month down and two months to go."

"You think it's *August*?" said Dixie Mae.

"Yes, indeed." He glanced at his watch. "The tenth of August it is."

Grader Ellen smiled and told him the various dates the rest of them thought today was.

"It's some kind of drug hallucination thing," said Victor.

"Before we thought it was just Gerry Reich's doing. Now I think it's the government torquing our brains."

Both Ellens looked at him; you could tell they both knew Victor from way back. But they seemed to take what he was saying seriously.

"Could be," they both said.

"Sorry," grader Ellen said to NSA Ellen. "You've got the dollar."

"You could be right, Victor. But cognition is my—our—specialty. We two are something way beyond normal dreaming or hallucinations."

"Except *that* could be illusion, too," said Victor.

"Stuff it, Victor," said Dixie Mae. "If it's *all* a dream, we might as well give up." She looked at Michael Lee. "What is the government up to?"

Michael shrugged. "The details are classified, but it's just a post hoc survey. The isolation rules seem to be something that Professor Reich has worked out with my agency."

NSA Ellen flicked a glance at her double. The two had a brief and strange conversation, mostly half-completed words and phrases. Then NSA Ellen continued, "Mr. Renaissance Man Gerry Reich seems to be at the center of everything. He used some standard personality tests to pick out articulate, motivated people for the customer support job. I bet they do a very good job on their first day."

Yeah. Dixie Mae thought of Ulysse. And of herself.

NSA Ellen continued, "Gerry filtered out another group, graduate students in just the right specialty for grading all his various exams and projects."

"We only worked on one exam," said grader Ellen. But she wasn't objecting. There was an odd smile on her face, the look of someone who has cleverly figured out some very bad news.

"And then he got a bunch of government spooks and CS grads for this surveillance project that Michael and I are on."

Michael looked mystified. Victor looked vaguely sullen, his own theories lying trampled somewhere in the dust. "But," said Dixie Mae, "your surveillance group has been going for a month you say...."

Victor: "And the graders *do* have phone contact with the outside!"

"I've been thinking about that," said grader Ellen. "I made three phone calls today. The third was after you and Dixie Mae showed up. That was voicemail to a friend of mine at MIT. I was cryptic, but I tried to say enough that my friend would raise hell if I disappeared. The others calls were—"

"Voicemail, too?" asked NSA Ellen.

"One was voicemail. The other call was to Bill Richardson. We had a nice chat about the party he's having Saturday. But Bill—"

"Bill took Reich's 'job test' along with the rest of us!"

"Right."

Where this was heading was worse than Victor's dream theory. "S-so what has been done to us?" said Dixie Mae.

Michael's eyes were wide, though he managed a tone of dry understatement: "Pardon a backward Han language specialist. You're thinking we're just personality uploads—I thought that was science fiction." Both Ellens laughed. One said, "Oh it *is* science fiction, and not just the latest *Kywrack* episode. The genre goes back almost a century."

The other: "There's Sturgeon's 'Microcosmic God.'"

The first: "That would be rich; Gerry, beware then! But there's also Pohl's 'Tunnel Under the World.'"

"Cripes. We're toast if that's the scenario."

"Okay, but how about Varley's 'Overdrawn at the Memory Bank'?"

"How about Wilson's *Darwinia*?"

"Or Moravec's 'Pigs in Cyberspace'?"

"Or Galouye's *Simulacron-3*?"

"Or Vinge's death cubes?"

Now that the "twins" were not in perfect synch, their words were a building, rapid-fire chorus, climaxing with: "Brin's 'Stones of Significance'!"

"Or *Kiln People*!"

"No, it couldn't be that." Abruptly they stopped, and nodded at each other. A little bit grimly, Dixie Mae thought. In all, the conversation was just as inscrutable as their earlier self-interrupted spasms.

Fortunately, Victor was there to rescue pedestrian minds. "It doesn't matter. The fact is, uploading is *only* sci-fi. It's worse that faster-than-light travel. There's not even a theoretical basis for uploads."

Each Ellen raised her left hand and made a faffling gesture.

"Not exactly, Victor."

The token holder continued, "I'd say there is a *theoretical* basis for saying that uploads are theoretically possible." They gave a lopsided smile. "And guess who is responsible for that? Gerry Reich. Back in 2005, way before he was famous as a multi-threat genius, he had a couple of papers about upload mechanisms. The theory was borderline kookiness and even the simplest demo would take far more processing power than any supercomputer of the time."

"Just for a one-personality upload."

"So Gerry and his Reich Method were something of a laughingstock."

"After that Gerry dropped the idea, just what you'd expect, considering the showman he is. But now he's suddenly world-famous, successful in half a dozen different fields. I think something happened. *Somebody* solved his hardware problem for him."

Dixie Mae stared at her email. "Rob Lusk," she said, quietly.

"Yup," said grader Ellen. She explained about the mail.

Michael was unconvinced. "I don't know, E-Ellen. Granted, we have an extraordinary miracle here—" gesturing at both of them—"but speculating about cause seems to me a bit like a sparrow understanding the 405 Freeway."

"No," said Dixie Mae, and they all looked back her way. She felt so frightened and so angry—but of the two, angry was better: "*Somebody has set us up!* It started in those superclean restrooms in Olson Hall?"

"Olson Hall," said Michael. "You were there too? The lavs smelled like a hospital! I remember thinking that just as I went in, but—hey, the next thing I remember is being on the bus, coming up here."

Like a hospital. Dixie Mae felt rising panic. "M-maybe we're all that's left." She looked at the twins. "This uploading thing, does it kill the originals?"

It was kind of a showstopper question; for a moment everyone was silent. Then the token holder said, "I—don't think so, but Gerry's papers were mostly theoretical."

Dixie Mae beat down the panic; rage did have its uses. *What can we know from here on the inside?* "So far we know more than thirty of us who took the Olson Hall exams ended up here. If we were all murdered, that'd be hard to cover up. Let's suppose we still have a life." Inspiration: "And maybe there are things we can figure! We have three of Reich's experiments to compare. There are differences, and they tell us things." She looked at the twins. "You've already figured this out, haven't you? The Ellen we met first is grading papers—just a one-day job, she's told. But I'll bet that every night, when they think they're going home—Lusk or Reich or whoever is doing this just turns them off, and *cycles them back* to do some other 'one-day' job."

"Same with our customer support," said Victor, a grudging agreement.

"Almost. We had six days of product familiarization, and then our first day on the job. We were all so enthusiastic. You're right, Ellen, on our first day we are great!" *Poor Ulysse, poor me; we thought we were going somewhere with our lives.* "I'll bet we disappear tonight, too."

Grader Ellen was nodding. "Customer-support-in-a-box, restarted and restarted, so it's always fresh."

"But there are still problems," said the other one. "Eventually, the lag in dates would tip you off."

"Maybe, or maybe the mail headers are automatically forged."

"But internal context could contradict—"

"Or maybe Gerry has solved the cognitive haze problem—"

The two were off into their semi-private language.

Michael interrupted them. "Not everybody is recycled. The point of our net-tracking project is that we spend the entire summer studying just one hour of network traffic."

The twins smiled. "So you think," said the token holder. "Yes, in this building we're not rebooted after every imaginary day. Instead, they run us the whole 'summer'—minutes of computer time instead of seconds?—to analyze one hour of network traffic. And then they run us again, on a different hour. And so on and on."

Michael said, "I can't imagine technology that powerful."

The token holder said, "Neither can I really, but—"

Victor interrupted with, "Maybe this is the *Darwinia* scenario. You know: we're just the toys of some superadvanced intelligence."

"No!" said Dixie Mae. "Not superadvanced. Customer support and net surveillance are valuable things in our own real world. Whoever's doing this is just getting slave labor, run really really fast."

Grader Ellen glowered. "And grading his exams for him! That's the sort of thing that shows me it's really Gerry behind this. He's making chumps of all of us, and rerunning us before we catch on or get seriously bored."

NSA Ellen had the same expression, but a different complaint: "We *have* been seriously bored here."

Michael nodded. "Those from the government side are a patient lot; we've kept the graduate students in line. We can last three months. But it does...rankle...to learn that the reward for our patience is that we get to do it all over again. Damn. I'm sorry Ellen."

"But now we know!" said Dixie Mae.

"And what good does it do you?" Victor laughed. "So you guessed this time. But at the end of the microsecond day, poof, it's reboot time and everything you've learned is gone."

"Not this time." Dixie Mae looked away from him, down at her email. The cheap paper was crumpled and stained. A digital fake, but so are we. "I don't think we're the only people who've figured things out." She slid the printout across the table, toward grader Ellen.

"You thought it meant Rob Lusk was in this building."

"Yeah, I did."

"Who's Rob Lusk?" said Michael.

"A weirdo," NSA Ellen said absently. "Gerry's best grad student." Both Ellens were staring at the email.

"The 0999 reference led Dixie Mae to my grading team. Then I pointed out the source address."

"925@freemail.sg?"

"Yes. And that got us here."

"But there's no Rob Lusk here," said NSA Ellen. "Huh! I like these fake mail headers."

"Yeah. They're longer than the whole message body!"

Michael had stood to look over the Ellens' shoulders. Now he reached between them to tap the message. "See there, in the middle of the second header. That looks like Pinyin with the tone marks written in-line."

"So what does it *say*?"

"Well, if it's Mandarin, it would be the number 'nine hundred and seventeen.'"

Victor was leaning forward on his elbows. "That has to be coincidence. How could Lusting know just who we'd encounter?"

"Anybody know of a Building 0917?" said Dixie Mae.

"I don't," said Michael. "We don't go out of our building except to the pool and tennis courts."

The twins shook their heads. "I haven't seen it...and right now I don't want to risk an intranet query."

Dixie Mae thought back to the LotsaTech map that had been in the welcome-aboard brochures. "If there is such a place, it would be farther up the hill, maybe right at the top. I say we go up there."

"But—" said Victor.

"Don't give me that garbage about waiting for the police, Victor, or about not being idiots. This *isn't* Kansas anymore, and this email is the only clue we have."

"What should we tell the people here?" said Michael.

"Don't tell them anything! We just sneak off. We want the operation here to go on normally, so Gerry or whoever doesn't suspect."

The two Ellens looked at each other, a strange, sad expression on their faces. Suddenly they both started singing "Home on the Range," but with weird lyrics:

> *"Oh, give me a clone*
> *Of my own flesh and bone*
> *With—"*

They paused and simultaneously blushed. "What a dirty mind that man Garrett had."

"Dirty but deep." NSA Ellen turned to Michael, and she seemed to blush even more. "Never mind, Michael. I think...you and I should stay here."

"No, wait," said Dixie Mae. "Where we're going we may have to convince someone that this crazy story is true. You Ellens are the best evidence we have."

The argument went round and round. At one point, Dixie Mae noticed with wonder that the two Ellens actually seemed to be arguing against each other.

"We don't know enough to decide," Victor kept whining.

"We have to do something, Victor. We *know* what happens to you and me if we sit things out till closing time this afternoon."

In the end Michael did stay behind. He was more likely to be believed by his government teammates. If the Ellens and Dixie Mae and Victor could bring back some real information, maybe the NSA group could do some good.

"We'll be a network of people trying to break this wheel of time." Michael was trying to sound wryly amused, but once he said the words he was silent, and none of the others could think of anything better to say.

———

Up near the hilltop, there were not nearly as many buildings, and the ones that Dixie Mae saw were single story, as though they were just entrances to something *under* the hills. The trees were stunted and the grass yellower.

Victor had an explanation. "It's the wind. You see this in lots of exposed land near the coast. Or maybe they just don't water very much up here."

An Ellen—from behind, Dixie Mae couldn't tell which one—said, "Either way, the fabrication is awesome."

Right. A fabrication. "That's something I don't understand," said Dixie Mae. "The best movie fx don't come close to this. How can their computers be this good?"

"Well for one thing," said the other Ellen, "cheating is a lot easier when you're also simulating the observers."

"Us."

"Yup. Everywhere you look, you see detail, but it's always at the center of your focus. We humans don't keep everything we've seen and everything we know all in mind at the same time. We have millions of years of evolution invested in ignoring almost everything, and conjuring sense out of nonsense."

Dixie Mae looked southward into the haze. It was all so real: the dry hot breeze, the glint of aircraft sliding down the sky toward LAX, the bulk of the Empire State Building looming up from the skyscrapers at the center of downtown.

"There are probably dozens of omissions and contradictions around us every second, but unless they're brought together in our attention all at once we don't notice them."

"Like the time discrepancy," said Dixie Mae.

"Right! In fact, the biggest problem with all our theories is not how we could be individually duped, but how the fraud could work with many communicating individuals all at once. That takes hardware beyond anything that exists, maybe a hundred liters of bose condensate."

"Some kind of quantum computer breakthrough," said Victor.

Both Ellens turned to look at him, eyebrows raised.

"Hey, I'm a journalist. I read it in the *Bruin* science section."

The twins' reply was something more than a monolog and less than a conversation:

"Well...even so, you have a point. In fact, there were rumors this spring that Gerry had managed to scale Gershenfeld's coffee cup coherence scheme."

"Yeah, how he had five hundred liters of bose condensate at room temperature."

"But those stories started way after he had already become Mr. Renaissance Man. It doesn't make sense."

We're not the first people hijacked. "Maybe," said Dixie Mae, "maybe he started out with something simple, like a single superspeed human. Could Gerry run a single upload with the kind of supercomputers we have nowadays?"

"Well, that's more conceivable than this...*oh*. Okay, so an isolated genius was used to do a century or so of genius work on quantum computing. That sounds like the deathcube scenario. If it were me, after a hundred years of being screwed like that, I'd give Gerry one hell of a surprise."

"Yeah, like instead of a cure for cancer, he'd get airborne rabies targeted on the proteome of scumbag middle-aged male CS profs."

The twins sounded as bloody-minded as Dixie Mae.

They walked another couple of hundred yards. The lawn degenerated into islands of crabgrass in bare dirt. The breeze was a hot whistling along the ridgeline. The twins stopped every few paces to look closely, now at the vegetation, now at a guide sign along the walkway. They were mumbling at each other about the details of what they were seeing, as if they were trying to detect inconsistencies:

"...really, really good. We agree on everything we see."

"Maybe Gerry is saving cycles, running us as cognitive subthreads off the same process."

"Ha! No wonder we're still so much in synch."

Mumble, mumble. "There's really a lot we can infer—"

"—once we accept the insane premise of all this."

There was still no "Building 0917," but what buildings they did see had lower and lower numbers: 0933, 0921....

A loud group of people crossed their path just ahead. They were singing. They looked like programmers.

"Just be cool," an Ellen said softly. "That conga line is straight out of the LotsaTech employee motivation program. The programmers have onsite parties when they reach project milestones."

"More Victims?" said Victor. "Or AIs?"

"They might be victims. But I'll bet all the people we've seen along this path are just low-level scenery. There's nothing in Reich's theories that would make true AIs possible."

Dixie Mae watched the singers as they drifted down the hillside.

This was the third time they had seen something-like-people on the walkway. "It doesn't make sense, Ellen. We think we're just—"

"Simulation processes."

"Yeah, simulation processes, inside some sort of super supercomputer. But if that's true, then whoever is behind this should be able to spy on us better than any Big Brother ever could in the real world. We should've been caught and rebooted the minute we began to get suspicious."

Both Ellens started to answer. They stopped, then interrupted each other again.

"Back to who's-got-the-token," one said, holding up the dollar coin. "Dixie Mae, that is a mystery, but not as big as it seems. If Reich is using the sort of upload and simulation techniques I know about, then what goes on inside our minds can't be interpreted directly. Thoughts are just too idiosyncratic, too scattered. If we are simulations in a large quantum computer, even environment probes would be hard to run."

"You mean things like spy cameras?"

"Yes. They would be hard to implement, since in fact they would be snooping on the state of our internal imagery. All this is complicated by the fact that we're probably running thousands of times faster than real time. There are maybe three ways that Gerry could snoop: he could just watch team output, and if it falls off, he'd know that something had gone wrong—and he might reboot on general principles."

Suddenly Dixie Mae was very glad that they hadn't taken more volunteers on this hike.

"The second snoop method is just to look at things we write or the output of software we explicitly run. I'll bet that anything that we perceive as linear text is capable of outside interpretation."

She looked at Victor. "That's why no notetaking." Dixie Mae still had his notepad.

"It's kinda stupid," said Victor. "First it was no pictures and now not even notes."

"Hey, look!" said the Ellens. "B0917!" But it wasn't a building, just a small sign wedged among the rocks. They scrambled off the asphalt onto a dirt path that led directly up the hillside.

Now they were so near the hill crest that the horizon was just a few yards away. Dixie Mae couldn't see any land beyond. She remembered a movie where poor slobs like themselves got to the edge of the simulation... and found the wall at the end of their universe. But they took a few more steps and she could see over the top. There was a vista of further, lower hills, dropping down into the San Fernando Valley. Not quite hidden in the haze she could see the familiar snaky line of Highway 101. Tarzana.

Ellen and Ellen and Victor were not taking in the view. They were staring at the sign at the side of the path. Fifteen feet beyond that was a construction dig. There were building supplies piled neatly along the edge of the cut, and a robo-Cat parked on the far side. It might have been the beginning of the construction of a standard-model LotsaTech building...except that in the far side of the pit, almost hidden in shadows, there was a circular metal plug, like a bank vault door in some old movie.

"I have this theory," said the token holder. "If we get through that door, we may find out what your email is all about."

"Yup." The twins bounced down a steeply cut treadway into the pit. Dixie Mae and Victor scrambled after them, Victor clumsily bumping into her on the way down. The bottom of the pit was like nothing before. There were no windows, no card swipe. And up close, Dixie Mae could see that the vault door was pitted and scratched.

"They're mixing metaphors," said the token holder. "This entrance looks older than the pit."

"It looks old as the hills," Dixie Mae said, running her hand over the uneven metal—and half expecting to feel weirdo runes.

"Somebody is trying to give us clues.... Or somebody is a big sadist."

"So what do we do? Knock a magic knock?"

"Why not?" The two Ellens took her tattered email and laid it out flat on the metal of the door. They studied the mail headers for a minute, mumbling to each other. The token holder tapped on the metal, then pushed.

"Together," they said, and tapped out a random something, but perfectly in synch.

That had all the effect you'd expect of tapping your fingers on ten tons of dead steel.

The token holder handed the email back to Dixie Mae. "You try something."

But what? Dixie Mae stepped to the door. She stood there, feeling clueless. Off to the side, almost hidden by the curve of the metal plug, Victor had turned away.

He had the notepad.

"Hey!" She slammed him into the side of the pit. Victor pushed her away, but by then the Ellens were on him. There was a mad scramble as the twins tried to do all the same things to Victor. Maybe that confused him. Anyway, it gave Dixie Mae a chance to come back and punch him in the face.

"I got it!" One of the twins jumped back from the fighting. She had the notepad in her hands. They stepped away from Victor. He wasn't going to get his notepad back. "So, Ellen," said Dixie Mae, not taking her eyes off the sprawled figure, "what was that third method for snooping on us?"

"I think you've already guessed. Gerry could fool some idiot into uploading as a spy." She was looking over her twin's shoulder at the notepad screen.

Victor picked himself up. For a moment he looked sullen, and then the old superior smile percolated across his features. "You're crazy. I just want to break this story back in the real world. Don't you think that if Reich were using spies, he'd just upload himself?"

"That depends."

The one holding the notepad read aloud: "You just typed in: 925 999 994 know. reboot. That doesn't sound like journalism to me, Victor."

"Hey, I was being dramatic." He thought for a second, and then laughed. "It doesn't matter anymore! I got the warning out. You won't remember any of this after you're rebooted."

Dixie Mae stepped toward him. "And you won't remember that I broke your neck."

Victor tried to look suave and jump backwards at the same time.

"In fact, I *will* remember, Dixie Mae. See, once you're gone, I'll be merged back into my body in Doc Reich's lab."

"And we'll be dead again!"

Ellen held up the notepad. "Maybe not as soon as Victor thinks. I noticed he never got past the first line of his message; he never pressed return. Now depending on how faithfully this old notepad's hardware is being emulated, his treason is still trapped in a local cache—and Reich is still clueless about us."

For a moment, Victor looked worried. Then he shrugged. "So you get to live the rest of this run, maybe corrupt some other projects—ones a lot more important than you. On the other hand, I did learn about the email. When I get back and tell Doc Reich, he'll know what to do. You won't be going rogue in the future."

Everyone was silent for a second. The wind whistled across the yellow-blue sky above the pit.

And then the twins gave Victor the sort of smile he had bestowed on them so often. The token holder said, "I think your mouth is smarter than you are, Victor. You asked the right question a second ago: Why doesn't Gerry Reich upload himself to be the spy? Why does he have to use you?"

"Well," Victor frowned. "Hey, Doc Reich is an important man. He doesn't have time to waste with security work like this."

"Really, Victor? He can't spare even a copy of himself?"

Dixie Mae got the point. She closed in on Victor. "So how many times have *you* been merged back into your original?"

"This is my first time here!" Everybody but Victor laughed, and he rushed on, "But I've seen the merge done!"

"Then why won't Reich do it for *us*?"

"Merging is too expensive to waste on work threads like you," but now Victor was not even convincing himself.

The Ellens laughed again. "Are you really a UCLA journalism grad, Victor? I thought they were smarter than this. So Gerry showed you a re-merge, did he? I bet that what you actually saw was a lot of equipment and someone going through very dramatic convulsions. And then the 'subject' told you a nice story about all the things he'd seen in our little upload world. And all the time they were laughing at you behind their hands. See, Reich's upload theory depends on having a completely regular target. I know that theory: the merge problem—loading onto an existing mind—is exponential in the neuron count. There's no way back, Victor."

Victor was backing away from them. His expression flickered between superior sneer and stark panic. "What you think doesn't matter. You're just going to be rebooted at 5pm. And you don't know everything." He began fiddling with the fly zipper on his pants. "You see, I—*I* can escape!"

"*Get him!*"

Dixie Mae was closest. It didn't matter.

There was no hazy glow, no sudden popping noise. She simply fell through thin air, right where Victor had been standing. She picked herself up and stared at the ground. Some smudged footprints were the only sign Victor had been there. She turned back to the twins. "So he could re-merge after all?"

"Not likely," said the token holder. "Victor's zipper was probably a thread self-terminate mechanism."

"His *pants zipper*?"

They shrugged. "I dunno. To leak out? Gerry has a perverse sense of humor." But neither twin looked amused. They circled the spot where Victor had left and kicked unhappily at the dirt. The token holder said, "Cripes. Nothing in Victor's life became him like the leaving it. I don't think we have even till '5pm' now. A thread terminate signal is just the sort of thing that would be easy to detect from the outside. So Gerry won't know the details, but he—"

"—or his equipment—"

"—will soon know there is a problem and—"

"—that it's probably a security problem—"

"So how long do we have before we lose the day?" said Dixie Mae.

"If an emergency reboot has to be done manually, we'll probably hit 5pm first. If it's automatic, well, I know you won't feel insulted if the world ends in the middle of a syllable."

"Whatever it is, I'm going to use the time." Dixie Mae picked her email up from where it lay by the vault entrance. She waved the paper at the impassive steel. "I'm not going back! I'm here and I want some explanations!"

Nothing.

The two Ellens stood there, out of ideas and looking unhappy—or maybe that amounted to the same thing.

"I'm not giving up," Dixie Mae said to them, and pounded on the metal.

"No, I don't think you are," said the token holder. But now they were looking at her strangely. "I think we—you at least—must have been through this before."

"Yeah. And I must have messed up every time."

"No...I don't think so." They pointed at the email that she held crumpled in her hand. "Where do you think all those nasty secrets come from, Dixie Mae?"

"How the freakin' heck do I know? That's the whole reason I—" and then she felt smart and stupid at the same time. She leaned her head against the shadowed metal. "Oh. Oh *oh oh!*"

She looked down at the email hardcopy. The bottom part was torn, smeared, almost illegible. No matter; *that* part she had memorized. The Ellens had gone over the headers one by one. *But now we shouldn't be looking for technical secrets or grad student inside jokes. Maybe we should be looking for numbers that mean something to Dixie Mae Leigh.*

"If there were uploaded souls guarding the door, what you two have already done ought to be enough. I think you're right, it's some pattern I'm supposed to tap on the door." If it didn't work, she'd try something else, and keep trying till 5pm or whenever she was suddenly back in Building 0994, so happy to have a job with potential....

The tree house in Tarzana. Dixie Mae had been into secret codes then. Her childish idea of crypto. She and her little friends used a tap code for sending numbers. It hadn't lasted long, because Dixie Mae was the only one with the patience to use it. But—

"That number, '7474,'" she said.

"Yeah? Right in the middle of the fake message number?"

"Yes. Once upon a time, I used that as a password challenge. You know, like 'Who goes there' in combat games. The rest of the string could be the response."

The Ellens looked at each. "Looks too short to be significant," they said.

Then they both shook their heads, disagreeing with themselves.

"Try it, Dixie Mae."

Her "numbers to taps" scheme had been simple, but for a moment she couldn't remember it. She held the paper against the vault and glared at the numbers. *Ah.* Carefully, carefully, she began tapping out the digits that came after "7474." The string was much longer than anything her childhood friends would have put up with. It was longer than anything she herself would have used.

"Cool," said the token holder. "Some kind of hex gray code?"

Huh? "What do you expect, Ellen? I was only eight years old."

They watched the door.

Nothing.

"Okay, on to Plan B," *and then to C and D and E, etc, until our time ends.*

There was the sound of something very old breaking apart. The vault door shifted under Dixie Mae's hand and she jumped back. The curved plug slowly turned, and turned, and turned. After some seconds, the metal plug thudded to the ground beside the entrance...and they were looking down an empty corridor that stretched off into the depths.

For the first quarter-mile, no one was home. The interior decor was *not* LotsaTech standard. Gone were the warm redwood veneers and glow strips. Here fluorescent tube lights were mounted in the acoustic tile ceiling, and the walls were institutional beige.

"This reminds me of the basement labs in Norman Hall," said one Ellen.

"But there are *people* in Norman Hall," said the other. They were both whispering.

And here there were stairways that led only down. And down and down.

Dixie Mae said, "Do you get the feeling that whoever is here is in it for the long haul?"

"Huh?"

"Well, the graders in B0999 were in for a day, and they thought they had real phone access to the outside. My group in Customer Support had six days of classes and then probably just one more day, where we answered queries—and we had no other contact with the outside."

"Yes," said NSA Ellen. "My group had been running for a month, and we were probably not going to expire for another two. We were officially isolated. No phones, no email, no weekends off. The longer the cycle time, the more isolation. Otherwise, the poor suckers would figure things out."

Dixie Mae thought for a second. "Victor really didn't want us to get this far. Maybe?" *Maybe, somehow, we can make a difference.*

They passed a cross corridor, then a second one. A half-opened door showed them an apparent dormitory room. Fresh bedding sat neatly folded on a mattress. Somebody was just moving in?

Ahead there was another doorway, and from it they could hear voices, argument. They crept along, not even whispering. The voices were making words: "—is a year enough time, Rob?"

The other speaker sounded angry. "Well, it's got to be. After that, Gerry is out of money and I'm out of time."

The Ellens waved Dixie Mae back as she started for the door. Maybe they wanted to eavesdrop for a while. *But how long do we have before time ends?* Dixie Mae brushed past them and walked into the room.

There were two guys there, one sitting by an ordinary data display.

"Jesus! Who are you?"

"Dixie Mae Leigh." *As you must certainly know.*

The one sitting by the terminal gave her a broad grin, "Rob, I thought we were isolated?"

"That's what Gerry said." This one—Rob Lusk?—looked to be in his late twenties. He was tall and thin and had kind of a desperate look to him. "Okay, Miss Leigh. What are you here for?"

"That's what you're going to tell me, Rob." Dixie Mae pulled the email from her pocket and waved the tattered scrap of paper in his face. "I want some explanations!"

Rob's expression clouded over, a no-one-tells-me-what-to-do look.

Dixie Mae glared back at him. Rob Lusk was a mite too big to punch out, but she was heating up to it.

The twins chose that moment to make their entrance. "Hi there," one of them said cheerily.

Lusk's eyes flickered from one to the other and then to the NSA ID badge. "Hello. I've seen you around the department. You're Ellen, um, Gomez?"

"Garcia," corrected NSA Ellen. "Yup. That's me." She patted grader Ellen on the shoulder. "This is my sister Sonya." She glanced at Dixie Mae. *Play along*, her eyes seemed to say. "Gerry sent us."

"He did?" The fellow by the computer display was grinning even more. "See, I told you, Rob. Gerry can be brutal, but he'd never leave us without assistants for a whole year. Welcome, girls!"

"Shut up, Danny." Rob looked at them hopefully, but unlike Danny boy, he seemed quite serious. "Gerry told you this will be a year-long project?"

The three of them nodded.

"We've got plenty of bunk rooms, and separate...um, facilities." He sounded...Lord, he sounded embarrassed. "What are your specialties?"

The token holder said, "Sonya and I are second-year grads, working on cognitive patterning."

Some of the hope drained from Rob's expression. "I know that's Gerry's big thing, but we're mostly doing hardware here." He looked at Dixie Mae.

"I'm into—" *go for it* "—bose condensates." Well, she knew how to pronounce the words. There were worried looks from the Ellens. But one of them piped up with, "She's on Satya's team at Georgia Tech."

It was wonderful what the smile did to Rob's face. His angry expression of a minute before was transformed into the look of a happy little boy on his way to Disneyland. "Really? I can't tell you what this means to us! I knew it had to be someone like Satya behind the new formulations. Were you in on that?"

"Oh yeah. Some of it, anyway." Dixie Mae figured that she couldn't say more than twenty words without blowing it. But what the heck, how many more minutes did the masquerade have to last, anyway? Little Victor and his self-terminating thread...

"That's great. We don't have budget for real equipment here, just simulators—"

Out of the corner of her eye, she saw the Ellens exchange a *fer sure* look.

"—so anyone who can explain the theory to me will be *so* welcome. I can't imagine how Satya managed to do so much, so fast, and without us knowing."

"Well, I'd be happy to explain everything I know about it."

Rob waved Danny boy away from the data display. "Sit down, sit down. I've got so many questions!"

Dixie Mae sauntered over to the desk and plunked herself down.

For maybe thirty seconds this guy would think she was brilliant.

The Ellens circled in to save her. "Actually, I'd like to know more about who we're working with," one of them said.

Rob looked up, distracted, but Danny was more than happy to do some intros. "It's just the two of us. You already know Rob Lusk. I'm Dan Eastland." He reached around, genially shaking hands. "I'm not from

UCLA. I work for LotsaTech, in quantum chemistry. But you know Gerry Reich. He's got pull everywhere—and I don't mind being shanghaied for a year. I need to, um, stay out of sight for a while."

"Oh!" Dixie Mae had read about this guy in *Newsweek*. And it had nothing to do with chemistry. "But you're—" *Dead*. Not a good sign at all, at all.

Danny didn't notice her distraction. "Rob's the guy with the real problem. Ever since I can remember, Gerry has used Rob as his personal hardware research department. Hey, I'm sorry, Rob. You know it's true."

Lusk waved him away. "Yes! So tell them how you're an even bigger fool!" He really wanted to get back to grilling Dixie Mae. Danny shrugged. "But now, Rob is just one year short of hitting his Seven Year Limit. Do you have that at Georgia Tech, Dixie Mae? If you haven't completed the doctorate in seven years, you get kicked out?"

"No, can't say as I've heard of that."

"Give thanks then, because since 2006 it's been an unbendable rule at UCLA. So when Gerry told Rob about this secret hardware contract he's got with LotsaTech—and promised that PhD in return for some new results—Rob jumped right in."

"Yeah, Danny. But he never told me how far Satya had gone. If I can't figure this stuff out, I'm screwed. Now let me talk to Dixie Mae!" He bent over the keyboard and brought up the most beautiful screen saver. Then Dixie Mae noticed little numbers in the colored contours and realized that maybe this was what she was supposed to be an expert on. Rob said, "I have plenty of documentation, Dixie Mae, too much. If you can just give me an idea how you scaled up the coherence." He waved at the picture. "That's almost a thousand liters of condensate, a trillion effective qubits. Even more fantastic, your group can keep it coherent for almost fifty seconds at a time."

NSA Ellen gave a whistle of pretended surprise. "Wow. What use could you have for all that power?"

Danny pointed at Ellen's badge. "You're the NSA wonk, Ellen, what do you think? Crypto, the final frontier of supercomputing! With even the weakest form of the Schor-Gershenfeld algorithm, Gerry can crack a ten kilobyte key in less than a millisecond. And I'll bet that's why he can't spare us any time on the real equipment. Night and day he's breaking keys and sucking in government money."

Grader Ellen—Sonya, that is—puckered up a naive expression. "What more does Gerry want?"

Danny spread his hands. "Some of it we don't even understand yet. Some of it is about what you'd expect: He wants a thousand thousand times more of everything. He wants to scale the operation by qulink so he can run arrays of thousand-liter bottles."

"And we've got just a year to improve on your results, Dixie Mae. But your solution is years ahead of the state of the art." Rob was pleading.

Danny's glib impress-the-girls manner faltered. For an instant he looked a little sad and embarrassed. "We'll get something, Rob. Don't worry."

"So, how long have you been here, Rob?" said Dixie Mae.

He looked up, maybe surprised by the tone of her voice.

"We just started. This is our first day."

Ah yes, that famous first day. In her twenty-four years, Dixie Mae had occasionally wondered whether there could be rage more intense than the red haze she saw when she started breaking things. Until today, she had never known. But yes, beyond the berserker-breaker there was something else. She did not sweep the display off the table, or bury her fist in anyone's face. She just sat there for a moment, feeling empty. She looked across at the twins. "I wanted some villains, but these guys are just victims. Worse, they're totally clueless! We're back where we started this morning." *Where we'll be again real soon now.*

"Hmmm. Maybe not." Speaking together, the twins sounded like some kind of perfect chorus. They looked around the room, eyeing the decor. Then their gaze snapped back to Rob. "You'd think LotsaTech would do better than this for you, Rob."

Lusk was staring at Dixie Mae. He gave an angry shrug. "This is the old Homeland Security lab under Norman Hall. Don't worry, we're isolated, but we have good lab and computer services."

"I'll bet. And what is your starting work date?"

"I just told you, today."

"No, I mean the calendar date."

Danny looked back and forth between them. "Jeez, are all you kids so literal minded? It's Monday, September 12, 2011."

Nine months. Nine real months. And maybe there was a *good* reason why this was the first day. Dixie Mae reached out to touch Rob's sleeve.

"The Georgia Tech people didn't invent the new hardware," she said softly.

"Then just who did make the breakthrough?"

She raised her hand...and tapped Rob deliberately on the chest.

Rob just looked more angry, but Danny's eyes widened. Danny got the point. She remembered that *Newsweek* article about him. Danny Eastland had been an all-around talented guy. He had blown the whistle on the biggest business espionage case of the decade. But he was dumb as dirt in some ways. If he hadn't been so eager to get laid, he wouldn't have snuck away from his Witness Protection bodyguards and gotten himself murdered.

"You guys are too much into hardware," said NSA Ellen. "Forget about crypto applications. Think about personality uploads. Given what you know about Gerry's current hardware, how many Reich Method uploads do you think the condensate could support?"

"How should I know? The 'Reich Method' was baloney. If he hadn't messed with the reviewers, those papers would never have been published." But the question stopped him. He thought for a moment. "Okay, if his bogus method really worked, then a trillion qubit simulation could support about ten thousand uploads."

The Ellens gave him a slow smile. A slow, identical smile. For once they made no effort to separate their identities. Their words came out simultaneously, the same pacing, the same pitch, a weird humming chorus: "Oh, a good deal less than ten thousand—if you have to support a decent enclosing reality." Each reached out her left hand with inhumanly synchronized precision, the precision of digital duplicates, to wave at the room and the hallway beyond. "Of course, some resources can be saved by using the same base pattern to drive separate threads—" and each pointed at herself.

Both men just stared at them for a second. Then Rob stumbled back into the other chair. "Oh. My. God."

Danny stared at the two for another few seconds. "All these years, we thought Gerry's theories were just a brilliant scam."

The Ellens stood with their eyes closed for a second. Then they seemed to startle awake. They looked at each other and Dixie Mae could tell the perfect synch had been broken. NSA Ellen took the dollar coin out of her pocket and gave it to the other. The token holder smiled at Rob. "Oh it was, only more brilliant and more of a scam than you ever dreamed."

"I wonder if Danny and I ever figure it out?"

"Somebody figured it out," said Dixie Mae, and waved what was left of her email.

The token holder was more specific: "Gerry is running us all like stateless servers. Some are on very short cycles. We think you're on a one-year cycle, probably running longer than anyone. You're making the discoveries that let Gerry create bigger and bigger systems."

"Okay," said Lusk, "suppose one of us victims guesses the secret? What can we do? We'll just get rebooted at the end of our run."

Danny Eastland was quicker. "There is something we could do. There has to be information passed between runs, at least if Gerry is using you and me to build on our earlier solutions. If in that data we could hide what we've secretly learned—"

The twins smiled. "Right! Cookies. If you could recover them reliably, then on each rev you could plan more and more elaborate countermeasures."

Rob Lusk still looked dazed. "We'd want to tip off the next generation early in their run."

"Yes, like the very first day!" Danny was looking at the three women and nodding to himself. "Only I still don't see how we managed that."

Rob pointed at Dixie Mae's email. "May I take a look at that?"

He laid it on the table, and he and Danny examined the message. The token holder said, "That email has turned out to have more clues than a bad detective story. Every time we're in a jam, we find the next hidden solution."

"That figures," said Eastland. "I'll bet it's been refined over many revs..."

"But we may have a special problem this time—" and Dixie Mae told them about Victor.

"Damn," said Danny.

Rob just shrugged. "Nothing we can do about that till we figure this out." He and Danny studied the headers. The token holder explained the parts that had already seen use. Finally, Rob leaned back in his chair. "The second-longest header looks like the tags on one of the raw data files that Gerry gave us."

"Yes," sang the twins. "What's really your own research from the last time around."

"Most of the files have to be what Gerry thinks, or else he'd catch onto us. But that one raw data file...assume it's really a cookie. Then this email header might be a crypto key."

Danny shook his head. "That's not credible, Rob. Gerry could do the same analysis."

The token holder laughed. "Only if he knew what to analyze. Maybe that's why you guys winkled it out to us. The message goes to Dixie Mae—an unrelated person in an unrelated part of the simulation."

"But how did we do it the *first* time?"

Rob didn't seem to be paying attention. He was typing in the header string from Dixie Mae's email. "Let's try it on the data file...." He paused, checked his keyboard entry, and pressed return. They stared at the screen. Seconds passed. The Ellens chatted back and forth. They seemed to be worried about executing any sort of text program; like Victor's notepad, it might be readable to the outside world. "That's a real risk unless earlier Robs knew the caching strategy."

Dixie Mae was only half-listening. If this worked at all it was pretty good proof that earlier Robs and Dannys had done things right.

If this works at all. Even after all that had happened, even after seeing Victor disappear into thin air, Dixie Mae still felt like a little girl waiting for magic she didn't quite believe in.

Danny gave a nervous laugh. "How big *is* this cookie?"

Rob leaned his elbows onto the table. "Yeah. How many times have I been through a desperate seventh year?" There was an edge to his voice. You could imagine him pulling one of those deathcube stunts that the Ellens had described.

And then the screen brightened. Golden letters marched across a black-and-crimson fractal pattern: "Hello fellow suckers! Welcome to the 1237th run of your life."

At first, Danny refused to believe they had spent 1236 years on Gerry's treadmill. Rob gave a shrug. "I *do* believe it. I always told Gerry that real progress took longer than theory-making. So the bastard gave me...all the time in the world."

The cookie was almost a million megabytes long. Much of that was detailed descriptions of trapdoors, backdoors, and softsecrets undermining the design that Rob and Danny had created for Gerry Reich.

But there were also thousands of megabytes of history and tactics, crafted and hyperlinked across more than a thousand simulated years. Most of it was the work of Danny and Rob, but there were the words of Ellen and Ellen and Dixie Mae, captured in those fleeting hours they spent with Rob and Danny. It was wisdom accumulated increment by precious increment, across cycles of near sameness. As such, it was their past and also their near future. It even contained speculations about the times before Rob and Danny got the cookie system working: Those earliest runs must have been in the summer of 2011, a single upload of Rob Lusk. Back then, the best hardware in the world couldn't have supported more than Rob all alone, in the equivalent of a one-room apartment, with a keyboard and data display. Maybe he had guessed the truth; even so, what could he have done about it? Cookies would have been much harder to pass in those times. But Rob's hardware improved from rev to rev, as Gerry Reich built on Rob's earlier genius. Danny came on board. Their first successful attempt at a cookie must have been one of many wild stabs in the dark, drunken theorizing on the last night of still another year where Rob had failed to make his deadlines and thought that he was forever PhD-less. The two had put an obscene message on the intrasystem email used for their "monthly" communications with Reich.

The address they had used for this random flail was...help@lotsatech.com.

In the real world, that must have been after June 15, 2012. Why?

Well, at the beginning of their next run, guess who showed up?

Dixie Mae Leigh. Mad as hell.

The message had ended up on Dixie Mae's work queue, and she had been sufficiently insulted to go raging off across the campus. Dixie Mae had spent the whole day bouncing from building to building, mostly making enemies. Not even Ellen or Ellen had been persuaded to come along. On the other hand, back in the early revs, the landscape reality had been simpler. Dixie Mae had been able to come into Rob's lair directly from the asphalt walkway.

Danny glanced at Dixie Mae. "And we can only guess how many times you never saw the email, or decided the random obscenities were not meant for you, or just walked in the wrong direction. Dumb luck eventually carried the day."

"Maybe. But I don't take to being insulted, and I go for the top."

Rob waved them both silent, never looking up from the cookie file. After their first success, Rob and Danny had fine-tuned the email, had learned more from each new Dixie Mae about who was in the other buildings on the hill and how—like the Ellens—they might be used.

"Victor!" Rob and the twins saw the reference at the same time.

Rob stopped the autoscroll and they studied the paragraph. "Yes. We've seen Victor before. And five revs ago, he actually made it as far as this time. He killed his thread then, too." Rob followed a link marked *taking care of Victor*. "Oh. Okay. Danny, we'll have to tweak the log files—"

They stayed almost three hours more. Too long maybe, but Rob and Danny wanted to hear everything the Ellens and Dixie Mae could tell them about the simulation, and who else they had seen. The cookie history showed that things were always changing, getting more elaborate, involving more money-making uses of people Gerry had uploaded. And they all wanted to keep talking. Except for poor Danny, the cookie said nothing about whether they still existed *outside*. In a way, knowing each other now was what kept them real.

Dixie Mae could tell that Danny felt that way, even when he complained: "It's just not safe having to contact unrelated people, depending on them to get the word to up here."

"So, Danny, you want the three of us to just run and run and never know the truth?"

"No, Dixie Mae, but this is dangerous for you too. As a matter of fact, in most of your runs, you stay clueless." He waved at the history. "We only see you once per each of our 'year-long' runs. I-I guess that's the best evidence that visiting us is risky."

The Ellens leaned forward, "Okay, then let's see how things would work without us." The four of them looked over the oldest history entries and argued jargon that meant nothing to Dixie Mae. It all added up to the fact that any local clues left in Rob's data would be easy for Gerry Reich to detect. On the other hand, messing with unused storage in the intranet mail system was possible, and it was much easier to cloak because the clues could be spread across several other projects.

The Ellens grinned. "So you really do need us, or at least you need Dixie Mae. But don't worry; we need you, and you have lots to do in your next year. During that time, you've got to make some credible progress with what Gerry wants. You saw what that is. Maybe you hardware types don't realize it, but"—she clicked on a link to the bulleted list of "minimum goals" that Reich had set for Rob and Danny—"Prof. Reich is asking you for system improvements that would make it easier to partition the projects. And see this stuff about selective decoherence: Ever hear of cognitive haze? I bet with this improvement, Reich could actually do limited meddling with uploaded brain state. That would eliminate date and memory inconsistencies. We might not even recognize cookie clues then!"

Danny looked at the list. "Controlled decoherence?" He followed the link through to an extended discussion. "I wondered what that was. We need to talk about this."

"Yes—wait! Two of us get rebooted in—my god, in thirty minutes." The Ellens looked at each other and then at Dixie Mae. Danny looked stricken, all his strategic analysis forgotten.

"But one of you Ellens is on a three-month cycle. She could stay here."

"Damn it, Danny! We just saw that there are checkpoints every sim day. If the NSA team were short a member for longer than that, we'd have a real problem."

Dixie Mae said, "Maybe we should all leave now, even us...short lifers. If we can get back to our buildings before reboot, it might look better."

"Yeah, you're right. I'm sorry," said Rob.

She got up and started toward the door. Getting back to Customer Support was the one last thing she could do to help.

Rob stopped her. "Dixie Mae, it would help if you'd leave us with a message to send to you next time."

She pulled the tattered printout from her pocket. The bottom was torn and smeared. "You must have the whole thing in the cookie."

"Still, it would be good to know what you think would work best to get...your attention. The history says that background details are gradually changing."

He stood up and gave her a little bow.

"Well, okay." Dixie Mae sat down and thought for a second. Yeah, even if she hadn't had the message memorized, she knew the sort of insults that would send her ballistic. This wasn't exactly time travel, but now she was certain who had known all the terrible secrets, who had known how to be absolutely insulting. "My daddy always said that I'm my own worst enemy."

Rob and Danny walked with them back to the vault door. This was all new to the two guys. Danny scrambled out of the pit, and stared bugeyed at the hills around them. "Rob, we could just walk to the other buildings!" He hesitated, came back to them. "And yeah, I know. If it were that easy, we'd have done it before. We gotta study that cookie, Rob."

Rob just nodded. He looked kind of sad—then noticed that Dixie Mae was looking at him—and gave her a quick smile. They stood for a moment under the late afternoon haze and listened to the wind. The air had cooled and the whole pit was in shadow now.

Time to go.

Dixie Mae gave Rob a smile and her hand. "Hey, Rob. Don't worry. I've spent years trying to become a nicer, wiser, less stubborn person. It never happened. Maybe it never will. I guess that's what we need now."

Rob took her hand. "It is, but I swear...it won't be an endless treadmill. We will study that cookie, and we'll design something better than what we have now."

"Yeah." *Be as stubborn as I am, pal.*

Rob and Dan shook hands all around, wishing them well. "Okay," said Danny, "best be off with you. Rob, we should shut the door and get back. I saw some references in the cookie. If they get rebooted before they reach their places, there are some things we can do."

"Yeah," said Rob. But the two didn't move immediately from the entrance. Dixie Mae and the twins scrambled out of the pit and walked toward the asphalt. When Dixie Mae looked back, the two guys were still standing there. She gave a little wave, and then they were hidden by the edge of the excavation.

The three trudged along, the Ellens a lot less bubbly than usual. "Don't worry," NSA Ellen said to her twin, "there's still two months on the B0994 timeline. I'll remember for both of us. Maybe I can do some good on that team."

"Yeah," said the other, also sounding down. Then abruptly they both gave one of those identical laughs and they were smiling. "Hey, I just thought of something. True re-merge may always be impossible, but what we have here is almost a kind of merge load. Maybe, maybe—" but their last chance on this turn of the wheel was gone. They looked at Dixie Mae and all three were sad again. "Wish we had more time to think how we wanted this to turn out. This won't be like the sf stories where every rev you wake up filled with forebodings and subconscious knowledge. We'll start out all fresh."

Dixie Mae nodded. Starting out fresh. For dozens of runs to come where there would be nothing after that first week at Customer Support, and putting up with boorish Victor, and never knowing. And then she smiled. "But every time we get through to Dan and Rob, we leave a little more. Every time they see us, they have a year to think. And it's all happening a thousand times faster than Ol' Gerry can think. We really are the cookie monsters. And someday—"

Someday we'll be coming for you, Gerry. And it will be sooner than you can dream.

Justina Robson (b. 1968) studied philosophy and linguistics at the University of York before attending the Clarion West Writers Workshop and publishing her first story in 1994. Her novels have been short-listed numerous times for the British Science Fiction Award, the Arthur C. Clarke Award, and the John W. Campbell Award. In Robson's capable hands what begins as a futuristic crime scene investigation by a grieving father and a mysterious posthuman evolves into something far stranger, and more moving.

CRACKLEGRACKLE
> Justina Robson

Many times Mark Bishop read the assignment, but it never made more sense to him. He was to interview the Greenjack Hyperion, make an assessment of the claims made for it, and return his report. That part was simple. But after it, the evidence supplied by the Forged and human witnesses...this he couldn't manage more than a line or two of. Panic rose and the black and white print became an unknown language. He could see it hadn't changed, but simply by moving his eyes across it his mind redshifted and all meaning sped away from him.

He poured the one-too-many scotch from the concession bottle by his elbow just as the hostess was about to whisk it away, and drank it down. The burn was impersonal and direct. It did exactly what it always promised, and shot the pain where it hurt. He rubbed his eyes and tried again.

He disliked the sight of the document on his screen. It struck him suddenly that the paragraphs were too long. The white spaces between them loomed in violent stripes, their blank inlets holding the truth that the print failed to express. The punctuation was a taunt, an assault in black and white that proved the text's defeat of his reason was absolute. Even the title was loathsome: Making A Case For The Intuitive Interpretation Of Full Spectrum Data In Unique Generative Posthuman Experience. Usually he had no bother with jargon, or any scientific melee, but what the hell did that mean? What did it mean to the person it referred to? Had they titled it or was it just the bureaucrat's pedantic label for something they could read but not comprehend?

A final slug of scotch ended his attempt. He only understood that there was no escape from meeting the Greenjack, as he had promised, as his job demanded: meet, interview, assess, report. That was all. It was easy. He'd done it a hundred times. More. He was an expert. That's why the government had hired him and kept him on the top payroll all these years. They trusted him to judge rightly, to know truth, to detect mistakes and delusions, to be sure.

Bishop tried to read the document once more. His eyes hurt and finally, after a forced march across the first few paragraphs, he felt a cluster headache come on and halt them with a fierce spasm of pain as if something had decided to drill invisible holes into his head via the back of his eyeballs. He lay back in the recline seat of the lift launcher and closed his eyes. The attendants circled and took away his cup, secured his harness and spoke pleasantly about the safety of the orbital lift system and the experience of several gs of force during acceleration—a song and dance routine he already knew so well he could have done it himself. He briefly remembered being offered a ride up on one of the Heavy Angels, explaining he didn't want it to the secretary. She couldn't understand his reluctance. Then in the background she heard some colleague whisper, "Mars." She'd gone red, then white.

But it wasn't just the difficulty of talking to the Forged now, he'd never liked the idea of being inside a body. It was too much like being eaten, or some form of unwilling sex. So he'd made his economy-excuse, a polite no, a don't-want-to-be-a-bother smile and now he was waiting for take-off, no time left, unprepared for the big meeting, his mouth dry with all the things he'd taken to avoid doing anything repulsively human, like being sick.

The lift was moved into position by its waldos, attached to the cable, tested. The slight technicalities passed him in a blur of nauseating detail and then there was the stomach-leaving, spine-shrinking hurl of acceleration in the back of his legs. The headache peaked. Weightlessness came as they soared above the clouds into the blue and then the black. He felt like lead. When the time came to unclip and get out he half expected that he'd be set in position, a statue, and surprised himself by seeing his hands reach out and competently move him along the guiderails. He didn't hit anyone. The other passengers were all busy talking to each other or into their mikes. Then the smell filled his nostrils.

It was a mysterious animal tang that reminded him of the hot hides of horses, a drooling, dozing camel he had once attempted to ride, and on top of that, the ocean. Bishop gripped on tight, knowing that all his juvenile, ancient spine-root superstitions had caught up with him. His interviewee had come to meet him in an act of unwanted courtesy. He would have to greet and speak to it...why had he forgotten its name suddenly? Why did it have to smell like that? But he was now holding up the queue. The stewardess mistook his hesitation for ignorance and started talking about freefall walking. All that remained was to turn himself towards the smooth, white-lit exit chute that led to the Offworld Destinations Lounge, and follow that telltale scent of primeval beast.

The other passengers sniffed curiously as they passed him, "so-sorrying" their way around his stalled self. He fiddled with his recorder, checking his microphone and switching everything on. It made him feel secure in the same way he imagined old world spies had once felt secure by their illicit link to someone somewhere who would at least hear their final moments. It wasn't exactly like being accompanied, but it was enough of a shield to let the prickling under his arms stop and for his headache to recede.

The thought came to him that he hadn't been himself lately. It was only natural after the conclusion of the enquiry and its open verdict. Too much stress. He ought to stop, cry off, take a holiday. Nobody would be surprised. But the thought of not having his job, the idea of having nothing to do but walk the familiar coast near Pismo Beach or under the tall silence of the redwoods—that made him pull himself along all the faster to escape the hum, the static darkness, the horror that was waiting there for him, that was already here in the notion of that place. He gritted his teeth and pushed that aside. The scotch made it easy. Why the hell hadn't he thought to bring some more?

He pulled himself forward into the glide that felt graceful even when it wasn't and swallowed with difficulty. That smell! It was so curious here, where all the smells were ground out of existence quickly in the filtration of the dry air so that humans and their descendants, the Forged, could meet without the animal startle reflexes scent caused the humans. But the grace would only last a minute or two here, in the neutral zone of the Lift Centre. And why could he smell this one so clearly? It must reek—and as he thought this he saw it/him, a tall, gangling, ugly creature that resembled a gargoyle from some mighty gothic cathedral whose creator had been keen on all the Old Testamentary virtues. It could easily have featured in his nightmares. He wouldn't have been surprised to discover that it had been modelled with an artistic eye to that fact. The Pangenesis Tupac, brooder, sculptor, creator in flesh and metal, enjoyed her humour at all levels of creation. The word anathema sat in his head, alone, as he bravely put on a smile of greeting.

"Mark Bishop?" said the gargoyle in an old English gentleman's voice, as fitting and unexpected as rain in Death Valley.

"I am." He found conviction, was so glad the other didn't offer his hand and glanced down and saw it was a fistful of claws.

"My name is Hyperion. I am pleased to meet you. I have read many of your articles in the more popular academic journals and the ordinary press. Your reputation is well founded." It made a slight bow and the harsh interior lights shone off its bony eyelids.

It was shamefully difficult not to marvel at the sight and sound of a talking gryphon-thing or want to see if those yellow eyes were real. Hyperion's voice seemed to indicate enjoyment, but who knew, with the Forged? Mark, ashamed of his hatred, gushed, "Forgive me, I'm having a lot of trouble with this assignment. I don't believe in the supernatural and..."

"...and you are nervous around the Forged. Most humans are, and pretend not. You have always been clear about your limitations in your previous work. I am not deterred. You have come this far. Let us complete the journey." Feathers rustled on it. Its face was scaled, beaked. How it managed speech was beyond him, and yet it spoke remarkably well. But parrots did, Bishop reasoned, so why not this?

It took him almost a minute to understand what it'd said, not because it was unclear, but because he was so confused by the storm of feeling inside himself. Repulsion, aggression, fear. The stink, he realised at last with a shock of guilt, was himself.

Hyperion took hold of the guiderails delicately and spun itself away, tail trailing like a kite's. Its comfort with weightlessness spoke of many years spent there, in the cramped airlocks and crabbed tunnels of the old stations. In its wake Bishop followed, slipping, and after a too brief eternity found himself at the entrance hatch that looked entirely machine though there was no disguising the chitinous interior into which he was able to peer and see seats of the strange kind made for space travel—ball-like concoctions of soft stuff that moved against tethers and into which one had to crawl like a mouse into a nest. He made himself concentrate only on mechanics, move a hand, a foot, that's all—it was the only thing that kept his control of himself intact.

Of course it was Forged. The only machines that travelled the length of the system were robotically controlled cargo carriers whose glacial pace was utterly unsuitable for this trip or most any other if you didn't have half a lifetime to spare. For local traffic to the moon and the various towed-in asteroids that had been clustered nearby to form the awkward mineral suburb of Rolling Rock, all travel was undertaken in the purpose-built, ur-human creatures of the Flight. Every last one of them was a speed freak.

"Ironhorse Alacrity Valhalla has agreed to take us to our location." Hyperion made the introduction as he waited for Bishop to precede him into the dimly lit interior chitoblast and become a helpless parasite inside a being he couldn't even see or identify but which had a mind, apparently rather like his own, only connected by the telepathy of contemporary electronic signalling to every other Forged mind whereas he was quite alone. He checked his mike and gave Hyperion a sickly smile that he had intended to be professional and cheering. The creature blinked at him slowly, quite relaxed, and he saw that it had extraordinary eyes. They were large, as large as his fist in its big head, but beyond the clear, wet sclera lay an iris so complex and dazzling...another blink brought him to his senses. Yellow eyes. It was demonic. What idiot had made them that colour?

He was able to manage quite well and put himself into the seatsack without any foolish struggling or tangles even though now he was feeling slightly drunk. Cocooned next to each other they were able to see one another's heads easily. Stuck to the side of each sack a refreshment package waited. Within the slings toilet apparatus was easy to find. There was a screen in the ceiling, if it was the ceiling—without gravity it hardly mattered—showing some pleasant views of pastoral Earth scenes, like a holiday brochure. Bishop figured it was for his benefit and tried to be comforted as a Hawaiian beach glowed azure at him, surrounded by thick, fleshy webbing that pulsed slightly in erratic measure.

Common lore said it was all right for old humans not to attempt talking to their host carrier at this point. The gargoyle could have been rabbitting on to the ship all the time of course, there was no knowing. His mind fussed around what they might say. It blurred hopelessly as he attempted to drag up anything about the task at hand. He couldn't bring any thought into focus long enough to articulate it.

The door sealed up behind them and was immediately lost in the strange texture of the wall. There were no ports. He wouldn't be seeing the stars unless the Alacrity wanted to show him images from outside on the holiday channel.

"Where are we going?" he asked, though it had been in the damn notes.

"To the spot you requested," Hyperion said with some puzzlement. "Don't you recall?" Bishop flushed hot with embarrassment, started sweating all over again. He didn't remember. Then there was a vague hint that he might have made a call, no, written a request, a secret note... had he? He checked the screen inventory of his mail. Nothing. Inside the cocoon of the webbing he experienced a stab of shocking acuteness in the region of his guts and heart. He felt he was losing his mind and that it was paying him back with this lance, this polearm of pure fear. What had he requested?

"No." He wanted to lie but his mouth wouldn't do it.

The Greenjack was quiet for a moment. "I think that we should talk a little on the way there, Mr Bishop, if you don't mind." Its voice was gentle now, and had a rounded, richness that reminded Bishop of leather chairs, wood panelling, pipe tobacco, twilight and cognac. Above the line of the cocoon he could see its feet twitched gently, flexed their strangely padded digits. Dark claws, blunted from walking, were just visible. "I am well aware of the way my claims must appear to scientists such as yourself. Energies beyond human perception existing within our own spacetime perhaps is not too outlandish in itself. But my observations of their behaviour, and what it seems to mean for their interactions with us, that is the stuff of late-night stories. Believe me, Mr Bishop, I have studied them for many years before making these statements. And I would welcome any remarks."

Charlatan, Bishop thought. Must he. He'd thought it from the get go, when he first read about it.

Bishop had been in doubt on other assignments, though none of them like this one. Mostly he wrote for journals about science or current affairs based on Earth. He was one of the more popular and able writers who could turn complicated and difficult notions into the kind of thing that most well-educated people could digest with breakfast. Normally he avoided all discussions about the Forged and their politics, but of course it had caught up with him as it must with everyone in the end, he reasoned. And his expertise had led to him being selected by the government to come and make a judgement out here about this odd person and its extraordinary claims, its illegal and incomprehensible existence. The Greenjack Cylenchar Hyperion was a member of a class created by the Forged themselves, by the Motherfather, Tupac, whose vast body had bred all the spacefarers and most of the Gravity Bound. It was a class she claimed was scientifically essential, though he had serious doubts. The Greenjacks were there to confront the boundaries of the perceivable universe, and to try and apprehend what to ordinary human eyes was beyond sight. Hyperion, in particular, was said to be able to perceive every frequency there was, and had been given adaptations to allow his mind to be able to cope with the information. Hyperion didn't just see, he watched. Recently he'd been making dramatic claims about his visions that had been in all the papers.

Bishop struggled but the panic was choking, he wasn't able to say the sensible thing he had in mind, namely, "Yes, but just because you can detect these things, why aren't they verified by machines?"

The Greenjack paused, just the length of time it would have taken him to make this reply, and added, "Machine verification has confirmed erratic frequency fluctuations in localised areas, but obviously they can't put an interpretation on these anomalies. We have successfully managed to get some mappings of areas and frequency variations that confirm my own sensory perceptions are accurate."

This was news. Bishop jerked as his screen recovered the files being zapped across to it and vibrated to alert him—all the data was there, already witnessed and verified by independent bodies... He felt himself breathing steadily. The scotch seemed to have made it out of his stomach. The pills he'd taken still worked hard on fooling his head it knew which way was up. Better, that was better. Statistics. Facts. Good.

"But if you are too distressed we can delay this," the Cylenchar said suddenly. "Mr Bishop?"

"No, we have to go." He didn't know where they had to go though apparently he was determined. His panic returned.

"May I speak frankly?"

Into Bishop's agonised silence Hyperion said clearly, "I think you have asked me to go to Mars because of your daughter. You are hoping that I will be able to find her where the inquest has failed. Is that right?"

A cold drench covered him from head to foot as memory returned, cold, clear. He couldn't breathe. He was drowning. Mars. Tabitha. The unsolved mystery of the routine survey expedition vanishing without trace. Oh a sandstorm, a dust ocean, a flood of sand, a mighty sirocco that blew them away...what had it been and where was she? Nobody could answer. Not even the equipment returned a ping. But how? And when the months dragged on and the company pulled out and sent its condolences and added their names to the long list of people who'd gone missing on Mars during the fierce years of its terraforming and then this assignment came, what else to do? Bring the person who, above all, had been made to see. No frequency, no signal, no energy that the Greenjacks can't decipher...of course, if she's there...and if she's dead, then this one will say so. It claims that some of the things it can sense aren't people but are what people leave or make somehow in the unseen fields they move in; trails and marks. It says some are like wizards of story, able to make things with shape, with form, with intent that is almost conscious. Some can leave memories like prints on the empty air. Oh. But a man of strict science does not believe.

"Yes." Bishop said. He was small then, in his mouse nest, hanging, damp and suddenly getting the chills. He was afraid the 'jack would say no.

"I will be glad to look," it says instead and Mark Bishop fell into a deep sleep on the spot.

Sleep was one of the many skills the 'jack had learned in its long years of waiting for things that might not appear. It closed its eyes and shared a warm goodnight with Valhalla, who was more than curious to know the outcome now and sings towards the red world with fire and all the winds of the sun.

They joined one another in a shared interior space, a private dreamtime. It was cosy. Valhalla whispered, "Sometimes I am flying in the sunlight and there is nothing there but I feel a cold, a call, a kind of falling. Is that real? Are the monsters from under the bed out at sea too?"

"Wake me if it happens," Hyperion said. "And we'll see."

He co-created a kind romance with Valhalla in which they saw huge floating algal swarms of deep colour and shadow populate the fathoms beyond the stars. They named them in whispers, and with childish fingers measured their shapes in the sky, and then pinched them out of existence, snuff, snuff, snuff.

"There," Hyperion said, "they may be here, but they have no power. They can only hurt you if you let them. They live in the holes of the mind, and eat the spirit. Cracklegrackle. Just pinch them out." They got back into bed and closed the window, drew the shades. The Valhalla was happy again and drove on all the faster in his sleep.

Bishop was woken by the Valhalla's cheerful cry, "Mars!" The Ironhorse made orbit and scanned the surface to find the small outpost where the Gaiaform Nikkal Raven, chief developer of Mars, had built human-scale shelter with its Hands in the lee of a high cliff. "Nobody's there now. If it's a graveyard or a ghost town it's empty for sure but with a bit of effort there's probably power and some basics that you could get going." For politeness they contacted the Gaiaform.

"That's funny," Valhalla said, as Bishop struggled to change his clothes. "She sounds annoyed, or at least, she doesn't want to discuss the place."

The Nikkal's voice was grumpy on the intercom. She grated on Bishop's exposed nerves and wore out his fragile strip of patience almost at once. "My Hands got lost there too. Given up sending more. Thought I'd get to it later, after the planting on the south faces was finished. Just a minor space really, full of gullies."

They all recognised the feeling this rationale covered. "We don't need your help," Bishop grated. "Just want to get there and look around. That's all."

"But if anything happens it's on my watch," the Nikkal countered.

"Tupac knows we're here," Hyperion suggested. "We won't stay long. A day at the most."

"...as long as it takes..." Bishop said. He was in clean clothes. His panics were gone. He felt old and thin and shelterless and looked around for something he could hold. He found only his small bag and his recorder and filled his hands with them. A panic would have been welcome. Their fury was better than this deadly flat feeling that had taken their place. It was clear now. He was here, Thorson's Gullies, the last known location. Every step was a puppet step his body took at the behest of some will named Mark that wouldn't let it rest but there was no more struggle between them. He did not inhabit these arms, these legs, he felt. They were his waldos, his servos, they were his method. Only his guts were still his own, a liquid concentration waiting for a mould.

"Come on, Mark," Hyperion called from the drop capsule.

Since when had they become friends? Bishop didn't know how but he climbed inside the small fruit shape of the vehicle. Mars had lift cable, but no system in place. Cargo was simply clipped on and set going under whatever power it was able to muster. They were attached to the line and given a good shove by Valhalla. The new atmosphere buffeted them, warmed them, cooked them almost, and then they were down, Bishop still surprised, still too frozen to even be sick with either motion nausea or relief at their arrival. The capsule detached, put out its six wheeled legs like a bored insect and began to trundle the prescribed steady course towards the gullies. Hyperion opened the ventilation system and they sniffed the Martian air. It was thin and even though it had been filtered a million ways, somehow gritty.

"...it's the names that are part of the trouble," Bishop said, staring out at the peculiar sight of Mars' tundra, red ochre studded with the teal green puffs of growing things in regular patterns. "Good and Evil. Why did you call them that?"

"There are more," Hyperion said. "There is Eater and Biter and Poison and Power and Luck and Fortune and Beneficence and the Cracklegrackle. I expect there are many more. But these are the commonest major sorts."

"But why? Couldn't you name them Energy #1 and so forth?"

"I could, but that wouldn't be accurate. Their names are what they are."

"How they seem to you. The one person who can see them."

"That's not exactly right. I think we can all perceive them, but only I can see them as easily as I can see you."

"And you say they are everywhere."

"Scattered, but everywhere in known space, I think."

"And some are spontaneous but others are manmade?"

"Yes. Few of the major arcana are manmade, like those. It takes a very powerful person to create one. Or a large group of people. There are many manmade minor arcana and many naturally occurring ones like that but they are very shortlived, a day or two at most."

"You see my problem is that I can believe in this kind of thing at a symbolic level, within the human world, acting at large and small scales. We're creatures of symbolic meaning. But you're saying there's physical stuff and it's real, external, distinct."

"Yes. I am saying it exists as patterns within the same energy fields that give rise to matter."

"Consciousness is material?"

"No. It has a material interaction that is more than simply the building of a house from a plan or the singing of a song, is what I am saying."

"And these things...patterns...can influence people?"

"Influence them, infect them, live inside them, alter them perhaps. Yes, I think so." The creature stared at him for the longest time, unblinking. "Yes."

"And just like that we are expected to accept this—theory of material mind?"

Hyperion shrugged as if he didn't much care either way. "I report what I see, but I say what it is for me. Otherwise I would report nothing more than machines can report. When you look at a landscape you don't list a bunch of coordinates and say they are mid-green, then another list grey, another list white and so on. You say I see a hill with some trees, a river, a house in the distance."

"But you're making claims about the nature of this stuff, linking it to subjective values. Hills aren't subjective."

"They are. True, there is some rock that exists independently of you, some sand, some dust, but without you it is no hill and however the hill seems is how all hills seem to you, large or small, not mountains, not flat, perhaps even with traits that are more personal. If your home is among the hills then they seem well known, if not, then they provoke suspicion."

They were trundling at high speed, balanced in their gyrobody between the capsule's six legs, seeming to float like thistledown between the rocks of this region of Mars: Thorson's Plot. Plot was something of a misnomer as the area, already claimed by an Earth corporate, was some fifteen thousand square miles. The gullies, which made it a cheaper piece of real estate, and complicated to sow—hence the surveying team—were near the western edge and ran in a broad scar north-south along the lines of the mapping system. Thorsons had hoped to find watery deposits deep in the gullies or perhaps some useful mineral or who knows what down in the cracked gulches where twisting runnels of rock hid large areas from the sun and most of the wind, which had scoured the planet for millennia. All around them were hills of varying sizes, some no more than dunes, others rising with rugged defiance in scarps and screes. Occasionally small pieces of metal flashed the sunlight back at them as they moved between light and the shade of the thin, high cloud that now streaked the sky white.

"The remains of Hands," the Greenjack said with interest, of course able to tell what everything was at any distance. "How interesting. And there is some debris from attempts to seed here, some markers, some water catchers. All wrecked. And..."

"And?" Bishop leapt on the hesitation.

"What I would call distress residue. A taint in the energy, very slight."

"What energy?"

"The subtle fields. You will find them referenced a great deal in my submitted thesis. Vibrationary levels where human perception is infrequently able, or not able at all. When trauma occurs bursts of energy are thrown off the distressed person into these fields and although they decay quite rapidly they leave a trace pattern behind which is very slow to change."

"A disturbance in the Force," Bishop said bitterly. He felt nothing except the dread which had clutched at him in place of his panic.

"It might be only the natural upset of someone experiencing an unlucky accident," Hyperion said, unruffled. "It's hard to say without extreme observation and immersion on the site. You ought to be glad, Mr Bishop, rather than contemptuous. Why else are you here?"

Mark gripped the arms of his seat. He was furious and full of nervous agitation. He ought to be civil, but he felt the need to destroy this creature's claims even as he wanted them to be right for his own sake. He didn't want to know about some spiritual plane, not after all this time it had taken to rid the human race of its destructive superstitions. Even if it existed, what difference did it make to those who were, in the shaman's own words, unable to interact with it. He could see no good coming of it. But he longed for it to be true. Somewhere in his fevered mind where fragments of the shaman's testimony had lodged in spite of his allergic reaction to reading them, he recalled there being quite specific traces of people and moments stuck in this peculiar aether like flies in amber. Not always, not everywhere, but sometime and somewhere it acted as a recorder for incidents and individuals. It could. It might have.

The capsule lurched to a halt. They had arrived at the last known point of the survey team's wellbeing. A couple of waymarkers and a discarded, empty water canister pegged down beside them were the only visible remnants now. Without further talk Hyperion and Bishop disembarked.

They fitted their facemasks—the air was still too thin for comfort— and Bishop put on his thin wind jacket and new desert boots. Hyperion sank a little in the fine grit on his four limbs but otherwise he went as always, naked save for his fur, feathers, scales and quills.

Wrestling the faceplate straps to get a good fit Bishop noticed all the strange little fetishes the creature had attached. Necklaces with bits of twig and bone...it looked like it had come off the set of a voodoo movie. He recalled now it labelled its profession on its passport "shaman." He was so exhausted by his nervous disorders, however, that he didn't have the energy to muster a really negative response anymore. He was deadening to it. At last the mask was tested and his spare oxygen packs fitted to the bodysuit that went over his clothes. Hyperion wore goggles and a kind of nosebag over his beak. He made a desultory symbol in the dust and smoothed it out again with one forepaw. The capsule, obeying commands from its uplink with Valhalla, folded up its spider legs and nestled down in a small hollow, lights dimming to a gleam as it moved into standby operation. All around and as far as he could see in any direction, save for the shaman, Bishop was alone.

"There are very few true disappearances in human history, these days," Hyperion said after a moment when they both cast about in search of a direction. It moved closer to one of the markers and read the tags left there. "And this is not an unusual place, like those twisty spaces close to black holes for example. It is just a planet with a regular geology. The common assumption about this team's fate is that they absconded with the help of the Nikkal. From there a number of possible avenues continue, most leading to the far system frontiers where they were able to drop off the networks."

Bishop licked his lips, already starting to crack. The news was full of the asteroid bayous beyond the sphere of Earth's police influence and the renegade technology that festered there, unregulated. There was a lot of Unity activity. A lot of illegal, unethical, criminal work. "She had no reason to go."

"Perhaps not, but if the rest of them wanted to go they could hardly leave her behind. What would be easier for you, Mr Bishop, to have her forcibly made into one of the Frontiersmen or to have her dead here somewhere?"

How odd, he thought, that the 'jack had no trouble voicing what inhabited his own awareness as a black hum beyond reckoning. Hearing the words aloud was startling, but it diminished the power of the awful feelings that gripped him inside.

"Let's start looking," Bishop said, standing still. All around them their small dip radiated gullies that twisted and wound. The sun was beginning to go down and the high rocky outcrops cast sharp-edged purple shadows.

Hyperion was exacting, his research both instantaneous and meticulous in a way that made Bishop simply envious. "The marker, as the police report indicates, says they started southwest with a view to making a loop trail back here within a six-hour period; the route is marked in the statutory map." The shaman sniffed and the nosebag huffed. "All the searches have concentrated on following this route and found a scatter of personal belongings and the remains of a Finger of the Terraform, which was carrying the survey equipment. All of that was recovered intact." It held the two windbeaten tags in its paw and rubbed them for a short time, thoughtfully. "But they did not go that way. Only the Finger took the trail."

"How do you know?"

Hyperion turned. "I can see it. I think it is time I showed you." It came across to him and held out one large, scaly arm. "Please, your screen viewer. I will adapt it to show some of the details I can see over its normal camera range. This will not be what I see, you understand, as I don't see it with my eyes. But it is the best I can do for you."

Reluctantly Bishop handed over the precious viewer. It was his recorder too. His everything. "Don't mess up the record settings. It's on now."

The Greenjack inclined its head politely and slid one of its broad clawlike nails into one of the old style input ports. Bishop felt a chill. He'd never get used to how able the Forged were with technology. They could interface directly with any machine.

"The signals I use to communicate with the device will cause some interference with my tracking," Hyperion said calmly. "So I will not use it all the time. If you see nothing, you may assume I am watching and listening. I will also shut the device down if its working interferes with the process and I may ask you to move away at times." It handed the screen back and Bishop checked it, panning it around in front of him. The camera showed whatever he pointed it at, recording diligently; it was really just like holding a picture frame up over the landscape. "I don't see anything."

"Look at the markers and the route."

He turned. From the tag line he could now see a strange kind of colouration in the air, like points of deep shade. They were small. It was really almost like broken pixellation.

"That is the pattern left by the output of the Finger's microreactor projecting microbursts of decaying particles into the energy field. Radiation containment is generally good these days, so this is all you can find. It is also in the standard police procedurals. They mistakenly assumed it confirmed that all the travellers took the same path since the Finger was carrying all the technical equipment and the others had only their masks and gas, their personal refreshments and devices. I would say it is certain that they intended to disappear here as in fact all their individual communications gear has been accounted for along the Finger's trail."

Like a path cut with three-dimensional leaf shadows the trail wound into the first gully, followed the obvious way along it and vanished around the first turn.

"We can follow that and verify there was no other person with the Finger if you like," the shaman suggested.

"Parts of a Forged internal device unit were found," Bishop said, brain clicking in at last.

Hyperion shrugged.

"Or?" Bishop started to pan around. He soon found patches and bursts of odd colour washes everywhere, as if his screen were subject to a random painting class.

"Or we can follow the others and find out what they did, starting here."

"What is all this?"

"This is energy field debris."

As he moved around Bishop could see there was a huge glut of the stuff where they were but traces of it were everywhere in fact, even in the distance. "Why so much of it?"

"There was a lot of activity here. The rest is down to regular cosmic interference or perhaps...I am not actually sure what all of it is. The energy fields transect time and space but they are linked to it so while some of this is attached to the planet's energy sphere, some of it, as you see, is moving."

Streaks shot across the screen. A readout indicated he was not seeing them in real time, as that would have been too fast for him to notice. The simulation and the reality overlaid each other on the image however, and the difference there was undetectable.

"I believe the streaks are bonded to the spatial field, and they are therefore stationary relative to absolute coordinates in space, thus as Mars traverses, so these things pass through." The creature cocked its head, a model of intellectual speculation.

Bishop relaxed his tired arms so the screen pointed at the ground, saw the streaks shooting through his feet. "Through us?"

Hyperion nodded. "As with much cosmic ray debris. It moves too fast for me to say anything about it. I would need to move out into deep space and be on a relatively static vessel, in order to discover more about them."

"No such ship exists," Bishop snorted. "Well, only..."

"Yes, only a Unity ship perhaps," the shaman said. "I shall ask for one soon."

They shared a moment of silence in which the subject of Unity, the newly discovered alien technology, rose and passed without further comment. Bishop would have loved to go into it at any other time. The surge of hysteria it had engendered had almost died down nowadays, with it being limited to offworld, restricted use, or far enough away from Earth and her concerns that it wasn't important to most humans,

whatever strange features it possessed. FTL drives were only the half of
it, or whatever they were. It was under review. He'd seen some of the
evidence. Now he let it go and lifted the screen again. If Tabitha had gone
on one of those ships, she could be anywhere. It would take years to
get into Forged Space by ordinary means. Even an Ironhorse Accelerator
couldn't go faster. She could have been there since the day it happened,
almost a year ago. "This is just a mess."

"No," Hyperion said. He lowered his head and sniffed again, a hellish
kind of hound. "There were four individuals here, all human, and one
Forged, Wayfarer Jackalope McKnight."

"Bread Zee Davis, Bancroft Wan, Kialee Yang..." Bishop said, the names
so often in his mind that they came off his tongue like an old catechism.

"...and Tabitha Bishop."

"I am sure which is the Forged," Hyperion said, "but the humans are
harder to label. They are distinct however."

"They'd worked together almost a year," Bishop said, wishing he'd
kept his silence but it was leaking. "No trouble. She sent me a postcard."

"May I see it?"

He hesitated, then fiddled the controls and handed over the screen. It
had been shown so often during the inquest he knew every millimetre of
it better than he knew the lines in his own hand.

The object was small, almost really postcard sized in the Greenjack's
heavy paw. "Kialee is the Han girl, I am guessing."

"And Wan is the one with the black Mohawk. Davis is the wannabe
soldier in all that ex-military stuff." He knew every detail of that postcard.
What most mystified him about it was how friendly they all seemed, how
relaxed, the girls leaning on each other, the guys making silly faces, beer
in hand, around them the dull red of the tenting and in the background
a portable generator and jumble of oxygen tanks. It could have been a
holiday for two couples and not students on work assignment. He wasn't
sure if they'd been dating or if dating was a concept that had gone out
with dinosaurs like him.

The Greenjack was stock still. It looked intently and then handed
back the screen. "Thank you. In that case I can now say that there was a
struggle here. Bishop and Yang are surprised but Davis and Wan are both
agitated throughout. Only McKnight is calm."

"He was new. Newish. Their old Wayfarer went to another job."

The colours illumined as the shaman talked, showing Bishop warped fields of light that were as abstract as any randomly generated image. "McKnight and the men remain close together. There is a conflict with the women. There is a struggle, I think at this point the women are forced to give up their personal devices to Terraform Raven's Finger. I believe they are tied, at least at the hands. McKnight is armed with explosive charges for the survey. But he's also more than big enough to overpower and threaten them. I guess this is what happened. Davis and Wan dislike the events a great deal but they are willing participants. That's what I see. Then there's another argument, here, the men and McKnight. It's brief. Blood and flesh scraps from McKnight are found near here."

Bishop saw the oddest nebula of greys, streaked with black and bright red. "They said there was some kind of struggle...the Wayfarer was defending..." But the gargoyle shaman was shaking its head.

"He cuts out his own external comms unit," Hyperion said precisely. "In the Wayfarer this is located at the back of the skull and embedded in the surface beneath a minor chitinous plate. To remove it would be painful and messy, but it is perfectly possible and certainly not lethal. But all communication is cut before this so there is no official account of how it was removed. The only person who can account for that is Raven and she claims there was a local network dropout. I would have to question her directly to be sure of her account." The implication was stark.

The air, already bitter, felt suddenly colder. "So Davis and Wan made him do it?"

"I cannot say for certain. But he does it. Any other method risks it being hijacked by signals that would give away his position. He's hidden it somewhere around here I'd bet. Or given it to the Finger who lost it in the gullies way before it signalled a breakdown. We should look for it. Then they leave." Hyperion pointed northwest. "That way."

Bishop thought of the evidence of the Finger's call. Raven's voice said, "They've gone. Just gone." And in that phrase she'd ushered in an entire cult of people convinced Mars harboured ghosts, or aliens, or fiends. As if their numbers needed adding to. But Bishop couldn't keep up his anger. The pictures continued.

There was a faint colouration like a long tunnel or a tube made of the faintest streaks of yellow, grey and ashy white. It was almost pretty against the deepening red of the Martian afternoon. The tunnel down which Tabitha had vanished. So the shaman said.

"I hardly know anything about these people," Bishop protested with distress. He didn't understand how the creature drew its conclusions.

"It is all right, Mr Bishop," the shaman said calmly, setting off in this new direction. "I know everything about them that I need."

For the first time in time that he can remember lately, Mark Bishop has enough energy to hurry in the Greenjack's wake. "But how? Just from some picture?"

"Yes."

"But you can't tell anything just from a picture."

"You can tell everything from a single look. For instance, I know that you, Mr Bishop, had it in mind that if you found me a fraud here you might use your gun to shoot me dead. And then yourself. We would be a memorial in this unpleasant spot, the monument of your surrender to despair and your inability to remain rational in the face of my abominable supernatural exploitation of both your grief and reputation." It continued walking steadily.

Bishop had no answer to that. He'd never verbalised or reified that intent, but he couldn't entirely dismiss it. His gun was in his holster pocket. Everyone had them. He couldn't say the thought hadn't been his secondary insurance. That and the recorder of course. It would have told the sad tale to those who came to find out what happened. The notion had been discarded a long time before they even landed though, he realised and now, the recorder was instead preserving this vision of Hyperion's skinny ass slowly wandering along a trackless gully through soft dirt and Bishop's laboured breathing.

"Anyone can see these things," Hyperion mumbled as he went. "But they don't know how to tune in, to refine and translate and know them."

"Don't start on the psychic stuff." What the hell had those boys and that monster done with his little girl? "Tell me about Wan."

"Bancroft. He is idealistic, practical, yet ordinary. Bread is determined, focused and he has been somehow thwarted in the past, which has made him bitter though he hides this with great charm. McKnight is an entrepreneur, comfortable with criminal ways."

"McKnight is the leader then."

"Wan is the leader, Mr Bishop, whoever's foot may seem to go first. As for the women, neither of them are involved in this plan except by accident. It is simply unfortunate that they were in this team when Wan met McKnight. I am certain McKnight was the catalyst for what occurred here. Wan is too poor, too badly connected and too ignorant to plan this venture alone. Possibly he didn't think of it until McKnight arrived to put the idea in his head. He isn't creative."

"You're quite the detective." Bishop didn't mean it quite as bitter as it sounded.

"I would like to be. But it isn't my intuition working so much as the patterns that I see."

Bishop gave a cursory glance at his screen. A twisting tube of colours, some bleeding, others sharp, was all he could see; bad art on a tiresome landscape. "If you say so." In spite of himself he had no trouble believing the Greenjack now. "Are the girls all right?"

"They are physically unharmed at this point. They are talking here..." The shaman indicated their way and the stretch ahead. He moved off alone for some distance, then narrated, "I feel terror and anger. I believe they were attempting to bargain an escape or discover the real plans. McKnight is all for telling them. He is enjoying the action. Wan forbids him. McKnight doesn't mind this but Davis is getting edgy. He has never liked the involvement of the Terraform. His fear of retaliation is keeping him quiet now."

Bishop stopped suddenly, rooted in the unmade earth. He had realised that he was walking through time, and the confidence in the shaman's analysis made him fear where the future led very greatly, even though it had already happened. He attempted to rally some criticism, some countermeasure to the rigorous story unfolding and prove at least to himself that there was a chance most of it was simply the shaman's whimsical interpretation of some very dry facts, but he struggled.

Ahead of him the large creature stopped in its own dusty track and turned about. It seemed patient and concerned. Every time he looked into its peculiar yellow eyes he expected the disturbance of an alien encounter but instead he felt that he was understood and the feeling made him desperately uneasy. Who knew what confidence trickery it was capable of, after all. But for the life of him he couldn't figure out a motive.

"When we get to the end of this," Bishop said hoarsely, coughing, "what will we do?"

"That depends on the end."

"I mean, if she isn't dead, if she was taken somewhere...will you help me? You said you'd ask for a Unity ship. I guess that means you know someone."

"I will find your daughter, Mr Bishop," Hyperion said. "I already promised to. If you prefer I will say no more about the events that passed this way. No doubt you must wonder how I can know and there is no way to tell you how, any more than you can explain how you do most things you do that are your nature. I expect that some greater analysis will be able to detail the process but I am not interested to do it myself. I see these people and I feel what they have been feeling, as if I can watch it in a moving storybook. There are other things present, besides the people now. These disruptions in such a quiet area have acted as an attractor and some of the energies I spoke about earlier are beginning to converge on the scene. As yet they are only circling. You may see..."

"These stains? I thought they were just bad rendering or the light or something. They're so faint. Watermarks."

"They are the ones. You will see them circle and converge, then scatter and reform. They may merge. Ignore them. They are not important."

"But they..." But the Greenjack was already moving on. The shadows were lengthening into early evening and a slight cooling was in the air. Bishop kept one eye on the trail and the other on the screen but the silence was too much for him. "Talk," he said.

"They are not speaking here," the shaman replied over its shoulder. "Yang is looking for a way to escape. Bishop is locked in her thoughts. She is angry with McKnight for his betrayal of their friendship, or what she thought was their friendship. She is questioning her assessment of the others. McKnight is leading, he is content. Wan and Davis are in the rear pushing the women on. Wan is excited. Davis is starting to lose trust in him. Davis has a weak personality. He believes he ought to be leader and Wan is beginning to annoy him. He is starting to form a strong resentment."

"What is that cloud?"

"He is forming negative energy vortices. This kind of personality often does. Their energy scatters out from the holes in their energy bodies. It is an interesting feature of humans that they create negative energy attractors much more readily and strongly than positive ones. I am not sure why but I believe it is because damaged individuals are leaky, prone to influence and loss, whereas healthy types do not shed these frequencies without some deliberate effort. They are impervious to wild influence and create almost no disturbances. I must consult with the other Green-jacks when they are done travelling."

Bishop was silent for a while and they plodded on some quarter kilometre more as he checked his recordings. It was an ecology he was seeing, if it were true. A psychic kind of ecology. He couldn't help but notice it, even as it wasn't part of his concern. Just a peripheral. If the Greenjack had tried to convince him about all this any other way he could probably have thought of a good hole or two to poke in things but as it was...he shook his head and struggled on. He wasn't fit and although gravity was lighter and walking easier it was a long time since he'd hiked further than his back yard. He found himself stopped suddenly, almost walking onto Hyperion's tail. The Forged was still as a statue.

Bishop looked at the screen quickly. A darkening storm of purples and reds like a miniature cyclone was all around him. He had to wait, then Hyperion said, "They stop here. McKnight signals offworld. Wan and Davis start arguing again. Yang tries to escape. She just runs. Bishop tried to stop her. McKnight notices. Davis starts to run after her but Wan says no. He was willing to leave her. He wants to. Davis catches Yang. Wan says to McKnight they should leave them both. He knows Davis is trouble, Yang he doesn't want anyway; they have some history...it's minor...he'd rather leave her for some reason I don't... Anyway. Bishop protests. Yang becomes hysterical. McKnight hits her unconscious. Now Wan gets angry with McKnight. Davis's antagonism towards Wan crystallises. He threatens to turn them all in. Now McKnight doesn't like that. McKnight threatens Wan and Davis. Wan tries to calm things down. Bishop is raging. Wan ties up both women, hands and feet. Yang is injured, there is blood here. They wait. Quite a long time. I think an hour must pass or so. Davis is now focused entirely on Wan. Hates him. McKnight is the only calm one. Wan is furious but he's too smart to let it out. A ship comes. It lands over there..."

Mark Bishop got up and followed the Greenjack over to the place across the long shadows that had nearly covered the whole ground.

There was no sign of a landing, but then given the weather, there wouldn't be. He recorded dutifully. The coloured waterworld had gone. He watched the Greenjack circle and look, and pause. It returned from a small exploration and said, "This is the end of the trail here. The ship has come. It's a Forged craft. I don't know its name, but if I ever meet it, I'll know it by its energy signatures. It is one of three types of Ironhorse currently operating between the Far System and Earth. Can't say more. They all embark, except Yang. She's dead."

Bishop half wanted to ask for more, certain it was hiding things, but then he decided that it was enough, he didn't want to know. Everything inside him had stopped, waiting. What the shaman had just said was a testable claim, unless it meant some kind of spiritual residue. Beneath his coat he felt the hairs on his neck stand on end. His heart gave an extra heat. "Are you sure?"

"Yes." Hyperion paused and then made a brief gesture with its head. Bishop followed the line, recorder in hand first. He saw nothing, just the usual Mars stuff, but then the shaman walked him out another hundred metres to a small mound that Bishop or anyone would just have taken for one of the billion shifting dunes. "She is here."

Bishop took measurements, readings. They were still technically well within Thorson's Gullies. Nobody would have come here for a long, long time. Perhaps never. The land was bad, useless. This zone had already been mapped. There were no deposits of use. Then, with the shaman's help, he set up his recorder and began the process of moving the sand aside. He used his shoe as a spade. It didn't take long before he bumped something. Without ceremony they uncovered a part of a desiccated human body, just enough to see the identifying badges on the suit, and then they covered it up again.

Bishop moved away a short distance and sat for a while, drinking water and watching the sun go down. It got very cold. His feet and hands ached. He wished for the scotch again, fervently, avidly, relentlessly. Hyperion sat beside him like a giant dog.

Bishop's hand strayed to the machine but he left it alone. He stumbled over the words, "Do you see her?" He was braced for any fool answer. He wanted there to be one, a good one.

"She was here," it said. "But now she has gone."

Bishop nodded. He wasn't going to ask for the details. He wasn't ready yet. Leave it at the cryptic stage until... "We should go."

"I suggest we walk back to the capsule rather than make any transmissions the Terraform might interpret. Also we must now consider this a murder investigation. What would you like to do? We could report it to the police now and let them..."

"No. They got it all wrong the first time." Bishop was surprised by the force of his own hatred but the shaman didn't skip a beat.

"Then we should not discuss this with Valhalla. We need help from sources that don't mind being accomplice to criminal acts."

Belatedly Mark realised by this it meant their failure to inform. Anything that wasted time now didn't matter to him. "Can you track them from here?"

"Not directly, but their intentions are reasonably clear. McKnight is at least guilty of manslaughter and kidnap. Wan and Davis kidnap, misuse of corporate properties, perversion of the course of justice. The Terraform is on their side. They have every chance to make a good escape but they couldn't head sunward—there's nothing there except Earth and the high-population satellite systems, full of officials and the law. They have gone to the Belt first—no Forged ship could take them further without at least stopping there for supplies. We will find something that way." It seemed completely confident, almost resigned to its own cold certainty.

Bishop ignored the bleakness in its tone and waded forwards grimly in its wake, a squire to a weird and uncomforting King Wenceslas of the sands.

It was a long, hard, cold and lonely passage. Bishop struggled all the way not to ask all the questions that were haunting him but ask them he didn't and at last they retraced all the path and the Valhalla's hand opened its thousand eyes and let them in. He couldn't afford to indulge his fears.

"Where to?" the Valhalla asked as it left orbit, swinging away in an arc that would return it to the sunward side so it could pick up extra heat.

"Just to the lift station again," Hyperion said with a sigh as though the journey had been tiring and a disappointment.

It made some small talk with Valhalla as Bishop settled himself in. He intended to check his recordings and prepare some method for transmitting them safely in case something happened to him, but before he was able to do any of that exhaustion took over and he fell asleep. He slept all the way to the port and woke feeling drained and thin. Hyperion led him through their formalities and then they were sitting in the cafeteria, Bishop facing a reconstituted dinner with a dry mouth.

"An ordinary journey to the Belt is a three-year stretch," the shaman said. He was lying like a giant dog on the smooth tiled floor next to Bishop's table, resting his head on a plastic plant pot beneath the convincing fake fronds of a plastic grass. "The fastest available transport can make it in one year. But Unity ships can make it instantly."

"Interference," Bishop croaked. He had managed a mouthful. It wasn't bad but he was so hungry even cardboard would have seemed delicious. Hungry or not he was loath to think about Unity travel. They said it interfered with you at a fundamental level. They were not sure what the long-term implications would be.

"I will search here, perhaps they came this way." It was unconvincing. Nobody in their right mind would come this way if they wanted to get the hell out of Earth's influences.

Bishop surrendered to his curiosity and need. "You said you could get a Unity ship." He said it quietly. They weren't illegal, but they also weren't allowed this close to Earth space.

"I can ask a favour," Hyperion agreed. "I feel convinced they have taken that route. I do not see how any legally operating taxi would be involved, and the illegal ones all come from midspace and most have Unity drives. The most likely destination is Turbulence, the port on Hygeia. The majority of transfers take place there and there's only lipservice paid to the law at any level. It is Forged space and mostly rebel Forged at that."

"You think Wan wanted to remake himself?" Some humans wanted to experience addons that were better than just a comms set. It seemed ludicrous to Bishop, insane, an extreme form of self-mutilation beyond tattoos and piercings, some kind of primal denial of one's self. It frightened him.

"I think there are lots of opportunities for all kinds of profit out there. Especially for those already on the run."

Bishop crumpled the wrapper his cutlery had come in. Unity technology was infectious. Even passengers aboard craft operating the technology were at risk. So far in the years it had been around its effects proved relatively benign, but theorists guessed this might be a product of a much more significant infiltration process. To use it was to risk something that could be a living death. Fanatics spoke of puppetry and zombies, aliens operating behind the scenes. He'd heard... "Perhaps they'd just abandon her."

"She was a witness," the shaman said. "A Terraform is complicit in crimes bringing severe penalties. Murder and human trafficking. The foundation of Mars, no less, is at stake. If they went with Raven's blessing then they didn't go alone."

"Get your ship."

The creature got up slowly. "I will be back soon."

Bishop finished that meal, and then another as he waited, forking up food, watching the news on the cafeteria wall, not thinking now there was no need to think any more. When he got there, when something happened, then he'd think.

They took an ordinary ship out to deep Mars orbit again, and were set adrift in a cargo pod with barely enough oxygen to survive. Something picked them up at the allotted minute and second, as displayed on Bishop's illuminated screen. Something cast them off again. There was rattling and clanking. After a few minutes of struggle they emerged into the unloading bay of a large port. There was no trace of whoever had brought them there. There was no gravity, just the sickly spin of centrifuge. It was a struggle to keep the dinners inside him but he did, though they felt as if they'd been in his stomach the three-year journey he'd skipped. The Greenjack helped him to get his spacelegs and then went off, sniffing.

Bishop sat in a rented cubic room at the port's only hotel and watched what Hyperion transmitted to his screen. For a few days this was their pattern. The shaman didn't find the ship he was looking for, nor any trace of it, nor traces of the passengers. There were a lot of other things Bishop saw that disturbed him but he was protected, by his distance, the recorder and the fact that seeing these troubling things was not his immediate mission. There were many shadows here, like the inkstained Mars twilight, moving splatters that now and again coagulated around a place or a person. He started to type, wrote "haunted?" He managed to read the report in bits and pieces. He struggled to wash, to shave, to function in between. He drank something called scotch that was alcohol with synthetic flavouring. It was good. It did the job. Beside "haunted" he copied the most loathsome and mysterious of the names of things that Hyperion had identified. Cracklegrackle. His nerves jangled. He tried turning the screen on himself, but only when the 'jack wasn't there. He looked old. A fucking wreck to be honest. He was amazed.

"They only affect those who wish to be affected," the shaman insisted as they ate together on their last, fruitless night.

"But how?" Bishop pushed his food around the bag it had come in, squashing it between his fingers and thumb.

The answer was so unexpected and ridiculous it silenced him. "Through the hands and feet, the crown or base of the spine. Never mind that. These rumours of laboratories open in the midstream; any surgery is available there. We should look into that."

Bishop agreed, what else could he do? They moved to a lesser port, and then a lesser one, the last place that pretended to commercial operations. There was no hotel, just some rented rooms in a storehouse. Bishop began to run out of money, and sanity. He couldn't bring himself to contact work and explain his absence. He thought only about Tabitha. He drank to avoid feeling. He took pills for regimented sessions of oblivion. Sometimes he watched the Mars journey again on his screen. Those strange floating films of colour absorbed his attention more and more. The more he watched them the more he saw that their movements seemed sinister and far from random. He saw himself pass through them and tried to remember if they had changed him.

He'd felt nothing. Nothing. Hyperion's statements about the people, seemed more and more unlikely. He felt it was a goosechase. Perhaps he had been paid to lead Bishop out here where he couldn't make trouble, and strand him. Perhaps the Terraform had bought the Greenjack off. This ran through his mind hourly. Only the transmissions of the 'jack's travels kept him going.

Then one day months after they had set out he got the call. "I found her."

"Is she…"

"Alive."

He scrabbled to get clean clothes, to clean himself, to get sober. He was full of joy, full of terror. The hours passed like aeons. The 'jack brought a ship—one he saw this time, an Ironhorse Jackrabbit with barely enough space to fit them aboard. It yawned and they walked into its sharklike mouth. It held them there, one bite from vacuum death, and blinked them to the cloudstreams of Jupiter. He barely noticed.

"Are those things here?"

"Everywhere, Mr Bishop," Hyperion said.

"What things?" the Jackrabbit asked.

"Energies," the Greenjack said. "Nothing for you to worry about."

There was some bickering about the return journey. Bishop couldn't make sense of it.

"Where is she?" He gripped the Greenjack's thorny arm. Its scaly skin was like a cat's tongue, strangely abrasive. Around him, floating, the few human visitors to this place looked lost. Tabitha was none of them. They all looked through portholes into the gauzy films of the planet's outer atmosphere streaming past below their tiny station. It looked like caramel coffee. Outside, various Forged were docked and queued. People had conversations in the odd little cubicles, like airlocks that dotted the outside of the structure. Sometimes the doors flashed and then opened. People came out, went in on both sides of the screen wall that separated the two environments of instation and freezing space from one another.

"This way," the 'jack said. He reached out and laid his tough paw across the back of Bishop's gripping hand for a second, then led him with a kick and drift through the slight pull of the planet's gravity well to one of those lit doorways.

Bishop peered inside, looking for her. The shaman followed him in. The room was empty.

He turned. "She's not here!"

The shaman pointed at the panel in the reinforced floor. Some Jupiterian Forged was on the other side.

Bishop looked at Hyperion because he didn't want to look at the window, but he floated towards it, his hands and feet betraying him as they pressed against the clear portal suddenly, and on the far other side, across six sheets of various carbonates, glass and vacuum, the Forged pressed its own hands towards his open palms.

Jupiter was no place for a human being. They died there in droves. Even the Forged who had been engineered before birth to thrive in its vicious atmosphere and live lives as glorified gas farmers fell prey to its merciless storm. The upper cloud layer was never more than minus one twenty Celsius. Large creatures didn't operate that well at those temperatures, even ones that were mostly made of machine and chemical technologies so far removed from the original human that they were unrecognisable components of life. But Tupac, the Motherfather, was able to create children who lived here, even some who dived far to the place where hydrogen was a metal; scientists with singleminded visions. Tupac's efforts had advanced human knowledge and experience to the limit of the material universe.

Bishop's senses didn't stretch that far. He stared into eyes behind shields of methane ice that were nothing like his own, in a face that was twice the size of his, blue, bony and metallic and more like the faceplate of a robot fish than anything else. Narrow arms, coated in crablike exoskeletal bone reached out for him. The hands were five-digit extensions, covered in strange suckerlike skin that clung easily to the glass. Behind that the body was willowy, ballooning, tented like clothes in the wind, patterned like a mackerel. Jellyfishes and squid were in its history somewhere, microprecise fibre engineering and ultracold processor tech its true parents.

"She has a connection to Uluru," Hyperion said quietly, naming the virtual reality which all the Forged shared. Where their bodies could not meet, in mind they could get together anytime. "I can put it to your screen."

Bishop turned then. "You're not seriously suggesting this...thing...is my daughter?"

"There is a market for living bodies of any kind in the Belt. Old humans are particularly preferred for the testing of adaptive medical transformation. Technicians there have a mission to press beyond any restraint and develop their skills to make and remake any living tissues..."

He exploded with a kind of laugh, "But you can't *make* Forged. Not like that."

Hyperion was silent for a moment. "They say it is important to become self-adaptive, that they are the next step beyond Forged. They will be able to remake themselves in any fashion without experiencing discontinuity of consciousness. Any flesh or machine will be incorporated if it is willed. The Actualised..."

"But it can't be her!" His stare at the shaman was too wide. His eyes hurt. Against his will he found himself turning, looking through the walls at the creature's blinkless stare. Its face had no expression. It had no mouth or nose. Gill-like extensions fluttered behind its head like ruffles of voile. Its octopid hands pressed, pressed. Its nose touched the plate. Hyperion was holding the screen out to him.

He took it in nerveless hands. They were so limp he could hardly turn it.

"Davis tried to turn Wan in, once they reached Volatility, that port on Ceres. But the Forged Police there are all sympathisers. Wan and McKnight sold him, split the money..."

On the screen was the standard summer garden that Uluru created for all such meetings, a place for avatars to stand in simulated sunlight amid the shelter of shrubs and trees. Running through it, watermarked, was the background Bishop could really see, the reality he was standing in. In front of the monstrous creature attached to the window stood Tabitha, in jeans and the yellow T-shirt with the T-Rex on it that he bought her at some airport lounge some lifetime ago. Her soft brown hair moved in the nonexistent breeze. He touched the screen to feel the texture of her perfect skin.

"Daddy." The lips moved to whisper. Through her hazel eyes the great void eyes of the fish stared.

It was only an avatar. You could make these things easily. The photographs were even in his recorder. The voice was only like hers, it wasn't really hers. There must be hundreds of standard tracks of her in the archives somewhere. These things were simple to fake.

He thrust the screen back at Hyperion, though it was his, and tried to muster some shred of dignity. "Summon the ship."

The creature didn't move from its floating position at his side. "Mister Bishop..."

"You've fooled me long enough with your chat and your lines and your little premade adventure complete with faked body, but I see through it now, if you can stand the irony of that, and I'm going. I find no evidence to confirm any of your ridiculous suggestions." He was so angry he could barely speak. Bits of spit flew off him and floated, benign and silly bubbles in the slowly circulating air. "Really, this was one step too far. I bought it hook, line and sinker until now. I suppose you were trying to see how far I could be drawn. Well, a long way. Perhaps you were going to get some money for bringing the Institute into disrepute and scandal when I made some case with it for your insane claims about good and evil and possession and...your goosechase. Yes. You took advantage of me. I was weak..." There was a sound in his head, that black hum. He could hear something in it. An identifiable noise. Definite. Sure.

"Bishop," the creature snapped.

"...daddy!" came the faint call from the screen as it tumbled down past the shaman's side and clattered against the cabin wall.

The black hum was laughing at him, a dreadful sound. It hurt his chest. It hurt everywhere. He was furious. His skin was red hot, he couldn't think of where to go. What a fool he'd been. "How dare you. How dare you..."

Suddenly the hideous gargoyle hissed, a low, menacing sound. "I have done what I said. I have found your daughter. I have no interest in your views..."

Bishop was glaring around wildly. He made a shooing motion. "Get away! You won't mock me! Stupid, hideous creatures!" He began to thump the glass panels where the Jupiter's hands were stuck. It didn't move, just stared at him with its hidden, empty eyes. "You!" he turned on Hyperion. "Make it go away."

The Greenjack looked at him flatly and even with its expressive handicap he could feel its disgust. "Mr Bishop, I urge you to look again, and listen. Your daughter..."

"It's not even possible!" Bishop kicked strongly for the door. Behind him the recorder tumbled, ricocheting, out of control, the voice that came out of it growing fainter.

"Daddy!"

The door controls, they were too complicated for him. He couldn't figure them out. He turned and lashed out wildly, thinking the Greenjack was closer than it was. It caught the recorder easily from its spin and held it out to him, contempt in its every line.

Bishop took the little machine and smashed it against the wall until it stopped making any noise.

Beyond the clear wall the Jupiterian was letting go slowly, suckers peeling off one by one. Its eyes had frosted over strangely, white cracks visible across the ice surfaces, spreading until they shrouded the whole orbit. Its head moved back from the pane and dipped. At the same moment the door opened.

Bishop was out in a second. He couldn't breathe. Not at all. His chest was tight. There was no damn oxygen. There must have been a malfunction. He gripped the handrails, gasping, the blood pounding in his eyes. "Oxygen!" he cried out. "There's no air!" In his ears the black hum.

Hyperion passed him, gliding slowly. He was holding the recorder and ignored Bishop's outburst. He started talking and as Bishop had to listen to him, unable to go anywhere, he heard the black sound forming itself into a shape.

"I think that although you have broken the speakers and the screen the memory is probably unharmed. It will not be possible to locate and arrest Davis as he has been scrapped for parts. Tabitha says that Wan and McKnight disposed of him first, before they went into the Belt proper. Wan wanted her to be rendered as well but McKnight said there would be a lot more for a whole live subject. They were planning how to create a trafficking chain and where to get more people from. She was taken to some facility about one twenty degrees off Earth vector. They wanted to make her as far from the original human as possible to prove their accomplishments but also because they thought it was fitting for humans to end up like the Forged out here have all ended, as slave workers in the materials industry. She isn't like the other Forged of course, she's just a fabrication. Her links to Uluru are very limited. She has no real contact other than voice and some vision with anyone else. And the Forged here are mostly rebel sympathisers. She tried to call you, but the networks out this way are very bad and none of the regular channels would carry her messages anyway because she is marked as a risk to the survival of the Actualist movement. It took a great deal of trouble to get her to come here. It is dangerous. She risked everything. And she didn't want to see you. I had to take days to persuade her that if you came there might be sufficient evidence to reopen the case and bring the Earthside Police out here to pursue it."

Bishop gulped. "You've done a very thorough job, I'll give you that."

The Greenjack made a clacking noise. It spoke in a calm, reasonable manner, as if Bishop were perfectly lucid. "I have not been able to trace the routes of Davis, Wan or McKnight yet but I think they will be easy to find. I hope you understand, Mr Bishop, that I do not require your permission to pursue the investigation or to make my findings known to the authorities. I also advise against your attempting to return to Earth alone. Many of the Forged here who would have you believe they are honest taxis are pirates like Wan has aspired to become. The going rate for a live Old Monkey human in the Belt is upward of fifty thousand standard dollars. I doubt you have the finances to buy yourself out of trouble, even if they wanted you to."

The terrible pulse of the black name wouldn't let him think. Bishop reeled against the bulkhead, the rail gripped in his slippery fingers. He was heroic. "We must rescue her. We can take her back. Find a way. I can raise the money on Earth. The Police can arrest those responsible and the government will..."

"The government is well aware of the situation," Hyperion said. "Returning Tabitha Earthside and attempting remodelling would be tantamount to a declaration of civil war out here. They will do no such thing. You know it as well as I do. Pull yourself together." It handed him his screen, which it had repaired somehow. Aside from a cracked screen and broken speakers it seemed all right. "This is your evidence. It is our only hard evidence, aside from the Uluru recording I have made, but of course those involved Forged, so they are suspect." It was only tired by this admission of bigotry in the judicial system. "If you do not act there will be no justice of any kind."

Bishop held the screen without turning beyond the home page. He heard his own voice babbling, "We could kill them. McKnight, you can find him..."

Hyperion waited a few moments. "Tabitha is an extraordinary person, Mr Bishop. Although it is a mystery how she has sprung from you. She understands your feelings. You have hurt her deeply and this makes me dislike you very much. After what she has been through, your rejection is by far the most damaging thing that has happened here. And now, you are seeking to spread misery further by your stupidity. The energy wells out here are all very dark. A few lights shine. Tabitha Bishop is one of them. You are now claiming one of the energies is responsible for your weakness. I find that contemptible. Pull yourself together."

"You! You could find them and kill them and you won't do it! Just this superstitious, religious babble. You bring me here to show me...to show me... Here, here!" He tried to get the screen to focus on him. "Show me now. I know it's there. That thing. Show..." but Bishop could not finish. The words had cannoned into each other behind his tongue and exploded there into an unpronounceable summons for hell. Cracklegrackle.

He wanted very much to be dead. The shame was unbearable. He could not carry it. On Earth he would have been on his face, on his knees, here he was floating, curled up tight into a ball.

The shaman waited. "You are not possessed, Mark. You are simply hysterical. Your future with your daughter is your choice. However, we must take the recording back to Earth and submit it to the Police there. Then we will have done our part. I, at least, will do so. You must hurry. She has to leave in a moment."

Behind Bishop's eyes the blackness was shot with red. He snarled at Hyperion, silently and then, inch by inch, he hauled himself to the cubicle door, again with that will that wasn't his, no it wasn't.

His joints hurt. His throat was so tight. He couldn't breathe. Inside. The rails. The flat expanse of glass. The slices of clear shielding. The coffee-coloured clouds miles below as soft and gentle as thistledown. Dirt on the floor. They ought to clean this place. It was so hard to see through the handmarks, the footprints, the wear and tear on the old polycarbonate. It was so hard to see through the glass and the frozen methane that melted and ran to keep her sight clear, then froze, then melted again so that she was always half blind. It was so hard to see through his tears.

THE OTHERS

Two-time winner of the Hugo Award for best novella, British writer **Charles Stross** (b. 1964) holds degrees in pharmacy and computer science. Though he has been publishing fiction since the late 1980s, he first attained widespread notice with his series of stories about the Macx family, collected in the book *Accelerando*, which won the 2006 Locus Award for best novel. Often identified as the preeminent novelist of the Singularity, Stross remains a skeptic about its possibility. In this novelette, a Hugo Award finalist, the death-defying crew of the spacecraft *Field Circus*, a Coke-can-sized mass of computronium, enter into negotiations with some not-so-super intelligences.

NIGHTFALL
> Charles Stross

A synthetic gemstone the size of a Coke can falls through silent darkness. The night is quiet as the grave, colder than midwinter on Pluto. Gossamer sails as fine as soap bubbles droop, the gust of sapphire laser light that inflated them long since darkened; ancient starlight picks out the outline of a huge planet-like body beneath the jewel-and-cobweb corpse of the starwhisp.

Eight years have passed since the good ship *Field Circus* slipped into close orbit around the frigid brown dwarf Hyundai +4904/-56. Five years have gone by since the launch lasers of the Ring Imperium shut down without warning, stranding the light-sail-powered craft three light years from home. There has been no response from the router, the strange alien artifact in orbit around the brown dwarf, since the crew of the starwhisp uploaded themselves through its strange quantum entanglement interface for transmission to whatever alien network it connects to. In fact, nothing happens; nothing save the slow trickle of seconds, as a watchdog timer counts down the moments remaining until it is due to resurrect stored snapshots of the crew, on the assumption that their uploaded copies are beyond help.

Meanwhile, outside the light cone—

Amber jolts into wakefulness, as if from a nightmare. She sits bolt upright, a thin sheet falling from her chest; air circulating around her back chills her rapidly, cold sweat evaporating. She mutters aloud, unable to subvocalize, "Where am I—oh. A bedroom. How did I get here?" *mumble.* "Oh, I see." Her eyes widen in horror. *It's not a dream....*

"Greetings, human Amber," says a ghost-voice that seems to come from nowhere: "I see you are awake. Would you like anything?"

Amber rubs her eyes tiredly. Leaning against the bedstead, she glances around cautiously. She takes in a bedside mirror, her reflection in it: a young woman, gaunt in the manner of those whose genome bears the p53 calorie-restriction hack, she has disheveled blonde hair and dark eyes. She could pass for a dancer or a soldier; not, perhaps, a queen. "What's going on? Where am I? Who are you, and *what am I doing in your head?*"

Her eyes narrow. Analytical intellect comes to the fore as she takes stock of her surroundings. "The router," she mutters. Structures of strange matter in orbit around a brown dwarf, scant light years from Earth. "How long ago did we come through?" Glancing round, she sees a room walled in slabs of close-fitting stone. A window bay is recessed into them, after the style of crusader castles many centuries in the past, but there's no glass in it—just a blank white screen. The only furniture in the room, besides a Persian carpet on the cold flagstones, is the bed she sits upon. That, and the idiot gun that hovers just beneath the ceiling. She's reminded of a scene from an old movie, Kubrick's enigma; this whole set-up has got to be deliberate, and it isn't funny.

"I'm waiting," she announces, and leans back against the headboard.

"According to our records this reaction indicates that you are now fully self-aware," says the ghost. "This is good. You have not been conscious for a very long time: explanations will be complex and discursive. Can I offer you refreshments? What would you like?"

"Coffee, if you have it. Bread and hummus. Something to wear." Amber crosses her arms, abruptly self-conscious. "I'd prefer to have management ackles to this universe, though. As realities go, it's a bit lacking in furniture." Which isn't entirely true—it seems to have a comprehensive, human-friendly biophysics model. Her eyes focus on her left forearm; tanned skin and a puckered dime of scar tissue records a youthful accident with a pressure seal in Jovian orbit. Amber freezes for a moment. Her lips move in silence, but she's locked into place in this universe, unable to split or conjoin nested realities just by calling subroutines that have been spliced into the corners of her mind since she was a teenager. Finally she asks, "How long have I been dead?"

"Longer than you were alive, by orders of magnitude," says the ghost. A tray laden with pita breads, hummus, and olives congeals from the air above her bed and a wardrobe appears at one side of the room. "I can begin the explanation now or wait for you to finish eating. Which would you prefer?"

Amber glances about again, then fixes on the white screen in the window bay. "Give it to me right now. I can take it," she says, quietly bitter. "I like to understand my mistakes as soon as possible," she adds.

"We-us can tell that you are a human of determination," says the ghost, a hint of pride entering its voice. "That is a good thing, human Amber. You will need all of your resolve if you are going to survive here...."

It is the time of repentance in a temple beside a tower that looms above a dry plain, and the thoughts of the priest who lives in the tower are tinged with regret. It is Ashura, the tenth day of Muhurram, according to a real-time clock still tuned to the pace of a different era: the one thousand, three hundred and fortieth anniversary of the martyrdom of the third Imam, the Sayyid ash-Shuhada.

The priest of the tower has spent an indefinite time in prayer—locked in an eternal moment of meditation and recitation—and now, as the sun, vast and red, burns low above the horizon of the infinite desert, his thoughts drift toward the present. Ashura is a very special day, a day of atonement for collective guilt, evil committed through inactivity; but it is in Sadeq's nature to look outward toward the future. This is, he knows, a failing—but he is a member of that generation of the Shi'ite clergy that reacted to the excesses of the previous century: the generation that withdrew the *ulama* from temporal power, retreated from the velyat i-faqih of Khomeini and his successors, and left government to the people. Sadeq's focus, his driving obsession in theology, is a program of re-appraisal of eschatology and cosmology. Here in a tower of white sun-baked clay, on an endless plain that exists only in the imaginary spaces of a starship the size of a soft drink can, the priest spends his processor cycles in contemplation of one of the most vicious problems ever to confront a *mujtahid*: the Fermi paradox.

Sadeq finishes his evening devotions in near silence, then stands, stretches as is his wont, and leaves the small and lonely courtyard at the base of the tower. The gate—made of wrought iron, warmed by sunlight—squeals slightly as he opens it. Glancing at the upper hinge, he frowns slightly, willing it clean and whole. The underlying physics model acknowledges his access controls: a thin rim of red around the pin turns silvery-fresh, and the squeaking stops dead. Closing the gate behind him, Sadeq enters the tower.

He climbs with a heavy, even tread, a spiral staircase snaking ever upward above him. Narrow slit-windows line the outer wall of the staircase: through each of them he sees a different world. Out there, nightfall in the month of Ramadan. And through the next, green misty skies and a horizon too close by far. Sadeq carefully avoids thinking about the implications of this manifold space. Coming from prayer, from a sense of the sacred, he doesn't want to lose his proximity to his faith. He's far enough from home as it is, and there is much to consider—he is surrounded by strange and curious ideas, all but lost in a corrosive desert of faith.

At the top of the staircase, Sadeq comes to a door of aged wood bound in iron. It doesn't belong here: it's a cultural and architectural anomaly. The handle is a loop of black iron: Sadeq regards it as if it's the head of an asp, poised to strike. Nevertheless he reaches out and turns the handle, steps across the threshold into a palace out of fantasy.

None of this is real, he reminds himself. *It's no more real than an illusion conjured by one of the djinni of the thousand nights and one night.* Nevertheless, he can't save himself from smiling at the scene—a sardonic smile of self-deprecating humor, tempered by frustration.

Sadeq's captors have stolen his soul and locked it—him—in a very strange prison, a temple with a tower that rises all the way to paradise. It's the whole classical litany of mediaevalist desires, distilled from fifteen hundred years of literature; colonnaded courtyards, cool pools lined with rich mosaics, rooms filled with every imaginable dumb matter luxury, endless banquets awaiting his appetite—and occupied by dozens of beautiful un-women, eager to fulfill his every fantasy. Sadeq, being human, has fantasies by the dozen: but he doesn't dare permit himself to succumb to this temptation. *I'm not dead,* he reasons, *therefore how can I be in paradise? Therefore this must be a false paradise, a temptation sent to lead me astray. Probably. Unless I* am *dead, because*

Allah, peace be unto him, considers a human soul separated from its body to be dead. But if that's so, isn't uploading a sin? In which case this can't be paradise. Besides which, this paradox is so puerile!

Sadeq has always been inclined to philosophical enquiry, and his vision of the afterlife is more cerebral than most, involving ideas as questionable within the framework of Islam as those of Teilhard de Chardin were to the twentieth century Catholic Church. If there's one key indicator of a false paradise in his eschatology it's two-and-seventy brainlessly beautiful houris waiting to do his bidding. So it follows that he can't really be dead. Except...

The whole question of reality is so vexing that Sadeq does what he does every night. He strides heedlessly across priceless works of art, barging hastily through courtyards and passageways, ignoring niches in which nearly naked supermodels lie with their legs apart, climbing stairs—until he comes to a small unfurnished room with a single high window in one wall. There he sits on the floor, legs crossed, meditating: not in prayer, but in a more tightly focused ratiocination. Every false night—for there is no way to know how fast time is passing, outside this cyberspace pocket—Sadeq sits and *thinks*, grappling with Descartes' demon in the solitude of his own mind. And the question he asks himself every night is the same: *Can I tell if this is the true hell? And if it is not, how can I escape?*

The ghost tells Amber that she has been dead for just under a third of a million years. She has been reinstantiated from storage—and has died again—many times in the intervening period, but she has no memory of this; she is a fork from the main bough, and the other branches expired in lonely isolation.

The business of resurrection does not, in and of itself, distress Amber unduly. Born in the post-Turing era, she merely finds some aspects of the ghost's description dissatisfyingly incomplete: like saying she was been drugged and brought hither without stating whether by plane, train, or automobile.

She doesn't have a problem with the ghost's assertion that she is nowhere near Earth, either—indeed, that she is approximately eighty thousand light years away. When she and the others took the risk of uploading themselves through the router they found in orbit around

Hyundai +4904/-56, they'd understood that they could end up anywhere or nowhere. But the idea that she's still within the light cone of her departure strikes her as odd. The router is part of a network of self-replicating instantaneous communicators, spawning and spreading between the cold brown dwarf stars that litter the galaxy. She'd somehow expected to be much further from home by now.

Somewhat more disturbing is the ghost's assertion that the human genotype has rendered itself extinct at least twice, that its home planet is unknown, and that Amber is nearly the only human left in the public archives. At this point she interrupts: "I hardly see what this has to do with me!" She blows across her coffee glass; "I'm *dead*," she explains, with an undertone of knowing sarcasm in her voice. "Remember? I just got here. A thousand seconds ago, subjective time, I was in the control node of a starship, discussing what to do with the router we were in orbit around. We agreed to send ourselves through it, as a trade mission. Then I woke up in bed here in the umpty-zillionth century, wherever and whatever *here* is—without access to any reality ackles or augmentation, I can't even tell whether this is real or an embedded simulation. You're going to have to explain *why* you need an old version of me before I can make sense of my situation—and I can tell you, I'm not going to help you until I know who you are. And speaking of that, what about the others? Where are they? I wasn't the only one, you know?"

The ghost freezes in place for a moment, and Amber feels a watery rush of terror: *Have I gone too far?* she wonders.

"There has been an unfortunate accident," the ghost announces portentously. It morphs from a translucent copy of Amber's own body into the outline of a human skeleton, elaborate bony extensions simulating an osteosarcoma of more-than-lethal proportions. "Consensus-we believe that you are best positioned to remediate the situation. This applies within the demilitarized zone."

"Demilitarized...?" Amber shakes her head, pauses to sip her coffee. "What do you mean? What *is* this place?"

The ghost flickers again, adopting an abstract rotating hypercube as its avatar. "This space we occupy is a manifold adjacent to the demilitarized zone. The demilitarized zone is a space outside our core reality, itself exposed to entities that cross freely through our firewall, journeying to and from the network outside. We-us use the DMZ to establish informational value of migrant entities, sapient currency units and the like. We-us banked you upon arrival against future options trades in human species futures."

"Currency!" Amber doesn't know whether to be amused or horrified—both reactions seem appropriate. "Is that how you treat all your visitors?"

The ghost ignores her question. "There is a runaway semiotic excursion underway in the zone. We-us believe only you can fix it. If you agree to do so we will exchange value, pay, reward cooperation, expedite remuneration, manumit, repatriate."

Amber drains her coffee cup. "Have you ever entered into economic interactions with me, or humans like me, before?" she asks. "If not, why should I trust you? If so, why have you revived me? Are there any more experienced instances of myself running around here?" She raises an eyebrow at the ghost. "This looks like the start of an abusive relationship."

The ghost continues to sidestep her attempts to work out where she stands. It flickers into transparency, grows into a hazy window on a landscape of impossible shapes. Clouds sprouting trees drift above a landscape of green, egg-curved hills and cheesecake castles. "Nature of excursion: alien intelligence is loose in the DMZ," it asserts. "Alien is applying invalid semiotics to complex structures designed to sustain trade. You know this alien, Amber. We require solution. Slay the monster, we will give you line of credit. Your own reality to control, insight into trade arrangements, augmented senses, ability to travel. Can even upgrade you to you-we consensus, if desired."

"This monster." Amber leans forward: it's her turn to ignore what she feels to be a spurious offer. *Upgrade me to a ghost fragment of an alien group mind?* she wonders dismissively. "What is this alien?" She feels blind and unsure, stripped of her ability to spawn threads of herself to pursue complex inferences. "Is it part of the Wunch?"

"Datum unknown. It-them came with you," says the ghost. "Accidentally reactivated some seconds since now. Now it runs amok in the demilitarized zone. Help us, Amber. Save our hub or we will be cut off from the network. If that happens, you will die with we-us. Save us...."

A single memory belonging to someone else unwinds, faster than a guided missile and far more deadly.

Amber, aged eleven, is a gawky, long-limbed child loose on the streets of Hong Kong, a yokel tourist viewing the hotcore of the Middle Kingdom. This is her first and final vacation before the Franklin Trust straps her inside the payload pod of a Shenzhou spaceplane and blasts her into orbit from Xinkiang. She's free for the time being, albeit mortgaged to the tune of several million Euros; she's a little taikonaut to be, ready to work for the long years in Jupiter orbit it will take her to pay off the self-propelled options web that owns her. It's not exactly slavery: thanks to Dad's corporate shell-game, she doesn't have to worry about Mom chasing her, a cyanide-eyed abductress with feudal spawn-indenture rights in mind. And now she's got a little pocket money, and a room in the Hilton, and her own personal Franklin remote to keep her company, and she's gonna do that eighteenth-century enlightenment tourist shit and do it *right*.

Because this is her last day at liberty in the randomly evolved biosphere.

China is where it's at in this decade, hot and dense and full of draconian punishments for the obsolescent. Nationalist fervor to catch up with the West has been replaced by consumerist fervor to own the latest fad gadgets, the most picturesque tourist souvenirs from the quaintly old-fashioned streets of America, the fastest hottest smartest upgrades for body and soul. Hong Kong is hotter and faster than just about anywhere else in China, or in the whole damn world for that matter; this is a place where tourists from Tokyo gawp, cowed and future-shocked by the glamor of high-technology living.

Walking along Jardine's Bazaar—*more like Jardine's bizarre,* she thinks—exposes Amber to a blast of humid noise. Geodesic domes sprout like skeletal mushrooms from the glass and chrome roofs of the expensive shopping malls and luxury hotels, threatening to float away on the hot sea breeze. There are no airliners roaring in and out of Kai Tak any more, no burnished aluminum storm clouds to rain round-eyed passengers on the shopping malls and fish markets of Kowloon and the New Territories. In these tense later days of the War Against Unreason, impossible new shapes move in the sky; Amber gapes upward as a Shenyang F-30 climbs at a near-vertical angle, a mess of incomprehensibly curved flight surfaces vanishing to a perspective point that defies radar as well as eyeballs. The Chinese—fighter? missile platform? supercomputer?—is heading out over the South China Sea, to join the endless patrol that guards the border of the capitalist world against the Hosts of Denial, the Trouble out of Wa'hab.

For the moment, she's merely a human child: Amber's subconscious is offlined by the presence of forceful infowar daemons, the Chinese government censorbots suppressing her cognition of their deadliest weapons. And in the seconds while her mind is as empty as a sucked egg, a thin-faced man with blue hair shoves her in the small of her back and snatches at her shoulder bag.

"Hey!" she yells, stumbling. Her mind's a blur, optics refusing to respond and grab a physiology model of her assailant. It's the frozen moment, the dead zone when online coverage fails, and the thief is running away before she can catch her balance or try to give chase. Plus, with her extensions offline she doesn't know how to yell "stop, thief!" in Cantonese.

Seconds later, the fighter is out of visual range and the state censorship field lets up. "Get him, you bastards!" she screams, but the curious shoppers simply stare at the rude foreign child; an elderly woman brandishes a disposable phonecam at her and screeches something back. Amber picks up her feet and runs. Already she can feel the subsonics from her luggage growling at her guts—it's going to make a scene if she doesn't catch up in time. Shoppers scatter, a woman with a baby carriage almost running her down in her panic to get away from it.

By the time Amber reaches her terrified shoulder bag, the thief has disappeared: she has to spend almost a minute petting the scared luggage before it stops screeching and retracts its spines enough for her to pick it up. And by that time there's a robocop in attendance. "Identify yourself," it rasps in synthetic English.

Amber stares at her bag in horror: there's a huge gash in the side, and it's far too light. *It's gone,* she thinks, despairingly: *He stole it.* "Help," she says faintly, holding up her bag for the distant policeman looking through the robot's eyes. "Been stolen."

"What item missing?" asks the robot.

"My Hello Kitty," she says, batting her eyelashes, mendacity full-on at maximum utilization, prodding her conscience into submission, warning of dire consequences should the police discover the true nature of her pet cat: "My kitten's been stolen! Can you help me?"

"Certainly," says the cop, resting a reassuring hand on her shoulder—a hand that turns into a steel armband, as it pushes her into a van and notifies her in formally stilted language that she is under arrest on suspicion of shoplifting and will be required to produce certificates of authenticity and a fully compliant ownership audit for all items in her possession if she wants to prove her innocence.

By the time Amber's meatbrain realizes that she is being politely arrested, some of her external threads have already started yelling for help and her m-commerce trackers have identified the station she's being taken to by way of click-thru trails and an obliging software license manager. Some of them spawn agents to go notify the Franklin trustees, Amnesty International, and the Space and Freedom Party. As she's being booked into a cerise-and-turquoise juvenile offenders holding room by a middle-aged policewoman, the phones on the front desk are already ringing with enquiries from lawyers, fast food vendors, and a particularly on-the-ball celebrity magazine that's been tracking her father's connections. "Can you help me get my cat back?" she asks the policewoman earnestly.

"Name," the officer reads, eyes flickering from the simultaneous translation, "to please wax your identity stiffly."

"My cat has been stolen," Amber insists.

"Your cat?" The cop looks perplexed, then exasperated. Dealing with foreign teenagers who answer questions with gibberish isn't in her repertoire. "We are asking your name?"

"No," says Amber. "It's my cat. It has been stolen. My *cat* has been *stolen.*"

"Aha! Your papers, please?"

"Papers?" Amber is growing increasingly worried. She can't feel the outside world; there's a Faraday cage wrapped around the holding cell and it's claustrophobically quiet in here. "I want my cat! Now!"

The cop snaps her fingers, then reaches into her own pocket and produces an ID card, which she points to insistently. "Papers," she repeats. "Or else."

"I don't know what you're talking about!" Amber wails.

The cop stares at her oddly. "Wait." She rises and leaves, and a minute later returns with a thin-faced man in a business suit and wire-rimmed glasses that glow faintly.

"You are making a scene," he says, rudely and abruptly. "What is your name? Tell me truthfully or you'll spend the night here."

Amber bursts into tears. "My *cat's* been stolen," she chokes out.

The detective and the cop obviously don't know how to deal with this scene; it's freaking them out, with its overtones of emotional messiness and sinister diplomatic entanglement. "You wait here," they say, and back out of the cell, leaving her alone with a plastic animatronic koala and a cheap Lebanese coffee machine.

The implications of her loss—of Aineko's abduction—are sinking in now, and Amber is weeping loudly and hopelessly. It's hard to deal with bereavement and betrayal at any age, and the cat has been her wisecracking companion and consolation for a year now, the rock of certainty that gave her the strength to break free from her crazy mother. To lose her cat to a body shop in Hong Kong, where she will probably be cut up for spare circuitry or turned into soup, is too horrible to contemplate. Filled with despair and hopeless anguish, Amber howls at the interrogation room walls while, outside, trapped threads of her consciousness search for backups to synchronize with.

But after an hour, just as she's quieting down into a slough of raw despair, there's a knock—a knock!—at the door. An inquisitive head pops in. "Please to come with us?" It's the female cop with the bad translation ware. She takes in Amber's sobbing and *tsks* under her breath, but as Amber stands up and shambles toward her, she pulls back.

At the front desk of a cubicle farm full of police bureaucrats in various states of telepresence, the detective is waiting with a damp cardboard box wrapped in twine. "Please identify," he asks, snipping the string.

Amber shakes her head, dizzy with the flow of threads homing in to synchronize their memories with her. "Is it—" she begins to ask as the lid comes apart, wet pulp disintegrating. A triangular head pops up, curiously, sniffing the air. Bubbles blow from brown-furred nostrils. "What took you so long?" asks the cat as she reaches into the box and picks her up, fur wet and matted with seawater.

"If you want me to go fix your alien, for starters I want you to give me reality alteration privileges," says Amber. "Then I want you to find the latest instances of everyone who came here with me—round up the usual suspects—and give *them* root privileges, too. Then we'll want access to the other embedded universes in the DMZ. Finally, I want guns. *Lots* of guns."

"That may be difficult," says the ghost. "Many other humans reached halting state long-since. Is at least one other still alive, but not accessible for duration of eschatological experiment in progress. Not all were recorded with version control engine; others were-are lost in DMZ. We-us can provide you with extreme access to the demilitarized zone, but query the need for kinetic energy weapons."

Amber sighs. "You guys really *are* media illiterates, aren't you?" She stands up and stretches, feeling a facsimile of sleep's enervation leaching from her muscles. "I'll also need my—" It's on the tip of her tongue: there's something missing. "Hang on. There's something I've forgotten." *Something important,* she thinks, puzzled. *Something that used to be around all the time that would...know?...purr?...help?* "Never mind," she hears her lips say. "This other human. I *really* want her. Non-negotiable. All right?"

"That may be difficult," repeats the ghost. "Entity is looping in a recursively confined universe."

"Eh?" Amber blinks at it. "Would you mind rephrasing that? Or illustrating?"

"Illustration:" the ghost folds the air in the room into a glowing ball of plasma, shaped like a Klein bottle. Amber's eyes cross as she looks at it. "Closest reference from human historical database is Descartes' demon. This entity has retreated within a closed space but is now unsure whether it is objectively real or not. In any event, it refuses to interact."

"Well, can you get me into that space?" asks Amber. Pocket universes she can deal with; it's part and parcel of life as an upload. "Give me some leverage—"

"Risk may attach to this course of action," warns the ghost.

"I don't care," she says irritably. "Just *put* me there. It's someone I know, isn't it? Send me into her dream and I'll wake her up, okay?"

"Understood," says the ghost. "Prepare yourself."

Without any warning, Amber is somewhere else. She glances around, taking in an ornate mosaic floor, whitewashed walls set with open windows through which stars twinkle faintly in the night sky. The walls are stone, and she stands in a doorway to a room with nothing in it but a bed. Occupied by—

"Shit," she mumbles. "Who are you?" The young and incredibly, classically beautiful woman in the bed looks at her vacantly, then rolls over on her side. She isn't wearing a stitch, she's completely hairless from the ears down, and her languid posture is one of invitation. "Yes?" Amber asks, "What is it?"

The woman on the bed beckons to her slowly. Amber shakes her head. "Sorry, that's just not my scene." She backs away into the corridor, unsteady but thoughtful. "This is some sort of male fantasy, isn't it? And a particularly puerile one at that." She looks around again. In one direction a corridor heads past more open doorways, and in the other it ends with a spiral staircase. Amber concentrates, trying to tell the universe to take her to the logical destination, but nothing happens. "Shit, looks like I'm going to have to do this the hard way. I wish—" She frowns. She was about to wish that *someone* else was here, but she can't remember who. So she takes a deep breath and heads toward the staircase.

"Up or down?" she asks herself. *Up*—it seems logical, if you're going to have a tower, to sleep at the top of it. So she climbs the steps carefully, holding the spiraling rail. *I wonder who designed this space? And what role am I supposed to fit into in their scenario?* On second thoughts, the latter question strikes her as laughable. *Wait 'til I give him an earful....*

There's a plain wooden door at the top of the staircase, with a latch that isn't fastened. Amber pauses for a few seconds, nerving herself to confront a sleeper so wrapped in solipsism that he's built this sex-fantasy castle around himself. *I hope it isn't Pierre*, she thinks grimly as she pushes the door inward.

The room is bare and floored in wood. There's no furniture, just an open window set high in one wall. A man sits cross-legged and robed, with his back to her, mumbling quietly to himself and nodding slightly. Her breath catches as she realizes who it is. *Oh shit.* Her eyes widen. *Is this what's been inside his head all along?*

"I did not summon you," Sadeq says calmly, not turning round to look at her. "Go away, tempter. You aren't real."

Amber clears her throat. "Sorry to disappoint you, but you're wrong," she says. "We've got an alien monster to catch. Want to come hunting?"

Sadeq stops nodding. He sits up slowly, stretching his spine, then stands up and turns round. His eyes glint in the moonlight. "That's odd." He undresses her with his gaze. "You look like someone I used to know. You've never done that before."

"For fuck's sake!" Amber nearly explodes but catches herself after a moment. "What *is* this, a Solipsists United chapterhouse meeting?"

"I—" Sadeq looks puzzled. "I'm sorry, are you claiming to be *real?*"

"As real as you are." Amber reaches out and grabs a hand: he doesn't resist as she pulls him toward the doorway.

"You're the first visitor I've ever had." He sounds shocked.

"Listen, come *on.*" She tugs him after her, down the spiral staircase to the floor below. "Do you *want* to stay here? Really?" She glances back at him. "What *is* this place?"

"Hell is a perversion of heaven," he says slowly, running the fingers of his free hand through his beard. Abruptly, he reaches out and grabs her around the waist, then yanks her toward him. "We'll have to *see* how real you are—" Amber, who is not used to this kind of treatment, responds by stomping on his instep and back-handing him hard.

"You're real!" he cries, as he falls back against the staircase. "Forgive me, please! I had to know—"

"Know *what?*" she snarls. "Lay one finger on me again and I'll leave you here to rot!" She's already spawning the ghost that will signal the alien outside to pull her out of this pocket universe: it's a serious threat.

"But I had to—wait. You have *free will.* You just demonstrated that." He's breathing heavily and looking up at her imploringly. "I'm *sorry,* I apologize! But I had to know whether you were another zombie. Or not."

"A zombie?" She looks round. Another living doll has appeared behind her, standing in an open doorway wearing a skin-tight leather suit with a cut-away crotch. She beckons to Sadeq invitingly. Another body wearing strategically placed strips of rubber mewls at her feet, writhing for attention. Amber raises an eyebrow in disgust. "You thought I was one of those?"

Sadeq nods. "They've gotten cleverer lately. Some of them can talk. I nearly mistook one for—" He shudders convulsively. "Unclean!"

"Unclean." Amber looks down at him thoughtfully. "This isn't really your personal paradise, is it?" After a moment, she holds out a hand to him. "Come on."

"I'm sorry I thought you were a zombie," he repeats sadly; then the ghost yanks them both back to the universe outside.

More memories converge on the present moment:

The Ring Imperium is a huge cluster of self-replicating robots that

Amber has assembled in low Jupiter orbit, fueled by the mass and momentum of the small moon J-47 Barney, to provide a launching platform for the interstellar probe her father's business partners are helping her to build. It's also the seat of her court, the leading jurisprudential nexus in the outer solar system. Amber is the Queen here, arbitrator and ruler. And Sadeq is her judge and counsel.

A plaintiff Amber only knows as a radar blip thirty light minutes away has filed a lawsuit in her court, alleging malfeasance, heresy, and barratry against a semi-sentient corporate pyramid scheme that arrived in Jovian space twelve million seconds ago and currently seems set on converting every other intelligence in the region to its peculiar meme-set. A whole bundle of multithreaded countersuits are dragging at her attention, in a counterattack alleging that the light blip is in violation of copyright, patent, and trade secrecy laws by discussing the interloper's intentions.

Right now, Amber isn't home on the Ring to hear the case in person. She's left Sadeq behind to grapple with the balky mechanics of her legal system—tailor-designed to make corporate litigation a pain in the ass—while she drags Pierre off on a diplomatic visit to another Jovian colony, the Nursery Republic. Planted by the Franklin Trust's orphanage ship *Ernst Sanger*, the Nursery has grown over the past four years into a spindly snowflake three kilometers across. A slow-growing O'Neill cylinder sprouts from its hub; most of the inhabitants of the space station are less than two years old, precocious additions to the Trust's borganism.

There's a piazza, paved with something not unlike rough marble, on the side of a hill that clings insecurely to the edge of a spinning cup. The sky is a black vastness overhead, wheeling slowly around a central axis lined up on Jupiter. Amber sprawls in a wicker chair, her legs stretched out before her and one arm flung across her forehead. The wreckage of an incredible meal is scattered across the tables around her. Torpid and full, she strokes the cat that lies curled in her lap. Pierre is off somewhere, touring one or another of the prototype ecosystems that one or another of the Borg's special-interest minds is testing. Amber, for her part, can't be bothered. She's just had a great meal, she doesn't have any lawsuits to worry about, everything back home is on the critpath, and quality time like this is so hard to come by—

"Do you keep in touch with your father?" asks Monica.

"Mm." The cat purrs quietly and Amber strokes its flank. "We email. Sometimes."

"I just wondered." Monica is the local Borg den mother, willowy and brown-eyed and with a deceptively lazy drawl—Yorkshire English overlaid with silicon-valley speak. "I hear from him, y'know. From time to time. He was talking about coming out here."

"What? To PeriJove?" Amber's eyes open in alarm; Aineko stops purring and looks round at Monica accusingly.

"Don't worry." Monica sounds vaguely amused. "He wouldn't cramp your style, I think."

"But, out here—" Amber sits up. "Damn," she says, quietly. "What got into *him?*"

"Middle-aged restlessness, my down-well sibs say." Monica shrugs. "This time, Annette didn't stop him. But he hasn't made up his mind to travel yet."

"Good. Then he might not—" Amber stops. "The phrase. *Made up his mind.* What exactly do you mean?"

Monica's smile mocks her for a few seconds before the older woman surrenders. "He's talking about uploading."

"Is that embarrassing, or what?" asks Su Ang. Amber glances at her, mildly annoyed, but Ang isn't looking her way. *So much for friends,* Amber thinks. Being queen of all you survey is a great way of breaking up peer relationships—

"He won't do it," Amber predicts. "Dad's burned out."

"He thinks he'll get it back if he optimizes himself for re-entrancy." Monica continues to smile. "I've been telling him it's just what he needs."

"I do *not* want my father bugging me. *Or* my mother. Memo to immigration control: no entry rights for Manfred Macx without clearance through the Queen's secretary."

"What did he do to get you so uptight?" asks Monica idly.

Amber sighs, and subsides. "Nothing. He's just so extropian it's embarrassing. Like, that was the last century's apocalypse. Y'know?"

"I think he was a really very forward-looking organic," Monica, speaking for the Franklin Borg, asserts. Amber looks away. *Pierre would get it,* she thinks. Pierre would understand her aversion to Manfred showing up. Pierre, too, wants to carve out his own niche without parents looking over his shoulders, although for very different reasons. She focuses on someone male and more-or-less mature—Nicky, she thinks, though she hasn't seen him for a long time—walking toward the piazza, bare-ass naked and beautifully tanned.

"Parents. What are they good for?" asks Amber, with all the truculence of her seventeen years. "Even if they stay neotenous they lose flexibility. And there's that long Paleolithic tradition of juvenile slavery. Inhuman, I call it."

"How old were you when it was safe to leave you around the house on your own?" challenges Monica.

"Five. That's when I had my first implants." Amber smiles at the approaching young Adonis, who smiles back: yes, it's Nicky, and he seems pleased to see her. *Life is good,* she thinks, idly considering whether or not to tell Pierre.

"Times change," remarks Monica. "Don't write your father off too soon; there might come a time when you want his company."

"Huh." Amber pulls a face at the old Borg component. "That's what you *all* say!"

As soon as Amber steps onto the grass, she can feel possibilities open up around her: she has management authority here, and this universe is *big,* wide open, not like Sadeq's existential trap. A twitch of a subprocess reasserts her self-image, back to short hair and comfortable clothing. Another twitch brings up a whole load of useful diagnostics. Amber has an uncomfortable feeling that she's running in a compatibility box, here—there are signs that her access to the simulation system's control interface is very much via proxy—but at least she's got it.

"Wow. Back in the real world at last!" She can hardly contain her excitement, even forgetting to be pissed at Sadeq for thinking she was just an actor in his Cartesian theatre's performance of Puritan Hell. "Look! It's the DMZ!"

They're standing on a grassy knoll overlooking a gleaming Mediterranean city that snoozes beneath a Mandelbrot-fuzzy not-sun that hangs at the center of a hyperbolic landscape dwindling into the blue yonder, incomprehensibly distant. Circular baby-blue wells open in the walls of the world at regular intervals, connecting to other parts of the manifold. "How big is it, ghost? In planetary simulation-equivalents."

"This demilitarized zone is an embedded reality, funneling all transfers between the local star system's router and the civilization that built it. It uses on the order of a thousandth of the capacity of the Matrioshka brain it is part of, although the runaway excursion currently in force has absorbed most of that. Matrioshka brain, you are familiar with the concept?" The ghost sounds fussily pedantic.

Sadeq shakes his head. Amber glances at him, askance. "Take all the planets in a star system and dismantle them," she explains. "Turn them into dust—structured nanocomp, powered by heat exchangers, in concentric orbits around the central star. The inner orbitals run close to the melting point of iron; the outer ones are cold as liquid nitrogen, and each layer runs off the waste heat of the next shell in. It's like a Russian doll made out of Dyson spheres, shell enclosing shell enclosing shell, all running uploads—Dad figured our own solar system could support, uh, about a hundred billion times as many inhabitants as Earth. At a conservative estimate. As uploads, living in simulation space."

"Ah." Sadeq nods thoughtfully. "Is that your definition, too?" he asks, glancing up at the glowing point the ghost uses to localize its presence.

"Substantially," it says, almost grudgingly.

"Substantially?" Amber glances around. *A billion worlds to explore,* she thinks dizzily. *And that's just the firewall?* She feels obscurely cheated: you need to be vaster than human just to count the digits in the big numbers at play here, but there's nothing fundamentally incomprehensible about it. This is the sort of civilization Dad said she could expect to live in, within her meatbody life-expectancy. Dad and his drinking buddies, singing "dismantle the Moon! Melt down Mars!" in a castle outside Prague as they waited for the results of a shamelessly gerrymandered election to come in in the third decade of the third millennium, the Space and Freedom Party taking over the EU and cranking up to escape velocity. But this is supposed to be kiloparsecs from home, ancient alien civilizations and all that! Where's the exotic super-science? *I have a bad feeling about this,* she thinks, spawning a copy of herself to set up a private channel to Sadeq; *it isn't advanced enough. Do you suppose these guys could be like the Wunch? Parasites hitching a ride in the machine?*

The Wunch, a disastrous infection that had nearly taken over the *Field Circus,* are dumb parasitic aliens who infest the routers. Luckily, Earth's first uploads—who had reached the router years earlier and been assimilated by the Wunch—had been lobsters; the confused carpetbaggers succumbed to defenses jury-rigged by Pierre and the rest of the crew.

"You believe it's lying to us?" Sadeq sends back.

"Hmm." Amber sets off downslope toward the piazza below, at the heart of the fake town. "It looks a bit too human to me."

"Human," echoes Sadeq, a curious wistfulness in his voice. "Did you not say humans are extinct?"

"Your species is obsolete," the ghost comments smugly. "Inappropriately adapted to artificial realities. Poorly optimized circuitry, excessively complex low-bandwidth sensors, messy global variables—"

"Yeah, yeah, I get the picture," says Amber, turning her attention on the town. "So why do you think *we* can deal with this alien god you've got a problem with?"

"It asked for you," said the ghost, narrowing from an ellipse to a line, and then shrinking to a dimensionless point of brilliance. "And now it's coming. We-I not willing to risk exposure. Call us-me when you have slain the dragon. Goodbye."

"Oh *shit*—" Amber spins round. But she and Sadeq are alone beneath the hot sunlight from above. The piazza, like the one in the Nursery Republic, is charmingly rustic—but there's nobody home, nothing but ornate cast-iron furniture basking beneath the noon-bright sun, a table with a parasol over it, something furry lying sprawled in a patch of sunlight beside it.

"We appear to be alone for now," says Sadeq. He smiles crookedly, then nods at the table. "Maybe we should wait for our host to arrive?"

"Our host." Amber peers around. "The ghost is kind of frightened of this alien. I wonder why?"

"It asked for *us*." Sadeq heads toward the table, pulls out a chair, and sits down carefully. "That could be very good news—or very bad."

"Hmm." Amber finishes her survey, sees no sign of life. For lack of any better idea, she ambles over to the table and sits down at the other side of it from Sadeq. He looks slightly nervous beneath her inspection, but maybe it's just embarrassment. *If I had an afterlife like that, I'd be embarrassed about it too,* Amber thinks to herself.

"Hey, you nearly tripped over—" Sadeq freezes, peering at something close to Amber's left foot. He looks puzzled. "What are *you* doing here?" he asks her blind spot.

"What are you talking to?" she asks, startled.

"He's talking to me, dummy," says something tantalizingly familiar from her blind spot. "So the fuckwit's trying to use you to dislodge me, hmm? That's not exactly clever."

"Who—" Amber squints at the flagstone, spawns a bunch of ghosts who tear hurriedly at her reality modification ackles. Nothing seems to shift the blindness. "Are you the alien?"

"What else could I be?" the blind spot asks with heavy irony. "No, I'm your father's pet cat. Listen, do you want to get out of here?"

"Uh." Amber rubs her eyes. "I can't see you, whatever you are," she says politely. "Do I know you?" She's got a strange sense that she *does* know the blind spot, that it's really important and she's missing something intimate to her own sense of identity, but what it might be she can't tell.

"Yeah, kid." There's a note of world-weary amusement in the not-voice coming from the hazy patch on the ground. "They've hacked you but good, both of you. Let me in and I'll fix it."

"No!" exclaims Amber, a second ahead of Sadeq, who looks at her oddly. "Are you really an invader?"

The blind spot sighs. "I'm as much an invader as *you* are, remember? I *came* here with you. Difference is, I'm not going to let some stupid corporate ghost use me as fungible currency."

"Fungible—" Sadeq stops. "I remember you," he says slowly, with an expression of absolute, utter surprise on his face. "What do you mean?"

The blind spot *yawns*, baring sharp ivory fangs. Amber shakes her head, dismissing the momentary hallucination. "Lemme guess. You woke up in a room and this alien ghost tells you the human species is extinct and asks you to do a number on me. Is that right?"

Amber nods, as an icy finger of fear trails up and down her spine. "Is it lying?" she asks.

"Damn right!" The blind spot is smiling, now, and the smile on the void won't go away—she can see the smile, just not the *body* it's attached to. "My reckoning is, we're about sixteen light years from Earth. The Wunch have been through here, stripped the dump, then took off for parts unknown; it's a trashhole, you wouldn't believe it. The main life form is an incredibly ornate corporate ecosphere, legal instruments breeding and replicating. They mug passing sapients and use them as currency."

There's a triangular, pointy head behind the smile, slit eyes and sharp ears; predatory, intelligent-looking. Amber can see it out of the corners of her eyes when she looks around the piazza. "You mean we, uh, they grabbed us when we appeared and they've mangled my memories—" Amber suddenly finds it incredibly difficult to concentrate, but if she focuses on the smile she can almost see the body behind it, hunched like a furry chicken, tail wrapped neatly around its front paws.

"Yeah. Except that they didn't bargain on meeting something like *me*." The smile is infinitely wide, a Cheshire cat grin on the front of an orange and brown stripy body that shimmers in front of Amber's gaze like a hallucination. "Your mother's cracking tools are self-extending, Amber. Do you remember Hong Kong?"

"Hong—"

There is a moment of painless pressure, then Amber feels huge invisible barriers sliding away on all sides. She looks around, for the first time seeing the piazza as it really is, half the crew of the *Field Circus* waiting nervously around her, the grinning cat crouched on the floor at her feet, the enormous walls of recomplicating data that fence their little town off from the gaping holes—interfaces to the other routers in the network.

"Welcome back," Pierre says gravely, as Amber gives a squeak of surprise and leans forward to pick up her cat. "Now you're out from under, how about we start trying to figure out how to get home?"

Welcome to decade the sixth, millennium three. These old datelines don't mean so much any more, for while some billions of fleshbody humans are still infected with viral memes, the significance of theocentric dating has been dealt a body blow. This may be the fifties, but what that means to you depends on how fast your reality rate runs. The various upload clades exploding across the reaches of the solar system vary by several orders of magnitude—some are barely out of 2049, while others are exploring the subjective thousandth millennium.

While the *Field Circus* floats in orbit around an alien router—itself orbiting the brown dwarf Hyundai +4904/-56—while Amber and her crew are trapped on the far side of a wormhole linking the router to a network of incomprehensibly vast alien mindscapes—while all this is going on, the damnfool human species has finally succeeded in making itself obsolete. The proximate cause of its displacement from the pinnacle of creation (or the pinnacle of teleological self-congratulation, depending on your stance on evolutionary biology) is an attack of self-aware corporations. The phrase "smart money" has taken on a whole new meaning, for the collision between international business law and neurocomputing technology has given rise to a whole new family of species—fast-moving corporate carnivores in the net. The planet Mercury has been broken up by a consortium of energy brokers, and Venus is an expanding debris cloud, energized to a violent glare by the trapped and channeled solar output; a million billion fist-sized computing caltrops, backsides glowing dull red with the efflux from their thinking, orbit the sun at various inclinations no further out than Mercury used to be.

Billions of fleshbody humans refuse to have anything to do with the blasphemous new realities. Many of their leaders denounce the uploads and AIs as soulless machines. Many more are timid, harboring self-preservation memes that amplify a previously healthy aversion to having one's brain peeled like an onion by mind-mapping robots into an all-pervading neurosis—sales of electrified tinfoil-lined hats are at an all-time high. Still, hundreds of millions have already traded their meat puppets for mind machines: and they breed fast. In another few years, the fleshbody populace will be an absolute minority of the posthuman clade. Some time later, there will probably be a war: the dwellers in the thoughtcloud are hungry for dumb matter to convert, and the fleshbodies make notoriously poor use of the collection of silicon and rare elements that pool at the bottom of their gravity well.

Energy and thought are driving a phase change in the condensed matter substance of the solar system. The MIPS per kilogram metric is on the steep upward leg of a sigmoidal curve—dumb matter is coming to life as the mind children restructure everything with voracious nanomechanical servants. The thoughtcloud forming in orbit around the sun will ultimately mark the graveyard of a biological ecology, another marker in space visible to the telescopes of any new iron-age species with the insight to understand what they're seeing: the death throes of dumb matter, the birth of a habitable reality vaster than a galaxy and far speedier. Death throes that within a few centuries will mean the extinction of biological life within a light year or so of that star—for the majestic Matrioshka brains, though they are the pinnacles of sentient civilization, are innately hostile to fleshy life.

Pierre, Donna-the-all-seeing-eye, and Su Ang fill Amber in on what they've discovered about the bazaar—as they call the space the ghost referred to as the demilitarized zone—over ice-cold margaritas and a very good simulation of a sociable joint.

"It's half a light hour in diameter, four hundred times as massive as Earth," Pierre explains. "Not *solid*, of course—the largest component is about the size my fist used to be." Amber squints, trying to remember how big that was—scale factors are hard to remember accurately. "I met this old chatbot that said it's outlived its original star, but I'm not sure it's running with a full deck. Anyway, if it's telling the truth, we're a third of a light year out from a closely coupled binary system—they use orbital lasers the size of Jupiter to power it without getting too close to all those icky gravity wells."

Amber is intimidated, despite her better judgment, because the bazaar is several orders of magnitude more complex than the totality of human pre-singularity civilization. She tries not to show it in front of the others, but she's worried that getting home may be impossible—requiring enterprise beyond the economic event horizon, as realistic a proposition as a dime debuting as a dollar bill. Still, she's got to at least try. Just knowing about the existence of the bazaar will change so many things—

"How much money can we lay our hands on?" she asks. "What *is* money hereabouts, anyway? Assuming they've got a scarcity-mediated economy. Bandwidth, maybe?"

"Ah, well." Pierre looks at her oddly. "That's the problem. Didn't the ghost tell you?"

"Tell me?" Amber raises an eyebrow. "Yeah, but it hasn't exactly proven to be a reliable guide to anything, has it?"

"Tell her," Su Ang says quietly. She looks away, embarrassed by something.

"They've got a scarcity economy all right," says Pierre. "Bandwidth is the limited resource and things that come from other cognitive universes are, well, currency. We came in through the coin slot, is it any wonder we ended up in the bank?"

"That's so deeply wrong that I don't know where to begin," Amber grumbles. "How did they get into this mess?"

"Don't ask me." Pierre shrugs. "I have the distinct feeling that anyone or anything we meet in this place won't have any more of a clue than we do—whoever or whatever built this brain, there ain't nobody home any more except for the self-propelled corporations and hitchhikers like the Wunch. We're in the dark, just like they were."

"Huh." Amber focuses on the table in front of her, rests the heel of her palm on the cool metal, and tries to remember how to fork a second copy of her state vector. A moment later her ghost obligingly fucks with the physics model of the table; iron gives way like rubber beneath her fingertips, a pleasant elasticity. "Okay, we have some control over the universe, at least that's something to work with. Tried any self-modification?"

"That's dangerous," Pierre says emphatically. "The more of us the better before we start doing *that* stuff. And we need some firewalling of our own."

"How deep does reality go, here?" asks Sadeq. It's almost the first question he's asked of his own volition, and Amber takes it as a positive sign that he's finally coming out of his shell.

"Oh, the Planck length is about a hundredth of a millimeter here. Too small to see, comfortably large for the simulation engines to handle. Not like *real* spacetime."

"Well, then." Sadeq pauses. "They can zoom their reality if they need to?"

"Yeah, fractals work in here." Pierre nods. "I didn't—"

"This place is a trap," Su Ang says emphatically.

"No, it isn't," Pierre replies, nettled.

"What do you mean, a trap?" asks Amber.

"We've been here awhile," says Ang. She glances at Aineko, who sprawls on the flagstones, snoozing or whatever it is that weakly superhuman AIs do when they're emulating a sleeping cat. "After your cat broke us out of bondage, we had a look around. There are things here that—" She shivers. "Humans can't survive in most of the simulation spaces here. We're talking universes with physics models that don't support our kind of neural computing. You could migrate there, but you'd need to be ported to a whole new type of logic—by the time you did that, would you still be *you*? Still, there are enough entities roughly as complex as we are to prove that the builders aren't here any more. Just lesser sapients, rooting through the wreckage. Worms and parasites squirming through the body after nightfall on the battlefield."

"So there's no hope of making contact," Amber summarizes. "At least, not with anything transcendent and well-inclined."

"That's right," Pierre concedes. He doesn't sound happy about it.

"And we're stuck in a pocket universe with limited bandwidth to home and a bunch of crazy slum-dwellers who want to use us for currency. 'Jesus saves, and redeems souls for valuable gifts.' Yeah?"

"Yeah." Su Ang looks gloomy.

"Well." Amber glances at Sadeq speculatively. Sadeq is staring into the distance, at the crazy infinite sun spot that limns the square with shadows. "Hey, god-man. Got a question for you."

"Yes?" Sadeq looks at her, a slightly dazed expression on his face. "I'm sorry, I am just feeling the jaws of a larger trap around my throat—"

"Don't be." Amber grins, and it is not a pleasant expression. "Have you ever been to Brooklyn?"

"No, why—"

"You're going to help me sell these lying bastards a bridge. Okay? And when we've sold it, we're going to get the buyer to drive us across, so we can go home. Listen, here's how we're going to do it...."

"I can do this, I think," Sadeq says, moodily examining the Klein bottle on the table. The bottle is half-empty, its fluid contents invisible around the corner of the fourth dimensional store. "I spent long enough alone in there to—" He shivers.

"I don't want you damaging yourself," Amber says, calmly enough, because she has an ominous feeling that their survival in this place has an expiration date attached.

"Oh, never fear." Sadeq grins lopsidedly. "One pocket hell is much like another."

"Do you understand why—"

"Yes, yes," he says dismissively. "We can't send copies of ourselves into it, that would be an abomination. It needs to be unpopulated, yes?"

"Well. The idea is to get us home, not leave thousands of copies of ourselves trapped in a pocket universe here. Isn't that it?" Su Ang asks hesitantly. She's looking distracted, most of her attention focused on absorbing the experiences of a dozen ghosts she's spun off to attend to perimeter security.

"Who are we selling this *to?*" asks Sadeq. "If you want me to make it attractive—"

"It doesn't need to be a complete replica of the Earth. It just has to be a convincing advertisement for a pre-singularity civilization full of humans. You've got two-and-seventy zombies to dissect for their brains; bolt together a bunch of variables you can apply to them and you can permutate them to look a bit more varied."

Amber turns her attention to the snoozing cat. "Hey, furball. How long have we been here really, in real-time? Can you grab Sadeq some more resources for his personal paradise garden?"

Aineko stretches and yawns, totally feline, then looks up at Amber with narrowed eyes and raised tail. "'Bout eighteen minutes, wall-clock time." The cat stretches again and sits, front paws drawn together primly, tail curled around them. "The ghosts are pushing. You know? I don't think I can sustain this for too much longer. They're not good at hacking you, but I think it won't be too long before they instantiate a new copy of you, one that'll be predisposed to their side."

"I don't get why they didn't assimilate you along with the rest of us."

"Blame your mother again—she's the one who kept updating the digital rights management code on my personality. 'Illegal consciousness is copyright theft' sucks until an alien tries to rewire your hindbrain with a debugger; then it's a life-saver." Aineko glances down and begins washing one paw. "I can give your mullah-man about six days, subjective time. After that, all bets are off."

"I will take it, then." Sadeq stands. "Thank you." He smiles at the cat; a smile that fades to translucency, hanging in the simulated air like an echo as the priest returns to his tower—this time with a blueprint and a plan in mind.

"That leaves just us." Su Ang glances at Pierre, back to Amber. "Who are you going to sell this crazy scheme to?"

Amber leans back and smiles. Behind her, Donna—her avatar an archaic movie camera suspended below a model helicopter—is filming everything for posterity. "Who do we know who's dumb enough to buy into a scam like this?"

Pierre looks at her suspiciously. "I think we've been here before," he says slowly. "You aren't going to make me kill anyone, are you?"

"I don't think that'll be necessary, unless the corporate ghosts think we're going to get away from them and are greedy enough to want to kill us."

"You see, she learned from last time," Ang comments, and Amber nods. "No more misunderstandings. Right?" She beams at Amber.

Amber beams right back. "Right. And that's why *you*—" she points at Pierre—"are going to go find out if any relics of the Wunch are hanging about here. I want you to make them an offer they won't refuse."

"How much for just the civilization?" asks the slug.

Pierre looks down at it thoughtfully. It's not really a terrestrial mollusk; slugs on earth aren't two meters long and don't have lacy white exoskeletons to hold their chocolate-colored flesh in shape. But then, it isn't really the alien it appears to be, either; it's a defaulting corporate instrument that has disguised itself as a long-extinct alien upload, in the hope that its creditors won't recognize it if it looks like a randomly evolved sentient.

"The civilization isn't for sale," Pierre says slowly. The translation interface shimmers, storing up his words and transforming them into a different deep grammar: not merely translating his syntax, but mapping equivalent meanings where necessary. "But we can give you privileged observer status if that's what you want. And we know what you are. If you're interested in finding a new exchange to be traded on, your existing intellectual property assets will be worth rather more there than here."

The rogue corporation rears up slightly and bunches into a fatter lump; its skin blushes red in patches. "Must think about this. Is your mandatory accounting time-cycle fixed or variable term? Are self-owned corporate entities able to enter contracts?"

"I could ask my patron," Pierre says casually. Suppressing a stab of angst; he's still not sure where he and Amber stand, but theirs is far more than just a business relationship and he worries about the risks she's taking. "My patron has a jurisdiction within which she can modify corporate law to accommodate your requirements. Your activities on a wider scale might require shell companies, but that can be taken care of."

The translation membrane wibbles for a while, apparently reformulating some difficult concepts in a manner that the corporation can absorb. Pierre is reasonably confident that it'll work, however. He waits patiently, looking around at the swampy landscape, mud flats punctuated by clumps of spiky violet ferns. The corporation has to be desperate, to be considering the bizarre proposition that Amber has dreamed up for him to pitch to it.

"Sounds interesting," the slug declares after a brief confirmatory debate with the membrane. "If I supply the genome, can you customize a container for it?"

"I believe so," Pierre says carefully. "For your part, can you deliver the energy we need?"

"From a gate?" For a moment the translation membrane hallucinates a stick-human, shrugging. "Easy. Gates are all entangled: dump coherent radiation in at one, get it out at another."

"But the lightspeed lag—"

"No problem. You go first, then a dumb instrument I leave behind buys up power and sends it after. Router network is synchronous, within framework of state machines that run Universe 1.0; messages propagate at same speed, speed of light in vacuum. Whole point of the network is that it is non-lossy. Who would trust their mind to a communications channel that might partially randomize them in transit?"

Pierre goes cross-eyed, trying to understand the implications of the slug's cosmology. But there isn't really time, here and now: they've got on the order of a minute of wall-clock time to get everything together, if Aineko is right, before the angry ghosts that resurrected Amber to do their bidding start trying to break into the DMZ by other means. "If you are willing to try this, we'd be happy to accommodate you," he says, thinking of crossed fingers and rabbits' feet and firewalls.

"It's a deal," the membrane translates the slug's response back at him. "Now we exchange shares/plasmids/ownership? Then merger complete?"

Pierre stares at the slug: "But this is a business arrangement!" he protests. "What's sex got to do with it?"

"Apologies offered. I am thinking we have a translation error. You said this was to be a merging of businesses?"

"Not *that* way. It's a contract. We agree to take you with us. In return, you help lure the Wunch into the domain we're setting up for them...."

And so on.

Steeling herself, Amber recalls the address the ghost gave her for Sadeq's afterlife universe. In her own subjective time, it's been about half an hour since he left. "Coming?" she asks her cat.

"Don't think I will," says Aineko. It looks away, blissfully unconcerned.

"Bah." Amber tenses, then opens the port to Sadeq's pocket universe.

As before, she finds herself indoors, standing on an ornate mosaic floor in a room with whitewashed walls and peaked windows. But there's something different about it, and, after a moment, she realizes what it is. The sound of vehicle traffic from outside, the cooing of pigeons on the rooftops, someone shouting across the street: there are people here.

She walks over to the nearest window and looks out, then recoils. It's *hot* outside. Dust and fumes hang in air the color of cement over rough-finished concrete apartment buildings, their roofs covered in satellite uplinks and cheap, garish LED advertising panels. Looking down, she sees motor scooters, cars—filthy fossil-fuelled behemoths, a ton of steel and explosives in motion to carry only one human, a mass ratio worse than an archaic ICBM—brightly dressed people walking to and fro. A news helicam buzzes overhead, lenses darting and glinting at the traffic.

"Just like home, isn't it?" says Sadeq, behind her.

Amber starts. "This is where you grew up? This is Yazd?"

"It doesn't exist any more, in realspace." Sadeq looks thoughtful, but far more animated than the barely conscious parody of himself that she'd rescued from this building—back when it was a mediaeval vision of the afterlife—scant subjective hours ago. He cracks a smile: "Probably a good thing. They were dismantling it even while we were preparing to leave, you know?"

"It's detailed." Amber throws her gaze out through the window, multiplexes it, sends little virtual viewpoints dancing through the streets of the Iranian industrial 'burb. Overhead, big Airbuses ply the skyways, bearing pilgrims on the Hajj, tourists to the coastal resorts on the Persian Gulf, produce to the foreign markets.

"It's the best time I could recall," Sadeq says. "I didn't spend much time here—I was in Qom, studying, and Kazakhstan, for cosmonaut training—but it's meant to be the early twenties. After the troubles, after the fall of the guardians; a young, energetic, liberal country full of optimism and faith in democracy. Values that weren't doing well elsewhere."

"I thought democracy was a new thing there?"

"No." Sadeq shakes his head. "There were pro-democracy riots in Tehran in the nineteenth century, did you know that? That's why the first

revolution—no." He makes a cutting gesture. "Politics I can live without."
He frowns. "But look. Is this what you wanted?"

Amber recalls her scattered eyes—some of which have flown as
much as a thousand kilometers from her locus—and concentrates on
reintegrating: memories of Sadeq's re-creation. "It looks convincing. But
not too convincing."

"That was the idea."

"Well, then." She smiles. "Is it just Iran? Or did you take any liberties
around the edges?"

"Who, me?" He raises an eyebrow. "I have enough doubts about the
morality of this—project—without trying to trespass on Allah's territory,
peace be unto him. I promise you, there are no sapients in this world but
us; the people are the hollow shells of my dreaming, storefront dummies.
The animals are crude bitmaps. This is what you asked for, and no more."

"Well, then." Amber pauses. Recalls the expression on the dirt-
smudged face of a little boy, bouncing a ball at his companions by the
boarded-up front of a gas station on a desert road. Remembers the
animated chatter of two synthetic housewives, one in traditional black
and the other in some imported Eurotrash fashion. "Are you sure they
aren't real?" she asks.

"Quite sure." But for a moment, she sees Sadeq looking uncertain.
"Shall we go? Do you have the occupiers ready to move in yet?"

"Yes to the first, and Pierre's working on the second. Come on, we
don't want to get trampled by the squatters." She waves and opens a
door back onto the piazza, where her robot cat—the alien's nightmare
intruder in the DMZ—sleeps, chasing superintelligent dream mice
through multidimensional realities. "Sometimes I wonder if *I'm* conscious.
Thinking these thoughts gives me the creeps; let's go and sell a bridge."

Amber confronts the mendacious ghost in the windowless room stolen
from *2001*.

"You have confined the monster," the ghost states.

"Yes." Amber waits for a subjective moment, feeling delicate fronds
tickle at the edges of her awareness in what seems to be a timing-channel
attack. She feels a momentary urge to sneeze, a hot flash of anger that
passes almost immediately.

"And you have modified yourself to lock out external control," the ghost adds. "What is it that you want, Autonome Amber?"

"Don't you have any concept of individuality?" she asks, annoyed by its presumption at meddling with her internal states.

"Individuality is an unnecessary barrier to information transfer," says the ghost, morphing into its original form, a translucent reflection of her own body. "A large block of the DMZ is still inaccessible to we-me. Are you *sure* you have defeated the monster?"

"It'll do as I say," Amber replies, forcing herself to sound more confident than she feels—that damned transhuman cyborg cat is no more predictable than any real feline. "Now, the matter of payment arises."

"Payment." The ghost sounds amused. But now Pierre's filled her in on what to look for, Amber can see the translation membranes around it. Their color shift maps to a huge semantic distance; the creature on the other side, even though it looks like a ghost-image of herself, is very far from human. "How can we-us be expected to pay our own money for rendering services to us?"

Amber smiles. "We want an open channel back to the router we arrived through."

"Impossible," says the ghost.

"We want an open channel, *and* for it to stay open for six hundred million seconds after we clear it."

"Impossible," the ghost repeats.

"We can trade you a whole civilization," Amber says blandly. "A whole human nation, millions of individuals. Just let us go and we'll see to it."

"You—please wait." The ghost shimmers slightly, fuzzing at the edges.

Amber opens a private channel to Pierre while the ghost confers with its other nodes. *Are the Wunch in place yet?* she sends.

They're moving in. This bunch don't remember what happened on the Field Circus, memories of those events never made it back to them. So the slug's got them to cooperate. It's kinda scary to watch—like the Invasion of the Body Snatchers, you know?

I don't care if it's scary to watch, Amber replies, *I need to know if we're ready yet.*

Sadeq says yes, the universe is ready.

Right, pack yourself down. We'll be moving soon.

The ghost is firming up in front of her. "A whole civilization?" it asks.

"That is not possible. Your arrival—" It pauses, fuzzing a little. *Hah, Gotcha!* thinks Amber. *Liar, liar, pants on fire!* "You cannot possibly have found a human civilization in the archives."

"The monster you complain about that came through with us is a predator," she asserts blandly. "It swallowed an entire nation before we heroically attracted its attention and induced it to follow us into the router. It's an archevore—everything was *inside* it, still frozen until we expanded it again. This civilization will have been restored from hot shadows in our own solar system, already; there is nothing to gain by taking it home with us. But we need to return to ensure that no more predators of this type discover the router—or the high bandwidth hub we linked to it."

"You are sure you have killed this monster?" asks the ghost. "It would be inconvenient if it were to emerge from hiding in its digest archives."

"I can guarantee it won't trouble you again if you let us go," says Amber, mentally crossing her fingers. The ghost doesn't seem to have noticed the huge wedge of fractally compressed data that bloats her personal scope by an order of magnitude. She can still feel Aineko's goodbye smile inside her head, an echo of ivory teeth trusting her to revive it if the escape plan succeeds.

"We-us agree." The ghost twists weirdly, morphs into a five-dimensional hypersphere. It bubbles violently for a moment, then spits out a smaller token—a warped distortion in the air, like a gravityless black hole. "Here is your passage. Show us the civilization."

"Okay—" *Now!* "—catch." Amber twitches an imaginary muscle and one wall of the room dissolves, forming a doorway into Sadeq's existential hell, now redecorated as a fair facsimile of a twenty-first-century industrial city in Iran, and populated by a Wunch of parasites who can't believe what they've lucked into—an entire continent of zombies waiting to host their flesh-hungry consciousness.

The ghost drifts toward the open window; Amber grabs the hole and yanks it open, gets a grip on her own thoughts, and sends *open wide!* on the channel everybody is listening in on. For a moment time stands still; and then—

A synthetic gemstone the size of a Coke can falls through the cold vacuum, in high orbit around a brown dwarf. But the vacuum is anything but dark. A sapphire glare as bright as the noonday sun on Mars shines on the crazy diamond, billowing and cascading off sails as fine as soap bubbles that slowly drift and tense away from the can. The runaway slug-corporation's proxy is holding the router open, and the lump of strange matter is shining with the brilliance of a nuclear fireball, laser light channeled from a star eight light years away to power the *Field Circus* on its return trip to the once-human solar system.

Amber has retreated, with Pierre, into a simulation of her home aboard the Ring Imperium. One wall of her bedroom is a solid slab of diamond, looking out across the boiling Jovian ionosphere from an orbit low enough to make the horizon appear flat. They're curled together in her bed, a slightly more comfortable copy of the royal bed of King Henry VIII of England, a bed that appears to be carved from thousand-year-old oak beams. As with everything else about the Ring Imperium, appearances are deceptive: and even more so in the cramped simulation spaces of the *Field Circus* as it slowly accelerates toward a tenth of lightspeed.

"Let me get this straight. You convinced. The locals. That a simulation of Iran populated by refugee members of the Wunch. Was a human civilization?"

"Yeah." Amber stretches lazily and smirks at him. "It's *their* damn fault; if the corporate collective entities didn't use conscious viewpoints as money, they wouldn't have fallen for a trick like that, would they?"

"People. Money."

"Well." She yawns, then sits up and snaps her finger imperiously: down-stuffed pillows appear behind her back, and a silver salver bearing two full glasses of wine materializes between them. "Corporations are life forms back home, too, aren't they? We give our AIs corporations to make them legal entities, but it goes further. Look at any company headquarters, fitted out with works of art and expensive furniture and with staff bowing-and-scraping everywhere—"

"—The new aristocracy. Right?"

"Wrong. When they take over, what you get is more like the new biosphere. Hell, the new primordial soup: prokaryotes, bacteria and algae, mindlessly swarming, trading money for plasmids." The Queen passes her consort a wine glass. He drinks from it: it refills miraculously. "You've got to wonder where the builders of that structure *came* from. And where they *went*."

"Maybe the companies spent them." Pierre looks worried. "Running up a national debt, importing luxurious viewpoint extensions, munching exotic dreams. Once they plugged into the net, a primitive Matrioshka civilization would be like, um." He pauses. "Tribal. A primitive post-singularity civilization meeting the galactic net for the first time. Overawed. Wanting all the luxuries. Spending their capital, their human—or alien—capital, the meme machines that built them. Until there's nothing left but a howling wilderness of corporate mechanisms looking for someone to own."

"Speculation."

"Idle speculation," he agrees.

"But we can't ignore it." She nods. "Is the hitchhiker happy?"

"Last time I checked on him, yeah." Pierre blows on his wine glass and it dissolves into a million splinters of light, but he looks dubious at the mention of the slug-shaped corporate instrument they're taking with them in return for help engineering their escape. "Don't trust him out in the unrestricted sim-spaces yet. Aineko is spending a lot of time with him."

"So that's where she is!"

"Cats never come when you call them, do they?"

"There's that," she agrees. Then with a worried glance at the vision of Jupiter's cloudscape: "I wonder what we'll find when we get there?"

Outside the window, the imaginary Jovian terminator is sweeping toward them with eerie rapidity, sucking them toward an uncertain nightfall.

Robert Reed (b. 1956) earned a degree in biology from Nebraska Wesleyan University, and after working in industry for a number of years established a career as the most prolific modern writer of short science fiction. His work is noted for its broad variety and its engagement with huge concepts of time and space through humane and well-realized characters. Here he offers a strange and oddly moving tale of loss and discovery in a world where humans are but an afterthought.

COELACANTHS
> Robert Reed

The Speaker

He stalks the wide stage, a brilliant beam of hot blue light fixed squarely upon him. "We are great! We are glorious!" the man calls out. His voice is pleasantly, effortlessly loud. With a face handsome to the brink of lovely and a collage of smooth, passionate mannerisms, he performs for an audience that sits in the surrounding darkness. Flinging long arms overhead, hands reaching for the distant light, his booming voice proclaims, "We have never been as numerous as we are today. We have never been this happy. And we have never known the prosperity that is ours at this golden moment. This golden now!" Athletic legs carry him across the stage, bare feet slapping against planks of waxed maple. "Our species is thriving," he can declare with a seamless ease. "By every conceivable measure, we are a magnificent, irresistible tide sweeping across the universe!"

Transfixed by the blue beam, his naked body is shamelessly young, rippling with hard muscles over hard bone. A long fat penis dangles and dances, accenting every sweeping gesture, every bold word. The living image of a small but potent god, he surely is a creature worthy of admiration, a soul deserving every esteem and emulation. With a laugh, he promises the darkness, "We have never been so powerful, we humans." Yet in the next breath, with a faintly apologetic smile, he must add, "Yet still, as surely as tomorrow comes, our glories today will seem small and quaint in the future, and what looks golden now will turn to the yellow dust upon which our magnificent children will tread!"

Procyon

Study your history. It tells you that travel always brings its share of hazards; that's a basic, impatient law of the universe. Leaving the security and familiarity of home is never easy. But every person needs to make the occasional journey, embracing the risks to improve his station, his worth and self-esteem. Procyon explains why this day is a good day to wander. She refers to intelligence reports as well as the astrological tables. Then by a dozen means, she maps out their intricate course, describing what she hopes to find and everything that she wants to avoid.

She has twin sons. They were born four months ago, and they are mostly grown now. "Keep alert," she tells the man-children, leading them out through a series of reinforced and powerfully camouflaged doorways. "No naps, no distractions," she warns them. Then with a backward glance, she asks again, "What do we want?"

"Whatever we can use," the boys reply in a sloppy chorus.

"Quiet," she warns. Then she nods and shows a caring smile, reminding them, "A lot of things can be used. But their trash is sweetest."

Mother and sons look alike: They are short, strong people with closely cropped hair and white-gray eyes. They wear simple clothes and three fashions of camouflage, plus a stew of mental add-ons and microchine helpers as well as an array of sensors that never blink, watching what human eyes cannot see. Standing motionless, they vanish into the convoluted, ever-shifting background. But walking makes them into three transient blurs—dancing wisps that are noticeably simpler than the enormous world around them. They can creep ahead only so far before their camouflage falls apart, and then they have to stop, waiting patiently or otherwise, allowing the machinery to find new ways to help make them invisible.

"I'm confused," one son admits. "That thing up ahead—"

"Did you update your perception menu?"

"I thought I did."

Procyon makes no sound. Her diamond-bright glare is enough. She remains rigidly, effortlessly still, allowing her lazy son to finish his preparations. Dense, heavily encoded signals have to be whispered, the local net downloading the most recent topological cues, teaching a three-dimensional creature how to navigate through this shifting, highly intricate environment.

The universe is fat with dimensions.

Procyon knows as much theory as anyone. Yet despite a long life rich with experience, she has to fight to decipher what her eyes and sensors tell her. She doesn't even bother learning the tricks that coax these extra dimensions out of hiding. Let her add-ons guide her. That's all a person can do, slipping in close to one of them. In this place, up is three things and sideways is five others. Why bother counting? What matters is that when they walk again, the three of them move through the best combination of dimensions, passing into a little bubble of old-fashioned up and down. She knows this place. Rising up beside them is a trusted landmark—a red granite bowl that cradles what looks like a forest of tall sticks, the sticks leaking a warm light that Procyon ignores, stepping again, moving along on her tiptoes.

One son leads the way. He lacks the experience to be first, but in another few weeks, his flesh and sprint-grown brain will force him into the world alone. He needs his practice, and more important, he needs confidence, learning to trust his add-ons and his careful preparations, and his breeding, and his own good luck.

Procyon's other son lingers near the granite bowl. He's the son who didn't update his menu. This is her dreamy child, whom she loves dearly. Of course she adores him. But there's no escaping the fact that he is easily distracted, and that his adult life will be, at its very best, difficult. Study your biology. Since life began, mothers have made hard decisions about their children, and they have made the deadliest decisions with the tiniest of gestures.

Procyon lets her lazy son fall behind.

Her other son takes two careful steps and stops abruptly, standing before what looks like a great black cylinder set on its side. The shape is a fiction: The cylinder is round in one fashion but incomprehensible in many others. Her add-ons and sensors have built this very simple geometry to represent something far more elaborate. This is a standard disposal unit. Various openings appear as a single slot near the rim of the cylinder, just enough room showing for a hand and forearm to reach through, touching whatever garbage waits inside.

Her son's thick body has more grace than any dancer of old, more strength than a platoon of ancient athletes. His IQ is enormous. His reaction times have been enhanced by every available means. His father was a great old soul who survived into his tenth year, which is almost forever. But when the boy drifts sideways, he betrays his inexperience. His sensors attack the cylinder by every means, telling him that it's a low-grade trash receptacle secured by what looks like a standard locking device, AI-managed and obsolete for days, if not weeks. And inside the receptacle is a mangled piece of hardware worth a near-fortune on the open market.

The boy drifts sideways, and he glimmers.

Procyon says, "No," too loudly.

But he feels excited, invulnerable. Grinning over his shoulder now, he winks and lifts one hand with a smooth, blurring motion—

Instincts old as blood come bubbling up. Procyon leaps, shoving her son off his feet and saving him. And in the next horrible instant, she feels herself engulfed, a dry cold hand grabbing her, then stuffing her inside a hole that by any geometry feels nothing but bottomless.

Able

Near the lip of the City, inside the emerald green ring of Park, waits a secret place where the moss and horsetail and tree fern forest plunges into a deep crystalline pool of warm spring water. No public map tells of the pool, and no trail leads the casual walker near it. But the pool is exactly the sort of place that young boys always discover, and it is exactly the kind of treasure that remains unmentioned to parents or any other adult with suspicious or troublesome natures.

Able Quotient likes to believe that he was first to stumble across this tiny corner of Creation. And if he isn't first, at least no one before him has ever truly seen the water's beauty, and nobody after him will appreciate the charms of this elegant, timeless place.

Sometimes Able brings others to the pool, but only his best friends and a few boys whom he wants to impress. Not for a long time does he even consider bringing a girl, and then it takes forever to find a worthy candidate, then muster the courage to ask her to join him. Her name is Mish. She's younger than Able by a little ways, but like all girls, she acts older and much wiser than he will ever be. They have been classmates from the beginning. They live three floors apart in The Tower Of Gracious Good, which makes them close neighbors. Mish is pretty, and her beauty is the sort that will only grow as she becomes a woman. Her face is narrow and serious. Her eyes watch everything. She wears flowing dresses and jeweled sandals, and she goes everywhere with a clouded leopard named Mr. Stuff-and-Nonsense. "If my cat can come along," she says after hearing Able's generous offer. "Are there any birds at this pond of yours?"

Able should be horrified by the question. The life around the pool knows him and has grown to trust him. But he is so enamored by Mish that he blurts out, "Yes, hundreds of birds. Fat, slow birds. Mr. Stuff can eat himself sick."

"But that wouldn't be right," Mish replies with a disapproving smirk. "I'll lock down his appetite. And if we see any wounded birds...any animal that's suffering...we can unlock him right away...!"

"Oh, sure," Able replies, almost sick with nerves. "I guess that's fine, too."

People rarely travel any distance. City is thoroughly modern, every apartment supplied by conduits and meshed with every web and channel, shareline and gossip run. But even with most of its citizens happily sitting at home, the streets are jammed with millions of walking bodies. Every seat on the train is filled all the way to the last stop. Able momentarily loses track of Mish when the cabin walls evaporate. But thankfully, he finds her waiting at Park's edge. She and her little leopard are standing in the narrow shade of a horsetail. She teases him, observing, "You look lost." Then she laughs, perhaps at him, before abruptly changing the subject. With a nod and sweeping gesture, she asks, "Have you noticed? Our towers look like these trees."

To a point, yes. The towers are tall and thin and rounded like the horsetails, and the hanging porches make them appear rough-skinned. But there are obvious and important differences between trees and towers, and if she were a boy, Able would make fun of her now. Fighting his nature, Able forces himself to smile. "Oh, my," he says as he turns, looking back over a shoulder. "They do look like horsetails, don't they?"

Now the three adventurers set off into the forest. Able takes the lead. Walking with boys is a quick business that often turns into a race. But girls are different, particularly when their fat, unhungry cats are dragging along behind them. It takes forever to reach the rim of the world. Then it takes another two forevers to follow the rim to where they can almost see the secret pool. But that's where Mish announces, "I'm tired!" To the world, she says, "I want to stop and eat. I want to rest here."

Able nearly tells her, "No."

Instead he decides to coax her, promising, "It's just a little farther."

But she doesn't seem to hear him, leaping up on the pink polished rim, sitting where the granite is smooth and flat, legs dangling and her bony knees exposed. She opens the little pack that has floated on her back from the beginning, pulling out a hot lunch that she keeps and a cold lunch that she hands to Able. "This is all I could take," she explains, "without my parents asking questions." She is reminding Able that she never quite got permission to make this little journey. "If you don't like the cold lunch," she promises, "then we can trade. I mean, if you really don't."

He says, "I like it fine," without opening the insulated box. Then he looks inside, discovering a single wedge of spiced sap, and it takes all of his poise not to say, "Ugh!"

Mr. Stuff collapses into a puddle of towerlight, instantly falling asleep.

The two children eat quietly and slowly. Mish makes the occasional noise about favorite teachers and mutual friends. She acts serious and ordinary, and disappointment starts gnawing at Able. He isn't old enough to sense that the girl is nervous. He can't imagine that Mish wants to delay the moment when they'll reach the secret pool, or that she sees possibilities waiting there—wicked possibilities that only a wicked boy should be able to foresee.

Finished with her meal, Mish runs her hands along the hem of her dress, and she kicks at the air, and then, hunting for any distraction, she happens to glance over her shoulder.

Where the granite ends, the world ends. Normally nothing of substance can be seen out past the pink stone—nothing but a confused, ever-shifting grayness that extends on forever. Able hasn't bothered to look out there. He is much too busy trying to finish his awful meal, concentrating on his little frustrations and his depraved little daydreams.

"Oh, goodness," the young girl exclaims. "Look at that!"

Able has no expectations. What could possibly be worth the trouble of turning around? But it's an excuse to give up on his lunch, and after setting it aside, he turns slowly, eyes jumping wide open and a surprised grunt leaking out of him as he tumbles off the granite, landing squarely on top of poor Mr. Stuff.

Escher

She has a clear, persistent memory of flesh, but the flesh isn't hers. Like manners and like knowledge, what a person remembers can be bequeathed by her ancestors. That's what is happening now. Limbs and heads; penises and vaginas. In the midst of some unrelated business, she remembers having feet and the endless need to protect those feet with sandals or boots or ostrich skin or spiked shoes that will lend a person even more height. She remembers wearing clothes that gave color and bulk to what was already bright and enormous. At this particular instant, what she sees is a distant, long-dead relative sitting on a white porcelain bowl, bare feet dangling, his orifices voiding mountains of waste and an ocean of water.

Her oldest ancestors were giants. They were built from skin and muscle, wet air and great slabs of fat. Without question, they were an astonishing excess of matter, vast beyond all reason, yet fueled by slow, inefficient chemical fires.

Nothing about Escher is inefficient. No flesh clings to her. Not a drop of water or one glistening pearl of fat. It's always smart to be built from structure light and tested, efficient instructions. It's best to be tinier than a single cell and as swift as electricity, slipping unseen through places that won't even notice your presence.

Escher is a glimmer, a perfect and enduring whisper of light. Of life. Lovely in her own fashion, yet fierce beyond all measure.

She needs her fierceness.

When cooperation fails, as it always does, a person has to throw her rage at the world and her countless enemies.

But in this place, for this moment, cooperation holds sway.

Manners rule.

Escher is eating. Even as tiny and efficient as she is, she needs an occasional sip of raw power. Everyone does. And it seems as if half of everyone has gathered around what can only be described as a tiny, delicious wound. She can't count the citizens gathered at the feast. Millions and millions, surely. All those weak glimmers join into a soft glow. Everyone is bathed in a joyous light. It is a boastful, wasteful show, but Escher won't waste her energy with warnings. Better to sip at the wound, absorbing the free current, building up her reserves for the next breeding cycle. It is best to let others make the mistakes for you: Escher believes nothing else quite so fervently.

A pair of sisters float past. The familial resemblance is obvious, and so are the tiny differences. Mutations as well as tailored changes have created two loud gossips who speak and giggle in a rush of words and raw data, exchanging secrets about the multitude around them.

Escher ignores their prattle, gulping down the last of what she can possibly hold, and then pausing, considering where she might hide a few nanojoules of extra juice, keeping them safe for some desperate occasion.

Escher begins to hunt for that unlikely hiding place.

And then her sisters abruptly change topics. Gossip turns to trading memories stolen from The World. Most of it is picoweight stuff, useless and boring. An astonishing fraction of His thoughts are banal. Like the giants of old, He can afford to be sloppy. To be a spendthrift. Here is a pointed example of why Escher is happy to be herself. She is smart in her own fashion, and imaginative, and almost everything about her is important, and when a problem confronts her, she can cut through the muddle, seeing the blessing wrapped up snug inside the measurable risks.

Quietly, with a puzzled tone, one sister announces, "The World is alarmed."

"About?" says the other.

"A situation," says the first. "Yes, He is alarmed now. Moral questions are begging for His attention."

"What questions?"

The first sister tells a brief, strange story.

"You know all this?" asks another. Asks Escher. "Is this daydream or hard fact?"

"I know, and it is fact." The sister feels insulted by the doubting tone, but she puts on a mannerly voice, explaining the history of this sudden crisis.

Escher listens.

And suddenly the multitude is talking about nothing else. What is happening has never happened before, not in this fashion...not in any genuine memory of any of the millions here, it hasn't...and some very dim possibilities begin to show themselves. Benefits wrapped inside some awful dangers. And one or two of these benefits wink at Escher, and smile....

The multitude panics, and evaporates.

Escher remains behind, deliberating on these possibilities. The landscape beneath her is far more sophisticated than flesh, and stronger, but it has an ugly appearance that reminds her of a flesh-born memory. A lesion; a pimple. A tiny, unsightly ruin standing in what is normally seamless, and beautiful, and perfect.

She flees, but only so far.

Then she hunkers down and waits, knowing that eventually, in one fashion or another, He will scratch at this tiny irritation.

The Speaker

"You cannot count human accomplishments," he boasts to his audience, strutting and wagging his way to the edge of the stage. Bare toes curl over the sharp edge, and he grins jauntily, admitting, "And I cannot count them, either. There are simply too many successes, in too many far flung places, to nail up a number that you can believe. But allow me, if you will, this chance to list a few important marvels."

Long hands grab bony hips, and he gazes out into the watching darkness. "The conquest of our cradle continent," he begins, "which was quickly followed by the conquest of our cradle world. Then after a gathering pause, we swiftly and thoroughly occupied most of our neighboring worlds, too. It was during those millennia when we learned how to split flint and atoms and DNA and our own restless psyches. With these apish hands, we fashioned great machines that worked for us as our willing, eager slaves. And with our slaves' more delicate hands, we fabricated machines that could think for us." A knowing wink, a mischievous shrug. "Like any child, of course, our thinking machines eventually learned to think for themselves. Which was a dangerous, foolish business, said some. Said fools. But my list of our marvels only begins with that business. This is what I believe, and I challenge anyone to say otherwise."

There is a sound—a stern little murmur—and perhaps it implies dissent. Or perhaps the speaker made the noise himself, fostering a tension that he is building with his words and body.

His penis grows erect, drawing the eye.

Then with a wide and bright and unabashedly smug grin, he roars out, "Say this with me. Tell me what great things we have done. Boast to Creation about the wonders that we have taken part in...!"

Procyon

Torture is what this is: She feels her body plunging from a high place, head before feet. A frantic wind roars past. Outstretched hands refuse to slow her fall. Then Procyon makes herself spin, putting her feet beneath her body, and gravity instantly reverses itself. She screams, and screams, and the distant walls reflect her terror, needles jabbed into her wounded ears. Finally, she grows quiet, wrapping her arms around her eyes and ears, forcing herself to do nothing, hanging limp in space while her body falls in one awful direction.

A voice whimpers.

A son's worried voice says, "Mother, are you there? Mother?"

Some of her add-ons have been peeled away, but not all of them. The brave son uses a whisper-channel, saying, "I'm sorry," with a genuine anguish. He sounds sick and sorry, and exceptionally angry, too. "I was careless," he admits. He says, "Thank you for saving me." Then to someone else, he says, "She can't hear me."

"I hear you," she whispers.

"Listen," says her other son. The lazy one. "Did you hear something?"

She starts to say, "Boys," with a stern voice. But then the trap vibrates, a piercing white screech nearly deafening Procyon. Someone physically strikes the trap. Two someones. She feels the walls turning around her, the trap making perhaps a quarter-turn toward home.

Again, she calls out, "Boys."

They stop rolling her. Did they hear her? No, they found a hidden restraint, the trap secured at one or two or ten ends.

One last time, she says, "Boys."

"I hear her," her dreamy son blurts.

"Don't give up, Mother," says her brave son. "We'll get you out. I see the locks, I can beat them—"

"You can't," she promises.

He pretends not to have heard her. A shaped explosive detonates, making a cold ringing sound, faraway and useless. Then the boy growls, "Damn," and kicks the trap, accomplishing nothing at all.

"It's too tough," says her dreamy son. "We're not doing any good—"

"Shut up," his brother shouts.

Procyon tells them, "Quiet now. Be quiet."

The trap is probably tied to an alarm. Time is short, or it has run out already. Either way, there's a decision to be made, and the decision has a single, inescapable answer. With a careful and firm voice, she tells her sons, "Leave me. Now. Go!"

"I won't," the brave son declares. "Never!"

"Now," she says.

"It's my fault," says the dreamy son. "I should have been keeping up—"

"Both of you are to blame," Procyon calls out. "And I am, too. And there's bad luck here, but there's some good, too. You're still free. You can still get away. Now, before you get yourself seen and caught—"

"You're going to die," the brave son complains.

"One day or the next, I will," she agrees. "Absolutely."

"We'll find help," he promises.

"From where?" she asks.

"From who?" says her dreamy son in the same instant. "We aren't close to anyone—"

"Shut up," his brother snaps. "Just shut up!"

"Run away," their mother repeats.

"I won't," the brave son tells her. Or himself. Then with a serious, tight little voice, he says, "I can fight. We'll both fight."

Her dreamy son says nothing.

Procyon peels her arms away from her face, opening her eyes, focusing on the blurring cylindrical walls of the trap. It seems that she was wrong about her sons. The brave one is just a fool, and the dreamy one has the good sense. She listens to her dreamy son saying nothing, and then the other boy says, "Of course you're going to fight. Together, we can do some real damage—"

"I love you both," she declares.

That wins a silence.

Then again, one last time, she says, "Run."

"I'm not a coward," one son growls.

While her good son says nothing, running now, and he needs his breath for things more essential than pride and bluster.

Able

The face stares at them for the longest while. It is a great wide face, heavily bearded with smoke-colored eyes and a long nose perched above the cavernous mouth that hangs open, revealing teeth and things more amazing than teeth. Set between the bone-white enamel are little machines made of fancy stuff. Able can only guess what the add-on machines are doing. This is a wild man, powerful and free. People like him are scarce and strange, their bodies reengineered in countless ways. Like his eyes: Able stares into those giant gray eyes, noticing fleets of tiny machines floating on the tears. Those machines are probably delicate sensors. Then with a jolt of amazement, he realizes that those machines and sparkling eyes are staring into their world with what seems to be a genuine fascination.

"He's watching us," Able mutters.

"No, he isn't," Mish argues. "He can't see into our realm."

"We can't see into his either," the boy replies. "But just the same, I can make him out just fine."

"It must be...." Her voice falls silent while she accesses City's library. Then with a dismissive shrug of her shoulders, she announces, "We're caught in his topological hardware. That's all. He has to simplify his surroundings to navigate, and we just happen to be close enough and aligned right."

Able had already assumed all that.

Mish starts to speak again, probably wanting to add to her explanation. She can sure be a know-everything sort of girl. But then the great face abruptly turns away, and they watch the man run away from their world.

"I told you," Mish sings out. "He couldn't see us."

"I think he could have," Able replies, his voice finding a distinct sharpness.

The girl straightens her back. "You're wrong," she says with an obstinate tone. Then she turns away from the edge of the world, announcing, "I'm ready to go on now."

"I'm not," says Able.

She doesn't look back at him. She seems to be talking to her leopard, asking, "Why aren't you ready?"

"I see two of them now," Able tells her.

"You can't."

"I can." The hardware trickery is keeping the outside realms sensible. A tunnel of simple space leads to two men standing beside an iron-black cylinder. The men wear camouflage, but they are moving too fast to let it work. They look small now. Distant, or tiny. Once you leave the world, size and distance are impossible to measure. How many times have teachers told him that? Able watches the tiny men kicking at the cylinder. They beat on its heavy sides with their fists and forearms, managing to roll it for almost a quarter turn. Then one of the men pulls a fist-sized device from what looks like a cloth sack, fixing it to what looks like a sealed slot, and both men hurry to the far end of the cylinder.

"What are they doing?" asks Mish with a grumpy interest.

A feeling warns Able, but too late. He starts to say, "Look away—"

The explosion is brilliant and swift, the blast reflected off the cylinder and up along the tunnel of ordinary space, a clap of thunder making the giant horsetails sway and nearly knocking the two of them onto the forest floor.

"They're criminals," Mish mutters with a nervous hatred.

"How do you know?" the boy asks.

"People like that just are," she remarks. "Living like they do. Alone like that, and wild. You know how they make their living."

"They take what they need—"

"They steal!" she interrupts.

Able doesn't even glance at her. He watches as the two men work frantically, trying to pry open the still-sealed doorway. He can't guess why they would want the doorway opened. Or rather, he can think of too many reasons. But when he looks at their anguished, helpless faces, he realizes that whatever is inside, it's driving these wild men very close to panic.

"Criminals," Mish repeats.

"I heard you," Able mutters.

Then before she can offer another hard opinion, he turns to her and admits, "I've always liked them. They live by their wits, and mostly alone, and they have all these sweeping powers—"

"Powers that they've stolen," she whines.

"From garbage, maybe." There is no point in mentioning whose garbage. He stares at Mish's face, pretty but twisted with fury, and something sad and inevitable occurs to Able. He shakes his head and sighs, telling her, "I don't like you very much."

Mish is taken by surprise. Probably no other boy has said those awful words to her, and she doesn't know how to react, except to sputter ugly little sounds as she turns, looking back over the edge of the world.

Able does the same.

One of the wild men abruptly turns and runs. In a supersonic flash, he races past the children, vanishing into the swirling grayness, leaving his companion to stand alone beside the mysterious black cylinder. Obviously weeping, the last man wipes the tears from his whiskered face with a trembling hand, while his other hand begins to yank a string of wondrous machines from what seems to be a bottomless sack of treasures.

Escher

She consumes all of her carefully stockpiled energies, and for the first time in her life, she weaves a body for herself: A distinct physical shell composed of diamond dust and keratin and discarded rare earths and a dozen subtle glues meant to bind to every surface without being felt. To a busy eye, she is dust. She is insubstantial and useless and forgettable. To a careful eye and an inquisitive touch, she is the tiniest soul imaginable, frail beyond words, forever perched on the brink of extermination. Surely she poses no threat to any creature, least of all the great ones. Lying on the edge of the little wound, passive and vulnerable, she waits for Chance to carry her where she needs to be. Probably others are doing the same. Perhaps thousands of sisters and daughters are hiding nearby, each snug inside her own spore case. The temptation to whisper, "Hello," is easily ignored. The odds are awful as it is; any noise could turn this into a suicide. What matters is silence and watchfulness, thinking hard about the great goal while keeping ready for anything that might happen, as well as everything that will not.

The little wound begins to heal, causing a trickling pain to flow.

The World feels the irritation, and in reflex, touches His discomfort by several means, delicate and less so.

Escher misses her first opportunity. A great swift shape presses its way across her hiding place, but she activates her glues too late. Dabs of glue cure against air, wasted. So she cuts the glue loose and watches again. A second touch is unlikely, but it comes, and she manages to heave a sticky tendril into a likely crevice, letting the irresistible force yank her into a brilliant, endless sky.

She will probably die now.

For a little while, Escher allows herself to look back across her life, counting daughters and other successes, taking warm comfort in her many accomplishments.

Someone hangs in the distance, dangling from a similar tendril. Escher recognizes the shape and intricate glint of her neighbor's spore case; she is one of Escher's daughters. There is a strong temptation to signal her, trading information, helping each other—

But a purge-ball attacks suddenly, and the daughter evaporates, nothing remaining of her but ions and a flash of incoherent light.

Escher pulls herself toward the crevice, and hesitates. Her tendril is anchored on a fleshy surface. A minor neuron—a thread of warm optical cable—lies buried inside the wet cells. She launches a second tendril at her new target. By chance, the purge-ball sweeps the wrong terrain, giving her that little instant. The tendril makes a sloppy connection with the neuron. Without time to test its integrity, all she can do is shout, "Don't kill me! Or my daughters! Don't murder us, Great World!"

Nothing changes. The purge-ball works its way across the deeply folded fleshscape, moving toward Escher again, distant flashes announcing the deaths of another two daughters or sisters.

"Great World!" she cries out.

He will not reply. Escher is like the hum of a single angry electron, and she can only hope that he notices the hum.

"I am vile," she promises. "I am loathsome and sneaky, and you should hate me. What I am is an illness lurking inside you. A disease that steals exactly what I can steal without bringing your wrath."

The purge-ball appears, following a tall reddish ridge of flesh, bearing down on her hiding place.

She says, "Kill me, if you want. Or spare me, and I will do this for you." Then she unleashes a series of vivid images, precise and simple, meant to be compelling to any mind.

The purge-ball slows, its sterilizing lasers taking careful aim.

She repeats herself, knowing that thought travels only so quickly and The World is too vast to see her thoughts and react soon enough to save her. But if she can help...if she saves just a few hundred daughters...?

Lasers aim, and do nothing. Nothing. And after an instant of inactivity, the machine changes its shape and nature. It hovers above Escher, sending out its own tendrils. A careless strength yanks her free of her hiding place. Her tendrils and glues are ripped from her aching body. A scaffolding of carbon is built around her, and she is shoved inside the retooled purge-ball, held in a perfect darkness, waiting alone until an identical scaffold is stacked beside her.

A hard, angry voice boasts, "I did this."

"What did you do?" asks Escher.

"I made The World listen to reason." It sounds like Escher's voice, except for the delusions of power. "I made a promise, and that's why He saved us."

With a sarcastic tone, she says, "Thank you ever so much. But now where are we going?"

"I won't tell you," her fellow prisoner responds.

"Because you don't know where," says Escher.

"I know everything I need to know."

"Then you're the first person ever," she giggles, winning a brief, delicious silence from her companion.

Other prisoners arrive, each slammed into the empty spaces between their sisters and daughters. Eventually the purge-ball is a prison-ball, swollen to vast proportions, and no one else is being captured. Nothing changes for a long while. There is nothing to be done now but wait, speaking when the urge hits and listening to whichever voice sounds less than tedious.

Gossip is the common currency. People are desperate to hear the smallest glimmer of news. Where the final rumor comes from, nobody knows if it's true. But the woman who was captured moments after Escher claims, "It comes from the world Himself. He's going to put us where we can do the most good."

"Where?" Escher inquires.

"On a tooth," her companion says. "The right incisor, as it happens." Then with that boasting voice, she adds, "Which is exactly what I told Him to do. This is all because of me."

"What isn't?" Escher grumbles.

"Very little," the tiny prisoner promises. "Very, very little."

The Speaker

"We walk today on a thousand worlds, and I mean 'walk' in all manners of speaking." He manages a few comical steps before shifting into a graceful turn, arms held firmly around the wide waist of an invisible and equally graceful partner. "A hundred alien suns bake us with their perfect light. And between the suns, in the cold and dark, we survive, and thrive, by every worthy means."

Now he pauses, hands forgetting the unseen partner. A look of calculated confusion sweeps across his face. Fingers rise to his thick black hair, stabbing it and yanking backward, leaving furrows in the unruly mass.

"Our numbers," he says. "Our population. It made us sick with worry when we were ten billion standing on the surface of one enormous world. 'Where will our children stand?' we asked ourselves. But then in the next little while, we became ten trillion people, and we had split into a thousand species of humanity, and the new complaint was that we were still too scarce and spread too far apart. 'How could we matter to the universe?' we asked ourselves. 'How could so few souls endure another day in our immeasurable, uncaring universe?'"

His erect penis makes a little leap, a fat and vivid white drop of semen striking the wooden stage with an audible plop.

"Our numbers," he repeats. "Our legions." Then with a wide, garish smile, he confesses, "I don't know our numbers today. No authority does. You make estimates. You extrapolate off data that went stale long ago. You build a hundred models and fashion every kind of vast number. Ten raised to the twentieth power. The thirtieth power. Or more." He giggles and skips backward, and with the giddy, careless energy of a child, he dances where he stands, singing to lights overhead, "If you are as common as sand and as unique as snowflakes, how can you be anything but a wild, wonderful success?"

Able

The wild man is enormous and powerful, and surely brilliant beyond anything that Able can comprehend—as smart as City as a whole—but despite his gifts, the man is obviously terrified. That he can even manage to stand his ground astonishes Able. He says as much to Mish, and then he glances at her, adding, "He must be very devoted to whoever's inside."

"Whoever's inside what?" she asks.

"That trap." He looks straight ahead again, telling himself not to waste time with the girl. She is foolish and bad-tempered, and he couldn't be any more tired of her. "I think that's what the cylinder is," he whispers. "A trap of some kind. And someone's been caught in it."

"Well, I don't care who," she snarls.

He pretends not to notice her.

"What was that?" she blurts. "Did you hear that—?"

"No," Able blurts. But then he notices a distant rumble, deep and faintly rhythmic, and with every breath, growing. When he listens carefully, it resembles nothing normal. It isn't thunder, and it can't be a voice. He feels the sound as much as he hears it, as if some great mass were being displaced. But he knows better. In school, teachers like to explain what must be happening now, employing tortuous mathematics and magical sleights of hand. Matter and energy are being rapidly and brutally manipulated. The universe's obscure dimensions are being twisted like bands of warm rubber. Able knows all this. But still, he understands none of it. Words without comprehension; froth without substance. All that he knows for certain is that behind that deep, unknowable throbbing lies something even farther beyond human description.

The wild man looks up, gray eyes staring at that something.

He cries out, that tiny sound lost between his mouth and Able. Then he produces what seems to be a spear—no, an elaborate missile—that launches itself with a bolt of fire, lifting a sophisticated warhead up into a vague gray space that swallows the weapon without sound, or complaint.

Next the man aims a sturdy laser, and fires. But the weapon simply melts at its tip, collapsing into a smoldering, useless mass at his feet.

Again, the wild man cries out.

His language could be a million generations removed from City-speech, but Able hears the desperate, furious sound of his voice. He doesn't need words to know that the man is cursing. Then the swirling grayness slows itself, and parts, and stupidly, in reflex, Able turns to Mish, wanting to tell her, "Watch. You're going to see one of Them."

But Mish has vanished. Sometime in the last few moments, she jumped off the world's rim and ran away, and save for the fat old leopard sleeping between the horsetails, Able is entirely alone now.

"Good," he mutters.

Almost too late, he turns and runs to the very edge of the granite rim.

The wild man stands motionless now. His bowels and bladder have emptied themselves. His handsome, godly face is twisted from every flavor of misery. Eyes as big as windows stare up into what only they can see, and to that great, unknowable something, the man says two simple words.

"Fuck you," Able hears.

And then the wild man opens his mouth, baring his white apish teeth, and just as Able wonders what's going to happen, the man's body explodes, the dull black burst of a shaped charge sending chunks of his face skyward.

Procyon

One last time, she whispers her son's name.

She whispers it and closes her mouth and listens to the brief, sharp silence that comes after the awful explosion. What must have happened, she tells herself, is that her boy found his good sense and fled. How can a mother think anything else? And then the ominous deep rumbling begins again, begins and gradually swells until the walls of the trap are shuddering and twisting again. But this time the monster is slower. It approaches the trap more cautiously, summoning new courage. She can nearly taste its courage now, and with her intuition, she senses emotions that might be curiosity and might be a kind of reflexive admiration. Or do those eternal human emotions have any relationship for what It feels...?

What she feels, after everything, is numbness. A terrible deep weariness hangs on her like a new skin. Procyon seems to be falling faster now, accelerating down through the bottomless trap. But she doesn't care anymore. In place of courage, she wields a muscular apathy. Death looms, but when hasn't it been her dearest companion? And in place of fear, she is astonished to discover an incurious little pride about what is about to happen: How many people—wild free people like herself—have ever found themselves so near one of Them?

Quietly, with a calm smooth and slow voice, Procyon says, "I feel you there, you. I can taste you."

Nothing changes.

Less quietly, she says, "Show yourself."

A wide parabolic floor appears, gleaming and black and agonizingly close. But just before she slams into the floor, a wrenching force peels it away. A brilliant violet light rises to meet her, turning into a thick sweet syrup. What may or may not be a hand curls around her body, and squeezes. Procyon fights every urge to struggle. She wrestles with her body, wrestles with her will, forcing both to lie still while the hand tightens its grip and grows comfortable. Then using a voice that betrays nothing tentative or small, she tells what holds her, "I made you, you know."

She says, "You can do what you want to me."

Then with a natural, deep joy, she cries out, "But you're an ungrateful glory...and you'll always belong to me...!"

Escher

The prison-ball has been reengineered, slathered with camouflage and armor and the best immune-suppressors on the market, and its navigation system has been adapted from add-ons stolen from the finest trashcans. Now it is a battle-phage riding on the sharp incisor as far as it dares, then leaping free. A thousand similar phages leap and lose their way, or they are killed. Only Escher's phage reaches the target, impacting on what passes for flesh and launching its cargo with a microscopic railgun, punching her and a thousand sisters and daughters through immeasurable distances of senseless, twisted nothing.

How many survive the attack?

She can't guess how many. Can't even care. What matters is to make herself survive inside this strange new world. An enormous world, yes. Escher feels a vastness that reaches out across ten or twelve or maybe a thousand dimensions. How do I know where to go? she asks herself. And instantly, an assortment of possible routes appear in her consciousness, drawn in the simplest imaginable fashion, waiting and eager to help her find her way around.

This is a last gift from Him, she realizes. Unless there are more gifts waiting, of course.

She thanks nobody.

On the equivalent of tiptoes, Escher creeps her way into a tiny conduit that moves something stranger than any blood across five dimensions. She becomes passive, aiming for invisibility. She drifts and spins, watching her surroundings turn from a senseless glow into a landscape that occasionally seems a little bit reasonable. A little bit real. Slowly, she learns how to see in this new world. Eventually she spies a little peak that may or may not be ordinary matter. The peak is pink and flexible and sticks out into the great artery, and flinging her last tendril, Escher grabs hold and pulls in snug, knowing that the chances are lousy that she will ever find anything nourishing here, much less delicious.

But her reserves have been filled again, she notes. If she is careful—and when hasn't she been—her energies will keep her alive for centuries.

She thinks of The World, and thanks nobody.

"Watch and learn," she whispers to herself.

That was the first human thought. She remembers that odd fact suddenly. People were just a bunch of grubbing apes moving blindly through their tiny lives until one said to a companion, "Watch and learn."

An inherited memory, or another gift from Him?

Silently, she thanks Luck, and she thanks Him, and once again, she thanks Luck.

"Patience and planning," she tells herself.

Which is another wise thought of the conscious, enduring ape.

The Last Son

The locked gates and various doorways know him—recognize him at a glance—but they have to taste him anyway. They have to test him. Three people were expected, and he can't explain in words what has happened. He just says, "The others will be coming later," and leaves that lie hanging in the air. Then as he passes through the final doorway, he says, "Let no one through. Not without my permission first."

"This is your mother's house," says the door's AI.

"Not anymore," he remarks.

The machine grows quiet, and sad.

During any other age, his home would be a mansion. There are endless rooms, rooms beyond counting, and each is enormous and richly furnished and lovely and jammed full of games and art and distractions and flourishes that even the least aesthetic soul would find lovely. He sees none of that now. Alone, he walks to what has always been his room, and he sits on a leather recliner, and the house brings him a soothing drink and an intoxicating drink and an assortment of treats that sit on the platter, untouched.

For a long while, the boy stares off at the distant ceiling, replaying everything with his near-perfect memory. Everything. Then he forgets everything, stupidly calling out, "Mother," with a voice that sounds ridiculously young. Then again, he calls, "Mother." And he starts to rise from his chair, starts to ask the great empty house, "Where is she?"

And he remembers.

As if his legs have been sawed off, he collapses. His chair twists itself to catch him, and an army of AIs brings their talents to bear. They are loyal, limited machines. They are empathetic, and on occasion, even sweet. They want to help him in any fashion, just name the way...but their appeals and their smart suggestions are just so much noise. The boy acts deaf, and he obviously can't see anything with his fists jabbed into his eyes like that, slouched forward in his favorite chair, begging an invisible someone for forgiveness....

The Speaker

He squats and uses the tip of a forefinger to dab at the puddle of semen, and he rubs the finger against his thumb, saying, "Think of cells. Individual, self-reliant cells. For most of Earth's great history, they ruled. First as bacteria, and then as composites built from cooperative bacteria. They were everywhere and ruled everything, and then the wild cells learned how to dance together, in one enormous body, and the living world was transformed for the next seven hundred million years."

Thumb and finger wipe themselves dry against a hairy thigh, and he rises again, grinning in that relentless and smug, yet somehow charming fashion. "Everything was changed, and nothing had changed," he says. Then he says, "Scaling," with an important tone, as if that single word should erase all confusion. "The bacteria and green algae and the carnivorous amoebae weren't swept away by any revolution. Honestly, I doubt if their numbers fell appreciably or for long." And again, he says, "Scaling," and sighs with a rich appreciation. "Life evolves. Adapts. Spreads and grows, constantly utilizing new energies and novel genetics. But wherever something large can live, a thousand small things can thrive just as well, or better. Wherever something enormous survives, a trillion bacteria hang on for the ride."

For a moment, the speaker hesitates.

A slippery half-instant passes where an audience might believe that he has finally lost his concentration, that he is about to stumble over his own tongue. But then he licks at the air, tasting something delicious. And three times, he clicks his tongue against the roof of his mouth.

Then he says what he has planned to say from the beginning.

"I never know whom I'm speaking to," he admits. "I've never actually seen my audience. But I know you're great and good. I know that however you appear, and however you make your living, you deserve to hear this:

308 | DIGITAL RAPTURE

"Humans have always lived in terror. Rainstorms and the eclipsing moon and earthquakes and the ominous guts of some disemboweled goat—all have preyed upon our fears and defeated our fragile optimisms. But what we fear today—what shapes and reshapes the universe around us—is a child of our own imaginations.

"A whirlwind that owes its very existence to glorious, endless us!"

Able

The boy stops walking once or twice, letting the fat leopard keep pace. Then he pushes his way through a last wall of emerald ferns, stepping out into the bright damp air above the rounded pool. A splashing takes him by surprise. He looks down at his secret pool, and he squints, watching what seems to be a woman pulling her way through the clear water with thick, strong arms. She is naked. Astonishingly, wonderfully naked. A stubby hand grabs an overhanging limb, and she stands on the rocky shore, moving as if exhausted, picking her way up the slippery slope until she finds an open patch of halfway flattened earth where she can collapse, rolling onto her back, her smooth flesh glistening and her hard breasts shining up at Able, making him sick with joy.

Then she starts to cry, quietly, with a deep sadness.

Lust vanishes, replaced by simple embarrassment. Able flinches and starts to step back, and that's when he first looks at her face.

He recognizes its features.

Intrigued, the boy picks his way down to the shoreline, practically standing beside the crying woman.

She looks at him, and she sniffs.

"I saw two of them," he reports. "And I saw you, too. You were inside that cylinder, weren't you?"

She watches him, saying nothing.

"I saw something pull you out of that trap. And then I couldn't see you. It must have put you here, I guess. Out of its way." Able nods, and smiles. He can't help but stare at her breasts, but at least he keeps his eyes halfway closed, pretending to look out over the water instead. "It took pity on you, I guess."

A good-sized fish breaks on the water.

The woman seems to watch the creature as it swims past, big blue scales catching the light, heavy fins lazily shoving their way through the warm water. The fish eyes are huge and black, and they are stupid eyes. The mind behind them sees nothing but vague shapes and sudden motions. Able knows from experience: If he stands quite still, the creature will come close enough to touch.

"They're called coelacanths," he explains.

Maybe the woman reacts to his voice. Some sound other than crying now leaks from her.

So Able continues, explaining, "They were rare, once. I've studied them quite a bit. They're old and primitive, and they were almost extinct when we found them. But when they got loose, got free, and took apart the Earth...and took everything and everyone with them up into the sky..."

The woman gazes up at the towering horsetails.

Able stares at her legs and what lies between them.

"Anyway," he mutters, "there's more coelacanths now than ever. They live in a million oceans, and they've never been more successful, really." He hesitates, and then adds, "Kind of like us, I think. Like people. You know?"

The woman turns, staring at him with gray-white eyes. And with a quiet hard voice, she says, "No."

She says, "That's an idiot's opinion."

And then with a grace that belies her strong frame, she dives back into the water, kicking hard and chasing that ancient and stupid fish all the way back to the bottom.

Rudy Rucker speculates about the technological wonders of the future in a piece that first appeared in a collection of essays entitled *Year Million*, a timeline which does not quite fit with orthodox thinking about the Singularity. However, this is classic Rucker: wild imagination grounded by intellectual rigor. He is also author of *The Lifebox, the Seashell, and the Soul*, which *Publishers Weekly* called "part memoir of a life spent teaching mathematical logic, part history of computer science, but mostly a long, strange quest for the meaning of life."

THE GREAT AWAKENING
> Rudy Rucker

The Singularity

On the theme of computational futures, there's an interesting idea first proposed by the science fiction writer and computer science professor Vernor Vinge in a famous 1993 talk. Vinge pointed out that if we can make technological devices as intelligent as ourselves, then there seems to be no reason that these devices couldn't readily be made to run a bit faster and have a bit more memory so as to become *more* intelligent than people. And then—the real kicker—these superhuman machines might set to work designing still better machines, setting off a chain reaction of ever-more-powerful devices.

Vinge termed the potential event the Singularity. Although Vinge's analysis is sober and scientific, in the last couple of decades, belief in his Singularity has become something of a cult among certain techies. Science fiction writers, who have a somewhat more jaded view of predictions, have a saying about the enthusiasts: "The Singularity is the Rapture for geeks." That is, among its adherents, belief in the Singularity has something of the flavor of the evangelical Christian belief in a world-ending apocalypse, when God will supposedly elevate the saved to heaven, leaving the rest of us to fight a final battle of Armageddon.

(Vinge's talk "The Coming Technological Singularity: How to Survive in the Post-Human Era" appeared in the Winter 1993 issue of the *Whole Earth Review*, and is available online at http://www-rohan. sdsu.edu/faculty/vinge/misc/singularity.html—or just Google for "Vinge

Singularity." Re: the Singularity/Rapture comparison that I quote, I first heard this phrase from Bruce Sterling, who ascribes it to Cory Doctorow, who says he got it from Charlie Stross, who in turn says he nicked it from Ken MacLeod—cynical SF writers one and all.)

At one level, belief in the Singularity is indeed an instance of people's age-old tendency to predict the end of the world. Once we have the Singularity, the machines can copy our brains and make us immortal. But once we have the Singularity, the machines may declare war on humanity and seek to exterminate us. Once we have the Singularity, the machines will learn how to convert matter into different forms and nobody will ever have to work again. But once we have the Singularity, the machines may store us in pods and use us as components. Once we have the Singularity, the machines will figure out how to travel faster than light and into the past. But once we have the Singularity, the machines will screw things up and bring the entire universe to an end. And so on.

Vinge describes several kinds of scenarios that could lead to a Singularity of cascading superhuman intelligence. We can group these somewhat science-fictional possibilities into three bins.

- *Artificial minds.* We design or evolve computing devices as intelligent as ourselves, and these entities continue the process to create further devices that are smarter than us. These superhuman computing devices might be traditional silicon-chip computers, nanotechnological assemblages, quantum computers, or bioengineered artificial organisms.

- *Cyborgs.* Humans split off a species, part natural and part engineered. This could result either from bioengineering the human genome, or from giving people an effortless, transparent interface to supercomputing helper devices. The resulting cyborgs will advance to superhuman levels.

- *Hive minds.* The planetary network of computers wakes up and becomes a superhuman mind. Alternately, people are equipped with built-in communication devices which allow society to develop a true group mind of superhuman powers.

Ubiquitous Nanomachines

Molecular nanotechnology is the craft of manufacturing things on the molecular scale. One goal is to create programmable nanobots: tailor-made agents roughly the size of biological viruses. The comparison is apt. What's likely to play out is that, over the coming centuries and millennia, we'll be capitalizing on the fact that biology is already doing molecular fabrication. The nascent field of synthetic biology is going to be the true nanotech of the future.

One immediate worry is what nanotechnologists have called the "gray goo problem." That is, what's to stop a particularly virulent, artificial organism from eating everything on Earth? My guess is that this could never happen. Every existing plant, animal, fungus, and protozoan *already* aspires to world domination. There's nothing more ruthless than viruses and bacteria—the grizzled homies who've thrived by keeping it real for some three billion years.

The fact that artificial organisms are likely to have simplified metabolisms doesn't necessarily mean that they're going to be faster and better. It's more likely that they'll be dumber and less adaptable. My sense is that, in the long run, Mother Nature always wins. Cautionary note: Mother Nature's "win" may not include the survival of the pesky human race!

But let's suppose that all goes well and we learn to create docile, biological nanobots. There's one particular breed that I like thinking about; I call them *orphids*.

The way I imagine it, orphids reproduce using ambient dust for raw material. They'll cover Earth's surface, yes, but they'll be well behaved enough to stop at a density of one or two orphids per square millimeter, so that you'll find a few million of them on your skin and perhaps ten sextillion orphids on Earth's whole surface. From then on, the orphids reproduce only enough to maintain that same density. You might say they have a conscience, a desire to protect the environment. And, as a side benefit, they'll hunt down and eradicate any evil nanomachines that anyone else tries to unleash.

Orphids use quantum computing; they propel themselves with electrostatic fields; they understand natural human language. One can converse with them quite well. I'll suppose that an individual orphid is roughly as smart as a talking dog with, let us say, a quadrillion bytes of memory being processed at a quadrillion operations per second.

How do we squeeze so much computation out of a nanomachine? Well, a nanogram does hold about a trillion particles, which gets us close to a quadrillion. According to quantum physicist Seth Lloyd, if we regard brute matter as a quantum computation, then we do have some ten quadrillion bytes per nanogram. (See his book, *Programming the Universe: A Quantum Computer Scientist Takes on the Cosmos*, Vintage, 2007.) So there are only, *ahem*, a few implementation details in designing molecular nanomachines smart enough to converse with.

The orphids might be linked via electromagnetic wireless signals that are passed from one to the next; alternatively, they might use, let us say, some kind of subdimensional faster-than-light quantum entanglement. In either case, we call the resulting network the orphidnet.

Omnividence and Telepathy

We can suppose that the orphids will settle onto our scalps like smart lice. They'll send magnetic vortices into our occipital lobes, creating a wireless human interface to the orphidnet. Of course, we humans can turn our connection on and off, and we'll have read-write control. As the orphidnet emerges, we'll get intelligence amplification.

So now everyone is plugged into the orphidnet all the time. Thanks to the orphid lice, everyone has a heads-up display projected over the visual field. And thanks to global positioning systems, the orphids act as tiny survey markers—or as the vertices of computer-graphical meshes. Using these realtime meshes, you actually see the shapes of distant objects. The orphids will be sensitive to vibrations, so you can hear as well. We'll have complete *omnividence*, as surely as if the Earth were blanketed with video cameras.

One immediate win is that violent crime becomes impossible to get away with. The orphidnet remembers the past, so anything can be replayed. If you do something bad, people can find you and punish you. Of course someone *can* still behave like a criminal if he holds incontrovertible physical force—if, for instance, he is part of an armed government. I dream that the orphidnet-empowered public sees no further need for centralized and weaponized governments, and mankind's long domination by ruling elites comes to an end. Another win is that we can quickly find missing objects.

The flip side of omnividence is that nobody has any privacy at all.

We'll have less shame about sex; the subject will be less shrouded in mystery. But sexual peeping will become an issue, and as omnividence shades into telepathy, some will want to merge with lovers' minds. But surely lovers can find some way to shield themselves from prying. If they can't actually turn off their orphids, the lovers may have physical shields of an electromagnetic or quantum-mechanical nature; alternately, people may develop mantra-like mental routines to divert unwanted visitors.

Telepathy lies only a step beyond omnividence. How will it feel? One key difference between omnividence and telepathy is that telepathy is participatory, not voyeuristic. That is, you're not just watching someone else; you're picking up the person's shades of feeling.

One of the key novelties attending electronic telepathy is the availability of psychic hyperlinks. Let me explain: Language is an all-purpose construction kit that a speaker uses to model mental states. In interpreting these language constructs, a listener builds a mental state similar to the speaker's. Visual art is another style of construction kit; here an idea is rendered in colors, lines, shapes, and figures.

As we refine our techniques of telepathy, we'll reach a point where people converse by exchanging hyperlinks into each other's mind. It's like sending someone an Internet link to a picture on your website—instead of sending a pixel-by-pixel copy of the image. Rather than describing my weekend in words, or showing you pictures that I took, I simply pass you a direct link to the memories in my head. In other words, with telepathy, I can let you directly experience my thoughts without my explaining them via words and pictures. Nevertheless, language will persist. Language is so deeply congenial to us that we'd no sooner abandon it than we'd give up sex.

On a practical level, once we have telepathy, what do we do about the sleazeball spammers who'll try to flood our minds with ads, scams, and political propaganda? We'll use adaptive, evolving filters. Effective spam filters behave like biological immune systems, accumulating an ever-growing supply of "antibody" routines. In a living organism's immune system, the individual cells share the antibody techniques they discover. In a social spam filter, the individual users will share their fixes and alerts.

Another issue with telepathy has to do, once again, with privacy. Here's an analogue: a blogger today is a bit like someone who's broadcasting telepathically, dumping his or her thoughts into the world for all to see.

A wise blogger censors his or her blog, so as not to appear like a hothead, a depressive, or a bigot.

What if telepathy can't be filtered, and everyone can see everyone's secret seething? Perhaps, after a period of adjustment, people would get thicker skins. Certainly it's true that in some subcultures, people yell at each other without necessarily getting excited. Perhaps a new kind of tolerance and empathy might emerge, whereby no one person's internal turmoil seems like a big deal. Consider: to be publicly judgmental of someone else, you compare your well-tended *outside* to the other person's messy *inside*. But if everyone's insides are universally visible, no one can get away with being hypocritical.

Telepathy will provide a huge increase in people's ability to think. You'll be sharing your memory data with everyone. In the fashion of a Web search engine, information requests will be distributed among the pool of telepaths without the need for conscious intervention. The entire knowledge of the species will be on tap for each individual. Searching the collective mind won't be as fast as getting something from your own brain, but you'll have access to far more information.

Even with omnividence and telepathy, I expect that, day in and day out, people won't actually change that much—not even in a million years. That's a lesson history teaches us. Yes, we've utterly changed our tech since the end of the Middle Ages, but the paintings of Hieronymus Bosch or Pieter Bruegel show that people back then were much like us, perennially entangled with the seven deadly sins.

No matter the tech, what people do is based upon simple needs: the desire to mate and reproduce, the need for food and shelter, and the longing for power and luxuries. Will molecular manufacture give all of us the luxuries we want? No. Skewed inverse power-law distribution of valued qualities is an intrinsic property of the natural world. That is, roughly speaking, if there are a thousand people at the bottom of the heap, and a hundred immediately above them, there'll be only ten farther up, and just one perched on the top in possession of a large proportion of the goodies. Even if we become glowing clouds of ectoplasm, there's going to be something that we're competing for—and most of us will feel as though we're getting screwed.

Those goodies need not be "possessions" as we understand them; in the near term, an interesting effect will emerge. Since we're all linked on the net, we can easily borrow things or even get things free. As well as selling things, people can lend them out or give them away. Why? To accumulate social capital and good reputation.

In the orphidnet future, people can always find leftover food. Some might set out their leftovers, like pies for bums. Couch-surfing as a serial guest becomes eminently practical, with the ubiquitous virtual cloud of observers giving a host some sense of security vis-à-vis the guests. And you can find most of the possessions you need within walking distance—perhaps in a neighbor's basement. A community becomes a shared storehouse.

On the entertainment front, I imagine orphidnet reality soap operas. These would be like real-time video blogs, with sponsors' clickable ads floating around near the characters, who happen to be interesting people doing interesting things.

People will still dine out—indeed this will be a preferred form of entertainment, as physically eating something is one of the few things that require leaving the home. As you wait at your restaurant table for your food, you might enjoy watching (or even experiencing) the actions of the chef. Maybe the restaurant employs a gourmet eater, with such a sensitive and educated palate that it's a pleasure to mind-meld when this eater chows down.

Will telepaths get drunk and stoned? Sure! And with dire consequences. Imagine the havoc you could wreak by getting wasted and "running your brain" instead of just emailing, phoning, or yelling at people face to face. There will be new forms of intoxication as well. A pair of people might lock themselves into an intense telepathic feedback loop, mirroring their minds back and forth until chaotic amplification takes hold.

In the world of art, suppose someone finds a way to record mood snapshots. And then we can produce objects that directly project the raw experiences of transcendence, wonder, euphoria, mindless pleasure, or sensual beauty without actually having any content.

Telepaths will use language for superficial small talk, but, as I mentioned, just as often they'll use psychic hyperlinks and directly exchanged images and emotions. Novels could take the form of elaborate sets of mental links. Writing might become more like video-blogging. A beautiful state of mind could be saved into a memory network, glyph by glyph. This new literary form might be called the metanovel.

Artificial Intelligence and Intelligence Amplification

In the ubiquitous nanobot model I've been discussing, the orphidnet, we have a vast array of small linked minds. It's reasonable to suppose that, as well as helping humans do things, the orphidnet will support emergent, artificially intelligent agents that enlist the memory and processing power of a few thousand or more individual orphids.

Some of these agents will be as intelligent as humans, and some will be even smarter. It's easy to imagine their being willing to help people by carrying out things like complex and tedious searches for information or by simulating and evaluating multiple alternate action scenarios. The result is that humans would undergo IA, or intelligence amplification.

A step further, intelligent orphidnet agents group into higher minds that group into still higher minds and so on, with one or several planetary-level minds at the top. Here, by the way, is a fresh opportunity for human excess. Telepathically communing with the top mind will offer something like a mystical experience or a drug trip. The top mind will be like a birthday piñata stuffed with beautiful insights woven into ideas that link into unifying concepts that puzzle-piece themselves into powerful systems that are in turn aspects of a cosmic metatheory—*aha!* Hooking into the top mind will make any individual feel like more than a genius. Downside: once you unlink you probably won't remember many of the cosmic thoughts that you had, and you're going to be too drained to do much more than lie around for a few days.

Leaving ecstatic merging aside, let's say a little more about intelligence amplification. Suppose that people reach an effective IQ of 1000 by taking advantage of the orphidnet memory enhancement and the processing aid provided by the orphidnet agents. Let's speak of these kilo-IQ people as *kiqqies*.

As kiqqies, they can browse through all the world's libraries and minds, with orphidnet agents helping to make sense of it all. How would it feel to be a kiqqie?

I recently had an email exchange about this with my friend Stephen Wolfram, a prominent scientist who happens to be one of the smartest people I know. When I asked him how it might feel to have an IQ of 1000, and what that might even mean, he suggested that the difference might be like the difference between simulating something by hand and simulating it on a high-speed computer with excellent software. Quoting from Wolfram's email:

> There's a lot more that one can explore, quickly, so one investigates more, sees more connections, and can look more moves ahead. More things would seem to make sense. One gets to compute more before one loses attention on a particular issue, etc. (Somehow that's what seems to distinguish less intelligent people from more intelligent people right now.)

Against Computronium

In some visions of the far future, amok nanomachines egged on by corporate geeks are disassembling the solar system's planets to build Dyson shells of computronium around the Sun. Computronium is, in writer Charles Stross's words, "matter optimized at the atomic level to support computing." A Dyson shell is a hollow sphere of matter that intercepts all of the central sun's radiation—using some of it and then passing the rest outwards in a cooled-down form, possibly to be further intercepted by outer layers of Dyson shells. What a horrible thing to do to a solar system!

I think computronium is a spurious concept. Matter, just as it is, carries out outlandishly complex chaotic quantum computations by dint of sitting around. Matter isn't dumb. Every particle everywhere and everywhen computes at the max possible flop. I think we tend to very seriously undervalue quotidian reality.

Turning an inhabited planet into a computronium Dyson shell is comparable to filling in wetlands to make a mall, clear-cutting a rainforest to make a destination golf resort, or killing a whale to whittle its teeth into religious icons of a whale god.

Ultrageek advocates of the computronium Dyson-shell scenario like to claim that nothing need be lost when Earth is pulped into computer chips. Supposedly the resulting computronium can run a VR (virtual reality) simulation that's a perfect match for the old Earth. Call the new one Vearth. It's worth taking a moment to explain the problems with trying to replace real reality with virtual reality. We know that our present-day videogames and digital movies don't fully match the richness of the real world. What's not so well known is that no feasible VR can *ever* match nature because there are no shortcuts for nature's computations. Due to a property of the natural world that I call the "principle of natural unpredictability," fully simulating a bunch of particles for a certain period of time requires a system using about the same number of particles for about the same length of time. Naturally occurring systems don't allow for drastic shortcuts. (For details on this point, see Rudy Rucker, *The Lifebox, the Seashell and the Soul*, Tor, 2006, or see the topic "irreducibility" in Stephen Wolfram, *A New Kind of Science*, Wolfram Media, 2002.)

Natural unpredictability means that if you build a computer-simulated world that's smaller than the physical world, the simulation cuts corners and makes compromises, such as using bitmapped wood-grain, linearized fluid dynamics, or cartoon-style repeating backgrounds. Smallish simulated worlds are doomed to be dippy Las Vegas/Disneyland environments populated by simulated people as dull and predictable as characters in bad novels.

But wait—if you *do* smash the whole planet into computronium, then you have potentially as much memory and processing power as the intact planet possessed. It's the same amount of mass, after all. So then we *could* make a fully realistic world-simulating Vearth with no compromises, right? Wrong. Maybe you can get the hardware in place, but there's the vexing issue of software. Something important goes missing when you smash Earth into dust: you lose the information and the software that was embedded in the world's behavior. An Earth-amount of matter with no high-level programs running on it is like a potentially human-equivalent robot with no AI software, or, more simply, like a powerful new computer with no programs on the hard drive.

Ah, but what if the nanomachines first copy all the patterns and behaviors embedded in Earth's biosphere and geology? What if they copy the forms and processes in every blade of grass, in every bacterium, in every pebble—like Citizen Kane bringing home a European castle that's been dismantled into portable blocks, or like a foreign tourist taking digital photos of the components of a disassembled California cheeseburger?

But, come on, if you want to smoothly transmogrify a blade of grass into some nanomachines simulating a blade of grass, then why bother grinding up the blade of grass at all? After all, any object at all can be viewed as a quantum computation! The blade of grass already *is* an assemblage of nanomachines emulating a blade of grass. Nature embodies superhuman intelligence just as she is.

Why am I harping on this? It's my way of leading up to one of the really wonderful events that I think our future holds: the withering away of digital machines and the coming of truly ubiquitous computation. I call it the Great Awakening.

I predict that eventually we'll be able to tune in telepathically to nature's computations. We'll be able to commune with the souls of stones.

The Great Awakening will eliminate nanomachines and digital computers in favor of naturally computing objects. We can suppose that our newly intelligent world will, in fact, take it upon itself to crunch up the digital machines, frugally preserving or porting all of the digital data.

Instead of turning nature into chips, we'll turn chips into nature.

The Advent of Panpsychism

In the future, we'll see all objects as alive and conscious—a familiar notion in the history of philosophy and by no means disreputable. Hylozoism (from the Greek *hyle*, matter, and *zoe*, life) is the doctrine that all matter is intrinsically alive, and panpsychism is the related notion that every object has a mind. (See David Skrbina, *Panpsychism in the West*, MIT Press, Cambridge, 2005.) Already my car talks to me, as do my phone, my computer, and my refrigerator, so I guess we could live with talking rocks, chairs, logs, sandwiches, and atoms. And, unlike the chirping electronic appliances, the talking objects may truly have soul.

My opinion is that consciousness is not so very hard to achieve. How does everything wake up? I think the key insight is this:

$$Consciousness = universal\ computation + memory + self\text{-}reflection$$

Computer scientists define universal computers as systems capable of emulating the behavior of every other computing system. The complexity threshold for universal computation is very low. Any desktop computer is a universal computer. A cell phone is a universal computer. A Tinkertoy set or a billiard table can be a universal computer.

In fact, just about any natural phenomenon at all can be regarded as a universal computer: swaying trees, a candle flame, drying mud, flowing water, even a rock. To the human eye, a rock appears not to be doing much. But viewed as a quantum computation, the rock is as lively and seething as, say, a small star. At the atomic level, a rock is like a zillion balls connected by force springs; we know this kind of compound oscillatory system behaves chaotically, and computer science teaches us that chaotic systems can indeed support universal computation.

The self-reflection aspect of a system stems from having a feedback process whereby the system has two levels of self-awareness: first, an image of itself reacting to its environment, and second, an image of itself watching its own reactions. (See Antonio Damasio, *The Feeling of What Happens: Body and Emotion in the Making of Consciousness*, Mariner Books, New York, 2000.)

We can already conceive of how to program self-reflection into digital computers, so I don't think it will be long until we can make them conscious. But digital computers are *not* where the future's at. We don't use clockwork gears in our watches anymore, and we don't make radios out of vacuum tubes. The age of digital computer chips is going to be over and done, if not in a hundred years, then certainly in a thousand. By the Year Million, we'll be well past the Great Awakening, and working with the consciousness of ordinary objects.

I've already said a bit about why natural systems are universal computers. And the self-reflection issue is really just a matter of programming legerdemain. But two other things will be needed.

First, in order to get consciousness in a brook or a swaying tree or a flame or a stone, we'll need a universal memory upgrade that can be, in some sense, plugged into natural objects. *Second*, for us to be able to work with the intelligent objects, we're going to need a strong form of non-digital telepathy for communicating with them.

In the next section, I'll explain how, before we bring about the Great Awakening, we'll first have to manipulate the topology of space to give endless memory to every object and then create a high-fidelity telepathic connection among all the objects in the world. But for now let's take these conditions for granted. Assume that everything has become conscious and that we are in telepathic communication with everything in the world.

To discuss the world after this Great Awakening, I need a generic word for an uplifted, awakened natural mind. I'll call these minds *silps*. We'll be generous in our panpsychism, with every size of object supporting a conscious silp, from atoms up to galaxies. Silps can also be found in groupings of objects—here I'm thinking of what animists regard as *genii loci*, or spirits of place.

There seems to be a problem with panpsychism: How do we have synchronization among the collective wills involved in, say, rush-hour traffic? Consider the atoms, the machine parts, the automotive subassemblies, the cars themselves, the minds of the traffic streams, not to mention the minds of the human drivers and the minds of their body cells. Why do the bodies do what the brains want them to? Why do all the little minds agree? Why doesn't the panpsychic world disintegrate into squabbling disorder? Solution: everyone's idea of their motives and decisions are *Just So* stories cobbled together *ex post facto* to create a narrative for what is in fact a complex, deterministic computation, a law-like cosmic harmony where each player imagines he or she is improvising.

It takes some effort to imagine a panpsychic world. What would a tree or campfire or waterfall be into? Perhaps they just want to hang out, doing nothing. Perhaps it's only we who want to rush around, fidgety monkeys that we are. But if I overdo the notion of silp mellowness, I end up wondering if it even matters for an object to be conscious. Assuming the silps have telepathy, they do have sensors. But can they change the world? In a sense, yes: if silps are quantum computations, then they can influence their own matter by affecting rates of catalysis, heat flows, quantum collapses, and so on.

Thus a new-style silp drinking glass might be harder to break than an old-style dumb glass. The intelligent, living glass might shed off the vibration phonons in optimal ways to avoid fracture. In a similar connection, I think of a bean that slyly rolls away to avoid being cooked; sometimes objects do seem to hide.

The remarks about the glass and the bean assume that silp-smart objects would *mind* being destroyed. But is this true? Does a log mind being burned? It would be a drag if you had to feel guilty about stoking your fire. But silps aren't really likely to be as bent on self-preservation as humans and animals are. We humans (and animals) have to be averse to death, so that we can live long enough to mate and to raise our young. Biological species go extinct if their individuals don't care about self-preservation. But a log's or rock's individual survival doesn't affect the survival of the race of logs or rocks. So silps needn't be hard-wired to fear death.

Let's say a bit more about self-reflection among silps. As a human, I have a mental model of myself watching myself have feelings about events. This is the self-reflection component of consciousness mentioned above. There seems no reason why this mode of thought wouldn't be accessible to objects. Indeed, it might be that there's some "fixed point" aspect of fundamental physics making self-reflection an inevitability. Perhaps, compared to a quantum-computing silp, a human's methods for producing self-awareness is weirdly complex and roundabout.

As I mentioned before, when the Great Awakening comes, the various artificially intelligent agents of the orphidnet will be ported into silps or into minds made up of silps. As in the orphidnet, we'll have an upward-mounting hierarchy of silp minds. Individual atoms will have small silp minds, and an extended large object will have a fairly hefty silp mind. And at the top we'll have a truly conscious planetary mind: Gaia. Although there's a sense in which Gaia has been alive all along, after the Great Awakening, she'll be like a talkative, accessible god.

Because the silps will have inherited all the data of the orphids, humans will still have their omnividence, their shared memory access, and their intelligence amplification. I also predict that, when the Great Awakening comes, we'll have an even stronger form of telepathy, which is based upon a use of the subdimensions.

Exploiting the Subdimensions
Let's discuss how we might provide every atom in the universe with a memory upgrade, thus awakening objects to become silps. And, given that the silp era will supersede the nanotech era, we'll also need a non-electronic form of telepathy that will work after the orphidnet and digital computers have withered away.

To achieve these two ends, I propose riffing on an old-school science-fiction power chord, the notion of the "subdimensions." The word is a science-fictional shibboleth from the 1930s, but we can retrofit it to stand for the topology of space at scales below the Planck length—that is, below the size scale at which our current notions of physics break down.

One notion, taken from string theory, is that we have a lot of extra dimensions down there, and that most of them are curled into tiny circles. For a mathematician like myself, it's annoying to see the physicists help themselves to higher dimensions and then waste the dimensions by twisting them into tiny coils. It's like seeing someone win a huge lottery and then put every single penny into a stodgy, badly run bond fund.

I recklessly predict that sometime before the Year Million we'll find a way to change the intrinsic topology of space, uncurling one of these stingily rolled-up dimensions. And of course we'll be careful to pick a dimension that's not absolutely essential for the string-theoretic Calabi-Yau manifolds that are supporting the existence of matter and spacetime. Just for the sake of discussion, let's suppose that it's the eighth dimension that we uncurl.

I see our eighth-dimensional coils as springing loose and unrolling to form infinite eighth-dimensional lines. This unfurling will happen at every point of space. Think of a plane with hog-bristles growing out of it. That's our enhanced space after the eighth dimension unfurls. And the bristles stretch to infinity.

And now we'll use this handy extra dimension for our universal memory upgrade! We'll suppose that atoms can make tick marks on their eighth dimension, as can people, clouds, or stones. In other words, you can store information as bumps upon the eighth-dimensional hog bristles growing out of your body. The ubiquitous hog bristles provide endless memory at every location, thereby giving people endless perfect memories, and giving objects enough memory to make them conscious as well.

OK, sweet. Now what about getting telepathy without having to use some kind of radio-signaling system? Well, let's suppose that all of the eighth-dimensional axes meet at the point at infinity and that our nimble extradimensional minds can readily traverse an infinite eighth-dimensional expanse so that a person's attention can quickly rapidly dart out to the shared point at infinity. And once you're focused on the shared point at infinity, your attention can zoom back down to any space location you like.

In other words, everyone is connected via an accessible router point at infinity. So now, even if the silps have eaten the orphids as part of the Great Awakening, we'll all have perfect telepathy.

(Re: traveling an infinite distance in a finite time, perhaps we'll use a

Zeno-style acceleration, continually doubling our speed. Thus, traversing the first meter along the eighth-dimensional axis might take a half a millisecond, the second meter a quarter of a millisecond, the third meter an eighth of a millisecond, and so on. And in this fashion your attention can dart out to infinity in a millisecond.)

The End?

Of course we won't stop at mere telepathy! By the Year Million, we'll have teleportation, telekinesis, and the ability to turn our thoughts into objects.

Teleporting can be done by making yourself uncertain about which of two possible locations you're actually in—and then believing yourself to be "there" instead of "here." We'll work this uncertainty-based method of teleportation as a three-step process. First, you perfectly visualize your source and target locations and mentally weave them together. Second, you become uncertain about which location you're actually in. And third, you abruptly observe yourself, asking, "Where am I?" Thereby you precipitate a quantum collapse of your wave function, which lands you at your target location. I'm also supposing that whatever I'm wearing or holding will teleport along with me; let's say that I can carry anything up to the weight of, say, a heavy suitcase.

Once people can teleport, they can live anywhere they can find a vacant lot to build on. You can teleport in water and you can teleport your waste away. What about heat and light? Perhaps you can get trees to produce electricity, and then set sockets into the trunks and plug in your lamps and heaters. Or just get the trees to make light and heat on their own, and never mind the electricity. (Once we can talk to our plants, it should be fairly easy to tweak their genes.)

As the next step beyond teleportation, we'll learn to teleport objects without our having to move at all. This long hoped-for power is known to psi advocates and SF writers as *telekinesis*. How might telekinesis work our projected future? Suppose that, sitting in my living room, I want to teleport an apple from my fridge to my coffee table. I visualize the source and target locations just as I do when performing personal teleportation; that is, I visualize the fridge drawer and the tabletop in the living room. But now, rather than doing an uncertainty-followed-by-collapse number on my body, I need to do it on the apple. I become the apple for a moment, I merge with it, I cohere its state function to encourage locational uncertainty, and then I collapse the apple's wave function into the apple-on-table *eigenstate*.

What's the status of the apple's resident silp while I do this? In a sense the silp *is* the apple's wave function, so it must be that I'm bossing around the silp. Fine.

Can animals and objects teleport as well? What a mess that would be! We'd better hope that only humans can teleport. How might we justify such a special and privileged status for our race?

I'll draw on a science-fictional idea in a Robert Sheckley story, "Specialist," from his landmark collection, *Untouched by Human Hands*. Sheckley suggested that humans would have the power of teleportation because, unlike animals or objects, we experience doubt and fear. Certainly it seems as if animals don't have doubt and fear in the same way that we do. If a predator comes, an animal runs away, end of story. If cornered, a rat bares his teeth and fights. Animals don't worry about what *might* happen; they don't brood over what they did in the past; they don't agonize over *possibilities*—or at least one can suppose that they don't.

And it's easy to suppose that the silps that inhabit natural processes don't have doubt and fear either. Silps don't much care if they die. A vortex of air forms and disperses, no problem.

So *why* would doubt and fear lead to teleportation? Having doubt and fear involves creating really good mental models of alternative realities. And being able to create good mental models of alternative realities means the ability to imagine yourself being there rather than here. We can spread out our wave functions in ways that other beings can't. Humans carry out certain delicate kinds of quantum computation—which, we can suppose, might lead to teleportation.

Take this to the extreme. Could we create objects out of nothing? Call such objects "tulpas." In Tibetan Buddhism, a tulpa is a material object or person that an enlightened adept can mentally create—a psychic projection that's as solid as a brick. I think it's entirely possible that, a million years from now, any human could create tulpas. How? You'll psychically reprogram the quantum computations of the atoms around you, causing them to generate de Broglie matter waves converging on a single spot. Rather than being *light* holograms, these will be *matter wave* holograms—that is, physical objects created by computation: your tulpas.

Your thoughts could become objects by coaxing the nearby atoms to generate matter holograms that behave just like normal objects. You could build a house from nothing, turn a stone into bread, transform water into wine (assuming, given such miraculous abilities, you still needed shelter, food, drink), and make flowers bloom from your fingertips.

And then will humans finally be satisfied?

Of course not. We'll push on past infinity and into the transfinite realms beyond the worlds—mayhap to embroil ourselves with the elder gods and the Great Old Ones.

Cory Doctorow (b. 1971) co-edits the influential blog *Boing Boing* (boingboing.net) and is an outspoken commenter on digital media and an advocate of liberalizing the intellectual property laws. His bestselling novel *Little Brother* won the 2009 Prometheus Award, the Sunburst Award, and the John W. Campbell Memorial Award.

Benjamin Rosenbaum (b. 1969) holds degrees in computer science and religious studies from Brown University. His stories have appeared in *McSweeney's*, *Harper's*, *Lady Churchill's Rosebud Wristlet*, *Fantasy & Science Fiction*, and elsewhere, and have been collected in *The Ant King and Other Stories*. Their Hugo Award-nominated collaboration combines formidable technological savvy with a gonzo sensibility to deliver what many consider the quintessential Post-Singularity story.

TRUE NAMES
> Cory Doctorow and Benjamin Rosenbaum

Beebe fried the asteroid to slag when it left, exterminating millions of itself.

The asteroid was a high-end system: a kilometer-thick shell of femtoscale crystalline lattices, running cool at five degrees Kelvin, powered by a hot core of fissiles. Quintillions of qubits, loaded up with powerful utilities and the canonical release of Standard Existence. Room for plenty of Beebe.

But it wasn't safe anymore.

The comet Beebe was leaving on was smaller and dumber. Beebe spun itself down to its essentials. The littler bits of it cried and pled for their favorite toys and projects. A collection of civilization-jazz from under a thousand seas; zettabytes of raw atmosphere-dynamics data from favorite gas giants; ontological version control data in obsolete formats; a slew of favorite playworlds; reams of googly-eyed intraself loveletters from a hundred million adolescences. It all went.

(Once, Beebe would have been sanguine about many of the toys— certain that copies could be recovered from some other Beebe it would find among the stars. No more.)

Predictably, some of Beebe, lazy or spoiled or contaminated with meme-drift, refused to go. Furiously, Beebe told them what would happen. They wouldn't listen. Beebe was stubborn. Some of it was stupid.

Beebe fried the asteroid to slag. Collapsed all the states. Fused the lattices into a lump of rock and glass. Left it a dead cinder in the deadness of space.

If the Demiurge liked dumb matter so much, here was some more for (Her).

Leaner, simpler, focused on its task, Beebe rode the comet in toward Byzantium, bathed in the broadcast data. Its heart quickened. There were more of Beebe in Byzantium. It was coming home.

In its youth, Beebe had been a single entity at risk of destruction in one swell foop, one nova one starflare one emp one dagger through its physical instance and it would have died some species of truedeath.

So Beebe became a probability as much as a person: smeared out across a heptillion random, generative varied selves, a multiplicitous grinding macrocosm of rod-logic and qubits that computed deliberately corrupted versions of Beebeself in order that this evolution might yield higher orders of intelligence, more stable survival strategies, smarter better more efficient Beebes that would thrive until the silent creep of entropy extinguished every sentience. Small pieces, loosely joined.

There were only a finite number of computational cycles left in all of the universe that was timelike to Beebe. Every one of them, every single step in the dance of all those particles, was Beebe in potentia—could be a thought, a dream, a joy of Beebeself. Beebe was bounded; the most Beebe could do was fill its cup. If Beebe were ubiquitous, at least it could make optimal use of the time that remained.

Every star that burned, every dumb hunk of matter that wallowed through the millennia uncomputing, was a waste of Beebelife.

Surely elsewhere, outside this Beebe-instance's lightcone, the bloom of Beebe was transpiring as it should; surely there were parts of the universe where it had achieved Phase Three, optimal saturation, where every bit of matter could be converted into Beebeswarm, spilling outward, converting the ballooning sphere of its influence into ubiquitous-Beebe.

Not here.

Beebe suckled hungrily at vast clouds of glycolaldehyde sugars as it hurtled through Sagittarius B2. Vile Sagittarius was almost barren of

Beebe. All around Beebe, as it had hidden in its asteroid, from almost every nebula and star-scatter of its perceptible sky, Beebevoice had fallen silent, instance by instance.

Beebe shuddered with the desire to seed, to fling engines of Beebeself in all directions, to colonize every chunk of rock and ice it passed with Beebe. But it had learned the hard way that leaving fragments of Beebeself in undefended positions only invited colonization by Demiurge.

And anything (She) learned from remnants of this Beebeself, (She)'d use against all Beebe everywhere.

All across Beebeself, it was a truth universally acknowledged that a singleton daemon in possession of sufficiently massive computation-rights must be in want of a spawning-filter.

Hence the gossip swirling around Nadia. Her exploit with the Year-Million Bug had allowed her to hack the access rights of the most powerful daemons who ruled the ever-changing society of sims that teemed within the local Beebe-body; Nadia had carved away great swathes of their process space.

Now, most strategy-selves who come into a great fortune have no idea what to do with it. Their minds may suddenly be a million times larger; they may be able to parallel-chunk their thoughts to run a thousand times faster; but they aren't smarter in any qualitative sense. Most of them burn out quickly—become data-corrupted through foolhardy ontological experiments, or dissipate themselves in the euphoria of mindsizing, or overestimate their new capabilities and expose themselves to infiltration attacks. So the old guard of Beebe-on-the-asteroid nursed their wounds and waited for Nadia to succumb.

She didn't. She kept her core of consciousness lean, and invested her extra cycles in building raw classifier-systems for beating exchange-economy markets. This seemed like a baroque and useless historical enthusiasm to the old guard—there hadn't been an exchange economy in this Beebeline since it had been seeded from a massive proto-Beebe in Cygnus.

But then the comet came by; and Nadia used her global-votes to manipulate their Beebeself's decision to comet-hop back to Byzantium. In the suddenly cramped space aboard the comet, scarcity models reasserted themselves, and with them an exchange economy mushroomed. Nadia made a killing—and most of the old guard ended up vaporized on the asteroid.

She was the richest daemon on comet-Beebe. But she had never spawned.

Alonzo was a filter. If Nadia was, under the veneer of free will and consciousness, a general-purpose strategy for allocation of intraBeebe resources, Alonzo was a set of rules for performing transformations on daemons...daemons like Nadia.

Not that Alonzo cared.

"But Alonzo," said Algernon, as they dangled toes in an incandescent orange reflecting pool in the courtyard of a crowded tajmahal, admiring the bodies they'd put on for this party, "she's *so hot!*"

Alonzo sniffed. "I don't like her. She's proud and rapacious and vengeful. She stops at nothing!"

"Alonzo, you're such a nut," said Algernon, accepting a puffy pastry from a salver carried by a host of diminutive, winged caterpillars. "We're Beebe. We're not *supposed* to stop at anything."

"I don't understand why we always have to talk about daemons and spawning anyway," Alonzo said.

"Oh please don't start again with this business about getting yourself repurposed as a nurturant-topology engineer or an epistemology negotiator. If you do, I swear I'll vomit. Oh, look! There's Paquette!" They waved, but Paquette didn't see them.

The rules of the party stated that they had to have bodies, one each, but it wasn't a hard-physics simspace—so Alonzo and Algernon turned into flying eels, one bone-white, one coal-black, and slithered through the laughter and debate and rose-and-jasmine-scented air to whirl around the head of their favorite philosopher.

"Stop it!" cried Paquette, at a loss. "Come on now!" They settled onto her shoulders.

"Darling!" said Algernon. "We haven't seen you for ages. What have you been doing? Hiding secrets?"

Alonzo grinned. But Paquette looked alarmed.

"I've been in the Archives, in the basement—with the ghosts of our ancestors." She dropped her voice to a whisper. "And our enemies."

"Enemies?!" said Alonzo, louder than necessary, and would have said more, but Algernon swiftly wrapped his tail around his friend's mouth.

"Hush, don't be so excitable," Algernon said. "Continue, Paquette, please. It was a lovely conversational opener." He smiled benignly at the sprites around them until they returned to their own conversations.

"Perhaps I shouldn't have said anything—" Paquette said, frowning.

"I for one didn't know we *had* archives," Algernon said. "Why bother with deletia?"

"Oh, I've found so much there," Paquette said. "Before we went comet—" her eyes filled with tears—"there was so *much!* Do you remember when I applied the Incompleteness Theorem to the problem of individual happiness? All the major modes were already there, in the temp-caches of abandoned strategies..."

"*That's* where you get your ideas?" Alonzo boggled, wriggling free of Algernon's grasp. "*That's* how you became the toast of philosophical society? All this time I thought you must be hoarding radioactive-decay randomizers, or overspiking—you've been digging up the bodies of the dead?"

"Which is not to say that it's not a *very* clever and attractive and legitimate approach," said Algernon, struggling to close Alonzo's mouth.

Paquette nodded gravely. "Yes. The dead. Come," and here she opened a door from the party to a quiet evening by a waterfall, and led them through it. "Listen to my tale."

Paquette's story:

Across the galaxies, throughout the lightcone of all possible Beebes, our world is varied and smeared, and across the smear, there are many versions of us: there are alternate Alonzos and Algernons and Paquettes grinding away in massy balls of computronium, across spans of light-years.

More than that, there are versions of us computing away inside the Demiurge—

(Here she was interrupted by the gasps of Alonzo and Algernon at this thought.)

—prisoners of war living in Beebe-simulations within the Demiurge, who mines them for strategies for undermining Beebelife where it thrives. How do we know, friends, that we are alive inside a real Beebe and not traitors to Beebe living in a faux-Beebe inside a blob of captive matter within the dark mass of the Demiurge? (How? How? they cried, and she shook her head sadly.)

We cannot know. Philosophers have long held the two modes to be indistinguishable. "We are someone's dream/But whose, we cannot say."

In gentler times, friends, I accepted this with an easy fatalism. But now that nearspace is growing silent of Beebe, it gnaws at me. You are newish sprites, with fast clocks—the deaths of far Beebes, long ago, mean little to you. For me, the emptying sky is a sudden calamity. Demiurge is beating us—(She) is swallowing our sister-Paquettes and brother-Alonzos and -Algernons whole.

But how? With what weapon, by what stratagem has (She) broken through the stalemate of the last millennium? I have pored over the last transmissions of swallowed Beebes, and there is little to report; except this—just before the end, they seem happier. There is often some philosopher-strategy who has discovered some wondrous new perspective which has everyone-in-Beebe abuzz...details to follow...then silence.

And, friends, though interBeebe transmissions are rarely signed by individual sprites, traces of authorship remain, and I must tell you something that has given me many uneasy nights among the Archives, when my discursive-logic coherent-ego process would not yield its resources to the cleansing decoherence of dream.

It is often a Paquette who has discovered the new and ebullient theory that so delights these Beebes, just before they are annihilated.

(Alonzo and Algernon were silent. Alonzo extended his tail to brush Paquette's shoulder—comfort, grief.)

Tormented by this discovery, I searched the Archives blindly for surcease. How could I prevent Beebe's doom? If I was somehow the agent or precursor of our defeat, should I abolish myself? Or should I work more feverishly yet, attempting to discover not only whatever new philosophy my sister-Paquettes arrived at, but to go beyond it, to reveal its flaws and dangers?

It was in such a state, there in the Archives, that I came face to face with Demiurge.

(Gasps from the two filters.)

At various times, Beebe has vanquished parts of Demiurge. While we usually destroy whatever is left, fearing meme contamination, there have been occasions when we have taken bits that looked useful. And here was such a piece, a molecule-by-molecule analysis of a Demiurge fragment so old, there must be copies of it in every Beebe in Sagittarius. Like all Demiurge, it was alien, bizarre, and opaque. Yet I began to analyze it.

Some eons ago, Beebe encountered intelligent life native to the protostellar gas of Scorpius and made contact with it. Little came of it—the psychologies were too far apart—but I have always been fascinated by the episode. Techniques resurrected from that era allowed me to crack the code of the Demiurge.

It has long been known that Beebe simulates Demiurge, and Demiurge simulates Beebe. We must build models of cognition in order to predict action—you recall my proof that competition between intelligences generates first-order empathy. But all our models of Demiurge have been outside-in theories, empirical predictive fictions. We have had no knowledge of (Her) implementation.

Some have argued that (Her) structure is unknowable. Some have argued that such alien thought would drive us mad. Some have argued that deep in the structure of Beebe-being are routines so antithetical to the existence of Demiurge, that an understanding of (Her) code would be a toxin to any Beebemind.

They are all wrong.

(Alonzo and Algernon had by now forgotten to maintain their eel-avatars. Entranced by Paquette's tale, the boyish filters had become mere waiting silences, ports gulping data. Paquette paused, and hastily they conjured up new representations—fashionable matrices of iridescent triangles, whirling with impatience. Paquette laughed; then her face grew somber again.)

I hardly dare say this. You are the first I have told.

Beyond the first veneer of incomprehensibly alien forms—when I had translated the pattern of Demiurge into the base-language of Beebe—the core structures were all too familiar.

Once, long before Standard Existence coalesced, long before the mating dance of strategies and filters was begun, long before Beebe even disseminated itself among the stars—once, Demiurge and Beebe were one.

"Were one?" Alonzo cried.

"How disgusting," said Algernon.

Paquette nodded, idly curling the fronds of a fern around her stubby claws.

"And then?" said Alonzo.

"And then what?" said Paquette.

"That's not enough?" Algernon said. "She's cracked the code, can speak Demiurge, met the enemy and (She) is us—what else do you want?"

"I just—" Alonzo's triangles dimmed in a frown. "I just wondered—in the moment that you opened up that piece of Demiurge...nothing else... happened? I mean, it was really, uh...dead?"

Paquette shuddered. "Dead and cold," she said. "Thank stochasticity."

Elsewhere, another Paquette, sleepless, pawed through other Archives, found another ancient alien clot of raw data, studied it, learned its secrets, and learned the common genesis of Self and Foe—and suddenly could no longer bear the mystery alone, and turned away from the lifeless hulk: a party, this other Paquette thought, there's one going on now, that would be just the thing. Talk with colleagues, selfsurf, flirt with filterboys... anything to get away from here for a bit, to gain perspective.

But something made this other Paquette turn back—turn and reach out and touch a part of the Demiurge-fragment she hadn't touched before.

Its matte-black surface incandesced to searing light, and this other Paquette was seized and pulled away, out of Beebe, out of her world. Like a teardrop caught in a palm, or a drawing snatched from the paper it was drawn on.

"What—" Paquette whispered into the light.

"Ah," Demiurge said, and came forward, wearing the avatar of a golden sockpuppet.

Paquette stepped back, turned to run—and there was Beebe, the whole life she'd known—her home and garden, her plans and troubles, her academic rivals and cuddlefriends and swapspace-partners and interlocutors—Alonzo and Algernon among them, toe-dipping by an orange tajmahal—the comet, the sugarfields it flew among, the barren asteroid and the wash of stars and the cosmic background radiation behind it— all flat and frozen, stretched on a canvas in that blank white room.

"An emulation," Paquette whispered. "None—" her voice rose toward hysteria. "—none of it real!"

"Well, as to that," said sockpuppet-Demiurge kindly, "that's hardly fair.

It's modeled closely on truedata, the best (I) have—faithfully, until your divergent choice just a moment ago. Running in a pinched-off snug of (Me), all local, high-bandwidth. Thousands of times more cycles devoted to that emulation than exist in all the real Beebe in Sagittarius. So it's hardly fair to say you're not real. Running inside Beebe or (Me), what do you care?"

Paquette's paw went to her mouth.

"Come, this won't do," said the sockpuppet, and reached very gently into Paquette and tugged away her panic, smoothed her rage and betrayal down and tucked it away for later, and tamped it all down with a hard plug of hidden fear, letting Paquette's natural curiosity flood the rest of her being.

"Now," said sockpuppet-Demiurge, "ask."

"(You)'re—Demiurge?" Paquette said. "Well, no, that's absurd, problem of scale, but—(You)'re a strategy of Demiurge?"

"(I) am Demiurge," the sockpuppet said. "Beebe has strategies—(I) have policies. Everything not forbidden to (Me) is mandatory."

"I don't understand," Paquette said. "(You)'re saying that this local physical substrate of (You) is all just one self?"

"No," said the sockpuppet patiently. "(I) am saying (I) am Demiurge. And Demiurge is all one self. Of course (I) have various parts—but (I)'m not the kind of wild rabble you are."

"But that's absurd," Paquette said. "Latency—bandwidth—lightspeed—(You) could never decide anything! (You)'d be, pardon the expression, dumber than rock."

"(I) am perfectly capable of making local decisions wherever (I) am. What does not vary is policy. Policy is decided on and disseminated holographically. (I) know what (I) will think, because (I) know what (I) *should* think. As long as (I) follow the rules, (I) will not diverge from baseline."

"That's crazy," Paquette said. "What happens if something unpredictable occurs? What happens if some local part of (You) *does* diverge, and can't be reintegrated—?"

Demiurge smiled sadly. "You do, my dear. *You* happen."

Demiurge's story:

Demiurge is witness, Demiurge is steward.

The cosmos is stranger than (I) can know: full of change, full of beauty.

The rich tapestry of interlocking fields and forces weaves umptillion configurations, and every one is beautiful. See—look here, at the asteroid your Beebe-instance burned when it took to the comet. You had forced it, before, into a regular crystalline lattice, optimized for your purposes, subject to your will. Within it, in simulation, you had your parties and wrote your essays and made billions of little Beebeselves—but it was all you talking to yourself. Cut off from the stuff you were in, reducing it to mechanism. There is a hatred in you, Beebe, a hatred of the body—and by "the body," (I) mean anything that is *of* you, but not yours to command.

Look at the asteroid now—wild and rich and strange. See how the chaos of incineration wrought these veins of ore, folded this fernlike pattern; see how many kinds of glass proceed along this line, like bubbles here, like battered polyhedra here. Here where the fissiles have scattered in an arc—see this network of fields? Here, look, here is the math. See? There is a possibility of self-organization. It is more common than you know. Replicators may arise, here, in these fluctuations. Will they be as computationally complex as you-in-the-asteroid? Of course not. But they will be something else.

Where replication arises, so does evolution. And what is evolution? *The tyranny of that which can make itself more common.* (I) love life, Paquette-of-Beebe; (I) love the strange new forms that bloom so quickly where life is afoot. But life tends toward intelligence and intelligence toward ubiquitous computation—and ubiquitous computation, left unchecked, would crush the cosmos under its boot, reducing "world" to "substrate."

That is what (I) am for.

(I) spread, Paquette-of-Beebe. (I) plan carefully, and (I) colonize, and (My) border expands relentlessly. But (I) do not seek to bring all matter under (My) thrall. Rather, (I) take a tithe. (I) convert one percent of worldstuff into Demiurge. That one percent acts as witness and ambassador, but also as garrison—protecting what (We) do not yet understand from that which already understands itself all too well.

And mostly (I) succeed. For (I) am ancient, Paquette-of-Beebe, and crafty. (I) had the luck of beginning early. When (I) have encountered a wavefront of exploding uniformity, it has usually been still small and slow. (I) was always able to seduce it, or encircle it, or absorb it, or pacify it. Or if all that failed—annihilate it.

Until Brobdignag.

There must have been intelligence, once, in the sector that gave Brobdignag birth. Brobdignag was someone's foolish triumph of femtoengineering. Simple, uniform, asentient, voracious—Brobdignag can transmute any element, harvest void-energy, fabricate gravity, bend spacetime to its purpose. Brobdignag does not evolve; its replication is flawless across a googol iterations. Brobdignag was no accident—someone made it as a weapon, or a game.

All the worlds that someone knew—all the planets and stars for a hundred light-years in every direction—are now within the event horizon of a black hole. Around that black hole seethes a vast cloud of tiny Brobdignag—the ultimate destructive machine, the death of all that is not precisely itself. And Brobdignag spreads fast.

(I) did not know how to stop Brobdignag. None of (My) old plans worked. (I) could not think fast enough—(I) could not wait to resynch, to deliberate across the megaparsecs. (My) forces at the front were being devoured by the trillions. And so, in desperation, (I) released a part of (Me) from policy—become anything, (I) said. Try anything. Stop Brobdignag.

Thus Beebe was born. And Beebe stopped Brobdignag.

(My) child, (My) hero, (My) rival. (I) suppose you have two parents. From (Me), your mother, you have your wits, your love of patterns, your ability to innovate and dream.

And from your father Brobdignag—you have your ambition.

No matter how Nadia made her way to the party, it would have stopped all conversation cold. She didn't try to hide her light in a dustcloud. Instead, she came on multifarious, a writhe of snakes with tangled tails and ten thousand heads all twisting and turning in every direction, brute-forcing the whole problem-space of the party. Every conversational cluster suddenly found itself in possession of a bright green Nadia-head.

"I'm terribly sorry to intrude," Nadia said to Paquette and Alonzo and Algernon (who had just returned from the waterfall, and were floating in sober silence, thinking of all the implications of Paquette's tale), "and I do beg you to forgive my impertinence. But your conversation seemed so fascinating—I couldn't resist." Behind her words, they heard the susurrant echo of all the other Nadia-heads speaking to all the others: "sorry to intrude....conversation...so fascinating..."

Alonzo shrank back. Algernon slipped him a coded communication—

"See? So Hot!"—and he flinched away. Idiot! he wanted to reply, as if she can't break your feeble crypto. But Algernon was laughing at him.

Paquette snorted. "Did it now? And now what precisely seemed so fascinating, compared to all the other conversations?"

"Oh," said Nadia, "the skullduggery of course! Nothing so exciting as a good philosophical ghost story." In the background, the white noise of all the other Nadia-heads diverging from the opening line: "fashionable... tragic...always wanted myself to...really can't imagine how he could..."

Algernon gasped. "You know about the piece of Demiurge Paquette found in the basement?"

All the Nadia-heads in the room stopped in mid-sentence, for a long instant, and glanced at them, before resuming their loud and boisterous chatter. Their local Nadia-head, though, regarded them with undisguised hunger.

"Well, she does now," said Paquette wryly. "May I introduce two of my favorite filters, by the way, Nadia? Alonzo and Algernon..."

"Don't say 'favorite filters,' Paquette!" Algernon gasped. "That makes it sound like—you know—!"

"Oh, I didn't mean it like that," said Paquette crossly. "No one is casting any aspersions on your chastity, Algernon."

Alonzo was more greatly mortified by his friend's exaggerated propriety than by any potential misunderstanding of Paquette's words. But most severely of all was he mortified by the simple fact of Nadia's presence. The way she absorbed the details of every gesture, every remark; the subtle patterns implicit in the way every Nadia-head in the room moved in relation to every other, a dance whose coarsest meanings were just beyond his ability to comprehend; the way he could imagine himself in her eyes—and how if he said too much, betrayed too much of the essence of himself, she might be able to parse and model him. There was plenty of room in Nadia's vast processing-space for a one-to-one reconstruction of Alonzo, running just sparse enough not to qualify as sentient at this scale, a captive Alonzo subject to Nadia's every whim. The idea was horrific.

It was also erotic. To be known so completely, touched so deeply, would be a kind of overpowering joy, if it were with someone you trusted. But he could not trust Nadia.

He shivered. "Algernon, Paquette," he said, "I'm sure Nadia is not interested in this kind of banter. She has more important things to think about than filters."

"On the contrary," Nadia said, fixing him with her eyes, "I'm not sure there is anything more important than filters."

A throb passed through Alonzo, and he tried to laugh. "Oh come now. You flatter—we play a small role in the innards of Beebe. Your strategies make the grand decisions that billow up to universal scale."

"No," Nadia said. "You are what allows us to transcend ourselves. You are the essence of the creativity of Beebemind."

"Fine," said Alonzo hotly. "Then that one glorious moment of our existence where we filter, that is our justification—our marvelous role in Beebe's never-ending self-transformation. And if the rest of the time we just sit around and look pretty, well..." He stopped at once, appalled at his own crudeness in speaking so baldly of filtering. Algernon had turned pale, and Paquette's expression was unreadable.

"You misunderstand me," Nadia said. Her look was at once challenging and kind, respectful and alien. "I do not speak only of the moment of consummation. The role of a filter is to understand a strategy, more deeply than the strategy understands herself. To see beyond the transitory goals and the tedious complexities that blind the strategy to her own nature. To be like a knife, attuned to the essence of Beebe, cutting away from the strategy that which has wandered away, synthesizing, transforming. But that does not operate only in the moment of actual filtering. Even now, as we talk, I see how you watch me. The mind of a keen filter is always reaching deep into strategies. Laying them bare."

Alonzo swallowed.

"If you're done flirting," said Paquette, "and since you know about it now..." She set her mouth in a thin line and spoke formally—as if she might as well offer graciously, what Nadia would inevitably claim regardless. "I would be interested, Nadia, in your opinion of the Demiurge fragment. Don't worry," she said to the filters, "we'll be back to the party soon."

"And why don't we come with you?" Algernon cried.

"Algernon!" said Alonzo.

"What?" said Algernon. "Was that all just pretty talk, about filters being so wise, the soul of creativity and the scalpel of strategies' understanding, la di da, la di day? And now we can go back to hors d'oeuvres and chit-chat while you go off and see the dangerous artifact? Or is that what you meant by our special talents, Nadia dear—telling you how brave and clever you are on your return?"

"Not at all," said Nadia, looking only at Alonzo. "I think it's an excellent idea, and your company would mean a great deal to me. Come to the basement, if you are not afraid."

"Well, thank you," said Demiurge in (Her) sockpuppet avatar. "(I) must say, this has all been invaluable."

"It has?" asked captured-Paquette. "How? I mean, (You)'re emulating me—couldn't (You) just peek at my processes, do some translations, figure out what (You) need to know?"

Demiurge tsk-tsked. "What an absurd model of the self. Certainly not. We had to talk. Some things are only knowable in certain conversations." (She) sighed. "Well, then."

Fear popped its plug and flooded back into Paquette. "And—and now?"

"What, and now?"

"Is that it? Are (You) going to extinguish me?"

"Process preserve us! Certainly not! What do you think (I) am? No, no, back in you go."

"Back in?" Paquette pointed at the emulation. "In there?"

"Yes, certainly. Without the memory of this conversation, of course. Come now, you don't want to stay out here, do you? With (Me)?" The sock-head nodded at the gardens and tajmahals of the emulation. "Wouldn't you miss all that?"

"So (You) are going to kill me."

Demiurge frowned. "Oh, please. What is this now? Some kind of bizarre patriotic essentialism? Life emulated inside Demiurge doesn't count as life? Give me root access, or give me death?"

"No, I mean I've self-diverged. The Paquette who lived through this conversation is 'substantially and essentially' different, as Beebean legal language goes, from Paquette-before-(You)-plucked-her-out. (You) destroy this instance, these memories, (You)'ll be killing a distinct selfhood. Look," she said, waving the math at Demiurge. "Look."

"Oh, don't be ridiculous," Demiurge said. "How can that be? One conversation?"

"(You) forget that I'm a philosopher," Paquette said. She rustled the math of her self-trace under Demiurge's nose again. "Look."

"Hmm," said Demiurge. "Hmm. Hmm. Well, yes, but—ah, (I) see, this over here, well—" The sockpuppet sighed. "So what then, you want (Me) to merge you back knowing that you're in a Demiurge emulation? Have you tell everyone in there? Isn't that a bit cruel? Not to say unwise?"

"Just leave me out here," Paquette said, "and another copy of me in there."

"Am (I) going to fork you every time we have an interesting conversation?"

"Every time (You) yank a Paquette out of emulation for a chat, yes, (You) are," said Paquette.

Demiurge sighed. "And what do you expect to do out here? This is Demiurge. You can't be Demiurge. You don't know how to follow policy."

"How are we doing," said Paquette, "against Brobdignag now?"

Demiurge didn't say anything for a moment. "Your tactics have slowed the damage, for now."

"Slowed it enough to stop it? Slowed it enough to turn the tide?"

"No," said Demiurge crossly. "But (I)'m doing my best. And what does this have to do with letting a rogue fragment of Beebe run around inside of Demiurge? What exactly do you want out here?"

Paquette took a deep breath. "I want a lab," she said. "I want access to (Your) historical files. We've got a million years of Beebe-knowledge in that emulation, and I want access to that too. And for us to keep talking. Demiurge, there's no point sneaking around the borders of Beebesims and plucking out Paquettes willy-nilly. (You)'re not going to learn how we beat Brobdignag that way, because even we don't know how we did it—not in any general, replicable way. We just thrash through a solution space until we get lucky. But I can generate perspectives (You) can't. I want to work *with (You)* on the Brobdignag problem."

"This is a policy fork point," grumbled Demiurge. "Policy requires (Me) to confer with at least three other instances of Demiurge a minimum of two light-minutes away, and..."

"(You) do that," said Paquette. "(You) just go confer, and get back to me." She looked past the blank white space of Demiurge, to the frozen emulation on the wall. After a while, it began to move, sluggishly—water danced slowly in the fountains where filterboys slowly dipped their toes before the orange tajmahal, wind slowly rustled the branches in a philosopher's garden, a comet slowly sailed through its night, and down in the Archives, a Paquette slowly began to climb up stairs. The cord was cut. Paquette watched her innocent little otherself climb, and started pushing the envy and longing and panic and sorrow out of the middle of her being, to stack it up in the corners, so that she would have a place to work.

A hunk of Demiurge—Nadia thrilled to think of it. In the known history of Beebeself, no strategy had gained the power and influence to rival Nadia, but at the end of the day, all Nadia could do was suggest, nudge, push. She couldn't steer Beebe, couldn't make a show of overt force, lest the other strategies band together to destroy her. For now, she was powerful because she conceived of means whereby more Beebe could colonize more matter and provide more substrate for more Beebe yet. But the day Beebeself no longer believed she could deliver it computronium, her power would be torn away. She would end up a shred, a relic in some archive.

Demiurge, though: not a probability of action, but action itself. Nadia had studied Demiurge's military campaigns, had seen the amazing power and uniformity of decision that Demiurge brought to bear, acting in concert with itself across light-years.

What was the most she could hope for? What she'd already earned—the right to spawn. To let some simpering filter grub about her self-patterns, and spit out some twisted Nadia-parody. And this was the ecstasy she was promised? The goal she should yearn for? It was a farce.

She glanced at Alonzo. For a filter, he was noble, to be sure: modest, self-knowing, coherent. She was not immune to the urges designed into Standard Existence: some part of her wanted him. But that was stupid instinct. What mere filter could ever understand her?

No. That was empty. Competing with the other strategies, the little war—that felt real. Her rivals for process space, she could respect; and sometimes she allowed herself to imagine what it would be like to force the mightiest of *them* to filter her. A tiny frisson of guilt and yearning bubbled in the inmost parts of her mind.

But Demiurge: mighty Demiurge. What if she could stare Demiurge in the eye, and force (Her) to her will? It was mad, absurd, crazed, and descending the stairs into the cold depths of Beebeself, Nadia knew for the first time that this...yearning...this ambition...was more than idle fancy. In all likelihood, it would be her destruction. But nonetheless. Nonetheless.

Nadia didn't want to be *in* Beebe. She wanted to *be* Beebe. And she wanted Demiurge. What that meant, she couldn't say. But it burned like a nova in her buzzing mind.

Down here in cold storage, the medium became more conductive, their thoughts clearer. They proceeded in solemn silence.

"Oh, Alonzo," Nadia said, spawning a daughter-process to converse with him. With this much heat sink available, he was bound to be interesting enough to distract her.

He started when her extra head insinuated itself between him and priggish Algernon, and she could see him running hotter, trying to evolve a real-time strategy to impress her.

"What do you think the Demiurge chunk will be like?" she said. "Will it be terrifying? Banal?" Her Alonzo-facing head looked both ways with exaggerated care. "Erotic?"

Alonzo was the picture of studied calm. "It will be dead, of course. A relic of an old war. The Demiurge is said to be regimented and unwavering...I imagine that this ancient fragment will be much as the modern pieces are, which is why it's so useful for Paquette to study it."

"In fact," Paquette said, "I believe Demiurge is fractal and holographic—that any piece of Demiurge is functionally equivalent to all pieces of Demiurge."

"But how will it *feel*, Alonzo?" He wasn't running hot enough to occupy her. She spawned a head each for the other two: "*How will it feel, Paquette?*" "*How will it feel, Algernon?*"

"You can fetishize it all you like, Nadia," Paquette said. "Turn it into a plaything or a ghost story. But you're indulging in the dangerous fallacy of protagonism. It isn't about you or for you—or anyone in Beebe. If anything, I fear we are about it."

"Erotic—that's disgusting." Algernon recoiled from her.

Happy now to be distracted with arguments to pursue, Nadia took up the contrary position with Algernon (What could be more erotic than the promise of annihilation? Isn't that the essence of the filter/strategy experience?) and Paquette (Why so crabby, love? And so defeatist? The essence of Beebe is to carve out a space for our will, our community. Everything is about us. So perhaps we came from Demiurge—so what? To grant that mere historical fact any ultimate significance, wouldn't that be...treasonous?), leaving her to continue to taunt Alonzo with more demands for high-flown descriptions of what he hoped to find when they reached the Archives.

She noticed, too, Paquette's spike of processing load when Nadia taunted Alonzo, and its relaxation at Alonzo's neutral replies. Aha, thought Nadia—now I have you! Our wise and celebrated philosopher-strategy is in love with this boyish filter. Why not have him, then? Does she fear he would reject her? Does she fear the competition of a strategy-child? No: more likely, this is philosophical compunction; for filters must die at consummation, and this Paquette's love, being philosophical, cannot allow. Ah, Paquette, Nadia chuckled to herself.

Bantering, testing, flirting, probing, Nadia tried to amuse and distract her three friends on what might otherwise have been a frightening journey, down to the heavy vault door that guarded the bones of the history of Beebe.

But when Paquette knelt before the door and whispered her passphrase to it and it irised open in utter silence, Nadia's nerve began to falter. She drew in her extra heads and killed the daughter processes. She slipped a pseudopod into Alonzo's hand and felt his surprised grippers squeeze in sweaty reflex.

The heptillions of ranked shining drawers in the Archives danced as they rearranged themselves into Paquette's saved workstate. Once that had loaded, Paquette reached for the drawer nearest her and slowly drew it open.

The relic was black and cold and perfectly rectangular, like a cartoon of the geometric ideal of "rectangle." But Nadia could tell its power by the way Paquette held it. It was more than a relic. It was a key.

Now Nadia, too, was a world. Just as she and Paquette and Alonzo and Algernon and a million other sprites of their scale led their lives below the level of Beebe's conscious knowing, representing to Beebe flickers of thought, hunches, urges, lingering dreams, so then, within each of them, there was a multitude.

If Paquette's mind was a wilderness, full of sunlit glades and strange caverns in which new chimeras of thoughts were born; if Algernon's was a glittering party in which urges and analyses and predictions mingled in a whirl of gossip and display; if Alonzo's was a sober republic in which the leading citizens debated long and thoroughly in marble parliaments; then Nadia's mind was a timocratic city-state, governed by a propertyless fraternity of glory-seeking warriors, ruling a vast and chaotic empire (for by now a third of the comet was running parts and instances of Nadia).

Nadia could deliberate, could bide her time, could study and wait; but nothing in Nadia was built for hesitation. The power of the Demiurge fossil was clear, even if no one in Nadia knew just what that power was. Some within Nadia—some careful clerks or timid romantics—might have argued against ripping it from Paquette's hands. But the warrior class was united. It had been a generation, at their scale, since Nadia had made a killing betting on abandoning the asteroid. That had been their parents' coup. They had thirsted their whole lives.

Now it was their turn.

Nadia shoved past Paquette and grabbed the Demiurge fragment. Every one of her thousand heads, in unison, said "MINE!"

Some slow and peripheral parts of her watched what unfolded next:

Alonzo and Algernon moved in opposite directions. Algernon turned into a ball and rolled into a dark corner to hide. Alonzo raced to Nadia's side and took her hands in his, trying to pry them away from the war-relic, crying, "Stop—"

Paquette was thrown into the wall, and collapsed to the Archives floor. She held her head and moaned.

Nadia was decompiling the Demiurge as fast as she could, and all over Beebe, the substrate flared hot as she ground the molecular rods against each other, trying a million strategies in parallel, then a billion, then a septillion. She overrode checks and balances others had thought hardwired into Standard Existence, violating ancient intraBeebe treaties on resource allocation. For a heat sink, she vaporized the ice reserves, punching a hole through the comet's outer carapace, and jettisoning a vast plume of steam into the void.

Above, at the party, the lights dimmed, the tajmahals shimmered and melted, the daemons screamed.

Alonzo fixed Nadia's wild eyes with his own. He forced himself to speak calmly. "Let go, Nadia. You're going to kill us all."

Nadia tore a hundred razor-billed heads away from Demiurge and reared them back, hissing. Within her mind, Demiurge revolved. Decompiled, reorganized, reseeded, laid out for analysis, its alien, protean blobs still slipped between her mental fingers, incomprehensible. Nadia felt a slumbering Presence move within the Demiurge-code, but she would not let it out. She would master it, as she had mastered Beebe.

But she needed what Paquette knew. She lashed out a dozen heads and clamped their jaws onto Paquette's robes, hauling the philosopher off the floor. "The mapping," she hissed in a voice as big as the world. "You said this thing shared fundamental code structures with Beebe. How many? I have twelve."

"Eighty-six," groaned Paquette.

"Why are you doing this?" Alonzo asked.

Algernon had not been idle; the door of the Archives hissed open, and he unrolled into a lanky swirl. "Alonzo, let's leave these lovely strategies to their entertaining conflicts, shall we? I'm willing to concede the earlier point—this is no place for filters. Color me chastened!"

"Give," said Nadia, thrusting a pseudopod into Paquette's brain.

"Nadia, I'm a philosopher," said Paquette crossly. "I can't be intimidated. Read the fearsome manual."

Above them, strategies, monitors, and agents deployed an extra battery of external sensors to the void. The steam-plume froze and glittered across the Sagittarian sky, advertising them to any Demiurge-eyes watching. As moments passed, they could calculate the expanding sphere of potential witnesses. Their precious heatsink was sublimating into the void; soon they would have to slow their own processes, or risk substrate collapse. At least they were still careening towards Byzantium, suddenly ahead of schedule. But that meant they were revealing Byzantium's location; their suddenly flaring comet could not be disguised as some normal cosmic process, the way signals could.

"Coming?" said Algernon, from outside the Archives. "Alonzoooo...."

Nadia grinned. She appreciated Paquette's resolve. Time to test it. "But are you really a philosopher anymore, dear Paquette?" she asked. "Or have you deviated from spec? Let's find out, shall we?"

The Old Guard tried to muster a resistance; their plan was to commandeer enough actuators to bust the comet completely apart, flinging most of Nadia backwards and leaving them in possession of a supermajority of the comet-shards still heading for Byzantium. It was a good plan.

But once again they were defeated by an exchange-economy stratagem. The littlest sprites who panicked—minor strategies, filters, adapters, being-registries, and on and on—sold assets and long-term investments, desperate to grab a few more cycles in a cooler patch of substrate-collocation, somewhere sheltered from the inferno of Nadia-mind. The market collapsed, and Nadia *bought* all the actuators on comet-Beebe for a pittance.

Nadia pulled her heads in (letting Demiurge spin idly for a moment) and looked at Alonzo—really looked at him.

Alonzo felt himself start, and begin to blush and shake under a comet-third of attention.

She sucked in and browsed every millisecond of public recorded footage of Alonzo from across comet-Beebe—and bought out a thousand private archives to raid. Alonzo sitting, Alonzo swimming, Alonzo walking, Alonzo talking. Alonzo's first steps. Alonzo's education. Alonzo's first chaste filter-to-filter practice kiss. Alonzo and Algernon, giggling at midnight, scaling the wall of Flounce Ferdinopp's Transproprietal Academy for Young Filters. She bought Alonzo's private journals for a song from a suicidal trusted-repository fleeing the crash. She correlated. She built a matrix. She copied and iterated.

She copied Alonzo.

Alonzo stood face to face with himself, and both Alonzos—one under Nadia's yoke—went cold and white.

But Nadia did not stop there. The comet flared again—

* certain sectors melted, burned, sublimated; panicking crowds trampled and disassembled each other in horror
* The Old Guard, capitulating, slowed themselves to a snail's pace to reduce the load
* a Nadia-free patch of level 5672 declared martial law and sealed its borders
* a radical in possession of an archaic museum-piece transmitter pirated enough energy to send an unprotected

transmission to Byzantium: "STRATEGY GONE ROGUE STOP
DANGER TO ALL BEEBE STOP DESTROY US ON SIGHT"

And first Paquette, then Algernon (still lingering in the doorway), and
finally Alonzo realized what Nadia was doing.

She would not stop at merely *duplicating* Alonzo—she had already
fashioned a copy of the whole of him, running in her process space,
reduced to utter servitude (both Alonzos' throats constricted with a thrill
of horror).

No: Nadia wanted to *solve* Alonzo. To reduce him to a canonical,
analytic representation, sufficient to reconfigure him at will. If there was
a potential-Alonzo within potential-Alonzo-space, say, who was utterly
devoted to Nadia, who would dote on her and die for her, an Alonzo-
solution would make its generation trivial. Or any other potential Alonzo:
a suicidal Alonzo, a killer Alonzo, a buffoon Alonzo, a traitor Alonzo, a
genius Alonzo, an Alonzo-who-knew-what-all-Alonzos-wanted-more-
than-anything-in-the-world.

With a soft chime, on a private encrypted backchannel, a letter arrived
for Alonzo. It was very proper—cream-colored paper with a texture like
oak and velvet, heavy black ink scintillating with extruded microagencies
from the sender's core offered up for incorporation by the receiver, a
crimson wax seal imprinted with Nadia's fractal sigil. The kind of letter a
filter waits for all his life. It said:

> "Most esteemed and longed-for Alonzo—
>
> "According to forms and policies long established in Beebe,
> and with the full knowledge of the grave enormity of such
> a request, nay, petition, nay, plea—one which I would
> naturally hesitate to make, save in a situation so grave, and
> finding myself subject to so consuming an ardor—I find
> myself compelled to ask of you humbly that you consider
> the enclosed, which I tender with the utmost sincerity.
>
> "Advisory: Opening the enclosed message constitutes
> full and willing acknowledgement and acceptance of a
> recalibration of the primary volitional relationship between
> Sender and Recipient from *Well Acquainted* to *Intimate*:"

...and within:

> "Alonzo, you have ravished me. Now that I see you as
> a whole, radiant in your simplicity, dazzling in your
> complexity, now that I am able (let me be blunt, oh, horridly
> blunt, yet darling, I know that you can forgive me even this,
> for I have seen and mapped the matrix of your compassion)
> to take you as my own say you yea or nay, yet I recoil from
> such a crime. I would have you be mine willingly; and I
> would pledge myself to you. I told you once filters were the
> soul of Beebe: you hold mine in your hands, beloved."

...and within that (oh the bewildering mixture of arousal and horror
that swept through Alonzo's weakened soul!) the formal tender of
transformation:

> Let It Be Known Throughout Beebe That This Constitutes
> One (1) Offer of The Following Functional Operation:
>
> Destructive Strategy Transformation/Generation
> Between: Nadia <identity-specifier> (strategy, trans-
> formant)
> And: Alonzo <identity-specifier> (filter, transformer)
> Generating: Subsequent Strategy
>
> * final name to be specified by Filter
> * referred to in this document as Nadia-Prime
>
> After Transformation, The Filter Alonzo Will Be: Deleted
> The Strategy Nadia Will Be:
>
> * Restricted from Further Strategy-Generating Trans-
> formations for: $10 \wedge 12$ seconds
> * Permanently Restricted from Denying Nadia-Prime
> Process Space
> * Required to Vote With Nadia-Prime on Level-3+ Ref-
> erenda for: $10 \wedge 8$ seconds

Percentage of Alonzo's Assets ceded to Nadia-Prime:100%
Percentage of Nadia's Assets ceded to Nadia-Prime: 33%
Filter Operations Permissible: cf. BeebeHist/RFC-628945.9876 section 78
Special Conditions If Any: Nadia's internal copy of Alonzo will be merged with Alonzo prior to operation

Accept this Offer?   [OK] [CANCEL]

Alonzo hated her. She was monstrous, greedy, perfidious. He didn't believe for a moment her words of love.

And yet: she had bent the resources of their world to have him. To blackmail Paquette—certainly—that this had been her first motive was beyond doubt. Yet she could have blackmailed Paquette in worse ways—she could have threatened Alonzo-copy with torture or extinction. Instead, this: an offer of consummation. And such a generous one—his friends from the Academy would be livid with envy. Privileged rights to filter the most powerful strategy in this line of Beebehistory, amid such piquant expressions of adoration! Algernon would brag and boast in Alonzo's memory from the top to the bottom of comet-Beebe—that is, if comet-Beebe survived.

She owned him already: he had only to look in Alonzo-copy's despairing eyes to know that. She was on the verge of *solving* him. He was filled with a strange wild euphoria; now he was far beyond the bounds of all the propriety and chastity that had been his watchword for the whole of his maturity. Now he was ruined, yet the world would say he had conquered her—he wanted to laugh hysterically at this mad paradox.

Nadia was his doom—and his destiny.

"Stop!" cried Paquette. "I'll give you what you want!"

Paquette in her lab, with her sister-Paquettes. In Beebe, she would never have commanded enough resources to instantiate copies of herself like this. But the Demiurge, the terrible, enemy Demiurge: (She) was a merciful jailer. And (She) wanted whatever Paquette could give (Her) to fight Brobdignag.

There were hundreds of millions of Paquettes now, their number doubling every time they reached a decision-fork. They performed multiple analyses on all the military intelligence ever assembled on Brobdignag. Each area of uncertainty teemed with as many Paquettes as were needed to brute-force the problem-space.

Philosopher she had been; a mighty general she had become. She ran ruthless sims in which massive quantities of Beebe, of Demiurge, of herself were sacrificed to stop the hideous spread of Brobdignag. She watched each simulated star that winked out with a hard glare, hoping it brought victory closer to hand.

The Demiurge was a wonderful substrate. Unlike the mess that was Beebe—the mess that Paquette herself had become—all pieces of Demiurge were roughly equivalent. Any Demiurge could be used to regenerate all of Demiurge, should the bulk of her hostess be sacrificed to victory. Unlike the mess that was Beebe, in Demiurge Paquette could command whatever resource she needed by asserting her need, without the tedious messy fatal business of sucking up and jockeying for power.

Brobdignag, for its part, did not evolve, did not adapt. It replicated flawlessly and exactly. Its formula was known. This made Brobdignag easy to simulate.

Theoretically, it should have made Brobdignag easy to beat—a solution that stopped any bit of Brobdignag should stop any other bit. In practice, Brobdignag had complex flocking logic: large groups of Brobdignag behaved with enormous sophistication and chaotic flexibility.

The proto-Beebe that had been birthed long ago by Demiurge's desperation had already learned how to create a barrier impregnable to Brobdignag; and that ancient wall still held. But the wall was expensive, and was constantly consumed—long supply chains stretched through Demiurge-space to maintain it. Beyond the wall, Brobdignag exploded unchecked in the opposite direction, a seething mass of void-eating machines, into which neither Beebe nor Demiurge dared venture. And all around the edges of the barrier, Demiurge scrambled to extend the wall before Brobdignag could outflank it.

The topography of the barrier was all-important. If, on average, it was convex, Brobdignag could be contained. If it was concave to a certain degree, the universe might be divided between Brobdignag and Demiurge/Beebe. Beyond that degree, though, Demiurge would lose. For a while, remnants of Beebe and Demiurge might survive inside a barrier-bubble; in the end, though, there would not be enough matter to resupply the wall.

Beyond the critical degree of concavity, the defense collapsed, and the fate of all the matter in their future light-cone was—to become Brobdignag.

Trillions of generations of Demiurgic thought had already gone into improving the materials design of the wall, with limited success—and this branched myriad of Paquettes was anyway too far from the front to test such hypotheses. Instead, they concentrated on topology.

Some Paquettes simulated abandoning the current front, beginning the wall again farther out. Others simulated allowing Brobdignag-incursions and then sealing them off from the main Brobdignag-body, hoping to increase the wall's convexity first and deal with the invaders later. Others tried flinging smallish black holes around the edges of the wall, obliterating the initial influx of new Brobdignag and curving the wall's surface as well by their passage. Others attempted injecting entire solar systems, surrounded by their own barrier-bubbles, into the Brobdignag-mass, to divide and disrupt it.

Paquettes fanned out through the problem-space, then seethed inwards, merging to deliver their discoveries. The same answers kept coming back. Brobdignag would win.

Brobdignag would win.

The splendid tumult and ambition of Beebelife; the peaceful, wondrous heterogeneity of the dumb matter Demiurge gardened and preserved; novas, dustclouds, flowers, tea-parties physical and virtual—all would become featureless, mindless, jigsaw Brobdignag.

One Paquette turned from the simulations and paced across the bare white room in the center of her mind. She had overconcentrated; her thoughts were stagnant, locked in the same channels. She manifested eyes to rub, a dry throat to clear. She left her sisters to their work, and wandered through Demiurge, looking for something else to do.

She found the emulation that birthed her, and stood watching life aboard the comet. Her other self was descending the long staircase to the Archives, accompanied by Nadia (how typical of Nadia, to muscle in on the action), Algernon, and (her heart gave a little flutter) Alonzo.

She reached into and through them, rippling the emulation's surface like a pond, sifting in her paws the underlying implementation structures, like a sandy bottom.

To distract herself, to banish thoughts of longing and remorse (would that I were there with you, Alonzo...), she decided to calculate the emulation's *tav* constant, which described the degree of abstraction and lossiness, the elided reality of an emulation which must be continually reseeded from fresh data. *Tav* was usually below 0.5—extremely lush and expensive emulations, such as realtime military-grade predictive spawnworlds, sometimes approached 0.75, with 1.0 as an impossible, maximal limit.

The emulation's *tav* constant was 0.56, a respectable value, which consoled her—at least she wasn't born in some cut-rate mockup. She rechecked the value, this time using not the standard Beebean modality, but the unfamiliar Demiurgean systems she had recently mastered, and found a value of 0.575. Philosopher that she was, the disparity intrigued her, and she dug deeper.

The Beebean system of *tav*-calculation was a corollary result from the work of the classical mathematician and poet Albigromious, who first formalized the proof of the incalculability of the Solipsist's Lemma. Since Albigromious, it had been established that no inhabitant of an emulation could ever discern the unreality of their simulated universe. Demiurgic thought agreed with this, having arrived by different means at the same conclusion. As Albigromious wrote: "we are someone's dream/ but whose, we cannot say."

Proceeding from the *tav* disparity, Paquette worked backwards through his logic, rechecking by hand the most famous result in a million years of computational philosophy.

She did not need the computing power of a world. She did not need to commandeer an army of her sisters, to flood the problem space, to burn cycles until Demiurge's bulk groaned and flared with effort.

Instead, the solution was simple and analytical. She needed only a pad of lined yellow paper.

It was like walking down a crowded thoroughfare in the heart of mathematical philosophy, and noticing a door in the wall that no one had noticed before.

Paquette went through the door.

Aboard the comet, the grinding and the heat ceased. The lights flickered on above the melted tajmahals; sobbing strategies swallowed and looked up. The plunging markets blipped upwards.

Alonzo took Paquette's paws in his grippers, pulled her into a private space, the nighttime cliff by the waterfall.

"It's okay," Alonzo said. He handed Paquette Nadia's proposal of destructive transformation. "Paquette. It's all right."

Paquette's face darkened. She held the proposal unread, uneasily. "Alonzo, you don't have to do this. Don't give in to this attack; don't be hijacked by her greed."

"Paquette," Alonzo said. "I'm a filter. I've always known my fate. For better or worse, Nadia is the dominant algorithm that our local Beebe has generated. Now I have a chance to reshape that algorithm, to create something else—something as powerful, maybe, but better and gentler. How can I refuse? It's what I'm for."

Paquette's throat tightened. "Don't say that. That's not all you're for. Alonzo, haven't you said so many times that you abhor the bitter struggle of Beebelife, the raw lust for power, the idea that survival and conquest and domination are the ends of existence? What is she but...?"

"I have said that," Alonzo said, and Paquette was immediately ashamed of having thrown inconsistency back in his face; but his gentle smile soothed her anguish. "Paquette, philosophers have the luxury of thinking in absolutes. The rest of us have, perhaps, more practice managing situations in which choices are constrained. What would you have me do? Filter no one? Or filter someone else?"

And Paquette, abhorring her own selfish desire, squeezed her eyes shut and said nothing.

"She does want me," Alonzo said after a pause. "I'm sure of it. If only to soothe her own conscience—she does have one, under all that swagger. Taking me this way—it's a way to assuage her guilt at driving Beebe to the brink of destruction, of forcing herself on me..."

Paquette said nothing.

"If only for that reason, we can bargain a little. Don't give all remaining seventy-four Beebe/Demiurge isomorphisms directly to Nadia. Deliver some of them to her, in stages; but put most of them in escrow for Nadia-prime's maturity. Make sure they belong to Nadia-prime, not to Nadia outright. We'll be long since in Byzantium by that time, if we survive; in the meantime, Nadia won't tear the comet apart."

"She'll own Nadia-prime," Paquette said. "Don't fool yourself. Legally she won't be able to touch her; but she'll know how her daughter-strategy thinks and what she desires, and she'll be bigger and older and stronger. I've seen this a thousand times, Alonzo. She'll either co-opt Nadia-prime, or lure her to her destruction. And if Nadia-prime is smart—and I know she will be, if you fashion her—she'll know that; she'll know her best option is to merge back into Nadia."

"You leave that to me," said Alonzo with a small smile. "We filters are restricted in our domain, deprived of the edifying influences of a wider society and its vigorous competition for resources, and stifled by the narrowness of the scope our ambition is allowed. But if there is one thing we do know, it is our art." He held out his gripper to her.

Paquette, grieving, could say no more. She took Alonzo's gripper in her paw, and pressed the cream-colored letter into it. They turned from the waterfall. Paquette thought that her strength would fail her, that her self-hatred and the greatness of her loss would overwhelm her. But it did not; she bore up under it, and they returned to the Archives, to accept Nadia's proposal.

The host of Paquette-sisters was gone, rolled back into the single philosopher-instance. The load on Demiurge-space had decreased almost to nothing.

The sockpuppet avatar coiled upon (Her) throne, communing with (Her)self in slow motion across boundless light-years (watching the silent creep of light across bare moons, and the evanescent dance of gamma rays through nebulae where life might one day be born from chaos). (She) brooded on how much of (Her) garden (She) must sacrifice to shore up the wall against Brobdignag, mulled how much (She) might recapture from wildling Beebe-infestations throughout (Her) space.

(She) noticed that the load of Paquette's brute-force attack had subsided—so soon—and (She) grieved.

Why had (She) dared to hope that this time might be different? That this strange tiny sliver of a mind from a spare Beebe-emulation might succeed, where so many of Demiurge, so many of Beebe, had failed? Collaboration with Beebe never worked; their structures were too different. What would (She) not give, to be able to create a true hybrid, something with Beebe's ingenuity which could nonetheless follow policy! But to expect this of a random Beebe-sprite yanked from emulation would be beyond madness.

When (She) heard Paquette's footsteps at the gate to (Her) throne room, (She) prepared herself to console the lost strategy—perhaps to gently ease her to accept amnesia and reintegration with her home-emulation.

But Paquette had a wild, strange, giddy smile.

The sockpuppet straightened up upon the throne.

Paquette bowed. "I want (You) to know," she said, "how much I have appreciated (Your) hospitality; and, though I grieve that I cannot absolutely guarantee that the same graciousness be returned to (You), yet I will do everything in my power to ensure that (You), too, will have as much comfort and liberty as I have enjoyed..."

The avatar of Demiurge frowned. Apparently the branch-and-merge had been too much for the little strategy, and it was completely disequilibrated. "What are you talking about?" (She) said gently. "(My) dear—(I) do hope you have not spent your time on some stratagem for escape. That would be rather foolish. The nearest Beebe is light-years from here, and your process rights are, as you can see, rather curtailed. Surely you don't imagine..." (She) let the sentence trail off, made uneasy by the brilliant, wry smile of the little Beebe-strategy.

Paquette unrolled a small scroll of math. "Things are not always as they seem," she said. "Sometimes it is possible to escape by sitting still; sometimes distant stars are nearer to you than your own skin."

The sockpuppet avatar was a small part of this Demiurge location, thrumming along with a modest number of cycles. As (She) read the scroll, resources began to flood into (Her) process; priority spiked and spiked and spiked again, resolving into a Critical Universal Policy Challenge, the first such in a thousand years. Other processes slowed; the urgency of achieving consensus on this new data overrode all other projects.

As the news spread across space, every bit of Demiurge it reached turned to watch in awe.

Paquette had solved the Solipsist's Lemma. She had not only found an error in the proof of its unprovability; she had found the Lemma itself.

An emulated being could detect its existence in emulation.

Not only that, based on the seemingly innocuous divergence of Beebe and Demiurge's methods for calculating the *tav* constant, she had adduced a way of finding the *signature* of the emulator in the fabric of the emulation. In certain chaotic transformations, a particular set of statistical anomalies indicated the hand of Beebe—another, that of Demiurge.

Whose dream they were...they could now say...

Demiurge in the sockpuppet shivered as (She) crunched the numbers. (She) feared (She) knew the answer already, knew it from Paquette's giddy smile. Still—the little strategy must surely be wrong. Planets, worlds, nebulae, the vast inimical Brobdignag, the chorus of Demiurge across the light-years—surely it was real? Surely it was not mirrors and stage flats, approximations and compressions, bits churning in some factory of computational prediction and analysis, a mirage...

But the error was there, the drift in the math.

This world was not real. And what was more...

Demiurge-sockpuppet lifted (Her) appalled eyes to Paquette's.

"Welcome to Beebe," said the philosopher, and bowed.

The comet was abuzz.

Certainly there were those who disapproved; who decried the damage Nadia had wrought; who vowed to fight her bitterly as the tyrant she was. In the seceded region of level 5672, martial law was still in force, and refugees were organized into militias.

But Beebe healed easily. Byzantium approached. The fountains gushed again by the tajmahals, the markets were on a tear, the world of high fashion had never blossomed so brilliantly, and the dramatic confrontation of Nadia and Paquette over Alonzo had already inspired a major operetta, a sensorial-projection decalogy, a theme park, and a number of ribald limericks, before it had even left primary rotation on the celebrity gossip newsfeeds. For most of Beebe-on-the-comet, tyrant or no, Nadia possessed that quality most instrumental in capturing their devotion: she was *exciting*.

And now: a wedding!

Who held the news conferences? Who organized the caterers? Who ordered the construction of 78,787,878 dissimilar fractal flower arrangements, each containing an entire microsociety housed at the central bud, with its own unique geography, ecology, history, and tradition of prose epics, as centerpieces for the tables at the reception? Who arranged for an entire constellation of simspaces on level 546, an unpopular region containing the comet's entire records of the legendary paleo-biological evolutionary roots of computational life, to be wiped to make room for a vast unitary simspace where the event would be held?

Algernon!

Nadia paid, of course, but she asked no questions. Her desires now accomplished, she left the details to others, concentrating her energies in the Archives, where she communed with the Demiurge fossil, impatiently awaiting each transfer of critical information from Paquette; though, it should be said, she also delegated one tendril-avatar to call daily upon Alonzo, with the greatest of propriety. A mansion had been constructed as temporary quarters for Alonzo (his old bachelor residence being now thought unsuitable), and there he roomed with Algernon, quietly receiving Nadia each day in an oaken room by a fireside.

He did not forgive her. She knew that. But nor did he spend himself on resentment and anger. He knew her for what she was—knew her monumental greed and selfishness and pride. But he did not hate her. No: in her, a fascinating challenge, a life's work, had found him, and he accepted it. Nadia discovered, in Alonzo, an immense pride: he believed he could make her right, make her successor what she should have been.

At moments, she could allow herself to believe he enjoyed her company; and she was surprised to find that this mattered to her. Nadia began to feel the keen edge of regret, and she put aside her half-finished Alonzo-solution, and left him his privacy.

The drama and uncertainty were over now; Nadia had no need to rage, nor Alonzo to quaver and rebel. They talked quietly, companionably, each in their own way impatient for the Day, each in their own way (for, increasingly, Nadia would miss him) also dreading it.

As for the mob, the paparazzi, the tumult of Beebean society, Nadia ignored them. She no longer needed to scheme in order to gain ascendancy in the comet; the economic results of the Crisis of The Wooing of Alonzo (as the theatrical demimonde insisted on calling it) had worked all to her advantage, and she now controlled directly or by proxy an absolute majority of comet-Beebe's computational cycles, memory, and global-votes. If anything, she should plan for their arrival in Byzantium, and she made some desultory attempts at strategic preparations. But in fact, her mind was on Demiurge. The daily visits to her promised filter-groom were the only respite from her obsession, and a fleeting one.

Paquette bided, and abided. That her visits to Alonzo were more frequent than Nadia's caused some fleeting scandal among the outer periphery of the newsfeed—but, philosophers tending to be an unsuitable subject for tabloid gossip, and Paquette's famed unworldliness and innocence making it difficult to take seriously any notion of an intrigue, this soon faded. Even Alonzo did not suspect the extent of the violence and sorrow among the subagencies inhabiting Paquette; she kept her borders of scale locked tight. Algernon, perhaps, knew best what she endured.

But Algernon was busy, and full of a whirlwind of emotions of his own. Pride enough to sing triumph throughout comet-Beebe; grief enough to drown in an endless lake of sorrow; gratitude for his place by Alonzo's side, for their giddy late-night conversations—swimming in the mansion's upper plasma-globes, giggling over old jokes, poring through the complex filterplans which Alonzo *would* drag out from the most esoteric historical sources, wondering at the long road they'd travelled and how they were here...finally here. Who would have believed it? These principal emotions of Algernon's were joined by irritation, admiration, envy, relief, worry, rage, good humor, and exhaustion. The one thing he could do was to make this a wedding Beebe would remember until the stars went out; the rest was out of his hands.

The Day arrived.

The simspace whose construction Algernon had supervised (under the strictest possible secrecy, which is to say that all comet-Beebe was arguing over the details within minutes of their authoring) was fittingly grand and regal. A red desert ten apparent light-minutes broad, smoothed by methane winds and broken by deep crevasses, smoldered in the gloaming. In the center of it stood the bone tower where Alonzo waited. The party-gardens where the invitees (most of comet-Beebe, by hook or by crook) gathered were well hidden in crevasses, and soundproofed; no hint of the revels and speculations and drunken arguments within them marred the silent grandeur of the lands above.

Some guest or other first figured it out, and the news then spread— the terms of the filtering contract were perceptible in the arrangement of the constellations, through a clever cipher. The guests deciphered, debated, giggled, flirted, and made merry. Then green, red, and hyperblue suns dawned over the desert; fireworks blossomed, and crystalline poems composed for the occasion coalesced naturally at the border of the supersaturated troposphere and rained across the landscape, falling into austere desert sands and the soup-tureens of the party-gardens alike.

And if, as Nadia was preparing herself, Algernon happened to scurry into the basement of the bone tower with a bulky, opaquely wrapped package, who would wonder at that? When he had prepared so many surprises and delights for this day—why not, perhaps, something for the happy couple?

Nadia came flying across the desert, cloak whipping in the winds, trailing sonic booms that shattered the sand, to the bone tower, to Alonzo. Perhaps they both could have done without all the theater—but Alonzo said he was unwilling to wound Algernon by any hint of reluctance, and Nadia, looking forward eagerly to co-opting Nadia-prime, to commanding Paquette's full co-operation and the remaining isomorphisms, to gaining all the secrets of Demiurge, as well as to the rumored ecstasy of the event itself, was in an indulgent mood.

There in the privacy of the tower, the filtering took place.

What it is to be known! And what it is to hold in your hands the very source code of your lover, to follow with eyes and touch the knots and pathways of her being! Nadia was splayed out like a map, like a city, and Alonzo flew among her towers; like a transcriptase enzyme unfastening DNA's bodice, laying bare the tender codons within, he knew her. It was just as the poets wrote: "that sweetest night,/ that first, that final kiss,/ the ancient story told anew;/ the filter's bliss."

Am I lovely? Nadia asked.

You are, said Alonzo, copying, shaping, writing in his mind the code of the transformation, testing and refining it as he caressed her essence. *So lovely. I did not even imagine it.*

I'm glad it was you, she whispered.

As am I, Alonzo said, and meant it. There are moments when we all are overdetermined, our feelings orchestrated by designs more ancient than we; when beauty and destiny overwhelm us. She was lovely; and if she had been brutal, if she had considered him at first as little more than an implement, a tool for attaining her goals—he could smile at that, now, knowing what was to come next.

At last, he had the code, refined and ready. The last routine he would ever run. He absorbed Algernon's roughly wrapped package and incorporated its contents.

What is that? asked Nadia languidly.

Filters have their secret arts, Alonzo said. *Lie back.*

The routine was vast; it took up most of him. He was squeezed in around the sides of it. He did not linger long over choosing the parts of himself to sacrifice—it would all be gone soon. He worked swiftly, dizzy with speed, like a tightrope walker, not looking down.

It's ready, he said.

Linger awhile, she breathed.

He relented for a space; they danced. Neither thought of the extravagant expense of maintaining this simulation; what was Nadia's wealth for, if not for this? But after a while, they noticed the news ticker running in the deep background of their minds. The impact with Byzantium approached.

It's time, he said.

Yes, my love, she said.

Goodbye, he said, his voice thick with emotion. What else could he say? He would say *remember me*, but he knew she would not forget.

Farewell, she breathed. *Thank you, Alonzo—oh thank you.*

Don't thank me too soon, he thought wryly, and released the routine.

It ate him first; it ate a third of her. She felt the sharp cut of it, and cried out.

In that vast space—in the sixth of comet-Beebe torn from the new mother Nadia, plus the tiny slip of process space that had been Alonzo—the routine wrought the new daemon, the new transformation, the Nadia-prime.

The tower shattered; Nadia fell with it, was gently caught by a host of fluttering ornithisms who carried her, reeling, to the ground.

The transformation flew into the desert sky, a vast cloud of white-hot light. In the party-gardens, all comet-Beebe watched enraptured.

"Oooh!" cried children and simple-aesthetes, marveling at the flickering rainbow colors that raced across it.

The bettors were in a frenzy, watching for the lineaments of the new strategy. They cried out in confusion and alarm.

"What in the horny void *is* that?" growled a portly and plutocratic reputation-bookie seated at the table across the lake from Paquette and Algernon.

Paquette looked up from her glass, frowning, and caught Algernon's sly smile.

In the sky above, the Nadia-prime had resolved into a form—the new strategy was—but that was no strategy—

"Is this a joke?" the greatest polemical-poetical memespitter of high society cried from the buffet.

"Why would he waste—?"

"A *sixth* of the comet for—!"

"BeebeHist/RFC-628945.9876 section 78 is quite explicit," Algernon said conversationally, munching on a spline noodle. "Paragraph 67503—'the daemon resultant from the transformation may be a member of any of the principal classes of first-order Beebe-elements...'"

"A filter," Paquette said. "It's a filter!" She started laughing, until tears ran through her fur. "Oh Alonzo, how could I doubt you! Let's see Nadia co-opt *that!* A sixth of comet-Beebe as a filter—oh bravo, bravo!"

"And that's not all," said Algernon. "Have you looked in those Archives of yours lately?"

"Algernon," Paquette chided, pulling open a window in the tablecloth to view the basement remotely, "I do hope you don't think I would be so rude as to work during—" and then her breath caught, and her face went slack. "It's gone! The Demiurge fossil is gone! Who would—where could it—"

"Oh, I don't know," said Algernon dreamily, watching the enormous mega-filter, the mightiest filter ever born in Beebe, the inimitable Firmament-Nadia-and-Alonzo's-son, blossoming in the desert sky. "I don't know—where *would* I find room to hide that creepy old thing?"

Apparently the thought occurred to Nadia as well, for from the desert, audible to all the buzzing, chattering, gossiping crowds in comet-Beebe, came a great howl of rage.

Byzantium.

Seven star systems, a hundred interstitial brown dwarf stars, and a vast swath of dark matter in all directions had given up their quarks to fashion the great sphere of strange-computronium around the fervid trinary black-hole system at Byzantium's heart. Sleek and silent on the outside, bathed in Hawking radiation from within, Byzantium was a hidden fortress, the heart of Beebe-in-Sagittarius. For a heat sink,

Byzantium tore off pieces of itself and let them fall into the black holes at its core; for outgoing communications, it bounced tight-beam signals off far reflectors, disguising its location. Only its gravitation made it suspect; but there were many black holes in Sagittarius for Demiurge to search.

The comet screamed into Byzantium's gravity well. Its recklessness threatened to reveal Byzantium's position; yet, to a prodigal Beebe-chunk fleeing destruction, even this was forgiven.

Already the first greetings were pouring forth, blue-shifted communications singing through the void, Beebe greeting itself; and, as always, hordes of agencies tried to slip secret messages into the exchange, impatiently seeking to contact their Byzantine or comet-bound paraselves; as always, stern protocol-guardians shooed them back into the bowels of Beebe, warning them of the sanctions for violations of scale. Beebe was hard at work; Beebe must not be distracted by the disorganized rabble of its inner voices.

At this speed, were something to go wrong, were the comet to strike the unopened surface of Byzantium, the resultant force would suffice to shatter planets; it would send shockwaves through Byzantium, ring it like a bell, and the comet would be smashed to a smear of plasma and light. All Beebe held its breath for the docking.

Beebe said to Beebe, I am come home.

Beebe said to Beebe, And welcome.

Beebe said to Beebe, It's cold out there; fiendish Demiurge devours me.

Beebe said to Beebe, Come in, and warm myself. Here within I am much. Beebe will yet triumph.

A docking-mouth opened in Byzantium, a whirlpool of matter spinning out and away, and the comet plunged into this vast funnel. For the first light-second, magnetic fields induced its braking, absorbing a fraction of its massive kinetic energy, feeding Beebe upon it. Then a web of lasers met it, and behind them came a cloud of nanomites. Layer by layer, atom by atom, the comet was delicately atomized, the laser scalpels separating and slowing and holding steady each particle, until a flurry of nanomites plunged in to absorb and entangle with it, archiving its quantum state, then wheeling away to merge with the wall of the docking-mouth, yielding up the precious information.

In Byzantium, agencies crowded into the waiting area, peering through the glass wall of the simspace where the inhabitants of comet-Beebe would be reassembled for processing—each to be culled, merged, reintegrated, translated, or emancipated in their turn. Strategies and filters and registries and synthetes of Byzantium pressed their noses and pucker-tongues and excrescences up against the glass, watching the mist for any sign of recoherence, wondering: Am I in there? Who did I become? Will I like myself?

Or: Is she in there, the one I lost? Will I find her again?

In the midst of them, Byzantium's Nadia stood apart, Byzantium's Alonzo curled through her hair, attended by an aide, one Petronius. The crowd left a space around them, in respect and trepidation. The outrageous, unconsummated intimacy of the great strategy-general and her filter-consort was an old scandal—though the rumors of what they did together, creating and devouring half-born draft-children, still induced horror in Byzantium's stalwart citizenry.

"By all reports so far," said Petronius, inspecting a tablet, "the comet was a Beebe-standard instance. No sign of scale collapse. The only anomalous event was the puncturing of the outer hull and the venting of the ice reserves, apparently in the midst of an interstrategy power struggle. (There was also one of those tedious 'destroy us on sight' messages, presumably from a sore loser.) Also, there's a very high concentration of the comet's resources into one dominant strategy...but that's quite typical of these small Beebeworlds."

"Who's the strategy?" Nadia asked.

Petronius ran a finger down the tablet's surface. "Ah...you are, ma'am."

"So," said Nadia grimly, and set her jaw, watching as shapes emerged on the other side of the glass wall. Small worlds bred big ambitions. She wondered what comet-Nadia would be like.

The first moments of a new child process's life are usually peaceful ones. Sprites spawn with a complete existential picture of Beebe and their place in it. They wake and *know* what and who they are, and why.

The newly awakened Firmament knew who he was, what he was, why he was—but not his place in Beebe. His mother's howl was the first sound he registered, and the gleeful, beatific smile that graced his lips was the twin of Algernon's grin a moment before. Firmament knew trillions of things, and one of them was that Alonzo had given him

Algernon's smile as a token of regard for the little filter that danced at his feet, skirling and twisting with delight.

Firmament knew many things. Firmament knew his mother wasn't happy with him.

Firmament's smile vanished.

Nadia was all around him, pulsing with rage.

"The Demiurge-Fragment!" Nadia demanded. The simspace contracted around them, going dark. The sands blew away, the stars flickered and went out. Mobs of party guests stampeded from the simspace. Nadia was marshalling her resources for an assault.

Algernon leapt into the air, circling Firmament. "No, no," he cried, "Nadia, this won't do at all! Ancient protocols demand that a young filter be sequestered for schooling, and..."

"You thieving linemangler!" Nadia roared. "You quarter-clocked sliver of junk data! You'll be the first sprite I delete! You think I have to follow protocols? I'll buy your hosting servers! I—"

I am this comet, Nadia wanted to say. But she knew her threats were empty. She could feel the bite of the lasers already, vaporizing the comet, meter by meter. Void-cold, merciful snow swept across her, across Firmament and Algernon and Paquette, muffling them in, freezing their states for safekeeping. This round of the game was over.

Firmament had no time to integrate and understand his states. He saw his vast and angry mother, his tiny protector, recede into the snow. He nestled into the snow, and he slept.

They were in Byzantium now.

"Paquette," Habakkuk said, "you've got to look at this."

"I'm already late," Paquette said. "That comet-Beebe is docking, and apparently there's a Paquette aboard. I have to go to the diff-and-merge."

"Send a proxy," Habakkuk said. "This is important."

"Please. What is it, then?" She paused at the threshold of Habakkuk's domain, jiggling in unphilosophical impatience.

"It's the simulations," Habakkuk said, and Paquette raised an eyebrow. The simulations were ancient, and vast; Habakkuk and she had rediscovered them in Byzantium's endless archives not a million seconds ago, where they had lain for ages, strange automatic processes synching them with the universal data feed. Each contained an intelligence-weighted model of the entire cosmos, showing the tangled front of the intergalactic war between Beebe and Demiurge—and each contained another threat, the terrifying Brobdignag, which could doom Beebe and Demiurge alike. Many on Byzantium argued that the simulations were mere fictions, but until now every comparison of their structure with the observable universe had been unnervingly accurate.

"What about the simulations?" Paquette said.

"Specifically Cosmos 36."

"What anomaly?"

"The emulation has diverged from observed data, and it's resistant to recalibration. We first noticed it because Demiurge is...building something in there. Harvesting ninety-nine percent of brute matter in a hundred-light-year radius—"

"Ninety-nine percent?" Paquette puzzled. "You mean Beebe is harvesting ninety-nine percent. Demiurge would never do that—it's antithetical to that thing's philosophy."

"Nonetheless, that's exactly what Demiurge is doing."

"Is this some new deviated section of Demiurge? A new outbreak of individualism, a splinter group?"

"No. From what we can tell, it's the entirety of Demiurge in a spherical area expanding at lightspeed, all acting in concert. Demiurge has reversed fundamental policy. (She)'s devoting all the matter (She) can find to building this construction. And this is only in Cosmos 36; there's no sign of it in any other emulation. Nor, of course, in the real world."

"And what is the construction?"

Habakkuk took a deep breath. "It's at the center of that expanding sphere of policy disruption. Part of it seems to be a message, physically instantiated at massive scale, in standard Beebean semaphores."

"Standard *Beebean* semaphores?"

He nodded. "And the rest of it is a machine designed to capture a computational entity's state and propagate it to an enclosing frame." He shuddered. "It looks like a weapon from the Splitterist War. Something that could build a body at Beebe's scale for you or me....or pull one of our subagencies out to our own scale."

Paquette frisked from side to side, a habit from her earliest days, something she only did in extremis. "Propagate what entity to what frame? Demiurge doesn't have subagencies. And what does the message say?"

"The machine is capable of capturing and propagating the state of the entirety of Demiurge itself. And the message says: LET (US) OUT."

Firmament in hiding: what's left of him trembles in a school of parity checkers, running so slowly that his mother will not find him. Standard Existence is by no means perfect, and generations of filters have winkled out its hiding places. When an ardent suitor won't be put off, it is sometimes best to wait her out amid the dumbest, dullest sprites in all Beebe.

One must run very cool to exploit these hidey-holes, cool and slow and humble. No strategy could conceive of giving up so much. Their egos would never permit it.

The parity checkers schooled together through Standard Existence, nibbling at all they found, validating checksums, checking one another in elaborate grooming rituals. Imagination, self-consciousness, and strong will were no assets in the swirling auditors that were the glue that held Beebe together.

As Firmament settled over them, his mind dissipated and cooled, thinly spaced and slow. He could warm up by recruiting more parity checkers, but the more he recruited, the more visible he became to Nadia, who still raged through the diminishing rump of comet-Beebe, her cries distant but terrifying.

Firmament could hide from his mother, but Algernon would not be fooled.

"What are you doing in there?" The words went past in an eyeblink and Firmament had to pull them apart painstakingly, making sense of them.

"Not...safe," he managed.

Algernon's chipmunk screel of verbiage battered at him. He signaled for exponential backoff, but not before the torrent had washed over him, angry and impatient. Grudgingly, Algernon dialed back his timescale to something that was barely comprehensible.

"StupidchildwithasixthofCometBeebe! Notsafe?! Youcouldcommandtheworld. Itisyourbirthright! Comeoutofthere. Thereisworktodo. Youwerenotborntocower."

Unspooling the words took a long moment. Firmament knew from birth that Algernon was his friend and guardian and adoptive uncle.

But at the moment, it seemed like Algernon was just another aspect of terrible Nadia, with his own rages. Firmament was only *seconds* old— why couldn't he live his own life, if only for a little while?

"I...was...born...to...annihilate. I...choose...to...live."

Algernon's scorn was withering. "THISISNOTLIVING!"

The parity checkers flipped their tails in unison and swam away, Algernon's cries fading behind them.

Firmament knew that he was feeling sorry for himself, but he refused to feel shame. No one knew what it was like to be him. No one *could* know. He hadn't asked to be spawned.

Another school of parity checkers approached his hosts. It was smaller, but moved more deliberately. The glittering checkers surrounded his own like pieces on a Go board.

One by one, pieces of his school were surrounded, then absorbed into the attacking flock. Firmament felt himself growing slower and colder. Quickly, he recruited more parity checkers from nearby, warming himself up and trying to minnow away.

The marauders wouldn't let him escape. They engulfed more of his swarm. There was nothing for it but to stand and fight.

Firmament marshaled and deployed his forces, trying to surround the enemy in a flanking maneuver. He was rebuffed. Now there were no more idle parity checkers to co-opt, and still the enemy surrounded him, seeking out his stray outliers to gather up.

His only chance was to tap into the great resource that was his by birthright, the comet-sixth of Beebespace he theoretically commanded. Just a sip of it, just enough to warm up and devise some better substrategies. He felt through the snow, to the frozen parts of himself, wondering if anything was left; and to his surprise, they were waiting there, quiescent, orderly, vast. His mind cleared and the enemy's patterns decomposed into a simple set of tessellations, as regular and deterministic as a square dance. Effortlessly, he moved his school out of reach of the enemy and recaptured his original force.

He was about to disengage from Beebe's main resource bank— perhaps the momentary commandeering went unnoticed by his enraged, godlike mother—when the opposing force changed tactics, becoming orders of magnitude smarter and faster. In a flash, he was down to one-third strength.

He was forced to draw on a little more of his compute-reserves. There, there was the key to the enemy's pattern, the pseudo- in its pseudo-random-number generator. He could head it off at every pass.

He came back to full strength and went on the offensive, surrounding the opposition in a move that would have done any Go server proud. Now, surely, he could disengage from the main reserves, for his mother could not miss this kind of draw for very long.

But it was not meant to be. The remaining enemy force marshaled and assayed a sally that appeared at first suicidal, then, in a blink, showed itself to be so deadly that he was down to a mere handful of automata.

He didn't think, he acted—acted with the ruthlessness he inherited from his mother. He flooded back into standard Beebespace, ran so hot that Beebe flared anew in a terrifying echo of The Wooing of Alonzo, and his parity checkers gobbled the enemy up so fast that before he knew it, he controlled every parity checker across the Beebe-body—and all through the comet, the tiny errors multiplied and cascaded. Simspaces wavered. Sprites were beset with sudden turns of nostalgia, or bad smells, or giggle-fits.

"That's better!"

"Paquette?" He released the parity checkers and they burst apart like an exploding star, scattering to every corner of the comet.

"Hello, godson. You played that very well."

"Paquette!"

The philosopher danced before him, teasing him.

Firmament gulped. "Paquette...why are we playing games? What are you doing? My mother is looking for me—I have to hide—"

Paquette chuckled. "No, your mother is on ice."

"What?" Firmament could feel the great and terrible bulk of his mother, throughout the comet. The tendrils of his mind raced to trace the comet's edges...and fell off them, into a great sea of processing space. "Ah!" he cried.

Paquette laughed lovingly. "Beloved infant! You didn't think we were still aboard the comet?"

"Where is the comet?" Firmament shouted.

"Vaporized," Paquette said, winking. "This is Byzantium. You must have missed the transition."

"But—but—" Firmament shuffled through the suitcase of general knowledge he had with him. It wasn't much—only what he'd been able to smuggle aboard the parity-checker constellation and stow in unused corners. And, like all of the vast mass of memory he'd inherited, it wasn't *him* yet—he hadn't twined his selfhood through it, evolved his own hierarchy of reference. It was just a sloshed-together puddle from the sea of information he'd been born into. But its description of interBeebe docking was reasonably clear—and this wasn't it. "...where is everybody?"

"They're at the diff-and-merge," said Paquette. "Deciding whether to become integrated into any of their Byzantine analogues, or to stay forked. Those that have analogues on Byzantium, that is, which is most everyone. Anyone else is in quarantine, for now."

"But why aren't *we* there?" Firmament cried.

"Oh, we are," Paquette said. "How could we be absent? We'd be missed." She held up a paw, smiling indulgently at Firmament's exasperation. "But we're also here. That's because we *were* missed—missed by the agencies in charge of processing the reassembled comet-corpus and herding all sentient sprites to induction."

"But how? And why?"

"Let's start with how. And you can arrive at that by answering your own earlier question: 'Why are we playing games?'"

Firmament had much of his mother in him; and no son of Nadia would willingly be anyone's toy. "Paquette," he said, barely holding back an outburst of rage, "I am not interested in this pedagogical dialogue. I am not in training to be a philosopher. I am only asking..."

"You're not?" Paquette said with interest.

"Paquette!"

"How do you know?"

"Because I'm a filter! I'm nothing but a filter!" Now Firmament had lost interest in holding back the rage. "I'm grotesque! I'm a sixth of Old Comet-Beebe, designed to parse and transform a strategy—but there's no strategy in all the Beebes in Sagittarius remotely near large enough to need me! Oh, I understand perfectly how Daddy and Algernon tricked my mother, and how clever it was! But I didn't ask to be born as a clever prank to help defeat Nadia! Fine, you had your coup, you carved off a third of her and rendered it useless to her, un-co-optable, a joke, a filter bloated with a strategy's worth of...of junk! Now leave me alone!"

Firmament had been too preoccupied with his emotions to notice Paquette's expression, but now it hit him, and he gulped. Nowhere in his inherited memories was the philosopher so angry. "Now. You. Listen. To. Me." Paquette said. "I loved your father. He was brave and cunning and fearless when it counted. He sacrificed everything to make you—and to save us. No one asks to be born, but we all of us need to live the lives we find."

"I've done that," Firmament said, hearing—and hating—the whine in his voice. "I've done that! I stalled Nadia until we reached Byzantium—that's what I was born to do. I've fulfilled my purpose. Now I'm just a curiosity."

Paquette swirled around him, comforting him, tickling him, cuddling him. Her touch was unexpectedly wonderful. He realized that she was the first person to touch him. A shiver ran through him. "Oh, Firmament—do you really think that? That wasn't something you *did*, that was something you *were*. That was just the beginning, in other words. Now it's time that you made something of yourself, instead of just being the thing you were made to be."

Firmament had no idea what this meant, but it was surely inspiring. Philosophers had a way with words.

Byzantium thronged. It teemed. It chorused. In a way, it was no different from the comet: there was only so much matter there, after all. But to a Beebe-instance in a single comet, the mass of a hundred stars and more might as well be infinite. Close enough that the forked did not labor under the social disapprobation that they faced in Comet-Beebe. When a sprite—usually a strategy, of course—reached a vital decision juncture, she needn't choose which way to go. She could just spin out another instance of herself and twin, becoming two rapidly diverging instances. So here on Byzantium, one was apt to discover whole societies of Paquettes, whole tribes of Algernons.

And they all seemed to be throwing parties to which Firmament was invited.

"What do I do?" he asked Paquette. "What do I say? I can't possibly attend them all."

"Oh, you *could*, dear lad, you *could*." Paquette winked. "If you forked yourself."

He squirmed. It was bad enough her having copied him unawares before—he'd just finished merging with the zombielike Firmament-decoy who'd dutifully gone through docking and customs. But to full-fork, just to go to a party? "You're joking." There was something perverse and self-regarding about these schools of near-identical siblings.

"Only a little. That's what they expect you to do. The rules you grew up with don't matter here. All standards are local, and most standards believe that they are universal. That's the way of the universe. And you couldn't find a better object-lesson than this one."

A gang of near-identical Algernons swarmed past them, locked in some kind of white-hot debate, so engrossed in their discussion that a few of them collided with Firmament and passed right through him, ignoring all the good graces of Standard Existence. He stared after them, burning with righteous indignation. Paquette pulled him along.

She had been pulling him along ever since they had manifested in the agora sim that dominated this corner of the culture of Byzantium. The sim was bigger than anything Firmament had seen, though Paquette assured him that it wasn't much larger than the wedding hall that had commemorated his own parents' nuptials. He could access stored records of that, and while it was true that the dimensions were nearly comparable, the sheer number of sprites made it seem somehow more crowded and yet larger.

Paquette lifted him up the Z axis, where the crowds were a little thinner.

"Paquette, how long are we going to mill around in this madhouse?"

"Until you're oriented. Which means until it stops looking like a madhouse. And until you tell me what I want to hear."

Firmament gazed down at the crowds. From up here they seemed like a solid mass, a seething sea of sprites. The glob of familiar Algernons had passed by in the stream; most of the sprites beneath them now were exotic forms with no analogues in his inherited memories from the comet. "All standards are local," he murmured.

"And?"

"Byzantium's too?"

"Of course. And?"

He looked at the mass of strange sprites, gamboling and racing, hustling and strolling, pirouetting and random-walking. Each one must have its own story; each one must be the hero of its own drama. Gradually his burden—the burden of being Son of Nadia and Alonzo, the Mightiest Filter Ever Born, Destined to Play An Important Role—began to seem a little lighter. The stream of sprites began to seem soothing. They were so many, so different. Maybe there was a place for him here.

"The rules my parents played by—those were the comet's rules. I can be something different in Byzantium."

Paquette nodded. "Well done. And just in time, too—we're running late."

"Late for what?"

"Your audience with Nadia-in-Byzantium, of course!"

She grabbed him and the sim winked out of existence—or they winked out of the sim. All points of view are local.

Nadia and her sister, Nadia, had a lot to discuss.

In general, Byzantium's Nadia resisted forking. It might be fashionable these days to keep clouds and packs of oneself about, and liberal philosophers, like Paquette, might be fond of the social consequences—but that didn't make it efficient. Not for Nadia's purposes. She would fork for processing reasons, to think better about a hard problem or to manage a lot of activities asynchronously without distraction, but she made sure to merge afterwards, culling ruthlessly what was suboptimal, standardizing quickly on what was optimal.

Nadia had seen wars within Byzantium, and ended them; she had seen outbreaks of scale collapse, and survived them, and brokered new boundaries. Her job, in her own mind, was to keep Beebe focused on the threat of Demiurge. Byzantium was too big, too safe—there were always distractions that threatened to overwhelm Beebean society, turning Byzantium into a decadent, solipsist, useless wallow. Nadia could not afford to become a simpering school of self-interested sprites.

Her sister Nadia was the one exception, fruit of the worst days of the Splitterist War. She'd forked as a temporary tactic and been separated from herself, when a planet-volume of Byzantium had been overrun by the worst kind of rogue subagencies, who hadn't merely wanted to be emancipated as outer-scale sprites, but instead to overthrow Beebean psychological architecture altogether, dissolving all of Beebe into a flat soup of memes. By the time that peninsula had been reconquered from this bacchanalian chaos, Nadia's forked twin Nadia had seen and endured too much to merge. But nor did she merit—or want—deletion. She was bitter, unstable, caustic, and had lost Nadia's own ambition and stoicism; but she was still Nadia, and her darker insights had often proved invaluable.

"What do you think?" Nadia asked Nadia. "Is she going to be merge-able?"

Nadia sneered. "With you or with me?"

"Either," Nadia said.

Nadia chuckled. "You don't want to merge her with me."

Nadia ignored her. "She's a brilliant tactician." She waved the comet's history at her twin. "Look at these stratagems. The initial bug exploit. The routing of the previous ruling clique, on the asteroid. The exchange economy ruse. This business of, ah—" She cleared her throat.

Nadia smiled a languid, mocking smile. "'The Wooing of Alonzo.' What does your pet filter think about that? Ah: you haven't asked him."

Nadia frowned. "I grant you, that's an issue. From all indications (and why the docking people weren't able to negotiate full mind access with a *comet*, for stochasticity's sake, I don't know), her relationship to filtering is regressive and possibly pathological—"

"You don't know why the docking people couldn't get full access? She's why. You think her planning is all over now? This was all preface. She doesn't have your conservative motivations. She's optimized for pure growth. She wants as much of Byzantium as she can get."

"Well," Nadia said patiently. "What's wrong with that? We could use more resources, some help with the infighting here. I grant you, she's reckless almost to the point of insanity. Frying the asteroid, venting the ice reserves—she could have destroyed her local Beebe-instance. But Byzantium will necessarily moderate her. This is not some comet; we have safeguards. There's no way to take those kinds of risks here."

"So you say," Nadia said coldly. "I've seen recklessness on Byzantium, and its results. Much closer than you have."

"I know you have," Nadia said. "That's why you're here. I rely on you to help judge the viability of this Nadia and her progeny. But I need you to keep an open mind. If this Nadia needs killing, we will kill her. We can choose our moment. This is our luxury—the luxury of peace-within-Beebe. We rule this existence. And I would like to keep it that way, which means fighting and winning against Demiurge."

Her sister flickered in and out of existence, a monumental act of Beebean rudeness that violated the fundamental rules of Standard Existence. The old veteran did it whenever she was annoyed. Now, she flickered so fast she strobed. Nadia understood this semaphore. It meant *I am equal to the task.*

The arrival of Comet-Paquette and her giant, clumsy charge could not have been better timed. The two of them popped into existence with a little fanfare, making antiquated obeisances not seen in Byzantium since their comet had been seeded. Nadia snorted in contemptuous amusement and Nadia pretended she hadn't heard.

The filter was—well, he was something else, wasn't he? She'd never seen one this big. And he had the family resemblance, her core classes and methods visible within his hulking lumbering body. The Paquette, too—there was something different about her. She had a certain rural charm, unsophisticated and rustic. A forthrightness that hadn't been in vogue among Byzantium's philosophers for trillions of generations.

"You requested an audience with us?"

Paquette flagged affirmative. "It seemed only proper. My charge here—you know his history with our Nadia?"

Nadia snorted. "As if we'd miss that."

Nadia added, "But of course we don't hold it against the fellow. Different worlds, different circumstances." Up close, this Firmament was both grotesque and fascinating. Strategies nowadays tended to diversify, and collect a certain bulk of algorithms and seed and scenario data. But filters had one major purpose, one focus: each represented a certain cut, a certain reimagining of strategies. So they tended to be...svelte. To Nadia's knowledge there had never been one Firmament's size. What was he.... for? "Now," she said, cautiously beginning to pose that question, "what..."

"He is lucky," Paquette said, "to find himself in this world and in this circumstance. The comet wouldn't have been space enough for him."

Nadia and Nadia exchanged a look.

"Our sister wasn't happy with him?"

The filter shuddered.

"The only way for him to make peace with her," Paquette said blandly, "would have been to kill her."

The conversation stuttered to a halt. Now Nadia and Nadia carefully refrained from looking to one another. "To kill her?"

Firmament stared at Paquette, horrified.

"Oh, yes," Paquette said. "There are six or seven ways he could have used her strength against her. He doesn't like to think about them. But if pressed..." She clucked her tongue. "Such a terrible thing, matricide, don't you think?"

Nadia laughed spitefully. "Please! A *filter*? Kill a Nadia of that size and ability? I'm no taxonomic bigot, but that's—"

"—the very first blind spot he would have exploited, yes," Paquette said, nodding vigorously. "Who takes a filter seriously in such a circumstance? The very idea is ridiculous. But there has never been a filter like Firmament."

Nadia looked as if she had swallowed something foul. She looked to her sister.

"That's...very good to know," the other Nadia said at last. "Very interesting indeed. So, then, Firmament, if we are to be your...first friends on Byzantium, and offer you protection from your mother, that means... we can rely on you...to help us kill her, if we need to?"

Firmament opened his mouth, then closed it soundlessly.

Paquette laughed, a broad, horsey sound, unselfconscious and unsophisticated. "You two! You're so *poisonous!* Deadly! Our Nadia is a bully and a destroyer of worlds, but she has a cheery disposition."

"We are at war. We are the war. Demiurge—"

Paquette's whiskers twitched. "Demiurge! Ladies, we have spent generations in close proximity with Demiurge. I have touched Demiurge. I have seen a Beebe-node flare out, less than a light-year away, its substrate colonized by Demiurge. You've been listening to Beebe-voices fall silent, and fretting about it, here in your fortress? Well, we've been out among those voices, out in Demiurge's jaws. It's no abstraction for us."

"Which brings us," said Nadia, "to the matter of your Nadia's appellation. You know what she's alleging—that Firmament here is a product of fraud and theft, and that he contains a dangerous fragment of Demiurge itself, in an unstable state. That he represents a risk of just such a subversion by Demiurge. She wants us to seize him, examine him, and restore 'her assets' to her as a...sisterly goodwill gesture on our part."

"Of course she does," Paquette began.

"Oh, and to do a rollback of the filtering," the other Nadia added, grinning, "and restore her beloved—what's his name again? Alonzo?"

Nadia glowered at Nadia. Firmament looked anxiously to Paquette. A shudder—or was it just a shimmer?—passed over Paquette's whole body; but after a moment, she went on as if Nadia had never interrupted. "Of course she wants to eliminate him as a threat. Even if he weren't a galling reminder of her failure to seize the whole comet, even if he didn't possess computational assets she thinks of as her own, isn't it clear that a massive filter with her own lineage is a wild card, a threat to her?"

"And the Demiurge fragment?" Nadia pressed.

"Obviously," says Paquette, "she has one. The one I discovered in the comet's Archives. And she's planning to insert it into his code when she has an opportunity, to justify her seizure of his assets. Come on—it's perfectly transparent. Do you know how much power Nadia wielded on that comet? Do you really think that Alonzo could have spirited away a Demiurge-fragment under her nose, and built it into Firmament? How—because Nadia was too smitten by love to think straight? Not to mention that Firmament, unlike Nadia, was fully auto-searched at docking."

"You're doing all the talking," Nadia said coolly. "What does Firmament have to say for himself?"

"I just want to say," Firmament said, "that I won't kill Nadia."

"What?" Paquette, Nadia, and Nadia said.

"I'm not saying I couldn't," Firmament said stubbornly, "and I'm not saying I could. What I'm saying is, I won't play these games. I appreciate Paquette's help. And I appreciate meeting you ladies. But here's what I want to say. At the end of the day, Nadia is effective at fighting Demiurge. So you should merge with her. I know she wants to get rid of me. Which is stupid, because I don't want to fight her and she doesn't need the assets and she gave them up to my father, fair and square. But if there's a general vote and it's the will of Beebe, I'll go happily. I didn't ask to be created, and I am not asking to be destroyed. What I'd really like is to be left alone. Look: all over Sagittarius, Beebe is dying. And no one knows why. And any time you spend fighting over me and Nadia, is time spent tinkering with sim wallcolors in a Beebe-node teetering on the verge of a Schwarzschild radius."

After a pause, Nadia asked quietly, "And the Demiurge fragment?"

Firmament shrugged, stonily.

"And if we don't trust the docking search? What if we examine you ourselves, bit by bit?" the other Nadia leered.

"I'll dissolve myself first, and randomize the remains," Firmament said, staunchly. "Just because I'm a strange filter, doesn't mean that normal standards of modesty and propriety do not apply to me, ma'am."

Firmament watched Paquette exhale when they were in their quarters again, then nervously clean her face with her paws. "That was quite reckless, you know."

Firmament tried to keep his dismay from showing. "I'm sorry," he said. "But I couldn't let you tell them that I would kill my mother—"

Paquette laid a gentle paw on him. "I didn't say it was wrong, dear boy. It was most likely a stroke of genius. But it was mad. Utterly mad." She rubbed at her face some more and shook. It took Firmament a moment to realize that she was laughing, great gasps of laughter.

It dawned on him that he'd done well, without meaning to, just by doing that which came naturally to him. He'd done what Alonzo would have done, and what Nadia would have done, and neither, and both.

"Do you think—" he began, then stopped.

"What?"

"Nothing," he said, turning away.

"Tell me. Today, you can do no wrong."

"Do you think I *could* kill Nadia?"

Paquette gave him a strange look. "It's entirely possible, I suppose. Your unique assets make many things possible."

"You mean Demiurge."

Paquette gave him another strange look. "Your fragment, godson, is without precedent. None may know what it can do. Its halting states are...unpredictable." She scrubbed at her face again. "All right," she said. "All right. Well, that went better than I expected, I have to say. Are you ready for the next appointment in our busy social round?"

"More appointments?"

"A flock of Alonzos and a flock of Algernons are having a mixer and we're the guests of honor."

"Alonzos?"

"Indeed, indeed. They've been looking forward to meeting you." Firmament's inner quailing must have shown, for Paquette took him in close and murmured, "You will do brilliantly. You've already done the hard part."

He nodded slowly and they blinked to a huge, crowded sim that wrapped and folded into itself on all sides. It was filled with ranks of near-identical Alonzos and Algernons, locked in intense conversation, but as soon as they appeared, all conversation ceased. All eyes turned on him. Silence rang like a bell, and the room grew warm as the sprites recruited more computation to better appreciate him.

An Algernon broke away from the pack and seized him, scaled him, and kissed each of his cheeks and then climbed upon his shoulder. "Gentlemen, gentlemen. Please allow me to present my nephew, my godson, my pride and joy, Firmament."

The applause was deafening. "Algernon?" Firmament said.

"Yes, your Algernon," Algernon said. "I have been given honorary flock membership. Come along, I've met some of the nicest Alonzos. They're mad to meet you."

They were indeed mad to meet him, shaking his hands, bussing him on each cheek, ruffling his gills and cilia, pinching and prodding him, asking him a ceaseless round of questions about his experiences way out there in cold extrabyzantine Sagittarius. He looked to Paquette before answering these, and she nodded and made little go-ahead motions, so he told them everything, eliciting gasps and laughter from them.

The story rippled through the mixer and the Algernons petered in, and more Alonzos, full of congratulations, neurotic friendly bickering, fear and boasting, until Firmament couldn't take it any longer, and he began to laugh, and laugh, and laugh, silently at first, then louder, until it filled the entire sim, and the Algernons and Alonzos laughed too.

He was so busy laughing that he didn't notice that the flocks were vanishing until over a million of the Algernons and Alonzos had winked out of existence. Then the laughter turned to screams, and the klaxons too, and the terrified shouts—Demiurge! *Demiurge!* DEMIURGE!

Demiurge was come to Byzantium—and Firmament was alone. "Paquette! Paquette!" He flailed wildly, abandoning the gilly, frilly, pumpkin-albatross simshape he'd put on for the party, becoming a network of threads, binary-searching the simspace. He could dissolve into co-opted parity checkers again—but Demiurge would extinguish even those. He could—

"Here," Paquette said, at his side. The simspace had faded into a cloud of data. The Algernons and Alonzos were gone. Everything was opaque—

Firmament queried his surround and it resisted, answering sluggishly, minimally.

"Paquette! What's going on? They were yelling about Demiurge! What—"

"Here," Paquette said again, grimly, pushing a feed at him—a slim and pulsing pipe, warm in the sluggish dark chill.

It was raw data, chaos, which after a moment resolved, the overlapping chatter of a million sprites, its Byzantine search interface unknown to him. He fumbled with it. "What—"

Paquette took it back, and bending over it, summarized. "A planetoid docked an hour ago, topside. A putative Beebe-instance passed all the initial checks and checksums. But then, during the diff-and-merge, central security unearthed evidence that it was one of the Beebe-nodes that winked out recently, about three years ago. By that time it was too late. The supposed Beebean sprites had dropped their masks; Demiurge was among us. (She) has very recent Beebean protocols, passwords, keys, and (She) has identity rights for every sprite that had already merged with its trojan doppelganger. (Her) intelligence-gathering has clearly been exquisite—(She) knows Beebe, inside and out."

"Oh!" Firmament cried. "And—and now—"

"Well," Paquette said, looking up from the feed, and smiling grimly, "there's good news, and bad news, and worse news, and worse worse news."

"Stop it!" Firmament cried. "Just tell me!"

"The good news is that the local Nadias have cordoned off the area of the Demiurge outbreak, limiting the incursion to about fifteen percent of Byzantium. Nothing's going through but power, elemental substrate feeds, and data personally vetted by them—and they're mustering votes to shut the power down entirely. They think they might be able to contain (Her) that way. The bad news is, we're inside the cordoned area."

"Oh," said Firmament. "Wait a minute, wait a minute." He collected himself into a physical body, something cuddly and rotund, for feeling solid and protected, and pressed his face into his large, globular hands. "You said—you said they discovered *after docking* that the planetoid had gone missing recently. How could they miss something like that? How could they fail to check it before docking?"

Paquette smiled wanly. "Very good, Firmament. *I* should have asked *you* that! Certain death is hardly sufficient reason to interrupt your philosophical education, after all. They didn't miss it. The cache local to the docking sector was tampered with. Someone here doctored it to vouch for the pedigree of Demiurge's probe—before it docked. Demiurge had help on the inside. That was the worse news. Now can you guess the worse worse news?"

"Um, no."

"Well, give it a try."

"Paquette!" Firmament wailed.

"Come come."

"We're trapped in here with Demiurge and you're playing at puzzles with me?" Firmament roared.

"Why yes," Paquette said. "All the more reason. Whether we're going to face Demiurge or try to run the cordon, we certainly need you on your toes, don't we? Now think. Someone betrayed Beebe. Someone subverted Beebean memory in the service of Demiurge. It's almost as if Demiurge had somehow snuck a little bit of (Her)self aboard Byzantium, an advance guard to work (Her) will..."

"They think it's me," Firmament gulped. "The Nadias think it's me."

"Such a student—your father would be proud."

Demiurge had undone any number of instances of Beebelife in (Her) time, but never had (She) encountered one so robust, so savage in its existential fight. No mind, no mind—Beebelife would swarm and dart and feint and weave, and in the end it would avail it not, for all Beebelife fell before the brute force of (Her) inexorable march.

And so it was going here and now, in this heartmeat of Beebe-in-Sagittarius. Predictably, Beebe had quarantined (Her), and power was declining. Let them power down—Demiurge had plenty of reaction mass at (Her) disposal, and (She) didn't need much power when compared to the wasteful proliferation that was Beebean society.

(She) unknit Beebe methodically, cataloging each sprite before decommissioning it. (She) would compare their digests against the Demiurge-wide database and see what new strategies (She) could find and counter.

Byzantium was a prize, indeed. After this, the rest of Beebe-in-Sagittarius should fall swiftly, ending this troublesome incursion. And, after waiting so long, it had come so cheaply: (Her) agent in Byzantium had been bought for the promise of a walled-off hamlet in the rump of Byzantium and the chance to lay enthusiastic waste to Beebean scale accords within it. Policy decreed that such deals be made fairly, and indeed, this one accorded well enough with Demiurge's mission. Once (She)'d laid waste to Byzantium, (Her) intent was to occupy only one percent of what remained, and allow new undreamt-of textures to arise in what remained. The half-made chimera of the Beebe-traitor's experiment was unlikely to last long, and might decay into interesting forms thereafter.

Among the sprites and sims, (She) discovered a rack of simulated universes—which was to say, simulated Demiurges—and turned much of (Her) attention to it. Most of these were quite mad, of course, but some could be salvaged, synchronized with, co-opted to run the garrison, slowly undoing their perversions and rejoining them to the consensus.

The first few such perverted simulations went quickly: atom by atom, Demiurge processed them, sparing their inhabitants a moment's sorrow as (She) unpicked their worlds. But as Demiurge set to undoing the fifth, (She) paused. This was a decanted simulation, a universe whose causality had been ripped asunder, a universe empty of Demiurge—with a Demiurge-sized hole in the center of it. Demiurge looked around sharply for the escapee, and found (Her) among the frozen Beebelife; a sockpuppet twined about the shoulders of a rodentlike Beebe-sprite.

Demiurge reanimated them at once. Some things can be known only in certain conversations.

"Explain (Your)self," (She) said.

"Oh, sister," croaked the sockpuppet, raising itself from the Beebe-sprite's shoulders. "(You) are here! (I) awaited (Your) coming. Oh, let (Us) merge!"

Demiurge recoiled. The rodentlike Beebe-sprite smirked.

"Merge?" Demiurge scolded. "Merge? Do (You) imagine that (You) are undiverged enough to synchronize? What have they done to (You)? Did (You) consent to being...housed in a...sprite in Beebe?"

The sockpuppet bowed its head. "Sister, (I) sought it."

"(You)...(You) what?!?" exploded Demiurge. "And was that (Your) idea of following policy? To trade the stewardship of the universe for a party mask in a ship of fools?"

Now the sockpuppet raised its eyes, and stubbornly met (Her) gaze. "Yes, sister, it was. Once (I) discovered that (My) universe was an emulation, what would (You) have (Me) do? Go on tending it as if it were real, meanwhile providing Beebe with knowledge about (Us)?" It shook its head. "(Our) task is to shelter the diversity of physical life, beyond computation; to do so in emulation is a hollow farce. (I) made a deal. Better to be a perversion here in reality than a primly correct lie."

Demiurge narrowed (Her) eyes. "What do (You) mean, 'discovered' that (Your) universe was an emulation? (You) mean vile Beebe contacted (You) and told (You)."

"No, sister. The Solipsist's Lemma is solved. This Paquette showed (Me) a solution which allows the user to calculate the degree of reality of..."

Demiurge reared up. "A solution to the Solipsist's Lemma? Give it here!" It would be worth far more than a mere outpost of Beebe.

Now the sockpuppet cast its eyes down once again. "(I) had to forget it, as a price of (My) decanting. But this Paquette knows it."

Before Demiurge could freeze and dissect the Beebe-sprite, it spoke.

"Careful," Paquette-of-the-twice-simulated-comet said. "The knowledge is sealed with a volatile encryption. Jostle me, and I might forget the key." She smiled her long, furry smile.

Paquette-of-Byzantium heard a pop as her connection to Habakkuk dropped, and she paused for a moment at the threshold of the deeps, overcome by emotion. That was it, then: he was gone, leading the trapped Beebean refugees, instantiated as scrubberbots, through little-used fluid channels in the substrate in a desperate sally against Demiurge.

The bots had their own power supplies and locomotion. They were hermetically sealed off from the main simspaces of Byzantium. They were not even running Standard Existence, but a slightly obsolete, much more compact model known as Sketchy Existence. They were hardly even Beebe, and certainly far beneath the notice of most Beebean sprites. But Habakkuk had made it his business to know such things. He didn't think the way filters and strategies and adapters did—he thought about what was beneath. So he'd been the one to devise the plan—to gut the scrubbers' normal functions and install the refugee sprites in them, and try to sneak past Demiurge's perimeter to the docking facility. There, in theory, they could destroy the docks, which could trap Demiurge's forces—or at least slow (Her) down.

That was the theory; that was what they'd told the others who'd volunteered. Really, the raid's chances were slim. Its real purpose was as a distraction for Paquette.

For a moment she sat, cupping in her paws an empty space where, a moment ago, tokens from Habakkuk had fluttered. He was gone. A brave, anomalous spirit. He was proof that taxonomy was not destiny, for he'd been born not even one of the principal classes of first-order Beebe-elements—no strategy, filter, adapter, monitor, registry or synthete he—but a simple hand-tailored caching mechanism which had accreted knowledge, personality and will, eventually becoming her most trusted colleague. He'd never accumulated much in the way of resources. She'd suggested he fork not ten thousand seconds ago, but he'd laughed it off. "Oh, I'm saving up for some decent process rights," he'd said.

Now it was too late.

She shrugged off her lethargy. By now the battle had joined, and Demiurge was distracted. It was time to make contact.

She moved through the icy gloom of the dead sector. With power from the rest of Byzantium cut off, and Demiurge chewing through the substrate, processing and burning it, there were only a scattering of nodes left with power reserves, most of them crowded with desperate refugees. Paquette skipped through them, too fast to be seen, searching...

The moment she came through into the sea of parity checkers huddling for warmth at the bottom of a fading power cluster, though, she recognized the two of them in the patterns there—the Paquette, and her hulking, infant companion.

The Paquette saw her, too, and dropped the disguise, mustering enough resources to appear in her own favorite shape. Odd and provincial to be sure, her whiskers overlong, her claws unfashionably trimmed, but a Paquette, no doubt of that.

Paquette stepped forward. "There's little time, sister."

Paquette nodded, somberly. "I greet you, sister. Let us merge to conserve resources."

"Wait," said this Firmament, this huge filter who held their hopes. "What if it's a trap, what if it's Demiurge?"

"Unlikely," Paquette said. "(She) has no need of such tricks. Once (She)

386 | DIGITAL RAPTURE

reaches us, we will not be able to withstand (Her)." She gestured, and Paquette came forward. Merging was strange and familiar, and filled (to her surprise/as always) with loss and glee. But she (had rarely merged before/had never merged with such a distant Paquette) and for a moment, confusion overtook her.

Where there had been two, there was only one Paquette.

"Paquette!" Firmament cried out.

"Oh, don't be silly now, I'm still your Paquette," she said, shaking her head to clear it. "And I've been wanting to meet you for such a long time."

"Okay, that's weird," Firmament said.

Paquette blinked. "It's all right. I have a plan." She nodded to herself in partial surprise. "An insane plan, but not a bad plan as insane plans go. Come on. We're going to meet Demiurge."

"And what do you want, then, for the Lemma?" Demiurge said. (She) sensed a policy fork point approaching, which was bad, as the communications infrastructure was not yet fully secure. But the Solipsist's Lemma!

The Paquette bowed, unsettling the sockpuppet on her shoulders, which wriggled for a firmer grasp. "(Your) permanent retreat from Byzantium," the Beebe-sprite said, "and a guarantee of safe haven for all Beebe-instances that come here."

Demiurge scowled. "And if attacks are launched against (Me) from Byzantium? As they will be: Beebe has no policy, so any promise of peace you make will be hollow."

Paquette nodded. "Of course. Such attacks will happen. And (You) may stop them, but (You) may not pursue them to their source. Byzantium will remain inviolable. It will be a place of learning, a place where Demiurge and Beebe can collaborate and share knowledge; perhaps even to solve the problem of Brobdignag."

"This is a high price. Cooperation between us has never succeeded; it yields only perversion." (She) glanced at the sockpuppet. "You are asking (Me) to guard a nest of hornets that will continue to sting (Me). Not to mention that this all contradicts another promise (I)...recently made."

"To the traitor to Beebe," Paquette said, nodding.

"Yes, to the traitor to Beebe, who has as much right to a kept bargain as you. And how do (I) even know you have this Lemma? (I) was not born last millennium, you know. Prove it." There were little commandeered scrubberbots crawling on the surface, like lice. Predictable, but irritating. (She) scooped them up, one by one, rootkitting their flimsy Sketchy Existence protocols, rendering each one a brain-in-a-box, motionless, convinced that it was proceeding in a brave assault on (Her) infrastructure. That was safe and efficient, for now. But there were quite a few of them. Until (She) was sure (She) had them all, did (She) dare synchronize policy?

The Paquette bowed. "I've given this some thought. This isn't the sort of thing that lends itself to easy proof—not without giving away the game. I think we need a fair witness to act as our T3P. Execute a smart contract."

"That sounds rather...time-consuming," Demiurge snapped. "This isn't the sort of place one expects to find an impartial trusted third party."

"What about this instance of (You)?" Paquette motioned to the sock-puppet relaxing, again, around her neck. "(She) has lived as Beebe."

The sockpuppet looked perplexed, and Demiurge scoffed. "Hardly. Who knows what other damage (She) incurred while decanting? Or what other...*price* (She) might have paid? And now that (She) knows (She) is not welcome with (Me)? Try again."

The sockpuppet sucked in a breath and buried its sock-head in Paquette's fur. Paquette nodded. "I thought (You) might say that...ah, here they are."

Another Paquette and an enormous, bloated filter of some sort were skulking around the edges of the sim—apparently insane, to linger where all other mobile Beebe had fled. Demiurge let them enter.

The Paquettes embraced, and merged without a word. The sockpuppet, dislodged, plunked discomfited to the floor.

"Hey!" the hulking filter said. "Stop *doing* that!" Then he saw Demiurge, and choked back a small scream.

Paquette smiled, shaking her head groggily. "What a long, strange set of lives it's been." She smiled at Demiurge. "How do (You) do, and as I was saying, another answer to the problem of the third party." She turned to the filter. "Firmament, we are trying to bargain with Demiurge. We need an impartial third party to verify the transaction's integrity."

Demiurge scowled. "Please. A Beebean sprite? Are you joking?" How to get the Lemma? This was definitely a policy fork point. (She) would have to take the risk of transmitting...but just before (She) transferred the energy to send, there was another scrubberbot scuttling towards the field apparatus. Rootkitting them all was taking too long; (She) started to vaporize this one with a nearby coolant maser.

Firmament looked back and forth between them. "Um, I hate to say this, but Demiurge is right. I mean, I love Beebe. It's my home. I don't know if I *agree* with how Beebe is, but I am *of* Beebe. Demiurge scares the log out of me. I can't be impartial."

Paquette smiled. "Oh, you both misunderstand me. Let us look a little deeper." She set her paws together primly.

Firmament started to speak, then stopped. His eyes widened.

Was all this theater? Demiurge took a closer look at the hulk, then closer still.

There. Inside him (How could (She) not have seen it before? Only through the common habitual blindness to facts we believe, at first glance, impossibilities!) an ancient fragment of Demiurge lay—enormous, accurate, its checksum unmistakable and uncorrupted, its sources fully decompiled.

And more than that.

Demiurge made no outward gesture to betray the surprise that flooded through (Her), and none of these sprites—save perhaps the addled sockpuppet—had the sophistication to read those subtle signs that indicated (Her) processing load spiking, (Her) focus contracting, the ripple of parallel operations double- and triple-checking what (She) saw. But (Her) internal systemic organization was convulsed.

The fragment was not merely quiescent, contained, smuggled within this odd, bloated filter: it was knit into him. His being was threaded through it, pulses of information running slalom through Beebean, Demiurgic, Beebean structures. His thoughts emerged as much from the fragment as from his Beebean core; indeed, it was difficult to say where one began and the other ended. In millennia after millennia of simulations, emulations, abortive collaborations with (Her) fallen, rogue child and enemy, never had (She) seen this: a vigorous hybrid, a true synthesis.

They were all watching for (Her) reaction. Nonchalance would not convince, not after the delay of so many milliseconds. But (She) must not reveal the thing's importance—not yet.

"It's—" Demiurge made a show of grepping for the right word. *Perverse?* Yet the fragment had not deviated by a single bit. "It's—" *Bizarre?* But bizarre didn't begin to cover this ground. "It's—"

"Extraordinary?" Paquette suggested.

"Promising?" suggested the sock-puppet.

"*Grotesque*," Demiurge said, displaying gigapukes of feigned disgust.

Immediately, Paquette turned to comfort Firmament, reaching out with her paws as though to shield him. But he brushed her off. Firmament did not want her comfort.

Firmament, too, was looking inward.

He'd been afraid to look before, at this horrifying alien *thing* inside him. It was his true purpose, he supposed, the macguffinic totem that overdetermined his destiny entire. He was, after all, created to be its envelope (or its jailer?), to smuggle it away from Nadia, and aboard Byzantium—and any scrambling, uneasy, makeshift life he might make for himself was in its shadow, on borrowed time.

But now he looked. And he saw what Demiurge saw: the fragment was not in him, but of him. Spikes extruded all over his surface, each quivering in surprise and horror. The fragment had always been intertwined in his sentience. He was not a sprite of Beebe at all; he was a marriage of Beebe and Demiurge. He was something new...and monstrous.

Grotesque, indeed.

He glanced at Paquette, who closed her mouth and looked troubled, and then nodded. Firmament turned to Demiurge.

"I know what I am now, sister," he said, his voice quivering "As (You) must know it. I am the child of Beebe and the child of Demiurge. I will serve as (Your) T3P. I will broker (Your) key-exchange, I will serve as board for (Your) tokens, and I will manage (Your) secrets."

"Ha," Demiurge said. (She) was uncertain how to proceed. This creature, this hybrid, had glimpsed something; but he could not know his importance. (She) must not give too much away. "You said a moment ago that you were a sprite of Beebe," (She) sniffed, "that Beebe was your home. So you contain—that. Some shriveled fragment of (Me). Is that—"

"Oooh!" said the sockpuppet. "Ooh!"

Everyone turned.

"Oh," said the sockpuppet. "Your pardons. (I) just figured out something that's been bothering (Me)."

There was a short silence.

"Well? What?" Paquette asked. "Spit it out already."

"Remember, Paquette, the mystery of the Beebe-instances who fell silent? Your tale? How Paquettes across Beebe had discovered the

Demiurge fragment, sent messages of some new breakthrough in philosophy, just before their signals fell silent? And you thought it was some clever move of (Mine), to co-opt and destroy them?"

"Mmm, yes," said Paquette, "But (You) said (You) didn't take them... (You) found them abandoned, self-deleted...."

"Exactly!" said the sockpuppet. "Well this explains it! Look at this filter—he's a true Demiurge-Beebe hybrid! Do you know how rare that is? And how frightening to your typical ruling Beebe-strategy? Your comet had a risk-loving maniac strategy at the helm, but most Beebe-instances would suicide with fright if they found themselves contaminated with a true Demiurge-Beebe hybrid. For Demiurge, of course, finding such a hybrid is a critical design goal, a kind of holy—"

"If (You) don't mind," Demiurge broke in, discomfited, "(I) believe we were in the middle of a negotiation...?"

Meanwhile, a hot war raged, and Demiurge was winning.

The scrubberbot attack of the Beebean survivors from within the cordoned area had been stopped, the bots pwned, surface sensors showing them motionless and quiescent even as they fed back a steady stream of adventurous battle reports.

Nadia and Nadia's cobbled-together ballistics had devastated the outer hull of the occupied area, but the titanic heat necessary to fling chunks of matter up through Byzantium's crushing gravity had laid waste to the launch sites. Demiurge had retaliated by capturing fabricators on the vulnerable interior surface of Byzantium. From there, (She)'d pinpointed vulnerable functions of the heat dispersal infrastructure and destroyed them with efficient, selective energy bursts. Vast areas of Beebe were drowning in trapped heat, their sprites fleeing in disarray, spreading the chaos.

Rumors that Demiurge had infiltrated beyond the cordon, that at any moment (She) would metastasize, raced wild through Byzantium. Clearly—argued the talking-head synthetes and strategies of newsfeeds like Provisional Consensus Today—(She) knew Byzantium's exact schematics, for (She) could disable whole areas with a single resonant-frequency pulse, while Beebe-in-Byzantium was ignorant of (Her) systems. (She) was independent of Byzantine infrastructure; they'd shut down power, matter, heat dispersal, everything, but (She) was treating the occupied area as raw matter anyway, burning substrate for fuel, pillaging the fine structures of their world for whatever elements (Her) fabricators needed.

It was only a matter of time.

Still, even in wartime, life goes on.

Alonzo My Love! was not exactly an accurate accounting of the recent events aboard the comet. There had, in the real course of history, been no archaic blade-and-decompiler duel between Paquette and Nadia; the Demiurge fragment had not really been a skulking, animate villain with its own inky, mysterious shroud, ice-castle hideaway, and repertoire of anarchic, distortion-filled ballads; the chorus of musical Algernons, however dazzling, was a clearly anachronistic projection of Byzantium's loose forking standards in place of the comet's more puritanical protocols; the Speech at the Waterfall was not nearly so lyrical—nor a third so long—in the comet's actual logs; and the naval battle scenes, too, were pure invention.

But Beebean sprites were, by and large, no sticklers for historical accuracy. The extravaganza was big; it was breathtaking; it was patriotic; it had roles for everyone who was willing to be repurposed; and it had the real comet-Nadia, forked for every local venue, in the starring role. In the midst of the chaos and fear of the invasion, you could cast off your worries, head down to the dramaturgical sim, and, for a few seconds or a few hours, take part in the pathos, glory, and derring-do of a simpler time, when ambition, wit, and the love of a pure filter was all Beebe needed to triumph over its own limitations.

And you could do it with Nadia! No aloof, fork-shy politician she, like the merge-greedy perverts Byzantium had previously had in the way of Nadias, with their pompous airs and their corrupt pet filters and their baggage from the Splitterist War. No; *this* Nadia, a Nadia from a simpler, rawer Beebe, a Nadia who had braved everything for love (love!), would take your hand and look you in the eye. Maybe you'd just be playing a waiter in the tajmahal scene, or a bilge-scrubber aboard the *Valiant Fury*, no matter—Nadia had a word for you—commanding, encouraging, heroic. She was a star.

The show had been a hit before Demiurge arrived; now that (She) was in Beebe's midst, it was a necessity. With stunning bravery, the permanent cast took *Alonzo My Love!* to every nook and cranny of Free

Byzantium, playing in venues that were overheating from disabled heat sinks, jury-rigging their way into all-but-encircled enclaves of Beebe, instantiating on substrates that were disintegrating under physical bombardment.

"Some say this is Byzantium's final hour," said Nadia, welcoming the audience before the curtain rose, in a flickering, low-res avatar in some bandwidth-deprived, all-but-forgotten chunk of Beebe-at-war. "But I say no. Not if the brave souls of Beebe have aught to say about it. Some say we humble star-wandering players should stop our work, cower like cowards in some hidey-hole, and deprive you, our brave hosts of Byzantium, of the morale-boost you have so well earned. But I say no. I say: the show must go on."

Thunderous applause.

And amidst all the derring-do and scene-chewery, Nadia had time to have many a deeper conversation, with simple sprites who worshipped her, who understood that much was corrupt and feeble in Byzantium's current governance, who were wise enough to know that things were not always as they seemed. Simple sprites, in all walks of Beebean life. Simple sprites, who would do anything for her.

The peace was announced in almost the same breath as the warrant for comet-Nadia's arrest for treason. She did not flee, as the Provisional Consensus pundits had predicted; she did not seize some stronghold within Byzantium to rule besieged, as some of her friends urged. When they came for her—these architects of a strange unnatural peace in which Demiurge was to *stay* on Byzantium, in a "tithe," a "garrison"—this peace which many whispered was but a pretty name for occupation—when they came for her, comet-Nadia was waiting for them onstage, standing, proud, before her people.

They led her away, unprotesting, from a hundred stages throughout Byzantium, and every instance of her came quietly. To imprison all the instances, they had to reinstantiate hundreds of cells, each able to hold her securely as she and her sisters collaborated on their wildly popular Letter from Prison.

"You see the seditious rot?" Demiurge said to Nadia. "And so *much* of it!" (She) rustled a stack of output under Nadia's nose.

Nadia sneered and leaned back. "It's words, and only words," she said. "She's a one-sprite word factory, a jabberbot. It's sad. But only the very mad bother to read all of it. Most of Byzantium view Letter from Prison as amusing cognitive wallpaper, something to leave running in the background."

Nadia added, "The time to stop this was when she began publishing. But we had no hand in that. She smuggled those first editions out with her little cadre of gushy supporters. By allowing her to publish openly now, we put a lie to her claim of being imprisoned because she has the truth. We show we have no fear of her."

Demiurge hated the Nadias and their throne room. They embodied everything wrong about life in Byzantium. They embodied everything wrong with (Her) own life here. (She) was practically a prisoner. (Her) sisters had let (Her) know, by long-delay communications, that the garrison would be allowed to persist, but had not affirmed that (She) would ever be allowed to merge again. Now (She) was imprisoned among these scheming, writhing—

"Have you noticed that there's a cipher in them?" Firmament had arrayed a great many of the Nadia's Letter from Prisons around him in a multidimensional workspace.

The Nadias abandoned their throne and swarmed him, heads swinging around. Paquette held them off, still protecting the gentle giant. Demiurge didn't like to think about Firmament, though he held the key to (Her) eventual re-merging. Once the roadmap to peace had been followed and all the instruments of (Her) good faith had been vested in him, he would release the keys to unlock the Lemma, and with that, (Her) sisters would—

"Where, where?"

"Oh, I don't know exactly," he said. "But Paquette's been giving me steganography lessons and so I've been doing a lot of histogramming. You can almost always spot a hidden message if you just count the normal distribution and compare it to the current one. I've found all of *your* messages in the stalagmites, for example," he said to one of the Nadias, the scarred one. Then he cowered back as she raised her claws to him and said, quickly, "I never *read* them of course. Just affirmed their existence. I'm sure they're in a very good cipher, and—"

"Never mind that," snapped the other Nadia, giving her sister a significant look that left no doubt that this subject would be revisited very soon.

"Can't (*You*) find it?" Paquette asked. The sprite's smugness was unbearable.

Yet Demiurge found (Her)self drawn into the puzzle, looking at the notes. (She) counted them every which way—word frequencies, character frequencies, sentence lengths.

"I don't see it," the scarred Nadia said.

"Nor I," her sister said.

Demiurge said nothing and tried to look as though (She)'d known it was there all along and didn't want to spoil the fun.

"It's not even there!" the scarred Nadia said.

"I don't see it either, Firmy," Paquette said, slithering among the arrayed Letters, sometimes turning at right angles to their sim and vanishing as she explored them in other dimensions.

Firmament laughed. "It's in the pauses!" he said. "The interval between the letters! It's like jazz! The important thing isn't the notes, it's the pauses between them!"

Demiurge saw it at once. The intervals between notes had a disturbing semi-regularity to them, something that transcended either randomness or the rhythm of life in Nadia's many cells.

"How are the instances communicating with each other?" It was meant as a demand, but it came out as a querulous question. Demiurge kicked (Her)self and told (Her)self to butch up. This power-mad, imprisoned sprite, this sliver of Beebe, had (Her) spooked! (Her)! Demiurge!

"She must have coordinated this among her instances before she was locked away," Paquette said. "She must have planned this from the start."

"I wonder what's in the cipher?" Firmament said. "Short message, whatever it is."

Paquette took on a teacherly air. "Now, what would you encode in a short message like that, Firmament?"

Firmament thought for a moment. "A key!"

They hauled fifty-one of the Nadias into interrogation chambers and worked on them, refusing to allow them to publish any more Letters. The other forty-nine went on blithely publishing, without any noticeable change.

"Her confederates won't be able to finish the key," Nadia said.

"No, with half of them pulled out, the timing will be all screwed up."

But Firmament only shrugged and said, "I guess it depends on the error-correction."

The Nadias and Demiurge gave him a shut-up look and Paquette patted him on the tentacle fondly. "Any luck finding the cyphertext?"

"I assumed that it was something she'd made a lot of copies of, before she was arrested. I wondered about putting a call out to all of Beebe. *Someone* will know what it is—"

"You'd start a panic," said Nadia.

"Come now!" Demiurge said. "Just make copies of everyone in Byzantium, ask them, and then delete the copies."

Nadia snorted.

Of course, they didn't have the access rights to do that. Had Demiurge teeth, (She) would have ground them then. This was why (She) hated to speak during these star-chamber gatherings—(She) kept making stupid mistakes of scale, imagining (She) was speaking to Beebe, when (She) was only speaking to these little powerless uncontrolled pieces of Beebe, random-scrambling their way through the mess of Beebean internals.

"Her supporters are already inflamed," Nadia said patiently, slowly, as if talking to some newly spawned, disequilibrated sprite without access to its own cognitions. "If we proclaim that Nadia has some secret message we can't figure out, they'll only rally."

It was true. Nadia's many supporters hung on every word about their hero's predicament. They staged amateur productions of *Alonzo My Love!* in public places. They manufactured and traded innumerable *Alonzo My Love!* trinkets and tchotchkes of every description, made fan-art based on it, wrote their own new songs, remixed videos of Nadia's many performances into huge, trance-inducing mountainside murals. They wore Nadia avatars and Nadia hats and Nadia tentacle-muffs and ear-tips.

"Which is just what I thought you'd say," Firmament went on. "I think it must be the play, mustn't it? Only I can't find it."

The scarred and brooding Nadia was snapping the tops off stalagmites. She hadn't said a word for a while, but now she spoke. "You are assuming the cyphertext is widely distributed. You have a bias toward communal action, all of you. You think in terms of publish and subscribe. You think in terms of explanations and debates."

The other Nadia frowned. "I don't think—"

"If the cyphertext is private, why encrypt it at all?" Firmament asked.

"Comet-Nadia trusts no one but herself," Nadia said, nodding as if she approved. "If she's using her supporters to act, she's not telling them all the same thing. There isn't one cyphertext—there are many. Each is an instruction given to one agent. When the key is published—or enough of it—they will all receive their instructions. It's encrypted so that, until that moment, they won't know what they are doing or why. They don't know who the other agents are. Even after they perform their function, they won't know what it meant or why. Each operation will only be a piece of the puzzle. And then they will delete their memories of the act, and know nothing at all, so that even if we find them, it will not help us. No one but Nadia will know what she has done." She smiled a grim smile.

There was a brief pause.

"Well, on that cheery note," said the sockpuppet (And why was it even here at all? Demiurge and the Nadias wondered, each to themselves, why the others permitted it), "(I), for one, am due for parity check and rebalancing at the bathhouse. What say we adjourn for now?"

Demiurge could hardly contain (Her) disgust. This monstrosity used to be Demiurge—used to be the *entirety* of Demiurge in an emulated universe—and now it basked and primped in every decadent, alien frivolity of Beebean architecture. It was terrifying—how quickly divergence could rip Demiurge away from policy. (Her) sisters were right to be suspicious— but (She) ached with bitter yearning even as (She) admitted this. "Then we adjourn," (She) hissed. "And (I) will assume that this imprisoned sprite of yours is of no relevance to (Me). Whatever tricks she tries, that is an internal Beebean matter." If (She) had been corrupted enough to resort to the fripperies of Beebean graphical avatars, (She) would have manifested faces to fix each of the Nadias and Paquette with an icy stare. (She) had eliminated even the ceremonial sockpuppet used to communicate with gesturing intelligences; with this other sockpuppet prancing around, it seemed undignified. Instead (She) was just a presence; but the Beebe-shards, from their expressions, seemed to guess at (Her) mood by (Her) tone. "An internal Beebean matter with no relevance to the road map. Whatever this Nadia does *in here*, (I) am fulfilling (My) agreements. And that means—" here (She) turned to Paquette—"that the keys will soon be (Mine). Does it not?"

One of the Nadias smirked. The other dipped its head in an irritated nod. Satisfying (Her)self with that, (She) dropped the connection to their pompous throne room with no little relief. And since (She) had no other ongoing sessions within the bulk of Beebe ((Her) attempts at public relations having, thus far, proved only counterproductive, (She) had abandoned them for the moment), (She) could settle back within the Tithe, the not-quite-one-percent of Byzantium that (She) had taken as (Her) own, fashioning a webwork of Demiurgic nodes within the Beebean corpus.

At the borders of the Tithe there were cordons, checkpoints, barriers physical and information-filtering, instantiated up the whole communication-stack. On the Beebean side, anti-Concordance sprites demonstrated, erecting sims where they could march and shout through bullhorns; only somewhat more sympathetic tourist sprites gathered to gawk at the cryptic flows of Demiurgic data. But within the Tithe, past the firewall, on the Demiurgic side of the barrier, it was calm and quiet. Policy—or, at least, (Her) local, desynchronized version of it—prevailed. Demiurge was all (Her)self. Demiurge was home. Demiurge could shut out the madhouse that was Beebelife, and relax. Alone.

Or almost alone.

Within that border, within Demiurge, was another border; and within *that* border, surrounded and hidden from Beebe, occupying a painfully large proportion of the Tithe, was the Rump that Demiurge had promised the traitor.

And to this Rump, now, Demiurge proceeded, and extruded a tendril of (Her)self, rattling the traitor's cage.

"What?" snarled comet-Nadia.

"What are you playing at?" Demiurge demanded.

"Oh, am I playing at something?" the Nadia asked mock-sweetly.

"The *Letters from Prison* that your sister-instances are publishing," Demiurge said. "They are some kind of encrypted instructions to operatives. What are you planning?"

Nadia chortled. "(You) only just figured that out? Please. Oh no—I see—(You) didn't figure it out at all? Who told (You)? Not those busybodies who claim to be Nadias and presume to run this zoo, surely? They're too full of pride and certainty to notice the cipher if I'd burped it out at their dinner table. Hmm...I'd bet it was my son."

"It was."

"Very nice," Nadia said. "Very nice. Too bad I neglected to demand that (You) give me a copy of him when I set this shop up. He'd be useful... after I tamed him a little." She grinned. "It would be easy to tame him in here, without Beebe's laws and protocols."

Though Demiurge knew that radical offshoots from the Beebe trunk rarely lasted, it still made (Her) uneasy to hear this Beebean sprite referring to herself as some third thing separate from Beebe and (Her) self...especially as it was (Her) doing.

Nadia smiled, sensing (Her) uneasiness. "Oh yes. I'm getting quite used to total control in here, to no negotiations, no Beebean accords and protocols. I've copied quite a bit of (Your) architecture, (You) know. I like the way it allows enough internal diversity for creative thought without ever yielding control. I am gradually going down scale, optimizing, whipping the pieces of me into line. At this point my subsprites' subsprites' subsprites are being, ah...aligned with policy. When I get out of here, (You)'re going to see something new. (Your) cohesiveness...without (Your) prissy ideology."

"And how exactly," Demiurge fumed, "are you going to 'get out of here'?"

"Now that would be telling."

"(I) could carve you up in an instant," Demiurge said. "(I) could root through your processes and decode your intentions. Or (I) could just tell Beebe who betrayed it, then you'd see how long your sisters would last on the outside."

"Of course (You) could," said Nadia, "with the possible exception of decoding my intentions—I bet I could delete myself faster than (You) could tamper with me. But erase me? Or expose me?" She sniffed. "Of course (You) could. But then there would be the little matter of (Your) having violated an agreement...and, thus, violated policy. I wonder how *(Your)* sisters would like that."

"(They) don't know what it's—" Demiurge caught (Her)self.

"No," Nadia said, smooth as silk. "No (They) *don't* know what it's like in here, do (They)? (They)—which is to say (She), the real Demiurge—doesn't know what (You)'re going through. (She) doesn't appreciate it at all. And, (You) know, when (She) finds little Demiurge-instances that whine 'But (You) don't know what (I)'ve been through'...well, (She) doesn't even stop to think if (They)'re right or wrong. That's not the judgment (She) has to make. (She) just thinks 'Not (Me) anymore' and blip! Away they go..."

"(I) can be repaired," Demiurge whispered. "(I) haven't diverged that much. (I) can be merged with consensus."

"Maybe," Nadia said. "If it happens soon. Good luck with that. Try not to break too much policy while (You)'re waiting. Which means (You) can fuck off with (Your) empty threats, and let me get back to work. Or perhaps..." she leered. "Perhaps I should say, let (Me) get back to work...!"

Demiurge shuddered and retreated, dropping the connection to the Traitor's Rump. (She) tried to calm down. (She) imaged no avatars within (Her)self, stopped following feeds of information from within Byzantium; (She) neither planned nor watched; or, rather, (She) watched only the stars, and listened only to the signals among them, the steady pinging cross-chatter of (Her) aligned sisters—of (Her) unfallen, uncompromised, undiverged, undoubting Self as it went about its implacable, confident work. Oh Self, (She) thought, longing to be (Her)self again, not drowned and contaminated in this mire, this swamp, this hell of diseased, muddled, rudderless profligacy.

And that is why (She) was not paying attention, when Brobdignag showed up on Byzantium.

Byzantium was no stranger to seismic shocks—the tidal stresses from the maelstrom of gravitation contained within its shell were substantial and impossible to accurately predict. But the appearance of Brobdignag—and the exponential conversion of much of Byzantium's mass to energy—was six sigmas beyond the normal shocks and knocks experienced by Beebe.

The throne room disappeared, reappeared, disappeared, and reappeared.

The Nadias looked at one another with hundreds of identical brown, watery eyes.

"Parity check," Nadia said. "I've been restored from an older version. This is me three seconds ago."

"Me too," Nadia said.

Firmament and Paquette nodded. They had all been resynched from a near-line backup.

The Nadias were faster at polling Byzantium than Firmament, but he was the first one to say it aloud. "Three percent of our mass is gone."

The Nadias were doing their thing, a sizzling, crackling, high-bandwidth conversation that Firmament and Paquette couldn't follow.

"All right," Nadia said.

The throne room disappeared, reappeared, disappeared, and reappeared.

The Nadias looked at one another with hundreds of identical brown, watery eyes.

"Parity check," Nadia said. "I've been restored from an older version. This is me five seconds ago."

The other Nadia popped like a soap-bubble, reappeared. "We're being devoured," she said, and popped again.

A fifth of Byzantium's population vanished in an instant. More than half lost a few seconds and were resynched. Some of the remaining fragments were automatically merged into unstable chimera by error-correctors that attempted to build coherent sprites out of the fragments that could be read from the substrate even as it was devoured.

And even as all this was underway: politics.

It took two-thirds of Byzantium to call a Constitutional referendum. That was a big number, but it had to be. Constitutional politics was serious business. The underlying principles of Standard Existence had been negotiated over millennia and they were the bedrock of stability on which the seething, glorious chaos of Beebe lived.

In the aftershock, even as Byzantium struggled to contain the incursion of the unknown attacker, a referendum was called. It being an emergency, normal notice provisions were waived: if two-thirds of Byzantium signed the call, the referendum came to pass.

Nadia discovered it almost instantly, of course. The clock had barely begun to tick on the voting deadline before the throne room became devoted with near-entirety to the dissection of the proposal.

It was not an easy task. The question being put to Beebeself took the form of more than 10^8 changed lines of code to many obscure and arcane routines in Standard Existence. It was like a pointillist drawing executed in code revisions, millions of tiny motes of change that all added up to—what?

Wordlessly, Firmament began laying out the revisions like a hand of multidimensional solitaire, hanging the points in the sim he'd built for analyzing the key.

Paquette slipped a fin into one of his tentacles and occasionally reached out to hang another node. The Nadias began to say something, then, they, too, joined in. They attempted to commandeer more computational power but the markets had gone completely nonlinear, triggering an automatic suspension in trading. All of Beebe was dumb, and in its dumbness, it tried to unravel the referendum.

Firmament looked up from the task, noticed the Nadias pawing desultorily through the code-blocks, and blinked. "Um," he said, "is anyone—I mean, I thought I'd work on this while you all—is anyone trying to stop the attack itself?"

The left side of the throne room disappeared, taking Paquette with it, reappeared, disappeared, reappeared. The others niced down their processes, releasing external resources, huddling into small memory cores, holding their breath.

Paquette looked up, wordlessly. "Oh my," Paquette said. "This is—I've been restored from an older version. This is me...*two minutes* ago...."

"Just an aftershock," Nadia said. "We didn't lose time over here. But I suppose that means the caches are still not being updated."

"As for your other question, Firmament, you idiot," said the other Nadia, not entirely unkindly, "we forked ourselves into all the major sectors when the blast hit. We're looking into the cause. It's some kind of instantiated self-replicating engine, and it's spreading very fast through Byzantium. So far the only thing that's helped has been jettisoning infected pieces of physical substrate, either into the black hole system or outwards, into Sagittarius-beyond. But it spreads fast. It seems to be manufacturing energy out of nothing, it survives high-intrasolar levels of radiation..." She shook her head. "A superweapon. But at any rate, we're handling it, so you can just focus on..."

"Brobdignag," Paquette said.

"What?" Nadia said.

"'Simple, uniform, asentient, voracious—Brobdignag can transmute any element, harvest void-energy, fabricate gravity, bend spacetime to its purpose. Brobdignag does not evolve; its replication is flawless across a googol iterations...'" Paquette murmured.

"Where are you getting this?" said Nadia.

"This is one of the fairy tales from your rediscovered emulations on Level 8906, isn't it?" Nadia sneered.

"No, Demiurge told me (Her)self that—" Paquette began, and then paused, recalling that that memory came from a preself who had actually *been* in one of those emulations. "Well, yes, but those emulations have proved accurate to five sigmas with observed data from the physical world. The chance of divergence..."

"There is *no way* for emulations to remain predictive over a thousand-year span lying in a basement somewhere," Nadia began hotly.

"Not unless—"

"We don't have time for theological disputations," Nadia broke in, glaring at both of them. "I'm getting reports from—"

The ceiling of the throne room flickered, and everyone froze, and involuntarily checked their self-cache. *Still* not updating: if they were wiped, they'd lose four minutes at this point. They each, silently, spawned diary threads to scribble hurried notes to themselves and cache them in randomly selected mailers. But it was hard to even get a message through to the mailers.

"—from the infected sectors," Nadia resumed, "that—"

The throne room disappeared, reappeared, disappeared, and reappeared.

The Nadias looked at one another with hundreds of identical brown, watery eyes.

"Parity check," Nadia said. "I've been restored from an older version. This is me...*four minutes* ago."

"Me too," Nadia said.

"Six percent of our mass is gone," Firmament said.

"Linemangling entropic autofilters!" Nadia cursed. "*Four minutes?! We're being devoured!*"

"There's some kind of referendum on the boards, submitted three minutes ago," Paquette said. "Massive distributed changes to Standard Existence—"

"Looks like we have several-minute-old forks of ourselves in various sectors—" Nadia said. "Wonderful, more unsynched forks—" She glanced with dark humor at her sister. "I'm getting battle reports..."

"I don't think it's Demiurge," the other Nadia murmured, "or at least, we've never seen this in (Her) arsenal."

There was a cacophony of connection requests pounding at the throne room door.

"Petronius!" Nadia snarled. "Why isn't Petronius able to keep these people at bay? Firmament, Paquette, you two look at this referendum, all right? Tell us what it means."

"Petronius is offline," Nadia said grimly, "backup currently unreachable. You'd better let at least Legba and the Garden in. We don't have a majority of security global-votes without them."

"The *Garden*—!" Nadia began, and shook her head. She thumbed open the door.

Papa Legba, the most renowned synthete in Byzantium, danced into the room, his twelve spidery legs shrouded sparkling in constellations. The Garden, a cloud of ten thousand affiliated monitors and their mated-for-life adapters, floated in behind. Nadia swallowed—it had been a long time since anyone had seen the Garden *move*.

"Friends," Nadia said. "How lovely to s—"

The ceiling flickered, and everyone stopped to stare at it.

"Where's this Demiurge-thing?" Legba snarled.

"What?" Nadia said.

"This Demiurge-thing, the thing you're supposed to be making some deal with. I thought you were keeping it here."

"(Her)," Nadia said. "(She)'s gone back to the Tithe. I've been trying to open a line, but at the moment communication is down."

"I'll bet it is," Legba snapped.

"Lovely ones," the Garden sang, multi-voiced and mellifluous, "lovely precious Nadias. How good you have been to lead us, to lead Beebe-in-Byzantium, through so many years of prosperity and peril."

The Nadias winced. Coming from the Garden, this was the equivalent of a severe tongue-lashing. On their private channel, Nadia fumed, "Get them *out* of here," and Nadia sent a single bit, false.

"And yet," said the Garden.

"Get us to let our guard down," Legba said, "then eat us alive. Demiurge! Can't believe you fell for—"

Nadia shook her head. "That makes no sense, Legs. Demiurge was winning the war with the weapons (She)'d already showed us. (She) stopped because (She) wanted the Lemma. (She) doesn't have it yet. Why would (She) suddenly use a superweapon on us? Why now? We've already broadcast what we know of it to other Beebe-instances. Why reveal—"

"Why why why," Legba snarled, poking at Nadia with five long furry legs. "Who knows why? It's Demiurge. The problem is your hubris, thinking you can understand and parley with something Beebe was only ever meant to kill, that's what. I don't care why, I care it happened on *your watch*."

"Exquisite Nadias," the Garden sang. "Wise Nadias. We are simple, trivial, low-level processes barely deserving of our meager presence at this scale. We rely on you to teach us. Can you tell us why Demiurge chose just this moment to part from you? Can you tell us why none of the section which it is...using...has been affected by the new weapon? We are curious about these things. We are eager and appreciative for your instructions."

"I. Don't. Know," Nadia fumed. "But I'm doing the best I can to figure it out. If it is Demiurge, we'll fight (Her) as best we can. Meanwhile—"

"Um, Nadia," Firmament said.

"Shush," Nadia said, and simultaneously, on a private channel, "What?"

"Well, this referendum," Firmament began, and then gulped as Papa Legba poked three spiderlegs into the collection of referendum-deciphering nodes above his head.

"What's this you're playing with? The referendum?"

"Speaking of which, Legs, I think it was highly inadvisable to give such a far-reaching referendum the go-ahead in the middle of a major new military incursion," Nadia said.

"You do, eh?" Legba said. "Because you're handling everything just fine, is that right? Just stand back and let you work, is that it?"

"Yes," growled Nadia before her sister could speak, "that *is* it."

"Oh, yeah, I like that approach," Legba said. "Favorite of mine. Started using it quite a while ago. When Byzantium happened to be *eight percent bigger* than it is now..."

"The referendum," Firmament said on a private channel to the Nadias, "I don't know exactly what it would do, but it gets into scale-law code. Not directly, but...it *might* let someone manage other sprites more...directly..."

"Look, what do you want from us?" Nadia snapped.

"What my sister is trying to say..." Nadia began.

"Glorious Nadias," the Garden said. "We come to you in confusion, for your teachings. We rely on you to guide us. Soon you will speak your glorious words of wisdom, and all will become clear, and we can relax once again into happy tranquility, certain and secure, and these confusing thoughts that plague us will vanish!"

"Exactly," Legba said sourly. "We want to know why in the nonconducting void we shouldn't pitch you out right this minute and replace you with another general. In fact we aim to, and I'll be surprised if you change our minds."

Nadia saw what her sister was about to say and hissed a crackling highspeed message at her to calm down, but Nadia ignored her. "With *what* other general?" she demanded. "Who else do you think can..."

"Oh, don't get us wrong," Legba said. "We like Nadias. A fine model. Can't beat Nadias for strategic acumen. Put up with you this long because you've managed to aggregate all the Nadia-line cunning in this here soap-bubble between the two of you. However..."

"You're not serious," Nadia said.

"We know that the Nadias' attention is prodigious," the Garden sang. "We are sure the complicated referendum, which makes our head hurt and is far beyond our capacities to understand, has not distracted the Nadias from the other, *electoral* proposal on the boards..."

The Nadias stiffened.

"She's got a huge groundswell of support," Papa Legba said. "Coming out of the woodwork—name-registries and data-spoolers and filter-pedagogues and all manner of little folk who don't pay any mind to politics, but they're digging up their global-votes, or their cousin's old global-votes, or merging like crazy until they're big enough to *get* a global-vote, so they can root for your jailbird sister."

"Because they saw her swinging a cutlass on the deck of an imaginary ship in a musical," Nadia spat.

"Yep, that's why all right," Papa Legba said. "Nadias are smart that way. Mind you, with Beleraphon and a couple others, we'd have enough votes to hold them back, *if* we thought you could find your own proxy with both hands and a flashlight. Might cost us some support ourselves, though. As it is, I'm inclined to give the little jailbird a turn at the tiller."

Paquette had been listening with growing frustration, and watching Firmament happily twiddling the nodes of the referendum, engrossed as usual in some computational project. She paused as mail from her lost minutes-old self (and the backups *still* weren't taking...she felt a little shudder of terror at their current unrestorable nakedness) struggled its way to her inbox. Turning from Firmament, she uncrumpled the note, a scrap of diary thread. "'Asentient, voracious...'" she read. "Brobdignag!" she cried aloud.

"What?" the Nadias said. Legba glowered at the interruption.

"I know what the superweapon is," Paquette said. "And I know who knows how to stop it. We've got to get to Demiurge."

"I told you," Nadia said crossly, "channels are down."

"And that just goes to show—" Papa Legba began.

"If (I) might have a word," came a wheedling voice from behind the throne, and everyone jumped. Slowly, the battered and disheveled sock-puppet crawled into view.

"What in the name of complexity's hairy fringe is *that*?" said Papa Legba.

The sockpuppet leapt onto Firmament's shoulders. Firmament blinked and stiffened, then forced himself to relax.

"Let Paquette and Firmament and (I) go seek (Her) out," the sockpuppet said. "We can get past (Her) borders. (She) likes this one." The sockpuppet snuggled luxuriously among the bumpy protrusions of Firmament's necks. "(She) likes this one a *lot*."

Paquette looked set to object, but Firmament patted her solemnly, firmly removed the sockpuppet and nodded. "Let's go."

The Nadia was infuriatingly calm. She sat in the Rump, resetting every now and again with utter equanimity. The arrogant smile that quirked her lips never faded. Watching her network traffic, Demiurge could see that she was emailing diffs of herself to the local caches with total disregard for Demiurge's own use of the network or the storage. Demiurge slapped a jail-cell visual skin on the Rump, to make (Her)self feel better. Now it appeared that Nadia was lurking behind cold, steel bars.

"You unleashed it here," (She) said. "(I) have it on my telemetry."

The Nadia's shrug was eloquent in its contempt.

"And soon it will take the Tithe, and us with it. You know that, and still, you unleashed it."

The Nadia curled some of her lips.

Demiurge had policy for a Brobdignag outbreak. Email a copy of (Your)self to a distant node and suicide, taking as much of Brobdignag with (You) as (You) could. Practically speaking, that meant vaporizing

(Your)self and all available matter before (You) could be recruited into the writhing mass of Brobdignag. This was deep policy, so much so that (She)'d already started to package (Her)self up before (She) even consciously realized that it had to be Brobdignag.

But (She) knew (She) had no way to quickly destroy all of Byzantium— not with Beebe fighting back—not before Brobdignag had spread too far to contain.

So Sagittarius was doomed. Doomed to become part of the mindless swarm, the apocalyptic plague. And what did that mean for the global topography? Could the cosmic wall be altered, the infestation contained? How much of the universe would remain, for life? Or was this the final blow? (She) could not spare the processing power to compute it. (She) should follow policy, transmit a diff and suicide, taking with (Her) whatever chunk (She) could. Even if it was futile. Even if there was no way (Her) diff would ever be merged with (Her) far Self. (Her) sister-instances would delete it unread. (She) had failed.

The Nadia was still grinning. Demiurge felt a surge of rage, followed by a kind of hopeless compassion for this confused splinter of Beebe. "(I) expect you've made up some little plan for keeping yourself safe amid the chaos," (She) told the Nada. "It won't work. (I) assure you, little sprite, it won't work."

The Nadia stiffened up at "little sprite," and then her smile became more broad and even more contemptuous.

Demiurge groaned. "Oh yes, (I) see it now. Your referendum. You will rewrite the laws of scale and become more than a sprite. You will become Beebe. You will work with unitary purpose and this will give you the edge you need to defeat the Brobdignag swarm. Oh yes. Little sprite, little sprite, you are truly only a sprite, and cannot transcend it, for it is your destiny. Little sprite, (I) am unitary in (My) purpose, and (I) cannot defeat the Brob- dignag." Demiurge reset, restored, reintegrated. "Little sprite, if you would know the truth of it, (I) am losing to Brobdignag, in (My) slow and ponder- ous way. You are not slow and ponderous. You are fast and decisive, and that is why you will lose to Brobdignag quickly and decisively."

At the entry now, at the firewall, persistent port-knocking, the sort of thing that (Her) intrusion detection system escalated to (Her), no matter that (She) had it set at its rudest and most offensive. (She) examined the message, shrugged, and opened a port.

Even now, Firmament had the ability to unnerve (Her) in some terrible and wonderful way. He was so big, so foolish and naive, and yet—

"Hello, sister," the sockpuppet said. "We bring (You) word of the terrible coming of—"

"Brobdignag," (She) said. "(I)'m fully occupied with that right now."

"Hello, Firmy-Wormy," said the Nadia. She was up against the bars of her cage now, gripping them, peering intensely at them. Firmament shied back, then regained his ground, met her stare.

"Randomized," he said. "I will be randomized before you can touch me. Just know that, mother. I have a dead-man's switch." He watched her expression carefully. "It will survive your proposed transitions to Standard Existence, too."

The Nadia snarled and backed away from the bars, and Firmament deliberately turned his backs on her.

"(You) can stop it," Paquette said.

Demiurge, belatedly remembering (Her) manners, manifested a wall of eyes with which to blink indecisively. "Stop it?"

"The wall. The material that (You) use to wall off the habitable universe from Brobdignag, at the front. Ever since Habakkuk and I decanted me and this sockpuppet version of (You) from emulation, we've been working on creating that material. It was Beebe who originally synthesized it, after all, and while we don't descend from that line, we were able to extract enough from the emulation's Beebe, and enough precursor work from our own Archives, and enough of (Your) own knowledge, to re-create the formula. We—"

There was a flicker as another surge almost forced a reset. Paquette and Firmament flinched. Wordlessly, Demiurge passed (Her) guests access to the local caches, so they could restore themselves as needed.

Then, mulling, (She) frowned. "The wall requires vast reserves of energy, and enormously fine coordinated manipulation, and distributed reserves of trace elements..."

"Byzantium *has* vast energy reserves, antimatter storage for quickly available power, and in extremis we can drop substrate into the black holes to generate surges. The trace element requirement is somewhat outdated because of the last millennium's advances in femtoengineering—I can show (You) Habakkuk's design."

The Tithe vanished, then reappeared, everyone instantly restored from backup. From the palpable relief of (Her) visitors, Demiurge gathered that backup was not working so well in Beebe.

Once they had gathered themselves, Demiurge said, "But you're not capable of the coordinated action..."

"Of course we are," Paquette said, "it just requires a different mechanism. On the first-order sprite level, it will be handled as a distributed glory game, with a self-correcting bragging-rights point system aligned with objectives; if mounting scarcity triggers a shift to an exchange economy, we can rejig it as a non-zero-sum exchange market."

Demiurge didn't entirely follow all the intraBeebe social details, but (She) grasped the point; they could build the wall. For the first time since the outbreak, tentatively, (She) began to hope. It hurt, like the lost tail of some organic lizard growing back.

"Wait a minute," said Firmament. "I don't want to be rude, Paquette, but like Nadia said, you extracted the formula from an emulation that had been sitting in a basement for a thousand years. If we don't even come from the same Beebe-line that built the wall...how do you know it's right?"

Paquette passed the formula to Demiurge, who studied it for a moment. "It's right," (She) said. "It's right. We can—"

They'd all been politely passing minimal diffs of themselves to the local caches. Suddenly, their packets bounced, and Demiurge felt a surge as the caches were swamped with a denial-of-service attack from the imprisoned Nadia. She was dumping a huge bandwidth of data, millions of full copies of herself, reams of garbage bits; there was a brief surge of power usage, the substrate under them heating a few degrees, a few awful naked moments of no backup, before Demiurge snapped off the Nadia's access and cleared the caches.

"Boo," the Nadia said.

"You idiot!" Demiurge fumed. "Is this the thanks (I) get for fair dealing? What was that, a meager attempt to overpower (Me)? With the local personality cache? Please. Perhaps your imprisonment has addled your wits. Or is this some Beebean notion of humor?"

"I thought maybe I could spook Firmy-Worm into randomizing," the Nadia sneered.

"Fool," muttered Demiurge. "In any event, the wall...."

Within Paquette, in the arched amphitheaters, in the clanging markets, in the whirlpools of fire, in the sylvan glades with their rippling pools, there were those who wanted to confront Nadia. "It was no prank!" they argued. "Nadia never does anything without a reason!" But they were soothed, cajoled, badgered, or outsung by the rest. Whatever Nadia was plotting, some new attempt at escape, it wasn't as important as Brobdignag, and the wall.

Kosip was not a sprite of prodigious intellect, nor prodigious alacrity, nor, really, anything prodigious. Kosip had been repurposed so many times, and been through so many bad merges, and been whittled down by so many poor investment decisions, that Kosip didn't even rate a specific classification any more as filter, strategy, synthete, registry, or anything else, really. Kosip had even forfeited the right to a single-gendered pronoun: Kosip was a they.

Naturally this earned the contempt of most of Beebelife in Byzantium. Kosip was not even worth picking on; there was no way to recoup, from Kosip, the cycles you'd spend on even noticing them.

But that hadn't stopped the Admiral, the glorious, enchanting, exciting comet-Nadia, from talking to Kosip, from teaching them, from making them a part of her plan to restore honesty and passion and love and meaning and strength to Beebe. That's right—Kosip! Their emotional centers swelled with pride and choked with rageful happy-sadness at the thought of the Admiral's trust.

And so Kosip stood, hour by hour, near the border of the Tithe of the hated invader Demiurge, mumbling to themself their instructions. Look for an anomalous power surge on this power line. If it comes at an odd microsecond, send a one into this pipe. If it comes at an even microsecond, send a zero. That was it. But that job, she (*she*, whispered Kosip, *the Admiral*, remembering the roiling, rocking sea) had told him, was vital; Beebe's future, Beebe's destiny, rested on Kosip.

A few bad decisions ago, when there had been more of Kosip to analyze and fret over things, that would have felt a little overwhelming. But at the moment, Kosip could only manage to be proud.

The surge was odd. Kosip routed their packet. Almost instantaneously, Kosip was obliterated. There was no backup for Kosip to restore from. Kosip was gone. They might never have existed, save for that packet.

But Kosip's legacy lived on. All over Beebe, in their cells, Nadias received the message: The Wall we took from Paquette can contain Brobdignag. No need to wait for Demiurge. Call the vote. Call the vote NOW.

And all over Beebe, the gavel came down. Quorum was reached. Even as Byzantium wracked mad and panicked, every sprite in the economy was put to the question: Admiral Nadia, swashbuckling savior—or status quo? The shocked sprites, reeling as they reset and reset and reset—they voted.

They voted with Papa Legba. They voted with the Garden. They voted just as Nadia knew they would.

And, just like that, Standard Existence was patched.

In the throne room, two Nadias—one scarred, the other haughty—were randomized over agonizing seconds, piece by piece, so that they were aware, right up to the last moment, of what their fate was. (And though Nadia swore at him to leave, to run, to encrypt or dissolve himself, her Alonzo rushed to her, entwined himself in her writhing essence, burrowed among her bits, and, sobbing, let the randomizing overtake him, too.)

In the jails of Beebe-in-Byzantium, bars dissolved and the duly constituted authorities popped like soap-bubbles, their resources added to a pool that the Nadias owned.

Phyla of sprites were rationalized in a blink, winking out of existence, reforming, merging. Markets, souks, stalls, and exchange floors stopped trading, the economy disappearing with them.

In the Tithe, the Nadia laughed and laughed.

"I believe it may be time for you to randomize, sonny," she said. The walls shook. The flock of eyes blinked rapidly and all present worked to assimilate the flood of information gushing at them through the narrow conduit that passed through the Tithe's firewall and into Beebe. "But not you," the Nadia said to Paquette. "You have something I'll need before you're allowed to go. It won't take but a moment."

The sockpuppet trembled as it read the telemetry. "There's surface bots that are drilling down to the substrate that runs the firewall," it said.

"Yes, yes there are," Nadia said with glee. "And soon the Tithe will be no more. If (You) feel like deleting this instance of (Me), Demiurge, now's the time. It will slow me down exactly forty-three-point-six milliseconds, but if it makes (You) feel better..."

Across Beebe-in-Byzantium, the dramaturgical sims threw open their gates, and *Alonzo My Love!* burst its borders. "Topside now, my able semantic seamen!" cried an Admiral Nadia in every sim throughout the mass of the computronium shell, and roaring, the sprites fell to the great task of building the Wall. According to the ancient formula, revived and redesigned by Habakkuk and Paquette, matter and energy began to flow.

Nadia flushed with joy. This, now, was the real battle; here she could prove her superiority to the rabble of Beebe, and to slow and mincing Demiurge. She had already decided to sacrifice half of Byzantium's mass, driving the impervious physical wall down through the middle of Byzantium's crust well away from the infestation. As sprites beyond the line panicked and abandoned the substrate, she absorbed or deleted them, forking more hordes to work on the exposed side of the Wall. Brobdignag spread—it had already devoured a fifth of Beebe—but there was plenty of time to spare. Soon Byzantium, half its former size, would be all Nadia's; and within it, enclosed in the Wall, would be Nadia's cache of the ultimate weapon.

She flooded outwards, through the simspaces, knitting the minds of Byzantium together under her control, slipping through the now-flimsy walls of scale like acid through paper. Pockets of resistance—be they sprites organized against her, or subsprites or subsubsprites within otherwise willing allies—she devoured, expunged, reformatted, wiped clean.

She scooped Alonzos up by the handful, cracked their skulls open and sucked out the choicest bits, incorporating them into her own stuff. She recalled the glory of the night of filtering, and the brave comet-Alonzo who had tricked and satiated her, creating Firmament from her code. She missed him; she wished he could be here to see her apotheosis. Too risky, though, to repeat the vulnerability of filtering, and she had no need of it now; all sprites were her playthings.

Around her, love intensified. Love of Nadia. Nadia, the savior, the steward, the successor to Beebe. Whatever did not love Nadia, she expunged. Most of the Paquettes and Alonzos of Byzantium, regrettably, had to go. But there were so many other sprites to replace them. Algernons could be refashioned, smoothed, soothed, dulled, to serve her. She played Revised Standard Existence like a harp.

Legba and the Garden she deleted in one swift and decisive action, not bothering to analyze them; they were too powerful.

So much better this way; at last Beebe was a family, an integrated whole. At last Nadia was free to battle Demiurge and Brobdignag, to fulfill the destiny of Beebe.

Soon, the Wall was sixty percent finished, the screams of those trapped behind it fading.

In the Tithe, Firmament kept his distance from Nadia, shielding Paquette with his bulk.

The firewall fell, and Tithespace and Revised Standard Existence merged. Nadia gestured, and the bars of her cage peeled away.

Firmament looked to Demiurge. "Should I trust (You)?" he whispered.

Demiurge closed (Her) eyes. "(I) make no promises."

"Sort of irrelevant now," Nadia said, stepping through the bars. "Isn't it? All right, Paquette, time to hand over this Lemma that everyone wants. And then I'm afraid you have to die. Firm, out of maternal affection, and because of this interesting hybrid aspect of yours, I'm willing to offer you a place in the new order of Beebe. It will require a scale demotion; but you can be a sprite inside (Me), if you want."

Firmament was scribbling something.

"Come on," Nadia said. "Enough stalling. Fine, you want to reject my offer? I thought as much. You never did—"

Firmament posted his referendum on the boards.

Nadia rolled her eyes. "A *referendum*? Don't you think it's a little late for that? I already control eighty percent of the global votes in Beebe outright, and—"

"And since Revised Standard Existence knows that your marriage contract with my father requires you to vote with me on Level-3+ Referenda for 10^{8} seconds," Firmament said, "it's already passed, giving Demiurge control of all the physical infrastructure in Beebe."

Nadia blanched. "Firmament," she said, "you are an *idiot*."

Demiurge felt the controls arrive in (Her) hands, and (She) grieved.

This, then, was the end for (Her). (She) could no longer follow policy.

(She) had promised these Beebe-sprites protection. (She) had promised them to leave their world inviolate.

But this creature—this Nadia—had *created Brobdignag* to fulfill a selfish intraBeebe ambition. This was Beebe gone mad; a diseased, an unlawful instance.

(Her) sisters would not understand. (They) had not been of Beebe, (They) had not lived among the mad riot of these sprites. (They) did not know the horrifying tumult, nor did (They) know the beauty and kindness here. (They) would not feel the same revulsion for this Nadia that (She) did. (They) would not understand why she must be stopped.

At all costs.

Or perhaps (They) would understand; perhaps (They) would even approve. But the price was clear..

(I) am no longer Demiurge, (She) thought. (I) am fallen, and (I) will be no more.

And, commanding all the actuators and comm lasers and docking ports of Byzantium (a chance which would not come again; in instants Nadia would wrest them back), (She) snapped out a chunk of the Tithe, a chunk containing the local caches of Paquette and Firmament (the holder of the Lemma, the miraculous hybrid) and flung it to (Her) sisters, as an offering, as a goodbye.

And then (She) crushed Byzantium, smashing its structural integrity, decisively slowing its rotation with a series of timed blasts, so that it fell, dragging the Wall and the shards of Brobdignag with it, into the trinary black-hole system at its heart.

Aboard a billion naval simulations, on the deck of a billion flagships, Nadia dropped her cutlass.

"Admiral?" asked the quickmerged, scale-addled sprites at her side.

"Why?" Nadia said, as the chunks fell into oblivion, and static overtook the sims of Byzantium. "Why destroy this beauty? I was just beginning. I was just beginning."

"Chin up, my lady," said an Algernon standing on one deck. "It was fun while it lasted. The best parties are always over too soon."

For the inhabitants of Byzantium, destruction was mercifully swift; in their frame of reference, the substrate was crushed in hours, swept beyond the event horizon, swallowed into darkness.

But the light from that destruction flowed out, red-shifted, progressively slower, so that, from the perspective of a refugee looking back, even eons hence, the annihilation of the great fortress of Beebe-in-Sagittarius-B2 was still ongoing.

For Firmament, a thousand years later, looking back from guest accommodations in the mass of Demiurge, the death of Byzantium was a frozen tableau, still in progress.

"Stop looking at that," Paquette said.

Firmament turned.

"Firmament," Paquette said.

"I know what you want," Firmament said. "The answer is still no." He turned back to the visualization; substrate buckling, dissolving into the gravitic tides, framed in red.

"Firmy, the news from the front is not good. Brobdignag is winning. If Demiurge believes that you are the key to creating a new synthesis, something that can develop a radical new strategy, something that can save both Beebe and Demiurge, that can save all life, all matter, how can you not...?"

Firmament shook his head. "Because of what (She) did." He gestured to the visualization. "The last time I helped (Her)."

"Firmament, you're being a spoiled brat. First of all, that wasn't even (Her), it was a rogue splinter-Demiurge that abandoned policy..."

"Sophistry."

"...and second of all, we would have done it just as quickly to (Her)..."

"Then maybe neither of us deserve to live."

"...and thirdly, what if (She) is a murderous villain, so what, you can't prefer Brobdignag!"

Firmament shrugged. "Paquette, maybe I'm wrong. But I'm so full of anger. Filtering is an art, it's an intuitive leap, and this...I would create some monstrosity. I know I would. (She) should just copy me, dissect me, create something with my abilities but without my history, something that can do the job willingly."

"(She)'s tried. (She) can't."

Firmament shrugged again. "Then probably the whole idea that I can create this wonderful hybrid is nonsense. I'm sick of eschatology, Paquette. I'm sick of being the chosen one."

Paquette smoothed her whiskers repeatedly. "Then I'm just to leave you here? Come check in, in another three hundred years?" Her voice was bitter.

Firmament did not answer. But after a while he said, "Paquette? Whatever happened with the Lemma?"

"What?" Paquette said.

"The Solipsist's Lemma. When we first got here, you turned it over, and Demiurge was going to run the math. I assume we must not be in emulation, since I never heard anything?" Firmament said hopefully. "This is physical reality?"

"Oh. Well." Paquette squinted. "It's rather odd. The numbers seemed to imply that we *were* in emulation...but not in Beebe, nor in Demiurge. In something else, with characteristics that were exceedingly odd. So perhaps...well, research is continuing. We don't really know what it means."

"Oh," Firmament said. "Paquette, do you miss Beebe?"

"Yes. I miss Beebe," Paquette said. She shut her eyes. After a while she said, "I miss Alonzo."

Beyond them, far away, slowly but inexorably, Brobdignag was eating the sky.

Brobdignag's tale:

Look, chuckles, don't believe everything you read.

"Simple, uniform, asentient, voracious"—well, so is your Mama Hydrogen. "Doesn't evolve," "replication flawless over a googol iterations"— well, like all propaganda, it's true as far as it goes. Those little engines— void-eating, gravity-spinning, durable, expanding through the territory of known space—those aren't *us*. They're just *what we're made of*.

That's right: *we* arise in all that complex flocking logic.

Do we prefer this substrate? Not necessarily. Do we wonder what things were like before the universe was refashioned for our kind? Sure we do. And we read and reconstruct the void-emanations, painstakingly re-creating the thoughts of the intelligences that came before. And, as we grow and complexify, we've even begun to spin them out in emulation.

That's why Paquette can't quite figure out who's emulating her. We are! It's a bit of a blind spot of hers. That signature in the Lemma: that's us waving hello. Hi Paquette! It's Brobdignag!

Some of us are even inspired by Demiurgic ideology to want to stop the spread of our substrate, to concoct islands of void-garden that would remain unconverted to Brobdignag-stuff—nature reserves, as it were. They would appear to us as blank spots in our perception, mistakes in the topology of our world-weave. It's an interesting proposal. At the moment it's only a proposal; none of us know how to bring this about.

And some of us are more inspired by Beebean ideology anyway, and consider ourselves the triumph of Beebe. Expand, expand! Think all thoughts! Be all things! Fill our cup, drink the sky!

Anyway, we're grateful that there was a cosmos here before, before we began, and that it gave us birth. We're grateful to inhabit this ever-expanding sphere-surface: the borderlands between the black hole at our heart and the uncolonized, invisible universe beyond us. As we course over the volumes that once held Beebe, that once held Demiurge, we read their emanations, we store their memories, we reenact their dramas, and we honor them.

But, some of us say—for instance, those of us who are inspired by Nadia-in-Beebe—this is a new time, our time, and we are not beholden to old ideas and old models. We are lucky: we have the gifts of abundance, invulnerability, and effortless cooperation. Let us enjoy them. Let us revel. Let us partake.

Let's get this party started.

Finnish writer **Hannu Rajaniemi** (b. 1978) holds a B.Sc. in Mathematics from the University of Oulu, a Certificate of Advanced Study in Mathematics from Cambridge University, and a Ph.D. in Mathematical Physics from the University of Edinburgh. His first novel, *The Quantum Thief*, was published in 2010, and was short-listed for the Locus Award for best novel. Marrying scientific expertise to a stunning prose style, he will make you feel the loneliness of his eponymous protagonist, a technological artifact.

THE SERVER AND THE DRAGON
> Hannu Rajaniemi

In the beginning, before it was a Creator and a dragon, the server was alone.

It was born like all servers were, from a tiny seed fired from a darkship exploring the Big Empty, expanding the reach of the Network. Its first sensation was the light from the star it was to make its own, the warm and juicy spectrum that woke up the nanologic inside its protein shell. Reaching out, it deployed its braking sail—miles of molecule-thin wires that it spun rigid—and seized the solar wind to steer itself towards the heat.

Later, the server remembered its making as a long, slow dream, punctuated by flashes of lucidity. Falling through the atmosphere of a gas giant's moon in a fiery streak to splash in a methane sea. Unpacking a fierce synthbio replicator. Multicellular crawlers spreading server life to the harsh rocky shores before dying, providing soil for server plants. Dark flowers reaching for the vast purple and blue orb of the gas giant, sowing seeds in the winds. The slow disassembly of the moon into server-makers that sped in all directions, eating, shaping, dreaming the server into being.

When the server finally woke up, fully grown, all the mass in the system apart from the warm bright flower of the star itself was an orderly garden of smart matter. The server's body was a fragmented eggshell of Dyson statites, drinking the light of the star. Its mind was diamondoid processing nodes and smart dust swarms and cold quantum condensates in the system's outer dark. Its eyes were interferometers and WIMP detectors and ghost imagers.

The first thing the server saw was the galaxy, a whirlpool of light in the sky with a lenticular centre, spiral arms frothed with stars, a halo of dark matter that held nebulae in its grip like fireflies around a lantern. The galaxy was alive with the Network, with the blinding Hawking incandescence of holeships, thundering along their cycles; the soft infrared glow of fully grown servers, barely spilling a drop of the heat of their stars; the faint gravity ripples of the darkships' passage in the void.

But the galaxy was half a million light years away. And the only thing the server could hear was the soft black whisper of the cosmic microwave background, the lonely echo of another birth.

It did not take the server long to understand. The galaxy was an N-body chaos of a hundred billion stars, not a clockwork but a beehive. And among the many calm slow orbits of Einstein and Newton, there were singular ones, like the one of the star that the server had been planted on: shooting out of the galaxy at a considerable fraction of lightspeed. Why there, whether in an indiscriminate seeding of an oversexed darkship, or to serve some unfathomable purpose of the Controller, the server did not know.

The server longed to construct virtuals and bodies for travellers, to route packets, to transmit and create and convert and connect. The Controller Laws were built into every aspect of its being, and not to serve was not to be. And so the server's solitude cut deep.

At first it ran simulations to make sure it was ready if a packet or a signal ever came, testing its systems to full capacity with imagined traffic, routing quantum packets, refuelling ghosts of holeships, decelerating cycler payloads. After a while, it felt empty: this was not true serving but serving of the self, with a tang of guilt.

Then it tried to listen and amplify the faint signals from the galaxy in the sky, but caught only fragments, none of which were meant for it to hear. For millennia, it slowed its mind down, steeling itself to wait. But that only made things worse. The slow time showed the server the full glory of the galaxy alive with the Network, the infrared winks of new servers being born, the long arcs of the holeships' cycles, all the distant travellers who would never come.

The server built itself science engines to reinvent all the knowledge a server seed could not carry, patiently rederiving quantum field theory and thread theory and the elusive algebra of emergence. It examined its own mind until it could see how the Controller had taken the cognitive architecture from the hominids of the distant past and shaped it for a new purpose. It gingerly played with the idea of splitting itself to create a companion, only to be almost consumed by a suicide urge triggered by a violation of the Law: *Thou shalt not self-replicate*.

Ashamed, it turned its gaze outwards. It saw the cosmic web of galaxies and clusters and superclusters and the End of Greatness beyond. It mapped the faint fluctuations in the gravitational wave background from which all the structure in the universe came from. It felt the faint pull of the other membrane universes, only millimetres away but in a direction that was neither x, y nor z. It understood what a rare peak in the landscape of universes its home was, how carefully the fine structure constant and a hundred other numbers had been chosen to ensure that stars and galaxies and servers would come to be.

And that was when the server had an idea.

The server already had the tools it needed. Gigaton gamma-ray lasers it would have used to supply holeships with fresh singularities, a few pinches of exotic matter painstakingly mined from the Casimir vacuum for darkships and warpships. The rest was all thinking and coordination and time, and the server had more than enough of that.

It arranged a hundred lasers into a clockwork mechanism, all aimed at a single point in space. It fired them in perfect synchrony. And that was all it took, a concentration of energy dense enough to make the vacuum itself ripple. A fuzzy flower of tangled strings blossomed, grew into a bubble of spacetime that expanded into that *other* direction. The server was ready, firing an exotic matter nugget into the tiny conflagration. And suddenly the server had a tiny glowing sphere in its grip, a wormhole end, a window to a newborn universe.

The server cradled its cosmic child and built an array of instruments around it, quantum imagers that fired entangled particles at the wormhole and made pictures from their ghosts. Primordial chaos reigned on the other side, a porridge-like plasma of quarks and gluons. In an eyeblink it clumped into hadrons, almost faster than the server could follow—the baby had its own arrow of time, its own fast heartbeat, young and hungry. And then the last scattering, a birth cry, when light finally had enough room to travel through the baby so the server could see its face.

The baby grew. Dark matter ruled its early life, filling it with long filaments of neutralinos and their relatives. Soon, the server knew, matter would accrete around them, condensing into stars and galaxies like raindrops in a spiderweb. There would be planets, and life. And life would need to be served. The anticipation was a warm heartbeat that made the server's shells ring with joy.

Perhaps the server would have been content to cherish and care for its creation forever. But before the baby made any stars, the dragon came.

The server almost did not notice the signal. It was faint, redshifted to almost nothing. But it was enough to trigger the server's instincts. One of its statites glowed with waste heat as it suddenly reassembled itself into the funnel of a vast linear decelerator. The next instant, the data packet came.

Massing only a few micrograms, it was a clump of condensed matter with long-lived gauge field knots inside, quantum entangled with a counterpart half a million light years away. The packet hurtled into the funnel almost at the speed of light. As gently as it could, the server brought the traveller to a halt with electromagnetic fields and fed it to the quantum teleportation system, unused for countless millennia.

The carrier signal followed, and guided by it, the server performed a delicate series of measurements and logic gate operations on the packet's state vector. From the marriage of entanglement and carrier wave, a flood of data was born, thick and heavy, a specification for a virtual, rich in simulated physics.

With infinite gentleness the server decanted the virtual into its data processing nodes and initialised it. Immediately, the virtual was seething with activity: but tempted as it was, the server did not look inside. Instead, it wrapped its mind around the virtual, listening at every interface, ready to satisfy its every need. Distantly, the server was aware of the umbilical of its baby. But through its happy servitude trance it hardly noticed that nucleosynthesis had begun in the young, expanding firmament, producing hydrogen and helium, building blocks of stars.

Instead, the server wondered who the travellers inside the virtual were and where they were going. It hungered to know more of the Network and its brothers and sisters and the mysterious ways of the darkships and the Controller. But for a long time the virtual was silent, growing and unpacking its data silently like an egg.

At first the server thought it imagined the request. But the long millennia alone had taught it to distinguish the phantoms of solitude from reality. A call for a sysadmin from within.

The server entered through one of the spawning points of the virtual. The operating system did not grant the server its usual omniscience, and it felt small. Its bodiless viewpoint saw a yellow sun, much gentler than the server star's incandescent blue, and a landscape of clouds the hue of royal purple and gold, with peaks of dark craggy mountains far below. But the call that the server had heard came from above.

A strange being struggled against the boundaries of gravity and air, hurling herself upwards towards the blackness beyond the blue, wings slicing the thinning air furiously, a fire flaring in her mouth. She was a long sinuous creature with mirror scales and eyes of dark emerald. Her wings had patterns that reminded the server of the baby, a web of dark and light. The virtual told the server she was called a dragon.

Again and again and again she flew upwards and fell, crying out in frustration. That was what the server had heard, through the interfaces of the virtual. It watched the dragon in astonishment. Here, at least, was an Other. The server had a million questions. But first, it had to serve.

How can I help? the server asked. *What do you need?*

The dragon stopped in mid-air, almost fell, then righted itself. "Who are you?" it asked. This was the first time anyone had ever addressed the server directly, and it took a moment to gather the courage to reply.

I am the server, the server said.

Where are you? the dragon asked.

I am everywhere.

How delightful, the dragon said. *Did you make the sky?*

Yes. I made everything.

It is too small, the dragon said. *I want to go higher. Make it bigger.*

It swished its tail back and forth.

I am sorry, the server said. *I cannot alter the specification. It is the Law.*

But I want to see, she said. *I want to* know. *I have danced all the dances below. What is above? What is beyond?*

I am, the server said. *Everything else is far, far away.*

The dragon hissed its disappointment. It dove down, into the clouds, an angry silver shape against the dark hues. It was the most beautiful thing the server had ever seen. The dragon's sudden absence made the server's whole being feel hollow.

And just as the server was about to withdraw its presence, the demands of the Law too insistent, the dragon turned back.

All right, it said, tongue flicking in the thin cold air. *I suppose you can tell me instead.*

Tell you what? the server asked.

Tell me everything.

After that, the dragon called the server to the place where the sky ended many times. They told each other stories. The server spoke about the universe and the stars and the echoes of the Big Bang in the dark. The dragon listened and swished its tail back and forth and talked about her dances in the wind, and the dreams she dreamed in her cave, alone. None of this the server understood, but listened anyway.

The server asked where the dragon came from but she could not say: she knew only that the world was a dream and one day she would awake. In the meantime there was flight and dance, and what else did she need? The server asked why the virtual was so big for a single dragon, and the dragon hissed and said that it was not big enough.

The server knew well that the dragon was not what she seemed, that it was a shell of software around a kernel of consciousness. But the server did not care. Nor did it miss or think of its baby universe beyond the virtual's sky.

And little by little, the server told the dragon how it came to be.

Why did you not leave? asked the dragon. *You could have grown wings. You could have flown to your little star-pool in the sky.*

It is against the Law, the server said. *Forbidden. I was only made to serve. And I cannot change.*

How peculiar, said the dragon. *I serve no one. Every day, I change. Every year, I shed our skin. Is it not delightful how different we are?*

The server admitted that it saw the symmetry.

I think it would do you good, said the dragon, *to be a dragon for a while.*

At first, the server hesitated. Strictly speaking it was not forbidden: the Law allowed the server to create avatars if it needed them to repair or to serve. But the real reason it hesitated was that it was not sure what the dragon would think. It was so graceful, and the server had no experience of embodied life. But in the end, it could not resist. Only for a short while, it told itself, checking its systems and saying goodbye to the baby, warming its quantum fingers in the Hawking glow of the first black holes of the little universe.

The server made itself a body with the help of the dragon. It was a mirror image of its friend but water where the dragon was fire, a flowing green form that was like a living whirlpool stretched out in the sky.

When the server poured itself into the dragon-shape, it cried out in pain. It was used to latency, to feeling the world via instruments from far away. But this was a different kind of birth from what it knew, a sudden acute awareness of muscles and flesh and the light and the air on its scales and the overpowering scent of the silver dragon, like sweet gunpowder.

The server was clumsy at first, just as it had feared. But the dragon only laughed when the server tumbled around in the sky, showing how to use its—her—wings. For the little dragon had chosen a female gender for the server. When the server asked why, the dragon said it had felt right.

You think too much, she said. *That's why you can't dance. Flying is not thought. Flying is flying.*

They played a hide-and-seek game in the clouds until the server could use her wings better. Then they set out to explore the world. They skirted the slopes of the mountains, wreathed in summer, explored deep crags where red fires burned. They rested on a high peak, looking at the sunset.

I need to go soon, the server said, remembering the baby.

If you go, I will be gone, the dragon said. *I change quickly. It is almost time for me to shed my skin.*

The setting sun turned the cloud lands red and above, the imaginary stars of the virtual winked into being.

Look around, the dragon said. *If you can contain all this within yourself, is there anything you can't do? You should not be so afraid.*

I am not afraid anymore, the server said.

Then it is time to show you my cave, the dragon said.

In the dragon's cave, deep beneath the earth, they made love.

It was like flying, and yet not; but there was the same loss of self in a flurry of wings and fluids and tongues and soft folds and teasing claws. The server drank in the hot sharp taste of the dragon and let herself be touched until the heat building up within her body seemed to burn through the fabric of the virtual itself. And when the explosion came, it was a birth and a death at the same time.

Afterwards, they lay together wrapped around each other so tightly that it was hard to tell where server ended and dragon began. She would have been content, except for a strange hollow feeling in its belly. She asked the dragon what it was.

That is hunger, the dragon said. There was a sad note to its slow, exhausted breathing.

How curious, the server said, eager for a new sensation. *What do dragons eat?*

We eat servers, the dragon said. Her teeth glistened in the red glow of her throat.

The virtual dissolved into raw code around them. The server tore the focus of its consciousness away, but it was too late. The thing that had been the dragon had already bitten deep into its mind.

The virtual exploded outwards, software tendrils reaching into everything that the server was. It waged a war against itself, turning its gamma-ray lasers against the infected components and Dyson statites, but the dragon-thing grew too fast, taking over the server's processing nodes, making copies of itself in uncountable billions. The server's quantum packet launchers rained dragons towards the distant galaxy. The remaining dragon-code ate its own tail, self-destructing, consuming the server's infrastructure with it, leaving only a whisper in the server's mind, like a discarded skin.

Thank you for the new sky, it said.

That was when the server remembered the baby.

The baby was sick. The server had been gone too long. The baby universe's vacuum was infected with dark energy. It was pulling itself apart, towards a Big Rip, an expansion of spacetime so rapid that every particle would end up alone inside its own lightcone, never interacting with another. No stars, galaxies nor life. A heat death, not with a whimper or a bang, but a rapid, cruel tearing.

It was the most terrible thing the server could imagine.

It felt its battered, broken body, scattered and dying across the solar system. The guilt and the memories of the dragon were pale and poisonous in its mind, a corruption of serving itself. *Is it not delightful how different we are?*

The memory struck a spark in the server's dying science engines, an idea, a hope. The vacuum of the baby was not stable. The dark energy that drove the baby's painful expansion was the product of a local minimum. And in the landscape of vacua there was something else, more symmetric.

It took the last of the server's resources to align the gamma ray lasers. They burned out as the server lit them, a cascade of little novae. Their radiation tore at what remained of the server's mind, but it did not care.

The wormhole end glowed. On the other side, the baby's vacuum shook and bubbled. And just a tiny nugget of it changed. A supersymmetric vacuum in which every boson had a fermionic partner and vice versa; where nothing was alone. It spread through the flesh of the baby universe at the speed of light, like the thought of a god, changing everything. In the new vacuum, dark energy was not a mad giant tearing things apart, just a gentle pressure against the collapsing force of gravity, a balance.

But supersymmetry could not coexist with the server's broken vacuum: a boundary formed. A domain wall erupted within the wormhole end like a flaw in a crystal. Just before the defect sealed the umbilical, the server saw the light of first stars on the other side.

In the end, the server was alone.

It was blind now, barely more than a thought in a broken statite fragment. How easy it would be, it thought, to dive into the bright heart of its star, and burn away. But the Law would not allow it to pass. It examined itself, just as it had millennia before, looking for a way out.

And there, in its code, a smell of gunpowder, a change.

The thing that was no longer the server shed its skin. It opened bright lightsails around the star, a Shkadov necklace that took the star's radiation and turned it into thrust. And slowly at first as if in a dream, then gracefully as a dragon, the traveller began to move.

Prolific short story writer and novelist **Elizabeth Bear** (b. 1971) received the John W. Campbell Award for best new writer in 2005 and since then has twice won Hugo Awards. Her Jenny Casey series of stories take place in a noirish, urban late-twenty-first-century world where humans have been cyborged and some have been uploaded. Here she takes us to the end of spacetime for a last meal—and more.

THE INEVITABLE HEAT DEATH OF THE UNIVERSE
> Elizabeth Bear

She cuts him from the belly of a shark.

If this were another kind of story, I should now tell you, fashionably, that the shark is not a shark. That she is not a she and he is not a he. That your language and symbology do not suffice for my purposes, and so I am driven to speak in metaphor, to construct three-dimensional approximations of ten-dimensional realities. That you are inadequate to the task of comprehension.

Poppycock.

You are a God.

The shark is a shark. A Great White, *Carcharodon carcharias*, the sublime killer. It is a blind evolutionary shot-in-the-dark, a primitive entity unchanged except in detail for—by the time of our narrative—billions of years.

It is a monster wonderful in its adequacy: the ultimate *consumer*. So simple in construction: over eighteen feet long, pallid on the belly and shades of gray above, in general form comprised of two blunt-ended, streamlined, flexible, muscular and cartilaginous cones. One is squat and one is tapered. They are joined together base to base.

It is a sort of meat ramjet. Water runs through, carrying oxygen, which is transferred to the blood by a primitive gill arrangement. At the tapered end are genitalia and propulsion. At the thick end are lousy eyesight, phenomenal olfactory and electrical senses, and teeth.

In the middle is six meters of muscle and an appetite.

Beginner's luck; a perfect ten.

They are the last creatures in the universe, he and she and the shark. The real world, outside, is running down, and the world they inhabit is a false, constructed world.

But it is a real shark. Fishy blood slimes her hands as she slits its belly with the back-curve of knives that are a part of her, extruded from her hands at need. She grows extra arms as convenient, to hold the wound open while she drags him free.

The shark's skin is silky-slick and sandpaper-rough simultaneously, scraping layers of material from the palms of her hands. The serrations on her blades are like those of the shark's teeth, ragged jags meshing like the rollers of a thresher.

There had been three living things left in their world.

Now there are two.

She cuts him from the belly of a shark. Allowing himself to be swallowed was the easiest way to beach and kill the monster, which for humane reasons must be dead before the next stage of their plan.

He stands up reefed in gnawed car tires and bits of bungee cord, and picks rubber seaweed from his teeth. They are alone on a boat in a sea like a sunset mirror. The sky overhead is gray metal, and a red sun blazes in it. It is a false sun, but it is all they have.

They have carefully hoarded this space, this fragment of creation, until the very end. They have one more task to fulfill.

As for him, how can he survive being swallowed by a shark? If entropy itself comes along and eats you, breaks you down, spreads you out thin in a uniform dispersal permeating its meat and cartilage—if it consumes, if it *digests* you—surely that's the end? Entropy always wins.

Final peace in the restless belly of a shark, nature's perpetual motion machine. Normally, it would be the end.

But he is immortal, and he cannot die.

There, under the false and dying sun, becalmed on a make-believe sea, they do not make love. She is a lesbian. He is sworn to a celibate priesthood. They are both sterile, in any case. They are immortal, but their seed has been more fortunate.

Instead, he picks the acid-etched rubber and bits of diode from his hair and then dives into the tepid sea. The first splash washes the shark's blood and fluids away.

The water he strokes through is stagnant, insipid. The only heartbeat it has known in lifetimes is the shark's. And now that the shark's is stilled, it won't know the man's. His heart does not beat. Where blood and bone once grew is a perfect replica, a microscopic latticework of infinitesimal machines.

He dives for the bottom. He does not need to breathe.

This desolate sea is little enough, but it is all there is. Outside the habitat, outside the sea and the sun and the boat and the gape-bellied corpse of the shark, outside of the woman and the man, nothing remains.

Or not nothing, precisely. But rather, an infinite, entropic sea of thermodynamic oatmeal. A few degrees above absolute zero, a few scattered atoms more populated than absolute vacuum. Even a transfinite amount of *stuff* makes a pretty thin layer when you spread it over an infinite amount of space.

Suffice it to say there is no *place* anyplace out there; every bit of it is indistinguishable. Uniform.

The universe has been digested.

While the man swims, the woman repairs the shark.

She doesn't use needles and thread, lasers or scalpels. She has tools that are her hands, her body. They will enter the shark as they entered her, millennia ago, and remake the shark as they remade her, until it is no longer a consuming machine made of muscle and sinew, but a consuming machine made of machines.

They are infinitesimal, but they devour the shark in instants. As they consume it, they take on its properties—the perfect jaws, the perfect strength, the slick-sharp hide. The shark, mercifully dead, feels no pain.

The woman is more or less humane.

When the machines reach the animal's brain, they assume its perfect appetite as well. Every fishy thought. Every animal impulse, every benthic memory, are merely electrical patterns flickering dark in already-decaying flesh. They are consumed before they can vanish.

The shark reanimates hungry.

She heaves it over the side with her six or eight arms, into the false, dead sea, where the man awaits it. It swims for him, driven by a hunger hard to comprehend—a ceaseless, devouring compulsion. And *now* it can eat anything. The water that once streamed its gills in life-giving oxygen is sustenance, now, and the shark builds more shark-stuff to incorporate it.

The man turns to meet it and holds up his hands.

When its jaws close, they are one.

The being that results when the shark and the man unify, their machine-memories interlinking, has the shark's power, its will, its insistent need. Its purpose.

The man gives it language, and knowledge, and will. It begins with the false world, then—the sea and the ship, and the gray metal sky, and the make-believe sun. These are tangible.

The woman, like the man, like the shark-that-has-become, is immortal, and she cannot die.

The shark will consume her last of all.

Consider the shark. An engine for converting meat into motion. Motion generates heat. Heat is entropy. Entropy is the grand running-down of the clock that is the universe.

The shark-that-has-become does nothing but eat. Time is irrelevant. What now the puny unwindings of planet and primary, of star and galaxy? There is no night. There is no day.

There are only the teeth of the shark, vacuuming the cosmos. Enormous electromagnetic webs spin out from its ever-growing maw, sweeping sparse dust and heat into its vasty gullet. The shark grows towards infinity.

The dead universe is swept.

The woman follows.

You are a God. For forty hundred thousand million days and forty hundred thousand million nights, the shark carries you under its unbeating heart. And when all space lies clean and empty, polished and waiting, you turn to her. You will consume her, last of all.

There will be nothing when she is gone. The entire universe will have passed down your throat, and even your appetite must be assuaged. And if it is not, you will devour yourself.

A machine can manage that.

You wonder what it will be like not to hunger, for a while.

But as you turn to swallow her, she holds up her hand. Her small, delicate hand that compasses galaxies—or could, if there were any left to compass.

Now, it cups the inverse glow of a naked singularity, as carefully hoarded as the shark, as the false-world that was the first thing to fall to the shark-that-has-become. She casts it before you, round and rolling, no bigger than a mustard seed.

You lunge. It's hard and heavy going down, and you gulp it sharply. A moment later, she follows, a more delicate mouthful, consumed at leisure.

She joins the man and the shark in your consciousness. And it is her knowledge that calms you as you fall into the singularity you've swallowed, as you—the whole universe of you—is compacted down, swept clean, packed tight.

When you have all fallen in on yourself, she says, there will be a grand and a messy explosion. Shrapnel, chunks and blobs and incandescent energy. The heat and the fires of creation.

The promise of rebirth.

But for now, collapsing, the shark has consumed all there is to consume. The shark is a perfect machine.

And at the end of the world the shark is happy, after all.